Other Books by
Alexander Jablokov

RIVER OF DUST
THE BREATH OF SUSPENSION
NIMBUS
A DEEPER SEA
CARVE THE SKY

dee

deepdrive

Alexander Jablokov

This is a work of fiction. Names, characters, places, and incidents either are the product of the author's imagination or are used fictitiously. Any resemblance to actual events, locales, organizations, or persons, living or dead, is entirely coincidental and beyond the intent of either the author or the publisher.

AVON BOOKS, INC.
1350 Avenue of the Americas
New York, New York 10019

Interior design by Kellan Peck
Visit our website at **http://www.AvonBooks.com/Eos**
ISBN: 0-380-97636-6

Library of Congress Cataloging in Publication Data:

Jablokov, Alexander.
Deepdrive / Alexander Jablokov. — 1st ed.
p. cm.
I. Title.
PS3560.A116D4 1998 98-11349
813'.54—dc21 CIP

First Avon Eos Printing: September 1998

Printed in the U.S.A.

FIRST EDITION

OPM 10 9 8 7 6 5 4 3 2 1

To Mary and Simon, one who aided, and one who, by his arrival, joyfully hindered, the completion of this book.

Acknowledgments

I would like to thank Jim Kelly, for this succinct title, and for the inspiration for Elward's walk among the stars; Richard Butner, whose lecture on the emotional economics of eight-track collecting inspired the pass,-tech posse; and the members of the Cambridge Science Fiction Workshop: David Smith, Sarah Smith, Steve Popkes, Kelly Link, Felicity Savage, Sari Boren, Pete Chvany, and, again, Jim Kelly, for monstrous editorial work.

One

1

Success often depends on the screwups of the competition, Soph thought as she examined the dark bulk of the spaceship *Argent*. The *Argent* had beaten Soph's team to Venus by more than a month but still hung in orbit, silhouetted against the protective dust clouds, farther from its goal than ever.

"Her second atmospheric shuttle is gone. Just like you said." Kun took a moment from his contemplation of the dust charts that floated around his head to examine the *Argent*. Soph wished he would leave that to her. Getting them safely to the surface should have been his sole concern.

"Yes." Soph didn't bother to tell him that it had been her irritating ex-husband, Lightfoot, who had told her that the *Argent*'s second atmospheric shuttle would be down on the surface ahead of them, probably at their intended destination. She hoped that didn't mean she'd have to reevaluate all the other things he had told her.

"Shit!" Kun took her mind off the *Argent*.

"Ah, that's not the kind of thing you like to hear your pilot *say*." Soph loosened her grip on her crash cocoon's webbing.

"Shit." Kun wiped his bald head. "This chart's a goddam liar!"

Venus's dust clouds swirled around his head. They blocked sunlight, keeping the Venusian surface human-habitable, and also protected the planet from intrusion by unauthorized vessels. Aside from these space reefs, Venus's orbital interception capability was limited, under treaties dating back to the first human settlement of the planet, centuries before.

"Tell me again how much you and Kammer saved by buying the cheaper version of the bootleg chart," Soph said.

"Never mind—"

The landing craft bucked. The cabin walls grew hot from dust friction. Soph heard the other team members muttering and cursing behind her.

All three of Kammer and Kun's craft were surplus Jupiter system gear. Soph and seven other members of the team hung aboard a narrow monocrystal hull with retrofitted drive pods. The crash cocoons had been ripped from an old Earth–Luna shuttle and still bore the smiling flower logos of the rebuild company. Soph noticed that each rubbery logo was carefully placed to conceal stress creases in the cocoon frame. Kammer and Kun loved saving money.

The flattening globe of Venus appeared below her lug-soled boots. Soph had seen ancient images of the planet when it had looked like a fuzzy ball bearing, covered with sulfuric acid clouds. Now vivid green lowlands surrounded pewter seas. Craters from the comets dropped by the alien Probe Builders pockmarked the plains. When the oceans finally filled, the planet would have two major continents: Aphrodite, a long landmass the size of Africa, along the equator; and Ishtar, the size of Australia, hanging off the north pole like a slipped toupee.

Their mission goal lay in the foothills of the Maxwell Mountains, which rose steeply in central Ishtar. There, a heavily fortified and protected alien named Ripi had made a deal for an extraction. Ripi had been a guest/prisoner of the Venusian government for eighteen years. He was the only representative of his species within the Solar System. The bored corruption of some of his low-level jailers had allowed him to make contact. It was worth a lot of risk to try to get him out.

The *Argent* had beaten them to the profitable pickup. But her captain, Tiber, had, for some unknown reason, descended to the Venusian surface alone—and disappeared. Since Tiber was the only one aboard his vessel who had communicated with Ripi, the *Argent* was stuck. The crew had apparently then sent the second atmospheric shuttle down directly to Ripi's covert, but that effort had failed as well. Ripi remained on the surface.

The terminator lay near Ripi's covert now. The fuzzy strip of extended sunset rippled over the high peaks of the Maxwells. The Venusian longnight was just falling there, which meant that Kammer and Kun's team would have almost two months of darkness in which to operate. Soph hoped for a quick in and snatch, but, clearly, things didn't always work out as planned.

Just inside the line of night, a few hundred kilometers south of Ripi, glowed Golgot, Venus's largest city, at what would someday be Ishtar's southern coast.

Kun peered at a coordination display that linked him with the other two penetration craft, one Kammer's and one piloted by a woman named Mura, and shook his head. He was young and had long eyelashes, as if to compensate for the lack of hair.

A whistling seemed to come from everywhere, even the inside of Soph's own skull, as the dust tore viciously at the hull's ablative shielding. That had been an expense Kammer and Kun had tried to avoid. But Soph had insisted on it as a requirement for her participation. A circum-Lunar orbital yard had sprayed it on at a good price. Its erosion would absorb the kinetic energy of the impacting dust. It was a means of survival as old as space travel.

"We'll be all right, Kun," she said. "We have redundancy."

"Sure," he said. "No question. Redundancy." The word did not seem to give him comfort. He swallowed. "Do you . . . do you suppose the *Argent* crew acted without Tiber? That they're trying to grab Ripi on their own?"

"No, of course not," said Soph, who suspected exactly

that. Otherwise, they would have sent that second shuttle down to recover Tiber, instead of trying for Ripi directly. God, she hated it when Lightfoot's warnings were borne out. She so wanted him to be wrong.

"Yeah," Kun said. "We'll get Ripi out."

"We will."

Soph rested back and felt her luggage rearrange itself to support her lower back. Its internal linkages, she hoped, would make up for any insufficiencies in the cocoon. The ship shook harder. A soft bag cupped the back of her head as the planet swelled.

Sophonisba Trost was a small woman, with a stocky, efficient body, sly black eyes, and a flat nose. She was some years older than fifty. She wore her still-black hair in a helmet, and her face crinkled all over when she laughed. She had always feared that she looked like a monkey.

She was slightly disappointed by the rising thunder as the ship made it past the last swirls of the inner dust clouds and entered Venus's stratosphere, and she blew a breath out between her lips. When they last talked, in his house on Luna, Lightfoot had told her to turn this mission down. It was suicide, he'd said. What he didn't understand was that that was one of its main attractions.

2

A broken dining room table tilted in the middle of the dimly lit storeroom like a sinking ship. Damaged decorative panels of synthetic stone from other parts of the vast house dripped with condensation.

"Ripi." Lightfoot wore a white shirt with a high collar, tailored to minimize his belly. "The Venusians haven't gotten anything from Ripi in the eighteen years since he blew into the System from Outside and crashed in the Ishtar back country. I'm sure he thought he was lucky to live through it, at the time. They stuffed him into that place they call his covert and haven't let him out since."

"I've done the research," Soph said. "I know the story."

"But do you understand it? That's the question."

"The question is why I even came here."

Lightfoot's creased face sagged even further: that basset hound expression he thought got him sympathy. "I invited you," he said. "You were kind enough to accept. I just want to talk." He pushed a steaming cup of tea at her. She caught it before it slid down the tilting tabletop.

"Lightfoot," she said, "you're not going to talk me out of it. If that's the only reason you've invited me here, we can go right on to the house tour. I understand there's some lovely ceiling carving on the upper floors. . . ."

"No, no. Please."

"What, then?" She calmed herself by building a teacup barrier out of toffee-colored chunks of carnelian.

"Some people used to think that Ripi entered the System with a functional deepdrive. After all, he'd come across interstellar space. Right?"

"If he had one, it vanished someplace between the orbit of Uranus and his impact point on Venus," Soph said, taking his rhetorical question at face value. "There's no sign of one. The Venusians do have his ship, what's left of it. They had to collect the pieces from the heights of the Maxwells."

"So, no deepdrive. Fine. What are you after, then? What makes it worth your while?"

"Something's up with Ripi. He's a Vronnan—the only example of that species in the Solar System. He was fleeing something when he came in, so he was just as glad the Venusians stuck him in velvet confinement when he landed there. He's let out dribs and drabs of Vronnan technology—it seems mostly biological—but nothing worth the amount the Venusians have sunk into him. Now, for the first time, he's let out that he wants to leave. Something's changed, either back in Vronnan space or here in the System. Something Ripi is involved in. It could be big."

"*Could* be." Lightfoot tugged at his jowls with thumb and forefinger. Soph thought he had waited all his life to have them, just for that ponderous gesture. "There still isn't any reason to risk your pretty little butt on this expedition, Soph. Kammer and Kun . . . amateurs. I don't trust them."

"Never mind my butt," Soph said, for form's sake. "And I know it's a risk. Since when have we not taken risks? Come on, Lightfoot."

"Calculated risks. For real gains." Lightfoot paused for a long moment. "It's against the order of nature for a mother to inherit her son's obsessions, Soph."

The mention of their dead son rocked her. They usually maneuvered around him, as if his body lay on the table between them, hands folded on his chest. Lightfoot never mentioned Stephan, not in fights, not in despair, never. In over two years, this was the first time. It had to mean something.

"Lightfoot—"

"Sorry, sorry." He turned away and slumped down against the chair arm, as if examining the flawed layers of blue-gray chalcedony piled in the corner. The storeroom was lit by flicker bulbs that had once provided romantic light to the huge ballroom upstairs. They had grown dim and beat in their fixtures like suffocating fireflies.

"It's against the order of nature for a son to die before his parents," Soph said to his back.

"Well, Stephan never did pay much attention to the rules, did he?"

"No, he didn't."

Stephan had been their only son. Soph and Lightfoot had talked about having more children, but somehow, between the oscillations in Lightfoot's fortunes and their endless operations, schemes, and missions, there had never been time for another. Stephan had become the repository of their warring ambitions.

Perhaps in response, his had been a life of risk. While still legally underage, he had served in the Earth–Mars War, with its far-flung battlespaces in the Asteroid Belt and the moons of Jupiter. Soph thought of that war as a futile riot against the alien species that had settled the System, from Gunners on Mercury and the Bgarth on Venus to Cruthans in the Titanian atmosphere. Stephan had seen it as a flare of romance in a grim, dark world.

There had even been fighting just off Earth itself, among the circum-Lunar asteroids of the Diadem. Those carefully neutral Lunarians who wished, watched the flare of Martian and Terran reaction drives through automated telescopes, and took bets. Soph had never wished.

After the war, Stephan had become a sporting guide on

Io, which, despite its inhospitable surface, had been a site of major fighting during the war. Io, the innermost large moon of Jupiter, was the most volcanically active body in the System. Its thin crust flexed dramatically under the gravitational pulls of Jupiter and Europa, the nearest of the other large satellites. Tidal friction kept a vast sea of sulfur and sulfur dioxide molten, ready to blast through the silicate crust. Volcanic plumes rose hundreds of kilometers above the surface. Continental floods of liquid silicate and sulfur poured across the torn surface, then seeped back down through the crust to the molten interior.

Uninhabitable by any of the alien species in the System, Io became a gigantic, dangerous playground after the war, with insulated swimmers chasing each other through bubbling pools of sulfur, gliders mounting almost to escape velocity on erupting volcanic plumes, surfers on breaking waves of rock.

It was there that Stephan had died, atop a volcanic eruption. The bloated face of Jupiter had stared down at him through the roiled atmosphere. Both his parents secretly wondered what he had seen there in those last moments. Somehow neither doubted that some revelation had come as he flew, arms outstretched, into the flaming sky.

Lightfoot sighed. "So you insist on going on this treasure hunt to Venus?"

"How often do I have to say it?"

"Once more, I think."

"Just once?" It was an old game, and she played it without thinking.

"Yes. The repetitions seem to be adding up."

"They are. I'm going, Lightfoot."

3

Once out of the dust cloud, they skipped down through the atmosphere over the Guinevere Sea, to the south of the future continent of Ishtar, and made their rendezvous. The landing craft now nestled into the underside of a hundred-meter-long biopackage built by the alien Bgarth, supported four thousand meters above the surface by vast airfoils filled with buoyant hydrogen, driven by biomechanical turbojets.

The Bgarth had landed only a few decades after the mysterious Probe, with its escort of ice comets, had begun the great transformation of Venus. The Bgarth accelerated the planet's human-habitability bootstrap by their presence beneath the crust and by complex biological packages like this one, intended for the continuing ecological growth of northern Ishtar.

The teams climbed out of their landing craft. The air at this altitude was thin but breathable. The airfoils hissed just like eroding orbital dust, as if death, an amateur poet, required an exact rhyme. The sea was an indigo pool, too far below to show any texture.

They faced a serious problem. Instead of three landing craft slid cozily into mushy growth under the flying biopackage, there were only two. The biopackage dirigible tilted perilously from the uneven weight.

"Are you sure she didn't make it?" Kammer paced the tilting floor. Pollinating beetles, escapees from their delivery modules, scuttled away from under her silver-trimmed assault boots.

"Positive." Kun stood absolutely still.

Behind him, half-sunk into the soft tissue, was the ship he and Soph had come down in. Reentry had scorched and puckered the shielding. The crystal hull shone from the bottom of dark holes. Beyond that was the second vessel, a converted water tug. Neither vessel retained enough ablative shielding to get back out through the dust cloud, Soph thought.

The rest of the team ignored the argument between their leaders and checked their gear with superstitious thoroughness.

"She might have veered off, realizing that the path was wrong. Mura's smart, Kun. That's why we hired her. She could still slide in and make the contingency rendezvous."

"She's a meteor." Kun seemed to think that if he moved so much as an eyebrow, it would mark him as untrustworthy. "I tracked her. Once the shielding burned through, the ship didn't last a split second. It's gone, Kammer. A third of our team is gone.''

''Dammit!''

Tall and long-necked, Kammer wore her golden hair in looped braids behind her head. In her reflective vest and hip-hugging insulated pants, hung with spiky combo climbing/fighting gear, she looked ready for a party, rather than an assault on a prison fortress holding an alien intelligence.

Too bad there was no party to go to.

''We'll have to change our plans,'' Soph said quietly.

Kammer tilted her head back to look down at Soph over her nose, a favorite gesture. ''Your job doesn't start until we hit the surface.''

''That's what I mean. That ship carried most of our all-terrain vehicles. We can't haul our gear up to Ripi's covert from the airhead without them. If we land as planned, I won't be able to do my job.''

''Isn't it a little early to start covering your ass, Ms. Trost?''

Soph controlled her temper. She'd argued about putting all the ATVs in one landing craft, but she'd been overruled. On fairly reasonable grounds, she had to admit: neither of the other two craft would have been able to hold them. The planning problems went deeper than she could have done anything about. Wasn't that what Lightfoot had warned her about?

''We'll have to abandon most of our heavy defensive gear at the landing site, then,'' Soph said. ''There's no way we can get it up into the Maxwells and still get back out with Ripi.''

''So what do you suggest?'' Kammer had an air of barely controlled patience.

''We'll have to hang on to this airship for longer, let it take us farther up into the Maxwells. There are some alternate landing spots nearer the target.''

Kun silently opened up topo displays of the Maxwells. Peaks thrust up from the floor. Proposed landing sites glowed yellow-green.

''You rejected those sites earlier,'' Kammer said.

''They're more dangerous,'' Kun said. ''More exposed.

Soph was right to reject them. Then. But now we don't have the ATVs to take us up from the proposed airhead, so the situation's different.''

"Goddammit, how was I supposed to know her ship was going to burn up in the dust cloud?'' Kammer sucked in a breath.

"Kammer, please.'' Kun almost whispered.

Kammer let the breath out and smiled. Suddenly she was again the competent team leader Soph had thought she was signing on with.

"All right, enough screwing around. Let's look at the backup sites and get on to busting Ripi out of jail.''

The Bgarth biopackage sank down toward the dark landscape of Ishtar. The sky still glowed with light refracted through the dust clouds—and would for weeks. It was as if a moon had been smeared out across the stars. By the cloud's vague light, Soph could see the peaks rising up at them.

Most of the team members were asleep, readying themselves for the landing and move toward Ripi's covert, which was planned to start in fourteen hours. It would still be night then, of course. It would be night for another two months. At Soph's direction, the team had set up perimeter proximity alarms, as if they were camped in the forest. They'd had very little time for practice back on Luna, and Soph felt the lack of actual field exercises keenly. It had taken them forever to lumber around the darkening biological platform to set up the alarms. Soph was not happy.

Soph's luggage had arranged itself near the platform edge in a broad V, its parasail configuration. Soph had decided not to depend on the descent gear purchased by Kammer and Kun and had instead invested her own money in adding air-assault capability to her own luggage. But the damn thing had sat too long in Lightfoot's house. It had always been his game to modify whatever gear she was setting up. An airfoil had already grown over the welter of chrome-cornered bags, striped gold and red: Lightfoot's school colors. The man had no decency.

The underside of the flying Bgarth biopackage was packed with translucent cylinders, like giant butterfly chrysalises.

Several had been bruised by the landing craft, and broken vesicles seeped yeasty-smelling fluid. The underlayers that supported the landing craft creaked as the dirigible's airfoils shifted out in the night, directing the biopackage to its destination.

"Look at this." Kun knelt by a swollen black mass at the base of a sagging chrysalis. "It's activated before hitting the surface. Kind of a crude thing, really. Penetrant explosive fungus. Breaks up the surface clinker."

Soph had been strolling with him while he examined the biopackage. "Explosive?"

He chuckled. "We don't have to worry about it. Takes a big electric charge to activate. Very specific. The Bgarth usually use a calculated lightning storm after they've sown an area. But this sort of mistake is unusual. This one is now useless."

Kun was the one who had arranged for them to conceal themselves in the Bgarth biopackage. He had contacts with the dissident human ecoteams in Aphrodite, who often covertly placed their own ecomodules aboard Bgarth airships.

Soph knew she should be asleep, charging herself up, instead of wandering around these distracting mysteries with Kun. But there was something charming about the young bald man with the long eyelashes. Despite all her efforts, Soph was still not sure whether he and the lovely Kammer were lovers. She rather hoped not.

"It's hard to tell anymore—what of Venus's life came from the Probe, what from the Bgarth, and what from these crazed ecoteam researchers down in Aphrodite," Kun said. "And it keeps going. New ecologies propagate themselves over the planet, each metastructure trying to bootstrap itself into dynamic dominance. It's kind of fun to watch."

"There are bookmakers on Luna who bet on ecotones moving as different environments expand and contract," Soph said.

Kun grinned, a little shyly. "Where do you think a lot of the money for the expedition came from?"

"I thought it was Kammer."

"Kammer spends money. She doesn't make it. I bet the lines and won big."

"Money. . . ." Soph said. "You know, Kun, I'm worried about these scapular credit stores of ours."

"The right of survivorship?" Kun looked surprised. "Surely, you don't think—"

"When an expedition falls apart, anything can happen."

Each member of Kammer and Kun's expedition carried cash in a secure module in his shoulder blade. In a true expression of trust, the cash was arranged in that ancient gentleman/adventurers' form of financial trust, the tontine. Survivors could call up the access codes of the dead and drain their valuta stores. Soph had visions of a failed expedition, its goal forgotten, but with various members hunting each other down for the remaining expeditionary cash in each others' scapulas.

"I don't think it will come to that," Kun said. "Really, Soph. I'll never kill you for the money in your shoulder."

A proximity alarm buzzed in Soph's mastoid bone. Too bad that it would wake up her team. They needed the sleep. But perhaps they needed the alert practice more. She leaned out into the rushing darkness, expecting to see some large high-flying bird curiously investigating the huge airship.

Instead, what she saw was the flicker of copter blades.

"Down, Kun!"

Together they rolled behind a chrysalis and scuttled backward. Soph could hear her team yelping questions in the darkness.

"Who the hell is that?" Soph asked. Now that she knew what to look for, she saw several more of the sound-screened aircraft hovering just beyond the first one. They vectored in.

"Enforcement & Joy. They won't fire yet. All this hydrogen, and no one wants to piss the Bgarth off by blowing up a biopackage carrier. Who knows what the Bgarth might do? Take away the oxygen atmosphere, maybe. People are always terrified that will happen."

Kun was panicked, babbling.

"Venusians are such worrywarts," Soph said. "Kammer!"

"No need to yell." Kammer appeared at her side and handed her a shoulder-launched antiaircraft munition from stores. Kammer's munition was already crouched tensely on her shoulder like a waiting hawk. She pulled on a control gauntlet and pointed at the nearest copter, which was only meters away. A thud, an almost subliminal flash of explosive, and it tilted and fell away into the darkness.

"I don't know who the hell they think they're dealing with," Kammer muttered.

Soph aimed her own munition and fired. But hers vanished into the darkness, and the copter she had aimed it at moved in unharmed. They had turned on their countermeasures—and Soph was sure that the penetration software in the munitions she had bought in Copernicus was months if not years out of date. The lead copter had been destroyed through its own overconfidence.

As the attackers came closer, they opened fire to cover their landing. Soph and Kammer ducked. A copter bounced against the underside of the biopackage at the stern, and troops with black image-amplification face masks spilled out of it. On each glared two green laser-grained eyespots, a visible sign of authority. They fanned out among the chrysalises.

"Back about ten meters," Kammer said. "There's a bottleneck amid these egg cases. They'll have to string out to get through. We can hold. Kun, get your butt into the ship and power up!"

Just like that, the mission was scrubbed.

Kammer yelled and swore and got some of the back people into Kun's shuttle while somehow preventing a general stampede. She seemed even taller than before. Soph took up her assigned spot, back toward the bulbous water tug, and her luggage. Kun dove through the shuttle hatch.

The E&Js did indeed get necked down by the arrangement of chrysalises, to be met with determined fire from the mission team. One of them dropped, to be pulled by one ankle back behind a chrysalis. Kun hesitated, hatches open, until Kammer screamed at him. Then he buttoned up and hit his side thrusters. Flames tore above Soph's head. The shuttle rolled slowly, then dropped over the side. Thunder sounded below as the shuttle's main drive came on.

Soph didn't have time to see whether Kun managed to avoid smashing into the sea below. The team members who remained had to try to get aboard the water tug and make their own escape.

Shouts came from behind her. Soph turned to see troops rappel down the biopackage's side and swing in to hit them in the rear.

They must have landed somewhere on the complex control surfaces above, a ticklish operation. For a brief instant, Soph felt admiration for their daring.

It was all over. A few more of the mission team went down, and the rest of them attempted to surrender. There was no escape. The E&J troops had cut them off from the tug.

But Kammer was not about to surrender. Not handicapped by the E&Js' fear of destroying any Bgarth biologicals, she fired straight through the bulging chrysalises to kill whoever was hiding behind them. Support fluid poured across the floor, filled with the dying shapes of incomprehensible embryos. The spotlights caught her bright hair, and Soph could hear her laugh above the high crack of small arms fire.

Most of the other team members had surrendered or died, leaving Soph as a holdout. She saw two of the black-helmeted figures turn toward her, their emerald eyespots glaring.

Soph dove, grabbed at her luggage handles. A burst of fire went through the space she had just occupied. She pushed her boot toes against the damp floor. Her luggage fell off the edge of the platform, pulling her after it.

Rushing wind, darkness. She held on to the handles as she fell down at the peaks of the Maxwell Mountains.

4

"Tiber, of course, is the key to the problem," Lightfoot said.

"How?" Soph asked.

"Because the question isn't why Ripi wishes to leave his upholstered jail in the Maxwells. I should think that would be obvious. The real question is why, out of all the vessels in the System, he would choose the *Argent.*"

Damn him, Soph thought. Lightfoot could find a surface irregularity in a null-g sphere of helium 2. She was not about to admit that that was the very question that had been worrying her.

"The *Argent* was hijacked from the MeshMatrix Krystal shipyard three years ago," she said. "It's been on the run from Terran recovery teams ever since. Tiber and his crew have sub-rosa contacts in the Belt and proven skills at evasion. Ripi had good reason to contact them."

"Proven skills? Really? How hard do you think Terran recovery teams are looking for that scow, anyway? They could be parked in orbit around Luna and no one would bother them. There were reasons Tiber was allowed to take off with the *Argent* . . . but this isn't the time to discuss Ulanyi internal politics. At any rate, I wouldn't put a lot of money on the *Argent*'s evasive capabilities. It's just good luck that the ship hasn't fallen apart already. After all, it wasn't designed for interplanetary transport but as a sort of broodship for conscious Ulanyi embryos shuttled up from Earth's northern hemisphere. It's a flying crèche."

"So Ripi made a mistake," Soph said. "He works in a situation of imperfect information, after all."

Lightfoot looked at her from under his brows. "No reason for you to think just as imperfectly, then. A month ago, Tiber descended to the Venusian surface near Golgot. There he vanished. He hasn't come back up to the *Argent* or made it across the Maxwells to Ripi."

"I'm well aware of that," Soph said. "That's how Kammer and Kun have an opportunity in the first place." She'd wanted to conceal exactly how shaky their operation's toehold was, but of course, Lightfoot knew a lot more than she wished he did. "He might reappear at any time, which would screw us—completely. I know that. But it's worth the risk."

"Tiber isn't reappearing," Lightfoot said. "Not without help. Do you know what happened to him?"

She hesitated. Lightfoot was not above pumping her for information while pretending to clarify things. "He seems to have gone down into the Bgarth facility at the Well, near Golgot."

"Quite right. Now what in the world would Tiber have to talk about with those crust-eating worms?"

"That I don't know, Lightfoot."

"Well, whatever it is, he'll have plenty of time to hammer out the details. There was surface action at the lip of the Well. Seems some kind of snatch team tried to grab him. Enforcement & Joy intervened, there was a lot of wild blasting away, and Tiber ended up stuck, his surface access destroyed. Who knows? Maybe those sentient mining machines just ate him, and you have nothing to worry about."

"You should ring for some cheese and crackers," Soph said. "You sound hungry."

"Ha. Maybe I am. You always were better at figuring that out than I was. You know, I'm not just interested in Ripi for your own sweet sake. He came into the System with a deepdrive. It disappeared. I'd like to know what happened to it. It's important to all of us. We need one to get out of this dust pit we call a solar system. Those Martians who launched the *Prismatic Bezel* just gave up on it and sent their colonization vessel through normal space. Crawling. Some other species do that, but they have much longer lives. And then the damn *Bezel* vanished before getting more than a fraction of a light-year away. . . ."

Lightfoot, like other tech hunters, sought the big score: a functional deepdrive. Not long before Stephan's death, he'd managed to lose a fortune on a brilliantly planned assault on a Cruthan nest floating in the thick atmosphere of the Saturnian satellite Titan that had netted nothing but dead growth infested with particularly virulent bacteria. Arguments still raged about whether the thing they had stolen had been a cleverly designed decoy, a big mistake and not a deepdrive at all, or whether deepdrives really were somewhat alive and thus could die and decay. Some even maintained that the essence of the deepdrive was somewhere concealed in the bacterial organelles and that the sterilization and quarantine had destroyed the results of what had actually been a successful mission.

But a deepdrive was more than a piece of useful technology. Since the arrival of aliens in the Solar System, it had taken on an almost spiritual meaning. To possess one was to possess the universe, to be a species equal to all the others in the Galaxy. Without it, humans were just crude islanders, standing on the beach and chanting at the passage of ships, hoping that something interesting would fall overboard and float up to shore.

Lightfoot denied this nonphysical meaning, even to himself, but Soph knew that it was what truly drove him. To become wealthy was one thing. To become Prometheus was something else again. Her plump ex-husband cherished ambitions that still excited her.

"We're not counting on any deepdrive information," Soph said. "We're interested in Ripi directly, for the reasons I've already explained to you. With Tiber out of the way, we have a clear shot."

"But do you have any idea of what Tiber was doing underground with the Bgarth?"

She considered a bluff. "No. Not specifically. Do you?"

"No idea at all. Like Ripi, I am dependent on my sources. How did you put it? I operate in 'a situation of imperfect information.' " He said it singsong, like a line from a children's rhyme. Lightfoot had a gift for presenting her own words and thoughts back to her in a way that made them seem impossibly foolish. "Soph, you have to wonder *why*. Tiber didn't just take a side trip. It had to be part of his plan. What part?"

"Don't hector me, Lightfoot."

"And Ripi wants *him*. Not you, Soph. Not Kammer and Kun. Tiber. You guys have been drafted as backup. And how much of a backup? The *Argent* has sent its second atmospheric shuttle down to Ripi's covert. They're waiting for Tiber. All of them. All he has to do is get out of the Well to achieve his purposes. And what those are, you have absolutely no idea."

"We're going, Lightfoot. We know the risks."

"No, you don't! You have no idea of what you are facing."

Soph stood. "Goodbye, Lightfoot."

"Goddammit, Soph, don't be so stupid!" It was amazing how fast his face turned red. "Don't get dragged down with those fools. It isn't worth it."

"Lightfoot—"

"First Stephan, now you. What drives intelligent people to bash their own heads out against a wall?"

The house was nothing but endless rooms laden with stone ornamentation. She stalked past long screens of carved synthetic jade, across pavements of rippled brown-and-white-striped sardonyx deliberately worn to seem ancient. Her luggage waited for her in the wide foyer. It stood against a curving wall, arrayed as if on display for a prospective purchaser. She had not left it that way.

"Soph." Lightfoot had followed some other route through the house and now stood above her on a curving flight of stairs made of purplish-red porphyry.

She ignored him. Perhaps he had built special access circuits into that wall when he finally convinced her to visit him. She wouldn't put that past him. Lightfoot had bought her the original active luggage years ago. That armored trunk and oval overnight bag were still constituents of the system. Lightfoot had always had good taste.

She'd done her best to clean the software of any trojan horse modules but had obviously not been entirely successful. Something in the house wall had issued a command, and the luggage, not mindful of its true allegiance, had responded.

"Soph. If things don't work out . . . I have a contact in Golgot. The one who knows about Tiber. And there's something about Tiber. . . . For God's sake, Soph, pay attention to me!"

He was almost crying. The bastard really had no idea. He always managed to peg the emotional price of his information at just a little more than it was worth. And this, she had to admit, was worth a lot.

"I'm not going to Golgot," she said. "And if I were going, I have my own contacts."

"Just take it! Please . . . her name is Ambryn Chretien. I have to say . . . she's not exactly *dependable*. But she's the best I've got. It may help you."

She had to force herself to listen. It was not often that Lightfoot just gave up information and even less often that he admitted that he was operating on the basis of a hunch. His apprehension about Tiber had no rational basis. He gave her contact procedures and identification codes, and she remembered it all, without acknowledging him once.

Her luggage rearranged itself into transport configuration, raised itself on its wheels, and slithered obediently after her as she walked down to her car. She would have to check it over thoroughly again on the long trip to Venus.

As she pulled the bubble car away from Lightfoot's house, down the fused-dust road across Aristarchus, Soph turned to look back at it. The place was visible from across the crater, a dark chunk of chondritic rock that looked as if an asteroid had lowered itself and nestled into the pale crater rim.

High up in the huge black boulder was a single glowing window, with a silhouetted figure in it looking down at her. Lightfoot would have had to put a light some distance behind him and project his shadow on a translucent screen to be visible from this distance.

It seemed like a lot of effort, but then Lightfoot had always been willing to work for those things he found important. Soph wished he would stop considering her so important.

5

The wings spread out and the parasail caught the air. Soph grabbed for the dangling harness just above her. At the touch of her hand, it slid down and hooked under her armpits. That gave her enough support to pull herself up. The rest of the harness clicked around her chest.

She was far from any of the surveyed landing sites. This region of the Maxwells was all volcanic rock that had been deeply shattered by subterranean Bgarth action.

The light that came from the nightglow of the Venus-girdling dust cloud was enough to hint at what lay below without giving her good detail.

It was all her own goddam fault. If she hadn't insisted on going farther, getting closer to Ripi's covert, they'd have glided out from under the Bgarth biopackage hours ago, headed for the original landing site. Their two spaceships would be buried in the high-altitude forest, awaiting their return. The E&J assault squads, having searched desperately for the interlopers after the other vessel burned up in the dust cloud, would have found nothing aboard the biopackage but some seemingly random vandalism to mark where they had been. As it was, due to Soph's decision, they'd bagged the team. Kammer was probably dead, perhaps Kun as well. When she had a chance, she would cry for them.

Her luggage chirped a couple of ultrasound pulses, disguised as the insect-hunting signal of a local bat species, then bleebled the derived altitude information through an earphone that had sprouted up from her shoulder. If she pulled in her wing tips and kept straight, she could land on the bottom of the fault ahead.

A sand dune came out of darkness and she slammed into it. She slid across its crest, pulling at the harness. Broken rocks jabbed at her thighs. She tasted blood in her mouth. A final yank, and she freed the harness before she got dragged any farther. Her luggage snapped through dry growth beyond. She lay in aromatic grass. The air was still warm from the just-departed day and she could feel the dryness of the thin leaves. Seed pods shattered against her and rattled down across her boots as she sat up. A small animal, panicked beyond sense, ran across her hand and dove into a hole beyond.

The luggage had been caught by a copse of shrubby trees. Dry leaves came down on her in a shower as she tugged it free. The trees had settled down for longnight.

A map of southern Ishtar appeared on the ground. A flicker of calculation, and her current location was marked. To the south, about eighty kilometers away, sprawled the giant metropolis of Golgot. Golgot then grew until it was itself a map, its tangled streets swelling out at her. She had her own contacts there. If she was lucky, she wouldn't have to resort to the contact Lightfoot had given her.

Her eyes adjusted to the dark. She looked up past the cracked stone walls on either side into the glow of the sky but could see no sign of the Bgarth biopackage or the Enforcement & Joy assault copters. She was utterly alone.

According to the map, this fault descended until it opened out on the shore of a stream. The stream was almost dry after the end of the longday. It would not have much water in it again until the morning, when the longnight's collected high-elevation snow melted and swelled it into flood. She could follow the muddy streambed down into the plains above Golgot, then make her way through the suburbs into the great city. It looked like there were a couple of steep drop-offs, waterfalls when there was water, but nothing too bad.

With much cracking of twigs, her luggage had reassembled itself. It now rested on high sets of triangularly arranged wheels, a transport configuration suitable for even the roughest country. With a rush of ventilators, it blew out any dust that might have worked its way into her clothing and gear. It shivered, ready to move.

She sat on a dry tussock and wept for Kammer, Kun, the other team members, Stephan, and everyone else. When there were no more tears, she stood up.

Two

1

"Why?" Ambryn looked at the Bgarth physiological image she had spilled across the table. The complex internal structures were a blur. "Oh, why?"

"Really, Ambryn." Derinda sat coiled on the other side of the table, her long body in a skintight leather suit stabbed through with hundreds of rusty blades. Fake blood had crystallized at the slash edges, where it glittered like citrine. "I came here for a skrying. Is that so odd? You *are* the best."

"I'm the *only* xenoanatomical skryer in Golgot," Ambryn said. "No different than when we were . . . together. Derinda, I—"

"So what am I looking at?"

Derinda rested her hands on the table. Since the last time Ambryn had seen her, she had put razor tips on her nails to keep from biting them. The edges were bent with tooth marks.

"These purple lumps are oxygen-generating nodes," Ambryn said.

"Ah." Derinda nodded eagerly. She'd shaved her hair, and the scarred scalp brought out the strength of her jaw. Ambryn was surprised by how well it suited her. "Oxygen."

"Derinda. Are you willing to learn this time?" Derinda

nodded. "Bgarth physiological processes are symbols only because they are also real. If you want to understand how they tell you the truth about your soul and your future, you have to understand the physical reality. The actual glands and organs. And they don't give up their secrets easily."

"I remember. I'll do my best. But it's hard. You *are* a good teacher, Ambryn."

Derinda was really trying, Ambryn thought. Her eyes were wide as she looked across the table at Ambryn. Derinda had never tried to understand when they were together. Not at all. She'd found the whole practice ridiculous.

There was a snort and clatter from the darkness at the back of the skrying parlor.

"Elward," Ambryn said. "That's a piece of Cruthan integument. It's fragile."

"Valuable?" Elward took his thick fingers off the beaded hide only reluctantly.

"Extremely."

"Huh. Looks like a big scab." He made a show of looking around. "Got any alien earwax?"

Elward had a huge torso, which made even his large arms and legs look spindly. His face, with its rosebud mouth, its aquiline nose, and its wide-set dark eyes, was inappropriately romantic-looking for the blocky head it had been slapped on to. Ambryn did not remember his being so offensive.

It was seeing him here, apparently working for Derinda, that frightened Ambryn. Ambryn had not even known the two of them had been in contact after that desperately botched operation at the Well. And, for that job, *she* had been the one who had hired Elward. That disaster had marked the end of her affair with Derinda. She'd spent the last few months trying to forget all about it.

"Why the Bgarth?" Ambryn asked Derinda. "I really don't think their bodies are appropriate for skrying your fate. If you remember, the Ulanyi—"

"I'm not interested in those thinking embryos," Derinda said. "We've dug around in their little shriveled bodies enough. That's the kind of thing Terrans worry about. Right? Like you. After all, you grew up with them. I'm from Venus. Bgarth are *my* aliens. So what about these axons here?"

Derinda ran her fingertips across the image. Ambryn remembered how delicate her touch could be. And how rough . . .

"These axons carry Bgarth neurotransmitters to the oxygen-producing reaction site. In one sense, you can think of the current atmosphere of Venus as a Bgarth thought."

Ambryn flicked a control and a full-sense image of a Bgarth bulked in the shadows at the ceiling. Manipulator palps and machinery interfaces dangled down into the cozy alcove where Ambryn did her fortune-telling.

"But what about the navigation gear?" Derinda looked up into the guts, but Ambryn could tell she was looking for something else altogether. "I mean, the Bgarth move around through the crust. How do they know where they are? That would be the best guide for me. Right? The most suitable metaphor."

That was a little too obvious. But that was Derinda's way. She tried to be subtle, but it just wasn't in her. It was the obviousness of her movements that had captivated Ambryn when they had first met. So Derinda must know about the chunk of Bgarth anatomical nav gear Ambryn had recently acquired, after long effort, and be here after it. But why should she care about it?

"Hey, get this." Elward held a book with a tooled binding. "This guy says that some race lived on Venus before the comets came. The water poisoned them all. Genocide, he says. Deliberate. By the Probe Builders." He shook his head. "You can still find the bodies, down in deep lava caves, he says. Is that true? I've never heard it." He looked disturbed.

"It doesn't matter." Derinda spoke sharply. "Come here and stand by us. Ambryn is nervous about her stuff, so don't touch it."

Elward loomed up at Ambryn's elbow. She remembered how comforting she had once found him, when they were on the same side. He'd saved their asses when things went bad at the Well, and Enforcement & Joy almost got them. Ambryn owed her freedom to him. Now he scared the hell out of her. The fact that he stared down her cleavage as he stood next to her didn't help matters.

Ambryn reached up with a long-fingernailed hand and

tugged out bioreactor guts. Reactive tissues spilled out across the floor and fetched up against the bases of the curio cabinets. Ambryn dug through them for the navigation connections.

"How much of this information comes from the Guts?" Derinda asked. "They're the ones who obsess over Bgarth bodies the most, aren't they?"

"They're willing to trade information," Ambryn said.

"Trade? For what? What do you give them?"

Derinda had uncoiled and now thrust herself across the table at Ambryn. She'd always felt like a cutting surface. Even when she rested her head on Ambryn's large breasts after love, the bones of her skull had seemed to dig for something.

"A variety of things," Ambryn said. "It's hard to know ahead of time what will please them. They're really odd people, you know. Living underground, trying to reach the Bgarth . . . that doesn't keep you on an even keel."

"Does living here among alien innards keep you balanced, Ambryn?"

"It keeps me fed."

Derinda laughed. "Not well. It's always a bitch, making a living in Golgot, isn't it? Everyone's always stepping on each other's faces."

Bgarth navigation organs bulked in the shadows. The magnetic coils warned Ambryn of danger. Everything looked ominous. You can find your way, they said, but the way will not be easy. Those you once loved will try to crush you. . . .

Derinda did not see the clear message of the Bgarth's navigation organs. But, of course, reading the message of the anatomy was Ambryn's skill. That was why Derinda was here. Wasn't it? A skrying—and an attempt to rekindle their romance.

She was working for someone else, Ambryn thought. Maybe she had always been working for someone else.

"It's been rough," Derinda whispered. "For me."

"Me too."

"I need someone to throw me a lifeline, Ambryn. I need . . . what happened at the Well . . . I lost a lot there." Her narrow eyes could grow wide when she wanted them to.

"What?" Ambryn asked, confused. "What did you lose?" The expedition to the Well had been her job, her idea. She had been after Tiber, down from the *Argent*. That was her big obsession. The escape after failure had been hairy, but Derinda had seemed to enjoy it, taken it as a lark. That night she had made love even more savagely than usual. And that night had been nearly the last time. The last pleasurable time, that was for sure.

"Energy, I guess," Derinda said. "Tiber . . . you know, Ambryn, I bet we could still get him out. If only there was a way to get the Guts to help us. They know the ways into the Well."

"No. I'm through with that." Ambryn had to lie. It was tempting to confide in Derinda when she seemed to open herself, but Ambryn had to do it on her own this time. She didn't know how, but she had to get in touch with Tiber herself. It was her only hope. Otherwise, she'd live out the rest of her life here, looking at the intestines of Ganymedean Turtles for old ladies wanting to talk to the ghosts of their dead children.

"Please, Ambryn. Think about it."

"I've thought about it."

"You should think about it a little more." Suddenly Derinda grabbed Ambryn's hair in her hand and pulled her face close. Ambryn thought she could see each individual tooth pressing out against Derinda's taut lips. "Don't you agree, Elward?"

"If you say so." Elward sounded reluctant.

"I do say so. Get me into the Well, Ambryn. You have a way. Don't you?"

"I—"

"Think carefully before you lie to me."

Ambryn had acquired the Bgarth nav organ from sources outside the Solar System. It had taken all she had left. She wanted to use it to negotiate with the Guts for a way into the Well, to talk to Tiber. She couldn't give it up now. Not even because she and Derinda had once loved each other.

Not entirely believing what she was doing, Ambryn reached her hand under the table for the charge prod. She'd bought it in case a client became hysterical at the truth that was revealed, but she had never had to use it. It was much farther under the table than she had thought. The thought of using it on Derinda gave her a thrill. It would put their relationship on a more even footing.

"You know," Ambryn said, "people once tried to skry using the constellations of the zodiac, patterns of stars along the ecliptic. Can you believe that? I mean, it's so arbitrary, to base your prognostic science on what is just a chance angle of perception. The aliens who come into the System are astrological signs made flesh. . . ."

Her fingers closed on the grip.

Ambryn gave Derinda one more chance. "I need to go my own way. Please. What's over is over. Let's each follow our own path."

Derinda snorted. "I thought you were smarter than that, Ambryn. Elward. She thinks she's getting clever with a weapon."

He smashed the side of her head without even seeming to move. She lost her grip on the charge prod and fell to the floor. Her head blazed in agony. He picked her up with huge hands and delicately set her back on the chair.

"Tie her up now," Derinda said. "I'll talk to her again after I have a look around."

Elward strapped Ambryn to her chair. The side of her head felt soft, like a rotting peach.

"Sorry," Elward said in her ear. "Contract provisions. Nothing personal. You understand."

"Get away from me." The room swam. She licked at the blood that trickled from the corner of her mouth. Her tongue felt a mile long.

"That's all for now, Elward," Derinda said. "I'll give you a call the next time I need you on a special."

"What?"

"You heard me. You can go back to our usual tasks. The day-to-day grind of our arrangement. Profitable, though, right? At least, I haven't heard you complain. The pickup tomorrow should fetch you a good amount."

"I don't think I should leave you alone with her," Elward said.

"Go," Derinda said. "Oh . . . take a souvenir from her collection. The Cruthan integument. Consider it a tip."

"I prefer my tips in cash."

The barest pause. "Consider it a tip."

2

The thunder of the blower that kept the patio bubble inflated also kept Soph from hearing the beating of her own heart. She tried not to peer too obviously at the door on the opposite side of the street. She huddled in her coat against the cold. The temperature had been dropping since she hit the wilds of Ishtar almost a month before, and the bubble did a poor job of insulation.

A waiter slumped past, ran a sponge across the table, exchanging new grease for old, and jammed a steam nozzle into Soph's soup bowl from the heating pipe that ran along the bubble edge. He had already reheated her soup twice and clearly resented the space she and her luggage took up, despite the fact that the bubble, intended to extend the restaurant's breezy longday patio into the coldest part of longnight, was otherwise empty.

An hour before, Soph had watched a big man in a long coat escort a slender woman from a heavily armored limousine into the doorway under the sign that said AMBRYN CHRETIEN, XENO-ANATOMICAL SKRYING, with a background of alien internal organs that flickered just at the edge of perception. Neither had come out.

Soph was here, waiting for Ambryn Chretien to be free, because both of Soph's other Golgot sources had already come up dry—and worse.

Hisan, a silver-haired executive in a tourist agency, had been imperviously bland, as if Soph was a deranged relative who had neglected to take her medication, and responded not at all to the code phrases that indicated disaster and a plea for help. A nervous assistant had escorted Soph off the premises and given her some money from Hisan, enough to buy the bowl of soup she was currently not eating.

Kopko, a pudgy man from a business bank, had met with Soph at his permanent table in the local restaurant where he made his data exchanges. There he had tried to turn Soph over to two local police officers hastily disguised as waiters. Soph had left behind a mess of broken plates, a dining room full of acrid smoke, and a screaming chef. Her luggage had punched a hole in the wall. She wondered if Kopko had lost his choice table as a result.

Now Soph was here, seeking the contact Lightfoot had desperately proffered. She had no choice.

The man in the long coat came out alone. He struggled with a bulky shape, irritatedly shrugging his shoulders as it bumped against the sides of the doorway and then almost fell onto his armored limo. Soph's cosmetics bag unfurled a mirror and she turned away, as if she wished to check her lipstick.

The driver opened a limo door and slung the bulky object into the rear seat. He glared in after at it, as if it had jumped in there on its own and now refused to come out, demanding that he drive it to some inconvenient location on the other side of Golgot. Then he slammed the door, got into the driver's seat, and drove away.

What had happened to the woman who was clearly his boss? Was she supposed to take a cab home? Why hadn't she had her driver wait? Soph gulped the rest of her soup, which was once again cold, and left the restaurant. Behind her, the waiter slammed shut the access door to the patio. He was tired of having to serve whoever decided to go out there.

Her luggage probed Ambryn Chretien's secure door. A soft-read popped up on the inclement-weather garment bag, showing the security codes. It had been a while since they had been upgraded. Soph was familiar with the problem. A moment later, the door unsealed, and she followed her luggage in.

The elegant skrying parlor was silent. Between high display cases she saw the actual skrying table, an image of some alien guts active on it. Next to it—

Soph sucked a breath through her nostrils. A lush woman in a tight green sheath dress and knee-high soft leather boots lay unconscious, head back, strapped to a chair. Her auburn hair spilled down the chair back. Blood covered the side of her head.

Soph sliced through the straps with a utility knife and lowered her to the floor as the med bag checked the woman's vitals. Soph was struck by the half-floral, half-feral scent that rose up from her warm skin.

Soph looked at the reads. No toxins, it seemed, just a slight concussion. The woman, presumably Ambryn Chretien, was in no immediate danger. Soph sprayed the head wound with an antiseptic and local anesthetic. But where was the other woman? Soph passed through the curtain at the back of the skrying alcove into the space beyond.

She found herself in a treatment room that must have come from a medical center. An oval pool of support fluid steamed in the center, an instrumentation cluster dangling down over it.

Beyond the treatment room was an arched hallway, rooms opening up to either side. The first door on the right was a utility room. A chunk of shale resting in a support cradle contained a partially excavated alien fossil, something lacy, like a chrinoid. Chiseled fragments littered the floor around it.

Soph heard a thump. The next door led to the bedroom, which smelled like a muskier variation of Ambryn's perfume. Expensive-looking clothing lay scattered and wrinkled on the thick carpet, around an altarlike bed on a tulip stem. A silver cooling bucket stood by the head, empty bottle still leaning in it, ice long gone.

"Help!" someone shrieked. "Oh, please, help! Someone!"

The slender woman lay huddled on the closet floor.

"Thank God," she murmured. "That terrible man . . . I thought he had come back."

Soph moved to help. As the woman reached up for Soph, she curled the fingers of her right hand and pointed. All the bones seemed to knot up. Soph slapped the hand away.

A crack—and the shot blew a hole in the wall. The hand turned again, and in the fingertip Soph saw the dark pinhole of the vapor projectile launcher that had replaced the interior of the woman's phalanges and ulna.

The second shot, panicked and too fast, blistered past

Soph's face. Pieces of the ceiling showered down on the bed.

Soph hit the summoning button in her knuckle and leaped out of the room and down the hall. She grabbed the fossil-bearing rock on its cart and rolled it. It trundled down the hall like an eager but elderly dachshund, and caught the woman in the legs just as she stepped through the doorway. That had to hurt. But she shoulder-rolled right over it. Soph only gained a few feet, making it into the treatment room.

"Stop," the woman said.

The surface of the black stone pool reflected the squid tentacle tangle of bioaccess gear that hung down over it.

Soph turned. The woman was young, with a lean, strong body. She wore an outfit covered with wounds. She smiled at Soph.

"Just like Ambryn to call for help. Are you another of her dear loves?"

"I'm sorry," Soph said. "I'm from—"

"Make it good. Back at the office, we like to trade the wild excuses people give us when we nail them. We have a contest every month for the most creative."

"I came in from tech support," Soph said. "But I must have the wrong office. If you'll excuse me, I'm late and—"

"Oh, well." The woman was disgusted. "I guess I lose again."

Her hand rose. Finally, in response to the summons, Soph's luggage slid into the room and hit the woman behind the knees.

The shot went wild.

Soph kicked up savagely, hoping to shatter the finger bones and to at least throw that damn gun out of alignment.

But instead of falling back, she smashed Soph in the cheek with her other hand. Soph's head jerked, and she saw stars.

The woman was on her.

It was now Soph's turn to feel something behind her knees: the edge of the pool. The woman's weight pushed her over, and they both toppled into the water.

Soph fought to the surface, took a breath, then was forced back under. The woman's hands tightened around her neck.

Maybe the gun seemed too impersonal now. Or maybe Soph had damaged it.

The woman tried to slam Soph's head against the side of the pool, but what looked like rock turned out to be soft padding.

She had no air. Soph flailed her arms but couldn't get a grip on anything. A layer of water separated her from the world. The woman's face swirled, growing larger, then receding. She maintained her dispassionate expression as she waited for Soph to see sense and die.

The water's refraction made it seem as though the instrument cluster was closer than it actually was. It looked like it hung right over the woman's shoulder. It loomed, unfurling each instrument control bulb for easy access.

It *was* close. Sensing something in the treatment pool, it had activated itself so that the therapist could get to work.

Maybe she could get enough of a grip to pull herself out and get some air. Surely it would be designed to present itself to a user's fingertips. . . .

Soph flailed, trying to make it seem random, the last throes of a dying woman. That wasn't hard.

She got a purchase, felt her fingers close around a soft bulb.

It did nothing for her. She yanked with every ounce of strength she had left, but the young woman was too strong and heavy for her. Soph did manage to pull her head up for one tiny gasp of air, a few more seconds of life, before she went under again.

Still she held on. The feel of the control bulb comforted her. It was all she had.

Instruments. Medical instruments above the pool. What were they? Tubes to aspirate mucus, muscle relaxants . . . surgical lasers? Deep anesthetics?

Feeling the quivering of her small muscles, she thumbed the knob until the indicator pulsed Maximum into her fingertip. She had no idea what she was maximizing. Then, with the last strength in her fingers, she hit activation, praying that it would not do something like clean the dead skin off her murderer's back with an ultrasound pulse.

The woman arched her back. Every muscle convulsed and she fell forward onto Soph.

Soph couldn't move her own right arm. It was dead meat on her shoulder, and when, in the course of her struggles, the hand happened to flop near her eyes, she did not recognize the fingers as her own.

Even dead or unconscious, the young woman was winning the fight. Soph scrabbled at the smooth walls of the pool with her one working arm. The woman's weight forced Soph back down.

The water closed back over her face.

3

Ambryn stood in the treatment room and watched the ripples on the water disappear. The sound of splashing had awoken her. The wound on the side of her head pounded. Nothing seemed real. The swirling clothes beneath the surface might have been some undersea plants, glowing here in the overhead lights of her treatment room.

Then what was under the water snapped into focus. Heads, hands . . . faces. Ambryn reached over, grabbed a handful of clothes, and yanked. Up came Derinda. Her hard face was serene, as if, beneath her closed lids, she dreamed of something beautiful. Ambryn lowered her to the floor, and another body floated to the surface. Ambryn pulled this woman out too. She was lighter than Derinda. She looked in the pool for another, but that seemed to be it.

Derinda had been hit by the neuromuscular depolarizer once used in presurgical prep. Her muscles were completely limp, and her diaphragm was goo. Ambryn flopped her back into the water, turned on the jets so that she floated, and pulled down the life-support sucker. She'd never had to use this—her clients weren't usually this far gone—and she hoped it hadn't been disconnected before she bought the setup. The mask attached itself to Derinda's face. The ventilator filled her chest with air. Her body shuddered as electrodes steadied her heart rate. All her muscle control was cooked. She wasn't going to be moving for a while, which was perfectly fine with Ambryn.

The woman on the floor choked. Ambryn turned her face-down and pushed the water out of her lungs. She was just a little thing, Ambryn thought, bony and wiry. Ambryn could feel ribs beneath her fingers. The woman coughed up water and drew a shuddering breath.

The woman was a bundle of taut springs. She twisted from Ambryn's embrace like a child who'd had enough affection from a parent. Her eyes, now that they were open, were dark and clear. Her face was slightly Asian, with a flat nose, wide cheeks, a narrow chin. Big creases on the sides of her mouth. She looked like she'd recently spent a lot of time being unhappy.

"Are you all right?" Ambryn asked.

"Are you Ambryn Chretien?"

"Yes. Yes, I am."

"And who is *she?*"

"She's . . . it's kind of complicated." Ambryn was taken aback by the speed of the woman's questions.

The woman gestured at a slithering stack of luggage. A bag opened and presented her with an ebony gun, very decorative. She pointed it over Ambryn's shoulder.

But Derinda was still unconscious.

The woman, her eyes still on Derinda, said: " 'The wolf, whose howl's his watch, thus with his stealthy pace, like Tarquin's ravishing strides, towards his design moves like a ghost.' "

It was the identifying code phrase for Ambryn's data contact on Luna. She'd picked it herself from an old play in archaic English, which, like all good students in the Ulanyi regions of North America, she had learned at school. *Mcdonald? Old Macbeth?* Something like that. She now wished she'd used a somewhat less ominous passage.

"Well," Ambryn said. "I'm glad my information has finally proved of use to someone. I must say, I never expected to actually see anyone. It's a little like having a picture step off the wall, to see someone from Luna."

"I hope you can be even more useful. My name, by the way, is Sophonisba Trost. Call me Soph."

"Are you here after Tiber?" Ambryn felt apprehensive.

She would be brushed aside and everything she'd worked for taken away. . . . "Where's the rest of your team?"

"I have no team."

Ambryn froze at Soph's tone.

"My team is dead. All of them. The mission is destroyed, and I only barely made it down to Golgot alive myself. I was hoping that we could reach an arrangement. All I need to do is get off-planet. Out of here."

"Oh, no," Ambryn said. "Oh, no . . . I'm sorry. I . . . I'm sorry. There's nothing I can do. Nothing I have."

"I just need to use your contacts to arrange transport," Soph said with forced patience. "If I can get from Ishtar south to Aphrodite, I can make contact with one of the eco-teams. We had dealings with them. And they have off-planet connections—"

"No," Ambryn whispered. "Those were all . . . Derinda's contacts. I knew them, used them . . . but I can't use them anymore. They had their reasons for dealing with her. . . ." She looked at her ex-lover's floating body. "And now they have their reasons for not dealing with me."

Soph looked dismayed, and Ambryn knew why. To bolster her value to her mysterious Lunar information buyer, Ambryn had claimed underground connections that were actually Derinda's. While involved with her, Ambryn had been able to back these claims up with hard evidence. Ambryn and Derinda had, in fact, helped two Martian researchers trapped in the Maxwells escape to Aphrodite, exactly as Soph now wanted to. Now Ambryn wondered why Derinda had done that, and how deep her game had actually been the whole time.

"There's nothing I can do," Ambryn said miserably. "And I need to escape as much as you do, now."

"Perhaps you have a place to wash up." Soph was brisk. "Then I can be on my way." As if in anticipation of her decision, her luggage had gathered itself together and waited by the door.

"Please! What are you after? Maybe I can—"

"The less we say to each other, the better." Soph nodded at Derinda. "Is this personal? Or is she Enforcement & Joy?"

Ambryn had been wondering that since Derinda's reappearance. She'd always thought that—whatever they had between them—it was entirely personal. "Both."

"Then we should both get the hell out of here. Now."

"Where? Where will you go?"

"As I said, the less we know about each other, the better."

Ambryn could see that despite her coolly professional demeanor, the other woman was at the edge. Soph had exhausted all of her other possibilities before coming here. And now Ambryn had disappointed her too. She'd taken that monthly retainer from that secret data buyer on Luna and in return was able to give nothing.

"Look." Ambryn decided to give it all up. She'd never get in to Tiber now, not alone. She needed any help she could get. "I have a way of contacting Tiber. A way through the Guts. I've been working at that ever since . . . ever since I got him trapped down there in the Well. I've just succeeded in finding something. I was thinking . . . Derinda was after it too."

"You're the one who trapped Tiber?" Soph said. Ambryn could see that she'd caught the other woman's interest. "When he came down to visit the Bgarth?"

"Yes. It wasn't . . . I meant to talk to him. That was all. I have my own reasons for it. But things went wrong. If you help me, I have a way into—"

"I'm not interested in Tiber." Soph's voice was flat.

"What? But—" Ambryn was close to crying. "He's valuable! Not just to me. My personal reasons . . . he came down to go after that alien up in the Maxwells, the really secret one that everyone knows about. And Tiber still has his atmospheric shuttle down there in the Well. That could be a way out! For both of us. Enforcement & Joy couldn't expect us to come up with an operational shuttle. We'll take them by surprise!"

Ambryn was flying. She could barely believe what she was saying.

"Tell me what you did to trap him." Soph said. Her flat face revealed nothing, but Ambryn knew she'd caught her interest.

"Do you want to help me get Tiber out?" Ambryn said. "It could be useful to both of us."

Soph looked at her for a long moment. What Ambryn had interpreted as a lack of expression was really a look of deep thoughtfulness, she realized. There was something attractive about it, as if thought implied vulnerability. Maybe that was because Ambryn got the impression that Soph's thoughts often hurt her.

"You understand that our goals most likely have nothing to do with each other," Soph said finally.

"I . . . understand." Did this mean that Sophonisba Trost had agreed to try to recover Tiber? Ambryn wasn't sure.

An alligator bag in her luggage opened and Soph picked up a detection device with a tortoiseshell handle. Ambryn found this evidence of style consciousness calming. Perhaps she and this dry, intense woman had something in common, after all.

"I don't want there to be any question." With quick movements that would have done credit to a pickpocket, Soph searched Derinda. The instruments scanned for body implants and electronics in the clothing. Soph found much of both. "We want Tiber for completely different things. You want—what?"

"I just want to talk with him," Ambryn said. "The *Argent* is packed with Ulanyi biological membranes. It was intended to house Ulanyi sentient embryos."

"I know," Soph said.

"Tiber hijacked it before it was ready. The place is, to all accounts, falling apart. I was raised as an Ulanyi embryo jockey. It's a family skill. When I heard the *Argent* was coming to Venus . . . well, I remembered. I fled all that, but . . . I have a lot to offer Tiber. I just wanted to do it."

Soph stared at her, as if uncertain of whether to take her seriously. Maybe all of Soph's decisions were carefully considered. That wasn't Ambryn's way.

"You want Ripi." Ambryn took a wild guess. "And you think you can use Tiber to reach him."

Soph winced. "Yes."

"I thought that if you weren't after Tiber specifically, you must be after Ripi." She felt pleased with herself for having hit the target. "So you still want to get to him, even though your team is . . . wiped out? I bet we can get you off Venus and aboard the *Argent*. Then you can go home. Why trek on up into the Maxwells?"

"Actually, I have no desire to go home." Soph pulled a small object out of Derinda's pocket and examined it. "I simply had no other alternatives. If I have something to do, I'll do it. How will you get access to the Well?"

"I have something to trade to the Guts—what are you doing? Don't kill her!"

Soph turned her ebony gun from Derinda and looked startled. "My ex-husband told me never to kill anyone in a strange city. You can never be sure of the consequences." She pushed the barrel against a couple of items she'd taken from Derinda and pressed the trigger. A dull thump—and dust sifted to the floor. "Do you have a secure room in this place? One that can be locked off separately?"

"Um, yes," Ambryn said. "What for?"

Soph grabbed Derinda's shoulders and pulled her out of the pool. Its job done, the support squid had pulled back up into the ceiling. Derinda breathed on her own. Water beaded on the leather suit. "We need somewhere to keep her, don't we? While we discuss the terms of our agreement."

Ambryn first met Derinda at a gallery opening. In the time they were together, Ambryn never quite figured out Derinda's connection to the art world. She seemed to be some kind of art finder, scoring odd works of orbital and convict art for discriminating gallery owners. But she was invited to all the parties.

As soon as she spotted Derinda slouching, drink in hand, near a polished cube of metal with fist marks in it, she knew she had made the right decision in coming. She later learned that the fist marks were Derinda's own, kind of an homage by the artist. After the party, they came back together to Ambryn's, where, for the first and last time, Derinda professed a deep interest in the practice of skrying.

A week after they got involved Ambryn learned that Tiber was coming down to the surface to visit the Bgarth at the Well. Ambryn had contacts with the Guts, humans who lived in Bgarth tunnels and sought to understand the crustal aliens by changing their own physiologies. They told her that Tiber would be trading membranes and other products that the *Argent*'s Ulanyi biological machinery was designed to produce.

When she was hijacked, the *Argent* was being built at MeshMatrix Krystal for a very specific purpose: to raise Ulanyi embryos in mental isolation from adult Ulanyi. Only human beings would control reality for those embryos. As the embryos grew to intellectual power, their entire worldview would be the creation of human beings. They would, essentially, be intellect slaves to the human-supremacist faction behind the building of the ship.

Ulanyi had colonized the wide, almost-uninhabited plains of North America and Eurasia in the first centuries of alien settlement in the System. They had quickly found humans among the seminomadic tribes of those regions who were willing to interpret the universe to the mind-hungry Ulanyi embryos.

A faction called the Pure Mind group arranged for the ship to be hijacked by Tiber before it could reach full functionality. Tiber had his own reasons for wanting the ship but was willing to accept help where he could get it. But, apparently, placental tissue for embryonic support was aboard when the *Argent* blew out of the construction bay. It was only that tissue that had kept the *Argent* financially viable.

And Ambryn had heard rumors that at least one Ulanyi embryo was aboard. Before fleeing Earth, and her family, she had been trained as an embryo jockey, someone specializing in mental contact with the developing Ulanyi mind. Now, after years of drifting aimlessly through the stew of Golgot, the prospect of contacting that embryo galvanized her into action. She decided she wanted to see Tiber and perhaps find a way to get aboard the *Argent*. It seemed that her earliest ambitions, drilled in before the fights with her family and disillusionment with the goals of human/Ulanyi civilization drove her from Earth, were not dead, after all.

Derinda found out what Ambryn was after and threw herself into the project. Ambryn was sure Derinda had no idea what the ultimate result of success would be: that Ambryn would leave Venus, never to return. It tormented her, sometimes, late at night. But Derinda was so goddam useful. . . . Ambryn was just starting to suspect why Derinda had had so many contacts.

One day they scouted the Well from the air. Ambryn's hobby was renting ultralights to fly into the savage updrafts of the Maxwells. This time she and Derinda flew into the dangerous vortices above the Well. They made love up there in the hostile air, taking turns controlling the aircraft with their toes, laughing, trying to drink from a squeeze bottle that always seemed to point in the wrong direction. They both got bruised from turbulence, and the act turned out to be more exciting than fun. Derinda bit her own tongue and made fun of her own inability to talk afterward. But that moment would hang perfect in Ambryn's memory, a spot of clarity in a jumble of dusty time.

The Well was a vast hole into Venus's crust, kilometers across, dug for unknown Bgarth purposes. The Bgarth grew a landing lip for Tiber's shuttle right at the Well edge. The atmospheric shuttle would land there and be taken into the Bgarth structure, where Tiber could negotiate a price for his membranes. Through her Gut contacts, Ambryn found a place she could meet Tiber as he came out. That was all. All she needed was a few minutes to convince him of her bona fides. If he needed her rare skills—and she was convinced that the *Argent* was dying without them—he could take her up in the shuttle. By this point, she had ceased to consider how insane this entire ambition was.

The Well was surrounded by an Enforcement & Joy security zone. The zone was vast and inadequately patrolled, but penetrating it was beyond Ambryn's capabilities. She needed someone who worked illicit access with corrupt joyboys.

Derinda offered her contacts, but Ambryn had reached her limit. She was starting to feel too guilty about using Derinda. Instead, she found her man herself. His name was Elward Bakst. He got his limo serviced in the lower levels of the Nubu Garage, the same place where Ambryn came more and more frequently to rent ultralights, in pursuit of some memory of innocent childhood when she had flown amid the cumulus clouds above the Canadian prairies.

Elward sat in shadow at the far end of his armored limousine, not smoking, not drinking, just sitting, elbows on knees. His questions had been calm, and she had fallen into trust with him. He had his own contacts with E&J. Those had been expensive. Very expensive. Ambryn had paid, heedless of consequence.

"Tiber was just coming out of the Well when the E&J assault hit." Ambryn's voice was unsteady. "I saw him. He stood at the valve head of the Gut tunnel, looking toward me, ready to say something. A very odd-looking man. . . ."

Soph watched as Ambryn poured herself another glass of the yellow wine she'd pulled from the lacquer cabinet by the head of her bed. Soph had considered forbidding it, but she'd been a mother and knew how to pick the battles that were worth fighting. Ambryn was so tight she was going to snap. Having her drunk was preferable.

"Enforcement & Joy wanted Tiber," Ambryn said. "Maybe as a trade to Earth. E&J helps finance itself from the bounty system."

Soph found something wrong with that reasoning. Lightfoot had pointed out how little Earth was interested in the *Argent*. "How much would Earth be willing to pay for Tiber, do you think?"

Ambryn curled a tendril of hair around a finger and thought about it. In the low-cut velvet dress into which she had changed, she looked like a Renaissance painting of a woman considering a suitor's proposal, even with the black silk bandage on the side of her face. The skrying alcove in which they sat, with its bronze incense tripods, its inlaid table, its fringed curtain, served as the perfect backdrop, which Soph did not think accidental.

"You're right," Ambryn said. "The Terrans *don't* want Tiber back. That would cause too many problems among the various factions. E&J must have been defending Ripi. They're very serious about that. He's their great alien resource, valueless though he has turned out to be."

"I've had experience with E&J's seriousness," Soph said.

"Oh, I'm so sorry!" Ambryn said, placing a warm hand on Soph's shoulder. "They're going overboard, though.

Someone at the Skullhouse is forgetting the only really important aliens on Venus. In Venus. No one knows how the Bgarth might react to a violent attack so near one of their . . . places. It's a senseless risk. The Bgarth have charge of the atmosphere, after all.''

The assault on the Bgarth biopackage had been a similar risk. ''Someone took it. How did you escape?''

''Elward got us out of there,'' Ambryn said. ''Down an escape route he'd set up ahead of time. Derinda made like it was something quite exciting, but we almost got killed, even though we weren't the target. I don't even know if the assault squad knew we were there.

''But that access point to the Well was destroyed. Tiber ducked back into the Gut facility and hasn't been able to get out since. I guess he's tried a couple of times, but E&J is all over the area now.''

Soph and Ambryn had brought Derinda to a small room in the back. It was a thick bubble, insulated against the sucking cold of the longnight outside. It was the only place that could be sealed separately from the rest of Ambryn's apartment. The lean bald woman, with sharp rusty blades torn through her suit, had seemed a frightening figure to Soph, but she could tell from the tender way in which Ambryn laid her out that some feeling still remained. Soph wondered if that feeling would survive what she would soon have to tell Ambryn about what she had found in Derinda's pocket.

''So why do you think you have access now?'' Soph asked. She answered her own question. ''You have something the Guts want. They're willing to defy E&J to get it from you and give you Tiber in return.''

Ambryn's wide gray eyes expressed startlement. She was a woman who had never learned to hide her emotions, because most people were eager to do the bidding of those emotions. Manipulating her must have been the least of Derinda's tasks.

''Yes,'' Ambryn said. ''I purchased a rare piece of Bgarth anatomy. It's something the Guts have never been able to get their hands on. The Bgarth guard themselves particularly against Gut investigation.''

''So where did you get it?''

"Do you ever do anything but ask questions?"

"When I get enough answers to act, I stop," Soph said. "I'm almost there. If you and I are to get Tiber out of the Well, I need all the information you have."

Ambryn did something and a freeze locker packed with human remains floated above the skrying table: arms, legs, internal organs, even heads, their features mercifully invisible under a layer of frost. Soph kept her expression noncommittal.

"Trade goods." Ambryn zoomed in on the frozen human corpses with what Soph thought was too much attentiveness. "From an old contact of mine, a salvage jobber who works out around the Uranus system. It's nothing terrible, despite how it looks. He picked it all up at bankrupt transplant centers. So he told me, anyway. He would rendezvous near Uranus with other collectors. From Outside."

The locker was replaced by a much larger array of low-value pieces of a variety of alien species: vestigial Turtle limbs, discarded Harf carapaces, sterile Tibrini reproductive segments, ambient-light Cruthan eyes.

"This is what he got in return. Not much of interest, right? Starter sets and stuff obsessives use to make their collections complete. But there was also this." She focused in on an irregular chunk of rock. Soph recognized what she had thought was a fossil on a rolling cart. Derinda had ignored it too. "This is a key part of Bgarth internal nav. Their sense of direction, if you will. The jobber held it for me, but I had to pay for it—big. What I didn't spend the first time at the Well, I've spent now. I have nothing left, Soph."

"So you've said."

"Immediately after I bought this, the trader got himself killed breaking into an organ bank that had somehow neglected to go bankrupt. His wife traded his body for a Very Fine set of Ganymedean Turtle mouthparts."

An image of them appeared. They really looked quite handsome against the polished mahogany panels of the grieving wife's foyer.

Just like Ambryn, what Soph wanted most of all now was money. The bodies of the Kammer and Kun expedition lay somewhere under E&J security. In their shoulder blades was enough free cash to finance another expedition. But without a good illegal contact, there would be no way for Soph to get into them.

"Ambryn," Soph said. "Who would be the best person for getting into an E&J secure area?"

"You need to do that?" Ambryn was apprehensive.

"I do."

"As I told you, I don't have a lot of contacts."

"I know." Damn Ambryn for puffing herself up so, and damn Lightfoot for not having caught it. His last loving gift to her had almost gotten her killed. "But you have at least one."

"Who?"

"Elward. Elward Bakst."

"Oh great idea. He's working for Derinda. For . . . E&J." Ambryn touched the bandaged side of her face. "He hit me."

"Anyone else, then?"

"You really need this?"

"I really do," Soph said. "It will finance the whole operation."

Ambryn sighed. "He probably still works out of the Nubu Garage. We can go there, but—

"I don't think we need to go there. I think he'll be back here and be willing to negotiate."

Soph pulled out something she had taken off of Derinda. It was a well-worn pocket stone, such as was carried by drivers, cops, and mothers: all those who have to stand and wait and thus need to fidget. She held it up to the light. It glowed a dark blue.

"Those are thrown up from somewhere in the Bgarth gut," Ambryn said.

Soph turned it over. On the unworn edge, just past where the thumb would rest, were silver initials. Soph squinted. EB.

"Unwise of old Elward to leave such an easily identifiable object behind, isn't it?" Soph said. "Most unwise."

"You found that in Derinda's pocket?" Soph watched a horrified realization grow in Ambryn's gray eyes. "She was going to kill me. No matter what happened, after she found what she was after, she was going to kill me."

"Now, we don't know—"

"I know!" Ambryn raised her hands and turned her head back and forth, as if looking for tears of sorrow but unable to find them. "She was going to set Elward up for it. The police investigation team would find that thing somewhere behind one of the cases, not too far from my body." Now the tears did come. Ambryn kept her hands raised and did not wipe them away. "She would get Tiber, and all of her past would be neatly put away. It would put her professional career right back on track. I'm sure that botched ambush really didn't make anyone at Enforcement & Joy very happy with her."

"If we work this right, they'll be even less happy," Soph said.

Three

1

Elward Bakst crunched across the frost-covered trash in the empty canal. He couldn't believe that he was actually walking across this abandoned turdscape, getting his driving boots dirty. But it was his own damn fault, wasn't it? He couldn't believe the mess Derinda had sucked him into.

The canal had never had water in it. Someone had built this place expecting the oceans to rise faster than they had. The seaside resort area with its little pavilions and shaded walkways was nothing but the fallen ruins of the future. Had the real estate developer believed some rock-chewing Bgarth's promise that it would spit that aqua up pronto? If so, he was as dumb as any Skullhouse politico. The ocean was still kilometers away. Might stay there forever, as far as Elward knew—or cared.

A bridge sagged broken-backed into the mounds of garbage. What was left of the gold trim glittered in a distant streetlight, and for an instant, Elward saw what it was supposed to be, arching over flowing water, ladies with slowly spinning ventilating parasols looking down at the fish. Hadn't worked out that way. Never did, in Golgot.

In the silence, he heard the crashing of a constant landslide as spoil from underground Gut excavations got piled up out on the flats. He could just see mounds of rock in the flare of work lights. They were hundreds of meters high, incredible monuments to pointless labor. People were already thinking of living on them, he'd heard, offering the Guts money for stuff they were throwing away. The rock piles would be islands when the water got higher. Good places for resorts, rich estates. Was everyone completely crazy?

He hadn't dropped the stone. He knew that. He always kept it in an inner pocket so that it wouldn't get scratched up. He'd bought it himself with some of the money from his first transport job. He thought about it. Derinda sometimes pretended to be interested in his body and touched him in a way he found hard to resist, even though he knew that his hard bulk held nothing for her. But the touch was good—when she did it.

Ambryn had never known who Derinda was. Hell, at the beginning, Elward hadn't either, which was really dumb. But Derinda had shown up at the Nubu Garage with a head of thick hair, Ambryn's girlfriend, and he'd always kind of liked Ambryn. She had good flesh, and she smiled at people. He'd let her talk him into something ridiculous and dangerous. And after it all came apart and they barely got out with asses intact, Derinda revealed herself to be the joyboy she'd always been, grabbed Elward's balls in a legal vise, and informed him that he was either working for her or going down for violation of an Enforcement & Joy security zone, conspiracy to transfer an alien resource, fleeing the scene of a legal assault, and so on. That hadn't been much of a choice.

Ambryn Chretien's building backed up onto the embankment. Elward climbed the railing of the fallen bridge. A mass of abandoned gear lay piled against the building rear. He climbed that too. It was covered with ice and snow, and he almost fell off twice. When he got up to the balcony, he was sweating.

He'd wanted this to be the approach in the first place. Ambryn's security was terrible. She always cut corners. Derinda could have gone in, gotten whatever the hell alien gland Ambryn had, and been out. But no. Derinda wanted a nice face-to-face, as if Ambryn had done something to her. Hell, maybe she had. Elward got the impression that Ambryn could be a bit casual with human organs herself. So: a little personal revenge. A bit messy for a supposedly professional job.

The balcony was buttoned down for the winter. The rippled black fabric parted with a single slash of his utility knife. Insulating foam puffed out. He reached in, grabbed handfuls, and threw it into the air to watch it drift off on the frigid longnight breeze. In the streetlights, the blobs of insulation looked like faraway clouds, like over the mountains. You could see the Maxwells from right here in the middle of Golgot, but Elward had never been there.

The place was dark and silent. That smell . . . something like animals, rich pets with clean silky fur, screwing. It gave him a shiver, that rich sex stink. He clipped through the temperature alarms so that the house wouldn't detect cold longnight air coming through the cut.

Someone lay on the floor. He pulled himself up against the curving wall and flipped out a gun.

Well, well. Derinda must have untied Ambryn so that she could have some fun and ended up having a little too much. He kneeled down next to Derinda and searched. No thinkstone.

But, goddammit, the door into the apartment was locked. It wasn't supposed to be. But, of course, Ambryn had confined Derinda in here. She didn't want the slinky little joyboy coming back in after her.

He pulled out a tube of spray-on insulation, the sort of thing every Venusian carried when out during longnight, and sprayed it over Derinda's too-fancy leather outfit. The foam puffed up and hardened until she looked like a fallen snowman. It would keep her alive in the bitterly cold air that spilled into the bubble through his cut. With the thinkstone missing, and probably other evidence of his presence around, he didn't want her to turn up dead either. If he played this smooth, she'd never know he'd been here.

He fiddled with the door lock. Ambryn hadn't expected someone equipped with full penetration gear, and it didn't take long. He crept down the dark rear hallway into the treatment room. Steam clung to the surface of the pool. He looked around for his thinkstone. The floor was wet. He didn't know what that meant. But where was Ambryn?

The skrying room was through a curtain. There she was, still in the chair. Hmm. Elward saw her shift her weight.

"Miss Ambryn?"

Somehow, when he felt the hardness of the gun muzzle under his chin, he wasn't a bit surprised. He dropped his own gun without even being asked. He hoped that gained him some points.

"Can I help you find something?" He didn't recognize the woman's voice. That didn't surprise him either.

The figure in the chair was . . . luggage, goddammit. Just some kind of mobile storage bags, now scurrying around, as if making fun of him. A leather purse bounced open and spit out some cable cuffs. The woman with the gun snatched them from the air.

"I came back to see if Ambryn was all right," he said. "Derinda had no call to go so far. My personal opinion."

"Please put your hands behind your back."

He liked that: "please." Who was this woman? She barely came up to his shoulder. Could he take her?

"Don't." She'd detected his minute weight shift. The gun jabbed into his larynx. "Your hands."

He put his hands behind his back. The cuffs snapped on around his wrists.

"No, really," he said. "I'm not just some kind of random sneak thief. I was here before. Just a little strong-arm job, I thought. You know, a warning with aversive conditioning. Nothing complicated, but it takes a professional. It's easy to overdo that kind of thing."

"Overdo! You almost smashed the side of her head in."

"No, I did not!" He was exasperated. People always overreacted to things. "I hit her, drew a good show of blood for Derinda, nothing a spray of skinseal and a couple of days won't get rid of. What's the story here?"

"Are you Elward Bakst?"

"No sense in denying it, I guess."

"Well, let's see what Elward Bakst would know, if he's as good as he thinks." A rustle as she put the gun away. "A few weeks ago, an illegal expedition was annihilated in the

Maxwells by an E&J assault squad. Do you know anything about it?"

"I heard about it. Gossip at the usual bunker watering holes, you know. Jaw, jaw."

"Anything about the disposition of the bodies?"

"Hmmm." He looked off, as if thinking deeply. He could still take her, he thought. He had no arms, but it would take her a second to get at her gun. She'd put it in an awkward pocket. That could be enough. He had heavy boots and knew how to use them. He could kick and then drop down on her. The cuff release had to be on her somewhere.

A noise made him glance at the luggage. A little bag on top was open, and a gun poked out of it, as if a team of trained hamsters was balancing and holding it up. It pointed right at him. As he watched, a display screen unrolled and brightened up with a picture. It showed his face. And in the middle of his forehead was the glowing ruby dot of a target indicator. For some reason, he didn't look happy. And he'd missed a spot when shaving.

The woman hadn't made a sound.

"I heard something about it." He felt like he had to show her that he had *something* on the ball. "There's a big fight inside Enforcement & Joy about them. A jurisdictional dispute. Seems that the assault squad that hit them didn't get their orders right. They were supposed to leave some of them alive, you know, for questioning."

"They didn't take any prisoners?"

"Nope."

She sucked in air. Her folks, then. Or maybe she was just a genuinely caring person.

"Anyway," he continued, "the instructional boys are all pissed off, because they have no one to interrogate. No one seems to want the bodies or know what to do with them, so they've dumped them in a reconditioned meat wagon over to the secure spaceport. Someone from the Skullhouse is supposed to stroll on over there and look them over, one of these longdays. That's about all I know."

"You once did a job for Ambryn Chretien."

"Total screwup," Elward said. "An ambush I should have

spotted even before I let her hire me. Almost got us all killed.''

''So you came here to apologize?''

''No. Wasn't my fault, anyway. She should have been smarter.''

''She judged your performance satisfactory. Exemplary, even. She particularly admired your sublevel contacts with E&J.''

''Sure, I can slide in anywhere. They always need someone deniable to rob their own organization. Hell, that's what Derinda's been using me for. Paying me well too, I have to admit. A push/pull thing, I couldn't resist. I got in a spot of financial trouble, never mind the details, but I needed the cash or I might lose the car. Without the car, I'd have to do something like bodyguard some snot-nosed kid while he struts around the play yard pissing on the scholarship students, then wipe him and tuck him back in when he's done.''

''Not your ambition.'' A bit of amusement in the voice. That was good. If brass knucks and guns didn't work, you used funny. At the moment, funny was all he had. ''So are you currently employed, Mr. Bakst?''

He didn't anticipate anything she said, but none of it surprised him. It felt fated. Maybe he'd done this all in another life. Maybe that Ambryn could find some alien guts that would explain it to him.

''Well, I still got Derinda's job to finish. . . .''

''Derinda was going to send you down for a murder. I might have something profitable enough for you to give you some wiggle. Would you like that?''

''I'd need to know the details. And, ah, I'd like my thinkstone back.''

The woman smiled. ''Of course. Sit down.''

He moved toward the big chair he'd tied Ambryn to.

''No. On that big blue trunk.'' The luggage shifted with a grunt, and there was a nice flat place to sit. The gun bag closed itself back up. ''It has a pressure sensor under the lid. If you try to get up without permission, it will jab nerve toxin into your buttock, and you'll be dead before you take a step.''

"Where do you *get* luggage like this?"

"Nowhere you shop. Please sit."

2

Soph stood in the darkness, breathing slowly. From glimpses of the mildewed remnants of large-breasted-woman-and-earth-moving-machine posters on the walls, Soph figured the trailer had once been a mobile office for a construction site. Someone had brought in panels to cover the windows, but they were the wrong size and so leaned uselessly against the wall, a deep kick mark on one a memorial to an installer's frustration. All that screened anyone's view of the inside was a desultory spray of black paint across each window.

The ground-surveillance lights of copters taking off from the nearby E&J landing pad stabbed in through the gaps in the paint, each time picking out a new view of a clenched hand, an exploded thigh, a disturbingly peaceful face. The body pallets had been jammed in without attempt at order, rolling one corpse up against another. There wasn't even room to walk between them, so Soph had been forced to clamber across the corpses of people she had worked with only weeks before, in order to suck money out of them.

It had been worse than she thought. Much worse.

Soph's breath puffed as she cut into Kammer's frozen shoulder. A thick cable dangled out of the trailer's rear, but there was no power hookup to plug into. Instead, longnight cold kept the bodies preserved. This ill-planned storage facility was temporary while the jurisdictional squabbles were settled.

One of her bags played an IR beam on Kammer's back while Soph viewed her surgery through close-up goggles. Soph had brushed Kammer's hair forward to hide the fact that most of her face had been shot away. It curled golden down to the scratched floor, as if Kammer had just fallen asleep in a deck chair and would have to be awakened soon to keep from getting sunburned. The fingers of her right hand were broken. Someone must have wrenched a gun from her death-tightened grip. But this shoulder looked perfect, ready for a low-cut dress, a night out. Soph sliced delicately down through the muscle layers until she saw the gray-white of the scapula.

There. Soph stuck the socket under her pinkie fingernail into the cut, down through the frozen flesh to the credit module. The pulse of data felt warm up her arm. My God. Kammer had been carrying a lot of cash. Soph was appalled. She could have used some of that, for better defensive precautions. All too late now.

Another copter rattled by overhead. Did its lights linger a little too long over the supposedly uninhabited body-storage trailer? Soph held her breath. The beams slid away, moved down the line of warehouses, illuminating Elward's limo, which was parked among some other cars by the black cube of a warehouse a hundred meters or so away, and then hunted across the torn rubble to the horizon.

Elward should be about done with his business in the warehouse now. He was proceeding with his smuggling job for Derinda, as if he knew nothing about her attempts to frame him for murder. This was simple prudence on his part, for during his negotiation with Soph, Derinda had escaped through the cut in the insulated bubble and disappeared, courtesy of Elward's sprayed insulation. Ambryn, weeping and frightened, had been hidden in the depths of the Nubu Garage, in a hidey hole Elward had set up, and Soph was working as fast as she could to get Tiber out of Golgot and off to Ripi's covert in the Maxwells. Elward needed deniability for when Derinda finally turned up. He'd get his share of the scapular cash, but there would be no evidence he'd had anything to do with the operation.

Soph turned her IR viewer off. There was nothing to cover Kammer with. Their gear was elsewhere. Everyone looked so cold lying on the floor. Soph had known them only for a few short weeks. They had never been friends. She wished there was something she could do for them. Kun must have escaped with a few of the others in the shuttle, but all those who had been left behind had died, even those who'd tried to surrender.

She picked up the bag, and it clung to her belt. She swung out and made the long drop from the battered door of the construction trailer. The air outside was so cold her nostrils seemed to crackle. Ice probed down her neck through gaps around her hood. Nothing lay around her but the rubble that was the basic structure of the Venusian surface, even after centuries of terraforming. Far off across the rubble plain, an orbital shuttle took off from the spaceport. Its light flickered across the rocks as it rose, then curved off to the west. The rest of her luggage, which had been standing watch outside, collected itself behind her.

The limo's engine purred in the darkness. A thin stream of condensation rose from a vent on the rear of the cab. Soph climbed the ladder to the warehouse. Like the body-storage trailer, the place was left over from some long-ago construction operation, perhaps the first building of Golgot. The metal skin was shredding off the fibrous skeleton.

''You're flush, you're heavy.'' Elward pushed a wheeled pallet stacked with metal slabs. ''You're full of money, like a tick.'' The slabs looked like hunks of spacecraft hull, with scorch marks and edges melted from reentry. One showed a cracked adhesion point where the descent parasail had been attached. ''You're about to explode.''

''Are we ready to go?'' Soph asked.

He looked at her. She'd said the wrong thing. ''We're ready,'' he said. ''But not to go. Not yet.'' Despite the coldness of the space, he unsealed his jacket. ''Let's do it. Here, right? Let's do it here. Within our agreement.'' He bared his muscled torso.

She stood behind him. ''We could just load up through the normal input channel.''

''No,'' he said. ''I like this way. It's more secure.''

''Fine.'' And with that, she sliced through the skin of his shoulder.

Blood streamed down his ribs. Keeping his data store so isolated showed a ridiculous fetish for security, she thought. Such a store was suitable only for black-edged security cash like this. It was like it wasn't even real money, but a spell, a knot of power, an ancient coin with an emperor's head stamped on it. The money was tied to his will, to his desire. If the spending did not arouse him, the money would not leave him.

''Take a look at this stuff,'' he said. ''This is what Derinda uses her joyboy status to get. It's made her rich. Maybe, if this Tiber thing doesn't work out for her, she'll just retire.''

Soph looked at what appeared to be pieces of what had once been a fuel tank. Graffiti was scrawled across it, some carved in with abrasion cutters, some with welded-on dust. They were mostly crude obscenities.

''Penal work,'' he said. ''Prisoners in orbit, working metal salvage. Old craft from the Outer System used to get sent down in minimum-energy-transfer orbits to Venus to help in its settlement. Some of them are still coming, will for centuries.

''True shit job, sorting that space junk, tossing it down to the surface. Disciplinary labor. They get used to it, addicted even. Their body-hugging spacesuits fondle them. They drink distillate of their own urine and sweat. Even carbonating it with CO_2 sucked out of their own breath can't really hide that. A pulsing fusion tube dug in along their spine, farting ionized plasma. Grab each incoming booster or support module, slap a wedge chute on, send the baby down to the surface. Like being a god, I guess. A little god, the idol kind unit dwellers dig out of a drawer and beat when the rent comes up short.''

He kicked at the wheeled pallet, bringing it around. The money flow into his scapular store was amazingly slow. He must want to feel every penny as it slid in and clicked into place. On the metal, Soph saw what looked like teeth marks, livid bruises, knife cuts.

''Leave their marks. Look.'' Elward leaned forward and rubbed his fingers across the patterns, lips pursed. ''Classic bite with suction bruise here. Little scalpel probing, sharp, the blood makes everything slick. Ah. Nice double-thumb press, snap the hyoid bone, clean strangle. Child, probably. Adults struggle too much for that particular grip.''

''What the hell is this?'' Soph said tightly.

''Criminals doing time in orbit, like I said. No one to exercise their talents on, so they create . . . art. And you know what the incredible thing is? They don't know. They don't know that their little scrawls sell for big money down here, that collectors have them on their walls, in their gardens, hanging on wires above their beds. No, they do it for pure love. Who the hell else does anything for love?''

The money was in. She pulled away. He turned, looked at her, smiled. His face glowed.

''Ripi, right?'' he said. ''That's what you're after.''

''I don't know who you're talking about.'' It was an effort to remain calm. Everyone knew her business. She slapped skinseal on his wound.

''No big deal. What do I care? It's just a guess, Soph. Just a guess. Lately there's been a lot of interest, is all. Why else would a sweet lady like you come to Golgot?''

''Tourist,'' Soph said. ''Seeing the sights.''

''Ah. Too bad your buddies ran into one of our major landmarks. Enforcement & Joy. A wonder of the Solar System.'' He shrugged back into his jacket. ''You know, these same guys, they drop all sorts of stuff down to Ripi. His house is built of old spaceship parts, did you know that? The Skullhouse gives him the pick. What they don't know is how much active stuff floats down along with the junk.''

She helped Elward load the heavy art into the limo. It was clearly Elward's home, as well as his center of operations. A bedroll and toiletry kit lay against one door, only cursorily tied down, so that drinking cups and epidermal cleaning sticks rattled around on the exposed corrugated subfloor. The car smelled sour, like a man spent too much time in it.

The limo's engine powered up and the tires spat gravel. Soph barely made it in the back door. She would never be sure whether Elward had meant for her to.

3

''Soph,'' Ambryn said. ''I heard her. She was here.''

''Who?'' Soph was distracted, looking up at the Nubu Garage's vaulted roof, where three gossamer-winged ultralight aircraft dangled from support lines, ready for launching.

''Who? Derinda! Who else?''

Soph's head snapped. ''What did you hear?''

''Silence.''

Soph didn't say anything.

''See? Just like that. This entire place roars and rattles. I was in that damn equipment closet Elward stuffed me into while you two were off doing whatever you were doing." She still resented being left out of Soph and Elward's plans. "I put my head on that damn Bgarth nav organ, but it couldn't tell me where to find sleep. People chattering, workers in the next bay . . . and then quiet as she passed. She was walking the skidgrids looking for me. For me, Soph. It was like hearing the shadow of a hawk."

"She gone now?" Soph asked.

"I think so. She always did have a short attention span. But she'll be back. Where the hell is Elward?"

"He has his cut." Soph sounded disappointed at Elward's being gone. That was insane. "He's gone. He had big plans, I gathered."

"Elward always had big plans. I had big plans too, come to think of it. Now . . ." Now the plans were all Soph's. Ambryn couldn't even figure out how that had happened. They were, after all, supposed to be equal partners in this operation.

Ambryn and Soph stood on the equipment platform that hung under the aircraft, high above the rest of the Garage.

"If you want to hire one of those, you'll have to negotiate with the aircraft themselves," Ambryn said. "They do the risk assessment and price accordingly. I've never been able to afford to rent any of these, but I'd suggest *Len-3*. From what I've heard, the other two are by nature more risk-averse. They'll probably reject your initial bid and shut themselves down. Think you can handle it?"

"You'll be the pilot," Soph said. "Perhaps you should—"

"It's your cash. Your operation. Everything is yours. It's an old expert billing system, upgraded over the decades. These craft are more than a hundred years old. There's a reason they've survived. They pay for their own repairs, buy their own parts and upgrades. Over the decades, each has hit on a survival strategy based on its inherent structural features. *Len-3* is physically tougher and can take more damage. So it can afford to push the risk curve in pursuit of greater profit."

"And the Garage provides the support system?" Soph looked at the manipulator arms, circuit furnaces, lubrication tubes, and power feeds that hung under the vault along with the aircraft. Dangling platforms were stacked with replacement parts.

Some of those parts, Ambryn suspected, came from aircraft that had gone too far into debt to the company store and lost their independent existences. All of *Len-3*'s negotiations would have, at their base, the need to avoid that fate.

"Yes," Ambryn said. "But these aircraft have good maintenance and supply contracts. They lease space and services from the Garage. If they decide to, they can fly off. There are plenty of other places that would be willing to cut a deal with them. The aircraft exchange information, keeping each other updated. Such craft have been known to swarm, taking their business elsewhere en masse. The Nubu Garage treats them well, believe me."

While Soph negotiated, Ambryn paced the platform, feeling it shift beneath her feet, and looked out the observation bubbles at the busy traffic of the surrounding neighborhood.

Soph's plan was risky but tight. The Guts, the Well, Tiber, the ultralight: it all fit together. There was nothing in the plan that Ambryn couldn't have come up with herself, and her Bgarth nav organ was a key part. There was no exotic piece of off-world technology, no use of forces from elsewhere, nothing but what was readily available for use, including Ambryn's own skills. But she hadn't come up with it. Soph had. Ambryn felt like someone who had been trying to scale a wall for days, only to have someone else come by, build a functional ladder out of corn shocks lying on the ground in plain sight, and clamber right over.

Outside, a tow truck grunted up one of the Garage's ramps, towing a flame-blackened vehicle with shattered windows, bent almost double from impact.

Ambryn recognized Elward's limo.

"I'm glad I have some money," Soph said, looking at the display. "*Len-3*'s asking for a heavy risk add-on."

For the first time, Ambryn felt disturbed. "How big a risk?"

Soph looked at her and smiled. "You'll be glad to know that *Len-3* will give us a 10 percent discount if you are the pilot. These craft do trade information all through the Garage, don't they? *Len-3* has a good measure of your skill. It seems that there was one particular high-risk procedure over the Well . . . at any rate, you just missed getting the 15 percent discount.''

''Sorry.'' Ambryn found herself embarrassed, wondering if Soph knew that that high-risk procedure had been screwing Derinda in midair.

She looked out at the ramp. The tow truck and burned car had disappeared. Let it get towed in, she thought, parts removed for salvage, the hulk dumped into the growing waste pile out on the flats that Garage managers labeled ''future reef development.'' Let Elward disappear. He already had disappeared. Then let him never return.

''Soph,'' Ambryn said. ''I think something bad has happened to Elward.''

4

Elward had his limo washed and quick-lacqued after maintenance. He admired its blue-black gleam in the overhead lights of its bay. He'd never had the money to spare for that before. It looked great.

He slid into his couch. A task list flickered above the dash, bright stars offering self-congratulatory assessments of quality. He'd gotten a quick adjust on the rear inductive rotor. He looked forward to feeling the extra power. Sensing his need to go, the bay door slid open. Now he could get the hell out of here and leave that Soph and her weird plans far behind. He had things to do.

A joyboy in a long leather coat stood in the lane, skidgrid shadows streaked across her bald scalp. It was Derinda. Elward considered gunning the engine and running her over. He could be out into the Maxwell foothills before anyone raised an alarm: the Nubu Garage resisted E&J penetration. But that would be stupid. After all, she was the one who had sent him away, at Ambryn's. As far as she knew, he had had nothing to do with what had happened afterward. She was after her art. She could have it. Then they would be done with each other.

"Keep driving, Elward." Derinda slid into the backseat. She had to have crossed a fair amount of Golgot in freezing longnight with nothing more than a layer of sprayed insulation to protect her. Now she hunched in the backseat, as if still holding the cold.

"Where to?"

"Just drive. I love the way you drive. Smooth yet powerful. Just the thought of it excites me." She failed to put any emotion into her voice.

He pulled out into the dark Golgot streets. She smiled and licked her upper lip. The mirror showed him a new addition: she had a miniature pellet gun under her pink tongue. A quick visit to the E&J surgery, it looked like. Its barrel briefly pointed at the back of his head.

"Got a good load this time, looks like," Elward said. "There's some real talent up there in orbit."

He heard a clank as she kicked the stack, but she did not examine any of it. Usually she dug right through it, her breath coming fast.

She leaned forward and stroked the back of his neck with cold metal nails. She wore nothing but a soft camisole under her coat. Her skin looked cold but felt hot.

"I got nailed by someone," she said. "I woke up covered with hardfoam. I walked home. I could barely remember who I was."

"At Ambryn's? After you sent me away, you mean?"

"Elward. Dear Elward." Her breath was hot on his ear. "You came back, didn't you?"

"I don't know what you mean. You sent me away. I went. I took that hide. My tip. It's still in the back."

"Where's your emergency hardfoam canister?"

"Around here somewhere. The car's a mess. I really should clean it up."

He felt like a jet of longnight air had gone straight up his ass. She knew. She knew he had come back.

"Don't slow down, Elward." She slumped back in her seat, far away from him. "I never knew this job would be so lonely. So devoid of real contact."

"What did you expect?"

"Ambryn never knew, did she? Who I really was."

"Ambryn never knew."

"But you did, smart boy."

"Not right away," Elward said.

"Soon enough."

"No," Elward said. "Not soon enough."

Derinda had been a joyboy from day one. She'd set up her first meeting with Ambryn. Derinda had known that the *Argent* was coming up on Venus for whatever the hell complicated operation. And Derinda had known to cover the Well. She'd gotten Ambryn, who had the contacts and information, all excited about getting into the Well to meet the *Argent*'s captain. Derinda had also known how to have a good time. It all worked out real nice until her operational boys had jumped the gun and started blasting away before the target was clear.

"Ambryn was protected," Derinda said. "She'd made contact with some kind of off-world extraction team. I never knew. Dear Ambryn. I never knew what she was capable of."

She sounded betrayed, as if Ambryn had deliberately lured her in. She huddled in the backseat, arms around her knees.

"It was my last chance, Elward. Oh, God!"

She shifted around in her seat. There were no options for her. She'd been assigned to pull in this Tiber, captain of the *Argent*, and she had blown it. She'd had too good a time with Ambryn, and none of her plans had worked out. Now she had to . . . what? What were her options?

"Elward. Please don't drive too fast. Look at that. Doesn't it look beautiful in the night?" Elward felt a surge of warmth toward her. She had suffered. She had been driven to work for E&J. She looked like a little girl back there.

"It does," he said.

A twisted, spotlit shape loomed above Golgot. The Skullhouse was the shell of the first Bgarth to have landed on Venus. It had crashed into the crust as cometary storms had torn the surface. When humans finally came, many years later, they found the shell completely empty. The Bgarth had injected itself into the crust in a new incarnation. The ragged top of the Skullhouse marked where the fusion drives that had carried this Bgarth into the System had lost their magnetic fields and novaed. The detonation had left the shell half-melted and useless for trying to figure out anything about the Bgarth that had supposedly once inhabited it. Skullhouse was a misnomer, but Elward supposed Butthouse just didn't have the right tone.

"I used to make wishes on it out my window when I was young."

"Ah, sure."

"Elward. What did you do when you came back?"

"I told you, I didn't—"

"You have your thinkstone back in your pocket. The one I took. You really should get rid of that habit, Elward. It will get you into trouble someday."

It suddenly seemed like a boulder against his hip. God damn it. Soph had given it back to him, as if she was doing him a favor.

"I saved your life," he said. "Put the foam on you."

"Why do you think you're still alive, dear Elward? I'm grateful. Very grateful. Can you . . . can you lower your couch? No, no, don't stop driving."

The ergonomic adjustment motors hummed as they brought his head back, and she slid up next to him. Her hands moved here and there on his body, and he found himself excited. And she talked. She spoke in an even monotone, giving him instructions, telling him how to feel, how to react. He obeyed, for a moment forgetting who she was. She pulled the thinkstone out, and he realized she'd just been guessing about it. Dammit.

A fingernail scratched at the healing wound on his shoulder and, freezingly, he understood everything.

He had to want to give the money up. That was the way it was stored in his scapula. Will released it. She knew that he had gotten the smuggled artwork only a few hundred meters from where those cash-full bodies had been lying. She wanted it. Her career was bust, she wanted to get the hell out, and here he had come driving up with just what she needed to do it: a good load of cash.

"Come on," he said. "Come on. I never knew."

"There was nothing to know." Her gleaming bald head moved down his chest.

He reached under his seat with his heel and deactivated all of the limo's safety systems, except for the ones protecting the driver. The factory-sealed interlocks had been devilishly hard to get through.

He'd steered by instinct through the tangled streets, the timing was right, and his destination lay ahead: an overpass with its abutments protected by solemn falcon statues, symbols of some long-defunct official cult. Shock-absorbent padding normally swathed them, but some fund had recently donated money to have their black bulks cleaned. The rightmost one stood in alabaster splendor, just a few streaks of black left on one side, as a steam-cleaning machine raised nozzles to its cruelly curved beak. Nothing but a stretched barrier separated its clawed feet from the stream of traffic.

''Let me take this off,'' Elward murmured, leaning over and tugging at his secondary safety harness. ''It'll be easier.''

She leaned back to let him.

As he did so, he jerked the wheel sharply, saying a prayer for the soul of his poor car. They'd been together for years.

Elward saw the startled white dot of the steam cleaner driver's face in the dark window, then the flimsy barrier was flying. The stone claws of the hawk smashed through the windshield.

Derinda lay on the buckled floor of the car, one hand under her cheek. Her coat had fallen away, and she looked incredibly beautiful. Blood sheened on her head.

He turned away and was just about to climb out through the smashed windshield when fingernails sank into his side.

Blood streamed down Derinda's face. Her left arm was broken. She smiled.

''Really, Elward. Is this how you show how much you love me?'' She put her mouth on his neck in a wide kiss, and he felt the barrel of the gun push against his spine.

5

A complex cloud, ruby in the light of early morning, climbed into the sky like the God of the Israelites. A heavy cyclonic stalk supported a vast thunderhead that smashed its way into Venus's upper atmosphere. Constant lightning flickered in the highest clouds. Soph paused in the street and looked up at the eternal storm of the Well's atmospheric column. Despite herself, she thought of her dear, dead, daredevil son, Stephan. He would have loved hang-gliding that thing.

That had to be Derinda's place, with the unobtrusive security seal around the door and the metal shutters, formidably locked, on the windows. Ambryn had, unwillingly, directed her, demanding to know why Soph thought she had to rescue Elward.

Soph had left before it became obvious that she didn't really know.

Behind the cluster of houses was an area of rocky soil covered with spiked plants. Derinda's personal defensive perimeter no doubt extended farther back here, so Soph's luggage generated a decoy and let it precede her.

Soph had devoted some effort to programming the decoy, and what strutted across the sharp-edged grass was a nattily dressed image of Lightfoot. If he tripped a detector and got raked by a UV laser, the clothes would scorch and the collar would become undone, but he himself would remain untouched, looking around in startled incomprehension, exactly the way he had when she told him she was leaving him.

Lightfoot prowled through the spike-tipped shrubs, rubbing his wide belly through his pleated shirt. He was, she knew, utterly in fashion. That made watching him risk his ass so much more pleasant.

During her last talk with Lightfoot on Luna, he had, without comment, given her a stylistic update with a complete image stack of his latest wardrobe. That was gutsy.

The booby trap made just the barest hiss as it went off. Transparent razor ribbon spiraled out from its buried packet and filled the field with what looked like mist.

It shaved grass stems off neatly, topping each with a milky droplet of sap. Shreds of bark hung off the trees and a single aggressive jay squawked once and became nothing but feathers and blood drops.

Soph had just been stepping ahead, sure that she had finally passed all the way through Derinda's perimeter. The ribbon tore past her face and sliced off a lock of hair. She froze for a second, seeing cold transparent death fluttering in front of her eyes, then threw herself backward.

Lightfoot stood there in the middle of it, clothes ripped into confetti. He looked at her pityingly and shook his head. Damn it, she hadn't loaded *that* favorite Lightfoot expression into the decoy. He must have bootlegged it in with the clothing data. The clever son of a bitch.

The dispenser sucked its razor ribbon back into itself, cleaning the edges with a high-pitched squeal. The jay's blood misted into the air. A security bag from her luggage took hold of the booby trap and deactivated it by lying on top of it and clamping it shut.

Ahead, the rear patio of Derinda's house. The insolent Lightfoot image shuffled polished loafers across the frost-heaved paving stones, peered into the pot of a frozen plant left outside during longnight, pushed hands against the rear door, jacket sleeves falling away just right to display fire-crystal shirt trim, then, no further booby traps detected, faded into nothing without looking at Soph again.

Soph pushed open the door and went in.

The interior reeked of shit and sweat. The hot air clung to Soph's face. The high rooms were surprisingly elegant, with white walls and tapestries showing misty mountains and earnestly meditating monks.

Someone clattered in the kitchen, exactly the sound of a normal morning—somewhere else in the Solar System. Derinda sang gently to herself. A coffeepot clinked and steam hissed through grounds. Derinda's light step went out the other side of the kitchen, and a door shut.

Elward lay in the living room, naked and bloody, on a tangle of sheets. The bonds that had once held him now dangled loose from the bed frame. The screws holding the bed to the floor had splintered the fine wood. Derinda had surely attached it with shaking, passionate hands, breath coming fast between her teeth. This was special, the damage said. Elward wasn't like all the others.

The white sheets under Elward were wet with blood and semen. The salty reek clogged Soph's nostrils. His wide back gleamed with sweat. Dried blood encrusted his fingernails.

Soph lay a hand on his shoulder. He shuddered and twisted

toward it, moaning deep in his throat. His hips twisted, and she saw that he was erect.

"There's no more," he said. "You've taken it all." His wheedling tone demanded further punishment.

"Elward."

At the sound of Soph's voice, his eyes opened. The dilated pupils contracted as he looked at her.

"No," he said.

"Shhh," Soph said, her hand still on his shoulder. She whispered, "Did she get it?"

He turned away, huddled up with his head hidden. The wound on his shoulder had not healed. That was hers, Soph thought. She had started this entire thing.

"The money, Elward," Soph said. "Your money. Did she get it?"

For a moment, she thought that the shame would make him ignore her. Then, reluctantly, he nodded. They both knew the deep meaning of the seemingly heartless question. For him to have given up that money . . . Soph didn't want to think about what had been done to him. Vastly worse that he had been made to want it.

"Well, Elward," Derinda's voice said at the kitchen door. "A little R&R will do us both some good. Then we can get back to accounting. Cash withdrawals are so much more fun with this technology, don't you think?"

The bald woman wore a pink robe and carried a breakfast tray with one hand. On it were two steaming porcelain coffee cups and a plate of shiny browned rolls. Upon seeing Soph, she opened her mouth in a round O of shock.

Derinda's chest puffed out under her robe and she fell backward into the kitchen. The cups shattered on the wood floor. She shuddered, tried to push herself up on her elbows, then flopped, loose and dead. Only then did Soph hear her pistol's detonation and feel the kick of recoil.

Soph looked at the gun in her hand, then down at the open security bag. After a moment of hesitation, she clicked the gun back into its mount, which had extended itself up to reach her. The bag sealed itself and then was again nothing but a peacock-green valise with slightly worn brass trim. Her luggage was getting to sense her moods a little too well,

Soph thought. She had not had any idea the gun was in her hand or even that she wanted it to be there.

Derinda's personal weapon gleamed at Soph from beneath her tongue. With her toe, Soph tried to snap the woman's jaw shut, but it kept falling open. Finally Soph rolled her completely over onto her face. Her left arm, she saw, was in a self-tensioning splint. Crude clamp points for tools had been added to it. Soph resisted the urge to kneel down and clean up the coffee. It would just have to pool there and stain the parquet.

Elward sobbed. It was amazing to see him with his bull-like torso curled in on itself, his head hidden, wanting to roll himself up and disappear.

"Elward."

Did he really think she was just going to leave him alone and go?

"Elward. Can you move?"

"She needed it to escape. She kept talking about getting back together with Ambryn, going back to Earth with her, meeting the family, staying safe. Sometimes it all seemed so sweet, like I really should help. Her voice. The way she talked. I wanted to do it."

Soph felt uncomfortable with the nakedness of his pain. He sat up on the bed now and looked to her, as if she had some solution from him, something to calm the fevered mind.

"It's really me in there somewhere," he said. "What I'm really like. That's a thing she understood."

Soph bent down, grabbed the collar of Derinda's robe, and tore it, exposing her shoulder. She stared at it. That money wasn't coming back out. When Enforcement & Joy got the body, they could dump the cash into their party fund.

"Still—" Elward choked. "Still need help? I'll work cheap. I need the money."

6

Elward activated the multiwheeled saurus. Despite its abandoned state, here in junk storage behind the Nubu Garage, the vehicle's motors hummed right up. It was equipped with a pincer claw for picking up abandoned junk on the streets of Golgot. With a remote control panel, he worked the claw through all of its movements, making sure it was not impaired at any joint. He focused on the turning of the joints, as if it was the most important thing in the world.

"What did she . . ." Ambryn's voice faded as she stared at his back. "And you . . . Soph just shot her?"

"Yeah. Just like that. Pretty rude when you think about it. Soph just barged into that cute little place and started blasting. Derinda was just making coffee."

"Look, Elward. I think I know what she—"

He turned on her. "You don't know a goddam thing."

Elward liked seeing her afraid. She really was a looker, and she dressed to show it: high boots, short loose skirt over tight leggings, a purple jacket that fell away, just right, to show the breasts under the ribbed sweater. Too bad none of it did him a damn bit of good.

She touched the black silk on the side of her head. That had to have healed by now. But she still wanted him to feel bad about it. He'd be damned if he would.

"No," she said in a small voice. "No, I don't know anything. I guess I never did. I never knew who Derinda was."

Now he was supposed to feel sorry for her. "Doesn't matter. I hired on after what happened at the Well, and I sure *did* know who she was."

"I'm a little curious as to why you—"

"Look, sweets. There's a lot you want to know, right? But I'm not going to tell you. I'd suggest we both just get on with it."

Elward kept his attention on the saurus. The thing was old. Since it had been designed to be self-modifying, incorporating bits and pieces of junk that it recovered from the streets, it had ended up looking pretty strange. He recognized the suspension of a high-speed bus above the front wheels and the remains of an urban antiriot vehicle in the side-mounted stun flails that settled arguments over towed vehicles. It sure wouldn't be much fun to drive.

"Derinda was going to send me down for that Well thing, okay?" he said. "And she offered me a good deal, smuggling that art for her. So we went to work together. Of course it went farther. It always does—with them. But I had to keep up the car, and that's not cheap, you know?''

''I saw it when they hauled it in. Can you afford to repair it?''

''Not any more.''

''You don't have any money left,'' Ambryn said.

He glared at her, wondering why she was picking a fight after he had just tried to make nice.

''I don't have any left either,'' she said.

''Well, aren't we both just a prize. We both work for Soph now, that right? All we can do.''

''She and I are cooperating,'' she said sharply. ''We share a common goal. She does have money, that's true. That's all she has. Taken from dead bodies. You helped her get it, didn't you?''

''That I did.'' The smuggled prisoner artwork still lay in a pile in Derinda's apartment. He hoped that would slow down the Enforcement & Joy investigation a little, give them a false trail, keep their minds off whatever insane thing Soph was planning.

Soph had taken him out of the house, through the red-glowing streets, to a public hot pool nearby. The heat came from metabolic exhaust from a Bgarth deep beneath the surface.

''Bgarth farts,'' he had said, sinking into the steaming water. ''A tonic for everything. Ain't Venus wonderful?''

Soph had calmed him, washed him, treated his wounds with one of those bags of hers. In the house, when he cried, she'd been almost cold, standing there, not looking at him, as if he'd messed himself and she was embarrassed. Hell, who was supposed to be embarrassed? There he'd been, tortured, covered with come, gasping for more, more . . . But in the pools, she had cared for him. She had held him while he floated in the water. He had tried to tell her about Derinda's voice, about how hard it had been to resist, but he hadn't made any sense, even to himself, and eventually had closed his eyes and slept.

''This whole plan's a little too simple,'' Ambryn said.

''It's only simple if nothing goes wrong,'' Elward said. ''It's the contingencies that always take up all the planning.''

"Sure." She was just pissed that she was now a subordinate, Elward thought.

"Hey," he said. "This alien she's after. Do you suppose she's really going to get something for him?"

"Yes," Ambryn said. "She's going to get something for him. Your cut will make you rich."

"Ha. I was rich before. I lost it in one night."

Ambryn looked up at the high vault of the Nubu Garage as it glowed in the horizontal sunlight of the long early morning. "She must be down in the Gut headquarters by now, with my nav device."

That was sad. Elward knew how hard she had worked to get that damn thing. Derinda had almost killed her to get it. And now Soph had it.

"You friends with them?" he said. "The Guts, I mean? They're crazy, right?"

She sat down on the lower rim of one of the saurus's wheels and crossed her legs. Elward found himself sitting down next to her, as if they were old friends chatting. He liked the feeling, even though he didn't believe it.

"I was at a Gut banquet once," she said. "Their banquet room is the anterior end of a Bgarth that died underground. Each guest sat in front of a big bowl with a shattered edge, as if someone had pallet-knifed it from a dinosaur egg. In it was a thick sludge, some kind of Gut . . . *preparation.* They kept offering us temporary intestinal extensions, like a trombone slide, they described it, fed in through incisions above and below our navels. No one went for it. You couldn't drink the water either. It was full of specialized protozoa. If you took a sip, they'd slide down your throat and start rebuilding your GI tract into a potent chemical engine for what they call the Grand Transformation of Venus."

"Think they'll offer Soph a snack?"

"I'd like to hear what she says."

They both found themselves laughing. When Ambryn laughed, she really did it, head thrown back, teeth white. Her whole body got into it. He liked seeing it.

"Oh, Elward," she said finally. "Do you ever wonder what happens after?"

"After what?"

"After we get Tiber out from under the ground and aboard *Len-3*."

"No," he said.

Four

1

"What happened here?'' Soph said, even though she already suspected the answer. ''An earthquake?''

She and her guide had come to the abrupt end of the curving dining room, where a cave-in had punched through the delicate layers above. Huge sheets of broken glass lay tilted among chunks of dark rock.

It could all have been cleaned up, Soph thought. But there was something memorial about it. She could see the pride of the secret act.

''No earthquakes on Venus.'' Mahmun, her guide, stated the fact as if it was a rule he occasionally had to enforce. ''No tectonic plates. Crust is one solid chunk. Living things make the only changes. A change that you, Sophonisba Trost, can be a part of.''

The inevitable recruiting ad. Ambryn had warned her.

Despite the folds of decorative cloth that concealed Mahmun's belly, his Gut, symbol of his devotion to a new world, Soph still sensed the things that moved beneath concealment, slithering ominously, waiting for an opportunity to spring out at her.

''It wasn't an accident, then,'' she said, resisting a step back.

"Oh, yes, an accident, of course." Mahmun grinned, revealing horse teeth with stainless-steel crowns. His augmented jaw musculature flexed like a weight lifter's biceps.

"Unfortunate."

"Someone was excavating, dozens of kilometers away. This particular Bgarth was digging its way to the surface. Don't know why. A coincidence of rock layers with different refractive indices lensed the shock waves and concentrated them on a fault here. It cut off the first anterior somite and a part of the second. We mourned for months."

"And then you moved in."

"We've learned a lot. There wasn't anything else to do. It was fate."

"And good luck for you."

"No," Mahmun said with a deep sigh. "A tragedy."

These spaces—the high-domed rooms, the slithering passages, the dark slots with their rumbling pumps—all were the insides of a dead Bgarth, abandoned here, deep under rock. This largest sinus, whose low end they stood at, was now the Guts' main ceremonial dining room. Soph wondered what a dinner would be like there.

Had the dead Bgarth been escaping from something? Perhaps it had been fleeing, in its geological way, from some political controversy down in the Well. It had been about to reach the surface when the Bgarth-focused Guts had struck, and thus created themselves a cozy clubhouse.

"Where is Tiber?" Soph had already turned in the Bgarth navigational organ as her part of the deal. Now she wanted to make pickup and get out of here.

"Tiber showed us." Mahmun spoke softly. "It was always there. We just didn't think about it. The pinched-off somites of this Bgarth are still alive, way below us. Tiber wants to ride them."

"Ride them?"

"You'll see."

A passage had been dug through the rubble. Soph and Mahmun climbed down through a maze of excavating machinery, some of it unspeakably primitive: jackhammers, conveyor belts, vibrating drills with power cables whose cracked insulation revealed ungrounded wires. All Bgarth were hybrids of the organic and the mechanical, but Soph had never known how wide the range really was.

"Are you managing to understand?" Soph asked.

"About our masters, the Bgarth?" Mahmun smiled with some satisfaction. "Oh, yes. They can't exist without us, you know. That's clear."

"I understand that they coevolved with a surface oxygen-breathing species of some sort."

"And that species is now vanished. That idea makes them hysterical up top, doesn't it? When they come down to talk to us, you can see the longnightmares they have. The air is gone, and they look out their windows and see Bgarth backs coming up through their gardens. They hope that we can give them some kind of guarantee that it won't happen."

The hypothesis was genocide, Soph knew. The Bgarth had wiped their co-species out in some sort of long-term planet-wide struggle. Then, lonely, unable to function properly without them, they left their planet and traveled long light-years to find a replacement.

"And are their fears misplaced?" Soph said.

"Only if we fail the way the other species did. If we fail to play our role properly." He gestured at the pile of archaic industrial machinery. "The Bgarth need our help. If we work together, Venus will be a garden—above and below."

Soph wondered how much of the Guts' existence was with Bgarth connivance. Those rock slugs did need heavy maintenance, and clever opposable-thumbed tree swingers, self-impressed descendants of *Homo habilis*, made excellent engineering symbionts. She did not believe the paranoid theory that human evolution had, as its secret real goal, the creation of just such a symbiont.

"And Tiber found a way to help you out?" Soph said.

"He wants to go below," Mahmun said. "We can free those lower somites and let them slide back down into the crust. The Bgarth seem to have a network of high-speed transport tunnels down there. Maybe maglev, maybe something else, nobody is sure. But Tiber has converted that shuttle of his into a bathyscaphe and attached it to the somites. We think there is a route back to the surface, in the Maxwells, through the throat of an extinct volcano."

"That's insane," Soph said. "Isn't it?" She had not based her plans on the shuttle's being operable, and this information confirmed her caution.

"Nothing to do with the Bgarth is insane," Mahmun said. "It just sounds like it."

Above them, on a platform supported by pitons sledgehammered into the rock face, stood a steaming food cart, pressure indicator on its domed top showing the readiness of its contents.

The Guts held complex metabolic simulations within their abdomens, in order to feel engineering revelations come from within. Some of them sought, it seemed, not just knowledge of, but identity with the Bgarth. Soph thought that Mahmun had gone further than most. Perhaps one of his descendants would someday, as some Gut extremists had it, swell out his spinal column, inhabit its inside, and burrow beneath the surface to compete with the Bgarth on their own turf.

Mahmun pulled a huge green sausage out of the steam. "The Well's edge is actually several hundred Bgarth fused into a ring. They share metabolic support, even nervous systems, and their nethers thrust down into the planetary mantle. Maybe deeper. This Bgarth was kind of a pseudopod of that structure."

He took a bite and the surface crackled between his teeth. The sausage was marked with silver lettering indicating its microbial substrates and trace minerals. Rows of colorful secretive organs had supplanted Mahmun's weepy pancreas and bile-seeping liver, his imitation of a Bgarth physiology.

"You shouldn't take him," Mahmun said.

"What do you mean?"

"I mean Tiber knows what he wants. And what he wants is to help us reach the Bgarth depths. You should let him do it."

All Tiber wanted to do was reach Ripi in the Maxwell Mountains. Soph was astounded at the lengths to which he would go to get there.

"Careful, Mahmun," she said. "We made a deal."

"I made no deal! Some of the higher-ups have lost touch with the true mission!" His pupils were dilated.

Mahmun, it seemed, was a renegade, a slave to the insinuating Connection whispering somewhere on the discursive highways between pylorus and cecum. It had to happen all the time, a constant fear for any right-thinking Gut. Such an extended amount of digestive innervation could lead to a takeover of the sensory cortex by purely internal signals. There was no time to deal with the outside world: the bubbling chemical plant inside required too much care. Intricate psychoses, chemically modulated, followed. Ambryn had briefed her.

He pushed Soph against a hydraulic drill face with his immense belly. She could swear she felt the vibrating peristalsis of his intestinal muscles, mimicking Bgarth processing of metal ore.

"Let me go, Mahmun," she said.

"No! You're bad substrate. You can't build a world on it. We can handle Tiber ourselves. We don't need your help."

Jesus. The Guts had a great deal to learn about public relations. Bad to have your flacks try to suffocate outside contractors. Puts a damper on negotiations.

She'd been searched at the entrance and all her toys taken away. But public relations wasn't the Guts' only shortcoming. She reached, two-fingered, into a sleeve and pulled out what looked like a silvery handkerchief. A snap of her wrist, and it stiffened into a gun.

Mahmun hesitated, pulled back. "What's that?"

"Oh, just some medicine. For my . . . spells. I like a remote hypo. That way I can cure other peoples' diseases too."

A pharmaceutical code floated above the gun, indicating what was loaded in it. Soph scratched the back of her neck with the corrugated barrel, then pointed it at Mahmun.

"You want to get cured?" she asked.

The code indicated that the hypo contained a tailored broad-spectrum antibiotic. One injection from a dart, and all of Mahmun's carefully nurtured intestinal flora would die. His gut, no longer able to survive with the meager chemical economy of *E. coli*, would rot from the inside.

He shrank back. "No need to threaten," he said sulkily. "I was just trying to explain the situation."

"I admire the clarity of your exposition," Soph said. "May we proceed?"

* * *

The *Argent*'s atmospheric shuttle had been hauled in from the Well lip by the Guts and brought down into the depths of their operation. It had become part of the lower body of the dead Bgarth. Its beetle-like shape squatted within a tangle of piping and wiring, a vast superconducting metal torus around it, as if it was an ore load being launched into orbit by a mass driver.

Laboring Guts squeezed between the overhanging rock face and the Bgarth. Protective meshes held up the crumbling rock. The heavy air had the acrid smell of doom that often clung to operations far under the surface. Soph felt a vibration through her feet and fancied that it was the Bgarth, trembling with anticipation at its release.

"Take him to the surface, then," Mahmun said. "We'll go below. We'll see what's down there ourselves."

That had to have been the plan all along, Soph thought. Tiber was not one of them, not a surgically modified Gut, not a Bgarth worshipper. His desperate need to reach Ripi had been useful to the Guts. It was useful to her too. She had no other way to gain access.

Soph dropped onto the shuttle's back. Light spilled out of the rear hatch, held open for a power cable running into the interior.

She climbed down. The shuttle was packed with Bgarth extrusions that had grown into it, and Tiber was just barely visible, sitting in a control couch, hunched over something. He turned toward her.

He was a big man and dominated the space inside the shuttle. His powerful shoulders matched almost equally wide hips, with a narrow waist between, giving him the proportions of two stacked triangles. His fingertips, as they rested on the back of the couch, had wide flat pads, like a frog's.

Tragic blue eyes sank deep into his oddly distorted face, whose bones seemed not to have known when to stop growing. The sweeping ends of black brows disappeared beneath a mass of long hair. His out-of-scale face was too large for the shuttle interior, like a theatrical property being carried away for storage, bumping against the walls.

"You have transportation to the Maxwells?" he said.

"If we can reach an agreement," she said. "Yes. Better than this, at any rate." The Guts had conveyed to him all the information about her mission as part of the deal for the nav part.

"They don't want to come up, you know." He kept his voice low, but it filled the small space. "They say that they do, that they can drive this thing right up a volcano in the Maxwells. But they're lying. They want to keep going down. That's all they want. What do you want?"

"I want to reach an agreement as to the disposition of the person of Ripi," Soph said. "Each of our missions has failed. Maybe, together, we can cobble together some sort of success."

"What do you *want*?"

She found the intensity of his gaze disconcerting. She didn't know what she wanted. "I want to find out Ripi's secrets."

He paused for a moment, as if that was a novel idea. "The *Argent*'s second atmospheric shuttle is at Ripi's. It was sent as backup. If we reach him, we can use it to get back up to the *Argent*."

Lightfoot had been right again. What that meant, this time, was that she could remain alive to be irritated with him.

"Is that what you needed?" Tiber asked.

"Yes," she said. "We can hammer the rest out as we go. You will give this vehicle up to the Guts for their purposes?" She didn't like operating without a solid agreement, but if they did not get out of Golgot and then off Venus as fast as possible, no agreement would matter.

"Yes, of course," he said. "It is useless to me now. Let's go get Ripi."

And, just like that, he lifted Soph up out of the shuttle, his wide hands on her hips. In turn, though he clearly did not expect it, she braced herself and reached a hand down. For a moment he was fearful of her touch, crouched like a frightened child. Then his fingers closed around her wrist. For all his bulk, he wasn't heavy, and when he stood next to her, she realized that he wasn't tall either, certainly nowhere near Elward's height. The sense of bulk came from his face alone.

As Tiber stepped among the Guts in the cavern, he grew large again, and everyone turned toward him. He had used them, they had used him, and in the end they had won, but she could see the bond that had grown between them. They gathered around him, touched him as if for luck, spoke softly. The Guts with their elaborate Bgarth-modeling abdomens, Tiber with his swollen bones and wide hips: Soph felt the misshapen one, with a body designed for hunting animals across a long-vanished veldt. Her anatomy had simply not kept up with the times.

It wasn't until much later that she realized that he had never told her why *he* wanted Ripi.

2

Elward settled the control helmet on his head and started the saurus's engines. He loved the control helmet. On its gleaming black front flared green laser-grained eyespots. They were the current fashion for anonymous authority figures in Golgot.

He should just go. He owned this damn vehicle now. The Garage had had no interest in leasing it out but had made him prepay a recovery fee if he should abandon it. It was quite a nifty deal for them, and he'd looked over the legal language with some interest. And all Soph wanted him to do was act as a complicated decoy and lumber around to catch E&J's interest. This thing had better uses.

The saurus could be an unusual freelance enforcement vehicle. He could pick up cars, dig out supposedly secure underground bunkers like new potatoes, quell rioting mobs. And he'd look great with this helmet. This saurus could become a mythic creature of the longnight, terrifying and fascinating.

Or maybe he could leave Golgot, grind out the long klicks across the flats of the someday-oceans, down to the long continent of Aphrodite. The ecoteams could use a vehicle like this, he bet. The Skullhouse restricted the technology available down there, trying to keep the Aphrodite ecoteams from taking over the entire planet with their experiments. The saurus would be useful not so much for planting moss colonies, or something, but for conflicts with other ecoteams. Elward understood that those philosophical disagreements sometimes got pretty violent. That would be interesting, smacking around down in the equatorial jungles, seeing the weird creatures those guys were working on, extinguishing an entire species if absolutely necessary.

A little girl watched him from an upper window of a building overlooking the yard. She had long hair, half-blowing across her face from a ventilator, and held something clutched against her chest: a toy truck, a doll, a toaster, Elward couldn't really tell. This yard was part of her entertainment, and the newly excavated saurus, standing tail-up among the abandoned vehicles, was probably the sharpest thing she'd seen in some time. He waved to her, but she just kept staring down at him, as if worried that he wasn't going to do his duty.

She turned to look at something inside the house. Someone was saying something to her. She waved her free hand with theatrical emphasis and pointed out the window. A parent wanted her for something, a meal, a nap, and she pleaded for a few more minutes to watch. She wanted to see what Elward would do, whether he would abandon Soph and escape with his vehicle or whether he would take it to the Well and do what he had agreed.

The parent was kind, and the girl settled back down at the window, chin now resting on her hand. The object she had been holding stalked away—a cat, its upthrust tail mocking the rear crane of the saurus.

He should show her. He should show her that things seldom worked out the way they did in little girls' dreams. The friend betrayed you, the lover infected you, the parent abandoned you. She should learn, damn it. It was about time she learned.

Elward put on his video-feed helmet and swung himself up into the cab, trying hard to look like a romantic figure on an important mission. He ran through all the equipment functions, raising and lowering both ends, whipping out the stun flails, twisting the crane. Then, after torquing the engine to its maximum, he tore out of the lot, sending up a cloud of dust. The thing was top-heavy, and he almost toppled it at the turn beyond the gate. That would have ruined the effect completely.

He looked back in a rear screen, but he couldn't see anything but gray-yellow dust, the buildings' dim looming shapes beyond. She wouldn't know where he had gone. She couldn't know. But she would hope, he knew, that he would achieve his goal and come back safe.

Len-3 spun up its turbines. Ambryn felt the responses of the control surfaces through the steering apparatus. In addition to giving her the physical pushes and pulls that mimicked the actions of the air outside, they provided texture, letting her know instantly about turbulent flow on any surface. The flexible wings folded back into launch configuration.

Ambryn shivered a little and the support lines catapulted the aircraft through the launch hatch. Ambryn felt the rocket assist as a push directly on her butt, a shiver-up-the-spine thrill.

The turboprops grabbed the air and pulled and she soared into the sun. Light, shadow, light, the glare of the Sun at the horizon, the long shadows stretching out across the ground. The yellow of drying grass, the patchy green of scrub woods. The land in shadow gleamed silver with frost, as if lit by a nonexistent Moon, while the ground in the sunlight had already turned dark.

The storm tower of the Well rose up before her, and she found herself remembering Derinda. Was what they had had together completely false? Was Ambryn stupid for having felt joy? She didn't think so. Even now, she didn't.

An illegal suburb of Golgot sprawled out to near the Well edge. Ambryn sank down toward the buildings and took a slow circle over the area, as if looking for something. Stacks of dwelling units in extensible matrix supports swayed in the morning breeze. Elevator tubes clung to their sides like parasitic worms. Golgot builders had taken construction scaffolding and turned it into cheap permanent habitation, though only the desperately poor or insane lived in it.

A multiwheeled saurus picked its way along the base of the buildings, grabbing mounds of garbage with a pincer claw and tossing them into its hoppers. Didn't Elward know how out of place it looked to be working so hard? No city services got provided to areas like this, even just before elections. A decoy should at least look like it was *trying* to conceal itself. Ambryn widened *Len-3*'s wings and slowed, as if to land. If those guys were at all on the ball . . .

An E&J copter bounced up above a line of dwelling units and fired a missile at *Len-3*.

She just had time to note the copter when the impact snapped her head back into the restraints. *Len-3* flipped over and hit full rocket assist. The Well storm rushed at her.

The missile had *Len-3* right in the belly. But the aircraft's countermeasures had kept the missile from knowing that it had reached its target. She imagined it lying in a vacant lot, fought over by rival gangs interested in increasing their firepower.

A second E&J copter clung to the edge of the high winds, perilously close to being swept away. There were no buildings here, just garbage plastered against the rocks. The Well served Golgot as a giant garbage disposal.

Ambryn heard a click as *Len-3* deployed a decoy drone. The detonation of the second copter's missile was just audible above the rush of the wind. It had hit the tiny decoy's giant radar image, but *Len-3* spun as if it had been hit itself. The outermost layer of the vortex grabbed the aircraft and sucked it into the Well.

''I tried to get out of one of these shafts,'' Tiber said, looking up at the sealed entrance. ''It was an ambush. I and the two Guts escorting me were almost caught.''

He punched a fist into his hand. Soph understood his frustration. He had lost some of his freedom of action in dealing with her. If he could have gotten out on his own . . . but, of course, the Guts had set that ambush up, in order to keep Tiber. It was his own fault for becoming so useful to them. If he'd been nothing but a drain on their resources, they might have let him go.

''These shafts are easier to enter than to leave,'' she said. ''Our decoy will be using this.''

''Then he'll be stuck down there too.''

"Elward? The Guts won't try to keep him. They'd be quite sorry if they did."

Bgarth movements through the crust had left tracks of softer rock through the granite. It had taken her and Tiber a few hours to climb up a narrow Gut-dug shaft. She could have just depended on Gut testimony that the entrance was easily accessible, but Elward deserved better than that. She had to check herself, and she had brought Tiber along to keep an eye on him.

The exit was blocked by an overturned bathtub, its bottom caked with some unsuccessful attempt to synthesize drugs or explosives: Soph pictured angry parents, an assignment to dispose of the evidence properly, an assignment adolescently neglected. Tiber pushed up and the bathtub rolled over, letting in sunlight. Leather-leaved weeds a meter high concealed them from view.

They looked out at a wasteland at the edge of a dense Golgot suburb. The soil was unreconstructed surface clinker. Once eternally stable in the preservative embrace of an inert carbon dioxide/nitrogen atmosphere, the rock and sintered dust now crumbled under atmospheric oxidation into an unpleasantly textured mineral felt, as if the mass of aluminosilicates had decayed without ever becoming organic.

Tiber tensed, as if thinking about making a break for it, despite her warnings.

"They'll nail you," Soph said. "Before you get ten meters."

"Those ten meters in the sun and air might make it all worth it," he said. "Just to feel it."

"You were raised orbital?" Soph said.

"I have never been anywhere where I was not surrounded by something on all sides. Looking out there scares me, but . . ."

Stephan had once tried to jump over the edge of a balcony in a Lunar atrium several hundred meters deep. Soph had not quite believed that he would do it and grabbed him only at the last minute. Then he had run off to play and never remembered the incident later.

She tapped Tiber's shoulder. Having made sure that Elward could use the shaft for his own escape, they now climbed back down. The Guts had an access point to the wall of the inner Well. If all went well, that was where Ambryn would be able to pick them up.

3

It would take a dozen of these sauruses a hundred years to even begin to make a dent in this mess, Elward thought. The winds blew trash in from all over Golgot, and people in this neighborhood seemed to think of it as nothing but good long-night insulation. He used the pincer arm to dig away at it.

Ambryn had put on quite an air show. That last little bit had been impressive, where she looked like she'd actually been hit and fell into the Well. He didn't think any farther about the possibilities. He had his own shit to worry about. That act had been Decoy One. He was Decoy Two, and he had to make it look good.

Once through the garbage, he hit rock and dirt. A Gut tunnel was supposed to run a few meters underneath here. They'd abandoned it a while ago, but E&J probably still had it marked as an active Gut route. Elward dug down toward it.

Those joyboys were set up all through this neighborhood, just waiting for Tiber to try to get back out again. They'd relax a little after they nailed *Len-3*. When they spotted Elward, they'd be sure that this was the real penetration. That was the plan, at least.

If he was successful, he'd never be sure whether the others made it. He'd sit out his time in some Gut hidey-hole, then make it back out once the heat was off, with all the money Soph had given him. Maybe he could manage to hold on to it for more than twenty-four hours this time.

God, he hoped they hadn't really shot Ambryn down.

He could feel the hollowness down below. He was about to break through—

Metal flared as a stream of UV pulses hit the saurus. He couldn't see. Everything was dust and flashing light. And the smell of metal tore into his face.

He turned and tore down a narrow road between the dwelling stacks. The saurus had an energy-absorbing coating, to deal with well-armed rioters, but it wasn't meant for this kind of attack. Hey, this thing was faster than he had thought. Faster than they thought too. He'd taken them by surprise. He was going to get away clean.

With a rending wail, an entire stack of living units tilted and slid in modules to the ground, blocking his path. E&J had booby-trapped the entire area. Elward couldn't believe it.

The modules flattened and smashed like ripe pumpkins when they hit. An old man wearing only shorts slid out of a crack in his house and shouted with rage as he wiped foaming impact gel from his skin. His eyes widened as he spotted Elward's saurus and he dove over his smashed house.

Elward would have to trust the impact-protection gear that was standard module issue to protect anyone left in the modules. Most people who lived in these things couldn't find anyone to sell them to. Elward torqued the engines and climbed up over the toppled living stack, praying no one was left inside.

Puffs of smoke rose from the buildings and the road.

Then he was over and clear. They hadn't expected that particular maneuver. Now, that rabbit hole Soph had planned for him was somewhere ahead to the left, behind the tile-fronted sewage reclamation center.

An armored car with spring wheels appeared in his rearview. Those huge blunderbusses on the side had to be for show. They put garlands of flowers on them for official parades. The real weapons were small, concealed in the headlights.

"Stop!" a voice bellowed. "Stop immediately!"

The damn thing was much faster than he was. A parked car exploded as he passed it. A couple of fragments thunked his cab.

He slowed. His breath was tight. His heart flexed his ribs. Goddammit, he was scared.

The E&J pursuit car disappeared. Elward blinked and stared at the rear display to make sure. Gone. Nothing but a puff of dust. He just caught a glimpse of the hole that had opened up in the street and swallowed the armored car. The Guts usually didn't give E&J one in the ass that way, Elward thought. Looked like whatever nav gadget the bellyboys had gotten from Ambryn had them all excited, and willing to take chances. They'd just saved Elward's sorry butt, that was for sure.

Elward took a sharp corner. There. A huge dump, big ugly plants growing all over it. The rabbit hole was somewhere over near the far side. He ground through the piles of garbage. There. He saw the landmark. Home free.

An assault copter slid out from behind a building. Its armored rear carried an incongruously cheery design of red and blue tulips, vestige of some failed E&J public relations effort. He could see its flechette launchers swivel toward him.

He was over the escape hole, the saurus between it and the copter. Out the door, dive, he was safe. The Gut hatch would close over him. He could sit down there and count his money.

He hit reverse, turned the saurus, and headed straight at the copter. You could only run so far.

Ambryn had never been this low down in the Well. The immense wall tore past her. It never ended. All sorts of structures bulked along it.

She'd barely lived through that attack. Looking like she was damaged had not been hard. When the vortex caught her, she almost smashed right into the rim. Fortunately, her flying reflexes had taken over. She hadn't had time for a thought until now.

Where the hell was the Gut access point? It was hard to tell where she was, even though *Len-3* kept giving her a precise location signal. It was like trying to find a particular spot on the porcelain while being flushed down the toilet.

A gigantic flap that could have been the Skullhouse's overcoat stuck out into the flow. She and *Len-3* swept over the sharp edge. Behind it, the wind was calmer. For the first time, she could open up her throat and take a breath.

The Guts had stimulated the growth here, not the Bgarth who had built the Well. So maybe they had learned something about the Bgarth, after all.

There, as tiny as a child's outthrust lower lip: the landing site. *Len-3* backed engines. The air here was just a smooth gale, nothing terrible at all. A hatch unsealed, and she saw Soph and Tiber. She moved toward them gently until the wings almost touched the wall and felt the aircraft rock as they stepped off onto its back. Each of them balanced for a terrifying moment. Then Tiber, followed by Soph, tumbled into the cabin, and she accelerated.

"Soph." Ambryn turned *Len-3* in a tight circle above the module stacks. One lay on its side, surrounded by a mob of citizens. "They'll be on us in a few seconds."

"I'm well aware of that," Soph said. She looked down at the field by the escape hole. What the hell was Elward doing?

The copter hovered right over the saurus. The saurus brandished stun flails that could not possibly reach the aircraft. For some reason, its pincer arm was not in action, but was folded at the rear. A flechette stream destroyed one of the saurus's wheels. Like a cat touching snow with a forepaw, it pulled it back and shook off the fragments of tire. The rest of the wheels shifted to maintain stability.

"Ambryn, can't we—"

"*Len-3* has no weapons," Ambryn said. "Banned by its maintenance contract."

They had to go. Soph knew that. Otherwise, her entire decoy operation would have been run for nothing. For his own reasons, Elward had not tried to escape, but instead had turned to a futile attack on the copter. If he didn't want to save his own life, there wasn't a thing she could do about it.

"Wait," Ambryn said. "I see his plan. If that thing would just get a little lower . . ." She flicked her finger.

A projectile arched out from *Len-3* and exploded. The bright burning dot and minor-chord wail showed that it was nothing more than an emergency flare.

Nevertheless, the copter, wary of attack, pulled itself farther down toward the saurus. The saurus's pincer arm swung up and passed through the copter's rear rotor. The blade smashed into it and tore free of its mounting.

The copter tilted. Its other rotor smacked tips on the hard ground. It bounced back up and smashed to the ground. Fragments flew. Impact foam sprayed in streams from ripped-through screw holes and formed staghorn sculptures as they hit the air.

The saurus crashed into the fallen copter.

"Land, Ambryn!" Soph said. "Land."

To her surprise, Ambryn had already done so. *Len-3* bumped across a rubble field and drifted to a halt.

The saurus bounded across the field toward them. Elward had one of those ridiculous emerald eyespot face masks on, Soph saw. Those dramatic spots were based on an anatomical feature of Ganymedean Turtles that was not actually an eye, but instead a reproductive indicator in fertile females.

Soph was almost mad enough at him to tell him that.

Five

A Chapter from the Life
of Ripi-Arana-Hoc

Later the surviving members of the Bru family would marvel at how long Ripi-Arana-Hoc must have been plotting his crime.

Ripi tugged at the seal-hatch. It clung on stubbornly, like the modified mollusc that it was. The ridges were thick and hard under his fingers. This was an old one. Old as the clanship, most likely, sucked from the sunlit shores of an ancient sea before Ripi's species first lifted from their native planet, a planet that now existed only as a bright memory resting in the back of the mind of every member of his race.

This dark corridor, its atmosphere thick with biological secretions, made Ripi uncomfortable. He was now far from familiar areas of this hostile clanship, and the clanship's places were important, individual, like the organs of the brain. He was not native to this place and had no inherited memories of Bru clanship. The discordant memories of the generations-familiar corridors of the Arana clanship in which he and his ancestors had been born and raised clashed with what he saw before him, sending out psychic moire patterns.

At any moment, a scavenger would come along and bump into him with its huge multimouthed head. It would do nothing, since he was alive, but his pheromones would later get reported to the cloaca when the scavenger vomited up its load. It might get ignored as irrelevant long-chain molecular noise. Ripi didn't think so.

Bru clanship's cloaca had more nervous system than it knew what to do with. In some Vronnan cities and clanships the cloaca's nervous system was purely vestigial, but in Bru clanship there were still substantial plexi, a cause of derision among other Vronnan colonies, since it indicated a primitive state of being. Ripi remembered mocking it himself. Now he feared it. So the cloaca floated there in the deep center of the clanship, swollen and gassy with bacteria, and thought constantly about the molecules that floated inside it. The vagrant trace of Ripi's presence would finally rise to the bubbling surface and get amplified into a signal perceptible to a directing intelligence: a half-memory-transferred Father, still anomalously conscious, was wandering near the memory crèche where his children grew slowly to consciousness.

Someone up the Bru clan hierarchy would surely be interested. They had gone through a great deal of trouble to acquire Ripi and his valuable memories from the Arana clan. Treaties between the clans of Arana and Bru had set what should have been a lasting peace by sacrificing Ripi, once a high-ranking Arana clan leader.

By this point in the memory-transfer process, Ripi should have been lying limp in his supportmouth, postlingual, pattern-sucked, ready to have what was left of his brain deliquesced, removed from his skull by the supportmouth's hollow incisors, turned into a preparation, and used as the final substrate for Ripi's children's growing memories.

It was supposed to be a Father's proudest moment, the last flickering of his consciousness comprehending gloriously the fact that his children had his memories, as well as the ancient and long-preserved memories of the family. Every story he'd heard since childhood, every transferred, specifically emphasized memory: they all told him of the transcendence of that realization.

His skin was still slick from the supportmouth's many tongues. He'd left the easily fooled supportmouth with a decoy, a preserved and chemically massaged lump of circuitgut a repairer had carved out of the wall of a chamber in Ripi's wife's family compound a few months ago when processing tumors had metastasized through its circuitry, changing its functions beyond repair.

The circuitgut had mostly ceased to function, but enough could be hormonally stimulated that its weight, temperature, and elementary movements fooled the primitive supportmouth.

Ripi hadn't known he was going to need the circuitgut when he stole it from the preliminary digestive system of a recycler moving slowly through the muck of the lower hall with its paddle-like paws. The knowledge of how to steal from a recycler was an inherited Arana-Hoc memory, a lucky one. Some ancestor had done it as a child, back in the early otherwise forgotten generations when children had little backed-up gene information and acted entirely on their own. Ripi had gotten a thrill from the bite of digestive enzymes on his hands and had even licked some off to feel the sting on his tasting palps.

He'd stored the circuitgut in a cooler, right in his wife's compound, until a use arose for it. So the circuitgut, with a little bacterial slickness on its surface, now rested in the caresses of the unintelligent supportmouth, which had issued no alarms and was content to keep the seemingly living meat floating on its tongues.

Ripi knew what would soon happen. One of his memory-strip chamber's mindnurses would hang down over the supportmouth to do a biocheck. For a moment, it would think that Ripi had turned into a hunk of rotting meat. Then it would sound the alarm.

Ripi did not have much time.

He squatted to tug harder at the hatch, then remembered that Ankur had given him a signal key. This secret crèche was Ankur's domain, after all. Ripi's sterile semisib ruled here, and Ripi was a desperate interloper.

Ripi-Arana-Hoc should not have had to be here. He should have been back aboard his ancestral Arana clanship, heading up the Hoc clan, as his memory of Departure entitled him to. But he was a short-lived male, so he had been made a political sacrifice to Arana's futile ambitions for interclan peace.

Departure was the marker memory of the Hoc family head,

a requirement for the possession of Ripi's rank. The feel of being pressed back into an acceleration couch as the primitive, dangerous spacecraft rose up from the native planet no one who lived in any of the clanships or clan-cities strewn across hostile and alien planets had ever seen—the memory defined its bearer. In mind-maintenance sleep, Ripi was tormented by the wide curve of that blue planet, Vron, for the memory was tinged with the regret of eternal loss.

The key wiggled in his hand. Its ancestors had been abyssal worms, underwater business colleagues of the mollusc's. Their symbiotic chemical recognitions had been made complex to an incomprehensible degree, to allow for essential security coding. An invisible exchange of information and a joining at a level of the clanship's culture that Ripi was incapable of comprehending, and the hatch silently unsealed. He was just an intelligent epiphenomenon of the clanship's complexity, foam atop a wave. The clanship's real functionings were concealed from him.

He climbed through the hatch.

"Empty," Ankur said. The support-fluid-gleaming body tossed among the lashing tongues of the crèche supportmouth like something boiling in a pot. "There is nothing left in his mind that we can use."

"He remembered." Ripi squatted by the unconscious form of the old Vronnan in the supportmouth. Neural cables had pushed their way past his eyes, into his mouth, and into his ears. Their surface was protected by a ridged green-gleaming shell derived from a beetle.

The unconscious Vronnan male's skin was cracked like dry mud. Many of his joints had fused into uselessness. Devoid of family, he had lived long past the point where a male usually gave up his memories.

"The memories remaining are all his own or, if ancient, do not match yours. Useless."

"He remembered Departure. The same couch, the same controls."

"He remembers Departure no longer. That memory has been transferred, stretched across your children's minds. No one will be fooled any longer."

"So now what do we do?" Ripi felt drained, as useless as this poor old Vronnan in the supportmouth.

"Now this."

Ankur stroked the supportmouth. Pin-sharp teeth emerged from the softly comforting tongues and sank into the flesh of the comatose, memory-drained body that lay there, all along the lines of the nerves. Useless neural deliquescence came. None of the memories this Vronnan had had could any longer conceal Ripi's betrayal so, instead of being ducted along the beetle-wingcase-sheathed neural cables to the brain of the Bearer who carried his growing children in her belly, the mass of neurons and all their irreplaceable information were dumped into waste disposal, another sign that would soon arouse suspicion.

Within a few moments, the Vronnan in the supportmouth was dead. Ripi looked down at him, obscurely saddened. His Brother in Memory had been useful to him, nothing more, but a deep identity of memory had now been shattered.

"Are you ready?" Ankur said.

Ripi looked at him helplessly.

"You must be ready. The next correlation check will reveal that your children have nothing of you in them save their genes."

Ankur slapped the dead body's chest. The supportmouth's tongues had pulled back, offended at the cessation of life they themselves had caused. Busy scavenger bugs already crawled on the skin. Primitive bugs, Ripi saw with horror. They had grown hard shells in defiance of the hormonal programs that were supposed to make them forget their planetary origins. They tore at the shells of the neural cables and devoured the delicate nerves underneath.

Ankur, Ripi's sterile semisib, was in charge of the memory-transfer process. That was his role, by rights so ancient they were reflex in all Vronnans, so the Bru had brought him here, even though they knew he was an enemy. He had been bred for this very action. His betrayal of the process was a crime as deep as Ripi's.

Ankur's kingdom, here in the depths of the enemy Bru clanship, was one of death and decay. Fecund air, thick with gold-green pollen choked Ripi's breathing tubes. The fibrillation of air-circulator wings poisoned by neglect. Bioluminescent bulbs scribbled with black lines of light-devouring parasites. When Bru security troops finally broke in, accompanied by their laser-armed Guardians, they would be horrified. For a moment, Ripi took pleasure in the thought.

Ripi thought of his wife, scion of a powerful Bru family. She rested now, in her postbirth chamber, vast and beautiful. He had met her years before, in the course of a surface assault Arana and Bru had cooperated on, and traded scents with her. If it had been just her, if they could have been together outside of the constraints of Arana and Bru policies, they could have been happy. But one could no more exist outside of family and clan policies than outside of air.

Bearers emerged from their secret kingdom to take away the body. Five of the mysterious beings, with their flat faces, their bald bulging skulls, their delicate soft skin. Ripi, like any adult Vronnan, preferred not to think about the Bearers' contribution to birth and memory transfer, to the very basis of what it meant to be a Vronnan. He could not suppress a vagrant feeling of disgust, which encompassed Ankur, who dealt with these creatures of dark, death, and birth.

Ankur spoke sharply to the Bearer leader, a bejeweled female. She reacted slowly, with seeming contempt. The Bearers knew the truth. Ankur and Ripi's elaborate charade did nothing to fool them.

Ripi knew he was a pervert. He had left his children with no real memories, save the ancient ones he had shared with his Brother in Memory. Two sons, three daughters. Their lives would have no status, no meaning. There would be no place for them, either here on the Bru clanship or back on the clanship of his own family.

Their Bearer, a young female carrying her first Vronnan clutch, hung mentally suspended within the life-supporting abdomen of a creature that had once, distant in evolutionary time, kept live prey within itself to feed its children, who hatched inside and ate the never-spoiled living flesh provided. Its functions had been altered until it could keep a Bearer alive as the Bearer's brain, linked by neural cables to the Father, transferred memories to the Vronnan embryos. Eventually, Bearers would cut the abdomen open with ceremonial knives and pull the barely breathing body of the one now known as the Memory Giver out into the light. But when Ripi's children were finally expelled from the body of the Memory Giver, who awoke to high status among her people, they would emerge into a hostile world.

But Ripi was alive. He had his memories, and he was alive.

He was going to stay that way.

"Are you coming with me, Ankur?" he said.

"No. No desire to visit that place. Nothing for me."

"It's perfect. A new species, hungry for technological data. The price they will pay for my knowledge will be high."

"You don't know what will happen. You know nothing about them."

"So what will you do?" Ripi asked.

"I have my own plans," Ankur said. "They need not concern you."

No more time. Without another word or gesture to his semisib, Ripi climbed through another hatch in the crèche wall. He'd planned this, his final exit. He followed a path through maintenance access, full of recycling insects and slowly frothing bacterial mats. He crawled through the muck, feeling the writhing of creatures of decay. It was degrading, a place he should not have been. That didn't matter. Nothing held him back.

He came to a weakened circle of tunnel wall. It was a zone of suspended decay, which had eaten through support members without sending a repair signal through the clanship's chemical nervous system. With a negligent flick of a razor-edged knife, Ripi cut his way through.

Now the signals screamed their chemical warnings. Oxidation block dripped from the edges of the newly cut hole. Beyond, nestled tumorlike in the very rind of the Bru clanship, was Ripi's escape vessel. Life connections had been shunted around it. The Bru clanship did not know it was there. Despite how he had been betrayed and his exile here to Bru, he still had secret allies aboard the Arana clanship. They had sent him the hormonal algorithms to create this vessel.

In response to his manipulations the ship had sprouted from the living shell of the Bru clanship, calling upon resources it had no right to. Ripi could only hope it was now mature enough for use.

Its hatch parted, and he entered.

The destination was already programmed into the navigation system, another hard-won piece of information: a planet circling newly contacted G3 star called, by the humans that had evolved under its light, Sol.

It was there that his new life would have to begin. Something pounded on the outside of his ship. They had reacted more quickly than he had thought possible.

He hit a switch and burst free of the Bru clanship.

Six

1

An explosion flashed far away off *Len-3*'s left wing.

"What was that?" Soph looked out at the tree-covered hills over which they flew.

"E&J copter," Ambryn said, after checking the displays. "Flying nap-of-the-earth in an attempt to reach Ripi ahead of us. Seems Ripi managed to get bootleg interception missiles along with the rest of his orbital junk. If there are other copters, they've gone to ground now. They didn't expect this."

"Maybe the next time the Skullhouse gets a valuable alien, they'll supervise him more closely," Soph said.

"Don't count on it," Elward said from a recumbent posture in his couch. "There's always someone to be paid off. Someone's rich now, and having Ripi gone is probably a good thing for them. Watch the interests, Soph. They're not always what they seem." He glanced at Tiber, to whom he had taken an instant dislike.

Tiber held his knees with his large hands and looked straight ahead. Because of his mass of curling brown hair, Soph thought of a male lion. He had that same air of strength developed to impress and overawe, rather than for mundane physical use.

The sharp slopes of the lower Maxwells poked up through morning mist. Ambryn banked *Len-3*. The sun hung above the horizon to the west, and the snow-frosted bulk of the main volcanic shield glowed to the east. Ripi's covert turned out to be three standing spacecraft, one tilting dangerously, and a collection of spacecraft parts that lay on a hillside like a child's abandoned toys.

Len-3 swooped below the level of the surrounding cliffs into a valley whose yellow-green was vivid against the darker trees that hemmed it in. Dead aspen littered the level ground, their trunks bone-gray amid the ferns. Ambryn, with *Len-3*'s cooperation, handled the landing nonchalantly. The aircraft spilled air through spread wing edges like a crow. The wheels bounced once, then settled on the soft ground. The engines hissed in reverse, and the aircraft slowed to a halt.

Len-3 opened itself up and dropped ramps to the needle-covered soil. Soph's luggage swarmed out and reassembled itself. While Ambryn, Elward, and Tiber stepped tentatively onto the ground, Soph remained a moment to finish another deal with *Len-3*. She wasn't ready to let the aircraft go, not until she was definitely free of Venus's gravity well. So, for a surprisingly reasonable charge, *Len-3* agreed to remain in the area of Ripi's before returning under autopilot to its nest at the Nubu Garage. Soph jumped out after the others.

Under Ambryn's direction, they all pushed the aircraft to a good takeoff position, nose pointed downslope. *Len-3* just had to make it over the pointy tops of the firs below.

Its jet assist rumbled, and the craft was off the ground. It climbed steeply over the trees, wings gleaming in the sunlight. It banked across the valley and was gone.

The cold morning air carried the resin of high-altitude pines and junipers. The hillsides sprouted with eager growth. Somewhere out here, Soph knew, were the products of the biopackage Kammer and Kun's expedition had hitched a ride on, now in combat with other ecological schemes. She wondered if any of the new plants she could see had been seeds aboard that craft.

Holes gaped in the standing spacecraft where equipment had been carelessly removed before tossing the hulks into salvage orbit, and the parasail landing had battered them further.

Soph pulsed the identity code Ripi had given the Kammer and Kun expedition. With a dull creak, an airlock hatch opened in the toppled thrust cylinder that formed the house's base. The thing was a wreck, creased by a long-ago explosion.

"Quite the mysterious golden city." Ambryn stood, hands on hips, and regarded it with disapproval.

"Don't be so fussy, Ambryn," Soph said.

2

"That's it?" Soph said.

They stood at the bottom of a vast silo, at least thirty meters across and twice that high. Light streamed in from overhead. Five mouths opened to passages, one of which they had come down. An atmospheric shuttle lay tilted amid junk like bent launch arms and oxygen pump lines, as well as a Martian emergency med cart still in its protective blister. Tiber nodded.

"So where the hell is our host?" Elward hunched his shoulders. "I thought he was desperate to get the hell out of here. I know I am."

"There." Soph pointed.

A transparent bubble bulged ten meters above the floor. In it, sitting in the middle of a bank of bleachers recycled from some centrifugal arena, was the alien, Ripi.

"Should we wave?" Ambryn said.

"He looks like he's waiting for the games to begin," Elward said. "I wonder who he bet on?"

Ripi was tiny, about the size of a ten-year-old boy. Despite his alienness, Ripi projected a distinctly aristocratic air. His eyes rested close together in the tiny face on the front of a head as sleek as a wind-powered racing vessel. The complex bone structure on what would have been a human's cheeks seemed to be air-inhalation vents. Soph could hear the soughing of his breath through speakers somewhere. The females, she understood, were much larger and stood centaurlike on a pair of secondary limbs on the chest. If Ripi had those, they were concealed by his expensive-looking robes. Space hulls and weaponry were not the only things he had had dropped down to him, it seemed.

"Proceed," Ripi said. "Quickly."

A channel change, and tense voices muttered map coordinates over the speakers. Ripi had either tapped into a secure E&J command channel or, more likely, into an in-clear propaganda signal, intended for their benefit. Ripi had shot down a copter. Hell, so had Elward. That was a declaration of war. Only flight would save them. Soph noted a few weapons pods hanging on the walls. Antipersonnel stuff, nothing too sophisticated. It could still kill them all—if Ripi got irritated with them. She didn't like that.

Soph turned to see that the shuttle's hatches were open, and Tiber had already entered. She scrambled after him, as if afraid he would leave without her.

The shuttle's interior showed generations of poorly systematized repairs. A too-large enviro module poked out through a hole cut in the floor. A soft-grip floor had been torn away, leaving a crunchy pattern of adhesive dots.

Ambryn slid over to the controls. "All right, all right," she said. "Not too bad, considering." Indicator lights came on, and Soph felt a puff of ventilation on the back of her neck.

Elward stood in the middle of the floor, carefully not touching anything, and watched Tiber suspiciously. Soph couldn't figure out why Elward was so distrustful. Tiber was just as stuck as the rest of them.

"Anything special I should know about this thing?" With her hands on the controls, Ambryn was quietly authoritative.

"I think we should be careful," Tiber said. "It looks like someone has—"

"You know, Soph," Elward said. "I never get into a car without giving it a security check first. A thorough one. Particularly if it has been sitting in some lot for a good long time, like, say, five minutes."

Ambryn's hands froze. "What are you saying?"

"He's saying I'm stupid," Soph said.

"That's not what I—" Elward began.

"And he's right."

Two of her bags hopped into the cabin and immediately snuffled around the control panels.

Tiber watched intently and showed no fear.

"Booby traps," Soph said. "Sabotage. Anything. I don't expect it—but Elward's right. It would be stupid to take a chance."

"I didn't say you were stupid."

"Well, Elward, that's because you're so polite."

He looked startled.

One of the bags had paused at Ambryn's couch. It extended a sensor into the magnetic clamps that held it to the floor. Ambryn started to get up.

"Wait," Soph said.

Indicator patterns crawled across its boa-hide back. Soph knelt next to it. A drawer opened and, without looking, she pulled out a self-closing ring with an iris cutter in it. The bag had already clamped around the anomalous addition to the couch's hardware: what looked like a makeshift connector box, fully in keeping with the rest of the repairs aboard the shuttle. Only this one had no apparent function. She fastened the ring around one end of it, and the iris cutter sliced through the fibers.

"What is it?" Ambryn said.

Soph pulled it out and held it dangling from the ring.

"A booby trap," Elward said admiringly. "Focused explosive. That thing would have turned your ass to jelly, sweetheart."

"Ambryn!" Soph shouted from the hatch. "Stop. Please."

Ambryn had rolled out of her couch and jumped out of the hatch. She had run across the silo floor, dodging odd chunks of surplus space gear, and now huddled against the opposite wall, sobbing.

Soph climbed out. She understood Ambryn's fear and felt like a fool. She had never anticipated that anyone would have managed to put a booby trap aboard the shuttle, which had been sitting here in Ripi's secure silo since it had landed. Had Ripi put it there? She looked up at the observation bubble. It was empty.

"Oh, God. Oh, God. They're here. They're everywhere." Ambryn quivered. "E&J. The joyboys. I thought we had gotten away. I could have . . . I had my hands on the controls. Oh, my God!"

Soph knelt next to her and suffered herself to be embraced by that lush flesh. That perfume . . . it should have been cloying, but it seemed to caress her nostrils. Ambryn pushed herself against her and sobbed.

Elward loomed over them. "You only just figured that out? Get used to it." He ran his eyes over Ambryn, enjoying either her terror or the effect it had on her body.

"Elward." Soph kept her voice level. "I know you're only trying to help . . ."

"Sure." He looked back at the shuttle. "Ha. I've got to admit, that's the most useful thing anyone has done so far."

Soph followed his gaze. Tiber squatted before the shuttle. He had pulled out a catalytic stove and unrolled a pan over it. As she watched, he chopped things and threw them into hot oil in the pan. He moved with total serenity. Even on the opposite side of the silo, she could smell the frying spices. She realized she was desperately hungry.

"But that guy is trouble," Elward said. "He's sucking you right in, Soph. He has his own reasons—"

"Back off, Elward." Soph said angrily. "Tiber is taking the same risks we are. I don't think you understand a damn thing about it."

Elward sucked in a breath and stepped back. "Maybe."

She was immediately ashamed. "Elward, I—"

"And maybe you should think about something. When was that booby trap put in? Here at this midget alien's little escape chamber or aboard the spaceship we're headed for?"

He walked away before Soph could say anything more. She was surprised to see him squat down next to Tiber and watch him cook. But maybe he was just hungry.

Ambryn looked at her with gray eyes gleaming with tears. "What does Tiber mean to you, Soph?"

"Mean? He means escape."

"Sure." Ambryn paused, as if thinking of saying something more, then pushed herself to her feet and drew a shaky breath. "I'm sorry I panicked, Soph. But . . . I'm so scared.

From now on, everything is dangerous. Anything could kill me in a second."

"Elward and I will do our best when we check over the shuttle, Ambryn," Soph said. "And our best is pretty good. You have to believe me. Before we launch, we'll take that thing apart."

"Sure. Sure. But I'll never be safe again." Ambryn looked up at the height of the silo. An open circle high above showed a patch of cloudy sky. "You know, Soph, this isn't a surplus spacecraft, not like the rest of this place. This is the hollow body of a Bgarth. A small one, of course. Maybe an infant. We've never seen one of those."

If the discussion would calm her . . . "Is it alive?" Soph asked.

"Well, let's see." Ambryn pulled a few paracrine communication capsules out of the Bgarth kit on her hip. Injection into the wall produced a slight but distinct shudder. "Yep. Still some activity here." She popped the capsules back in their kit. "At least I didn't waste my effort by bringing this stuff."

"What is it doing here?" Soph asked.

"Maybe it came up through the soft rock of the fumarole, got stuck, and pulled back, leaving just its shell," Ambryn said. "A little bit of exuberance that took a few decades. You have to understand the scale on which they live. We're all just a flicker to them. For all I know, they don't perceive us in real time at all. Maybe they'll just store it all up—for centuries—and then experience it as one thunderous burst of revelation after human beings have once again departed Venus."

"Do you suppose that this was what Tiber had been aiming for?" Soph asked. "In his descent into the crust aboard his shuttle? There's probably a passage upward from those high-speed passages the Guts believe are down there."

"The Guts think with their bellies," Ambryn said. "They're crazy."

Soph looked over at where Tiber was cooking. "Maybe we should go eat."

"Elward's right about one thing." Ambryn started back

toward the shuttle, every step a visible effort of will. "Making lunch is the smartest thing anyone's thought of so far."

3

"Vronnans," Tiber's voice said from the darkness. "Do you know anything about Vronnans?" Then the key light came on, and his face became visible. He stared up at the low ceiling.

"Ripi's people?" Ambryn said. "Very little."

She brushed her image display, and a few flickers floated through the air: a Vronnan limb, scorched as if from a flaming explosion, found in another cache of smuggled alien body parts; a massive Vronnan female spotted on a raft in an internal sea by a human researcher visiting Epsilon Eridani; a Vronnan city dug into the bedrock of an airless planetoid. Now that she saw it, Ambryn recognized that Ripi had, crudely, mimicked the structure of such a city in setting up his own fortress. And he'd hidden himself somewhere within it. No one had seen him since they'd discovered the booby trap aboard the *Argent*'s shuttle.

Tiber breathed hard as he watched the Vronnans. His skin was very fine, and she could see the beating of a blood vessel in his neck. Ambryn and he were in what she thought had once been part of a Martian orbital research station. Soph and Elward were checking the shuttle over for more booby traps, and she had suggested a skrying to Tiber as a way of calming herself, as the cooking seemed to have calmed him. Tiber had been eager. She had sensed his need. Soph, distracted, had agreed after issuing Tiber a comm link to her luggage. He and Ambryn had found a space in a shuttle bay.

"You show the soul via the bodies of others," Tiber said.

"Something like that," Ambryn said. "Let's see what I can show you."

"Not these. No."

"Okay."

It was just as well that he didn't want to use the Vronnans, because she didn't have enough material about them for a decent skrying. But his reaction to them was powerful—and instructive. She pulled up the bodies of other aliens. "You're an excellent cook. I think that lunch doubled everyone's intelligence. Something we badly needed."

"A friend taught me," Tiber said. "His name was Hlobane. Cooking was a hobby of his. It takes your mind off your problems, he said. And when you're done, you can eat."

He'd done wonders with the ingredients he had brought in his pack. It had been a sort of curry, with a jangle of competing flavors somehow brought into overall harmony. Ambryn could still smell it on her hair, but that didn't bother her. The food had brought them all into harmony as well, and the fear and pressure that seemed to push under everything had been, for the moment, released. Even Elward had seemed happy.

She watched Tiber's reactions to the various alien species, from the Turtles of Ganymede, to the pillbuglike trading Tibrini. She breathed through the top of her head and felt the cool relaxation come up from the smooth functionings of the diencephalon, the oldest part of the brain, which sat on the end of the spinal cord like a ball joint and let the hemispheres of the cerebrum tilt crazily about it while itself remaining still.

"Home," he said. "Do you know where that is?"

"No," she said.

"How do you know when you've returned?"

A solar prominence, vivid with deviant isotopes, crawled across the ceiling, climbing up from the Sun's chromosphere. What did that image mean?

"Home," Ambryn said, "is the place that gains as much by your return as you do." Why the hell had she said that? "If you can't find it, you have to create it."

"Ah," he breathed, as if she'd said something meaningful.

"The Gunners." She looked up at the image of the prominence. "Their home is lost."

"They always look for it," he said. "But the only thing they ever find is someone else's home."

"Of course," she said, not knowing what he was talking about.

The image dropped down to the surface of Mercury. The Gun appeared, standing stark and straight across the concentric landscape of Caloris, the basin that dominated one face of the planet. The image closed in on the base of the vast trussed object, which was a thousand kilometers long.

All around the base of the Gun, a structure larger than cities, Ambryn could see signs of activity. Radiation flared across the ground, incredibly dangerous to most life. Gamma rays poured through the surrounding rocks, Cherenkov radiation glared blue behind the gigantic bastions that supported the Gun's base.

Tiny figures were just visible, but the time for examining the actual Gunners was not yet. She tracked along the Gun itself as it readied itself to launch an isotope barge. At first the vibration was subliminal, a possible illusion of strained eyeballs. Then it became more obvious, a series of harmonics snapping through what suddenly seemed like a plucked violin string.

"The barges," Tiber said. "Do they contain something for me?"

"Of course," she said. "Of course they do."

"No." He was seeing something. She could tell. "Not the barges. The Gunners themselves. They know—" He stopped himself. "They know. . . ."

The solar prominence continued to crawl across the ceiling, its unnatural path guided by the incomprehensible plasma dynamics implicit in the Gunner isotope barge that had been dropped into the solar photosphere to set it off. Beneath it, a flare pulsed as stored magnetic energy was released, sending out cascades of everything from hard X rays to long-wave radio. An entire region of the Sun's surface was convulsed from Gunner intervention.

Dropping those stupid barges seemed to be the Gunners' main purpose in life. This tiny colony of Gunners on Mercury—a few hundred of them at most—spent their time preparing for and launching isotope barges or examining the flares and prominences that resulted from the atmospheric penetrations.

Some on Earth feared that eventually, through their interference with the solar atmosphere, the Gunners would set off a nova that would sterilize the terrestrial planets and that this was actually the normal culmination of their activities, and had been, in other systems.

But the Mercurian Gunners had suffered a secret disaster, of which only hints were available. They missed something essential to their faith and sat on Mercury, furious at the Sun that rose methodically every one-hundred-seventy-six Earth days, always exactly the same, seeming to have sworn an oath to exist forever. Each time they punched it with one of their isotopic barges, it grew a colorful zit, which then faded. They had arrived in the Solar System in a pupated state, aboard a seedship. That seedship had disappeared, and indications were that they were still looking for it.

"The barges vanish," Tiber whispered. "Halfway between Mercury and the Sun they . . . skip. A gap. Eighteen, maybe twenty light-seconds. Pop—over in a nanosecond. Twenty light-seconds, six million kilometers, in a millionth of a second. Imagine that if you can."

This was an odd focus, though it was one that obsessed a lot of people. Ambryn didn't understand this passion for faster-than-light travel, for hunting down deepdrives. Let others worry about bursting free of the Solar System, as if they had exhausted its possibilities. The universe could be seen perfectly well from where Ambryn sat. It sent its signals down to her in the form of exploratory alien species, who did not achieve their true meaning until they got here.

"All right," Ambryn said. "Look there, then. Look into the gap. Maybe your answer lies there."

"There," he said. "I could go there and ask . . . they will pay. They pay with information. I could find the answer. . . ." He drew a choking breath. "No!"

"Tiber—"

"No, no. Turn it off. Please." He sat up. Ambryn brought the lights up. He was sweating. His long hair dangled down about his face. "I don't need those answers. She will . . . I will be safe."

"I hope so," Ambryn said.

They locked eyes for a moment, and she sensed his desperate need. Except she had no idea what it was he needed. He lay back down on the metal floor. "I'm sorry. Let's proceed."

He stared up at a Gunner isotopic barge as it was readied for launching. Ambryn would continue the skrying session, but she knew that the truth—whatever it was—had already been revealed. All either of them would get from it now was the comfort of ritual.

Elward had never been off Venus and was surprised at how flimsy all this orbital stuff proved to be. Everywhere panels were torn away, frames were bent, modules were squashed. He had no trouble finding a way to the outside. Of course, the poor quality of the Skullhouse-hired crews that had first built the place didn't help. Maybe it was a miracle any of it was standing up at all.

He crawled through a hole and found himself standing on the ground amid plants. The tilting spaceship stood over him. Ambryn had called the big trees "pines." Their needles covered the ground in a soft brown carpet. All sorts of fungi grew there—and lacy-leaved plants just opening out into the sunlight. It was still morning cold, and Elward shivered. A rumble of thunder came from somewhere downslope. He'd finished his job. The shuttle was clean.

The big volcanic shield rose above him, broken into subsidiary peaks. Mist poured down the steep valleys as the sun melted the snow. Elward squinted at the silver line of a waterfall sketched down the gray rock. It must be a hundred meters high, at least, for it to be that size at that distance. He wondered what it sounded like, up close. And a spaceship lay just at its base, its prow in the soft ground. One of Soph's landing vessels, it looked like. That Bgarth biopackage must have come apart right here.

He strolled across the uneven ground, feeling it through the soles of his feet, all fresh and huge, the air moving around him, as if he had never heard of Golgot or Enforcement & Joy. Hell, he should just take off. Up into the hills. He could—what did they call it?—live off the land. He didn't quite know what that meant, but it didn't sound too hard. You just had to eat the plants, right?

A rock hit against another. He walked around the spacecraft's stern to find Tiber digging at something in the ground.

Seeing Elward, he stood up and brushed the dirt from his knees. Soph had sent Elward after him. Well, here he was.

"I've never been here," Elward said, looking up at the mountains. "Actually, I've never been out of Golgot. I've seen the mountains but only from far away, over buildings."

"This is my first planetary surface."

"Raised in orbit?" Elward said.

"Yes."

"Your parents live out there?"

"I don't remember them."

"My parents took off before I could remember them," Elward said. "They gave me a picture, at the crèche, of a couple standing on a bridge, but I found out later that it was a computer-generated image based on my DNA. I have my mother's cheekbones."

"You were raised there?" Tiber did have a soothing voice, deep but smooth.

"Oh, I was raised sort of holographically. Ah, let's see, 'every part of the child's environment containing the essential information needed for his emotional formation.' " Elward frowned. "I used to have a little display that explained the process to me. I must have lost it."

"That's sad."

"Yeah, well. Could have been worse."

He remembered the Preceptor in charge of his education. Its synthetic voice had been deliberately flat and mechanical to remind him of his fallen condition. And suddenly he understood. Derinda had known his past, of course. She had access to the records. And she had imitated that flat tone, the voice that Elward had always thought of as his parent. And he had obeyed without even knowing why.

"I was raised on a spaceship." Tiber started walking between the trees. Elward followed. "Though my mother told me I'd been born on a planet. I wasn't sure what that meant. Actually, I never did learn—until I came here." He looked up at the mountains.

Elward swallowed. "What was it like?"

"You could watch our ship—all over it—and my friend Rampo and I liked to do that. The ship's name was the *Bezel*. The *Prismatic Bezel*. It was supposed to go far. There was a room you could go to. They had screens showing everything about the ship. The people working would even answer questions—if they weren't too busy. You could see the people in the corridors, and all the stored animal embryos in the library, and felt like you'd put the ship on, like a wrestling suit.

"Rampo and I were watching one day, the way we liked, when a bunch of things suddenly popped out around the ship. One second they weren't there, the next they were. They looked like sections of a cylinder, curved on the inside to match our hull. For a little bit, I thought they were part of the ship we'd forgotten, and someone had finally found them and brought them to us.

"Everybody was yelling. Someone grabbed Rampo and me and pulled us out of there. We thought it was because we weren't supposed to see what was up there on the screens and we wanted to and we started yelling too. But it was really to protect us. I don't know where my parents were. I never saw them again.

"The hull blew in where those cylinder-section things were attached. I could hear it from my hiding place, which was in a secret place in the hull. They gave me food and water and reminded me what to do. They'd spent a lot of time teaching us this, and we had thought it was just a boring game. I don't remember now how we were supposed to survive, but I remember the taste of the air mask and the way it sucked onto your teeth to make a seal. If you blew into it right, there was a way to make a loud buzzing noise, and they'd tell you to cut that out.

"There was a lot of noise—explosions, shouts—and then everything was quiet. I waited there until someone finally found me. I guess it was just a matter of time."

"Who?" Elward asked. "Who found you?"

"I was rescued." Tiber's voice had no more life to it. "Eventually."

"Lucky," Elward said. "You could have died there."

"Yes," Tiber said. "I was lucky."

They stopped together beneath an open slope. Tiber frowned at where big black boulders poked up through the fresh grass. A fresh breeze riffled through. Dark clouds loomed up, and lightning flickered through their upper parts. Elward heard the echo of thunder.

"Oh, no. . . ." Tiber breathed.

"What is it?"

"A biological explosive," Tiber said. "A sort of fungus. It's all over this slope. Ready to detonate."

Elward looked back. They were right above Ripi's covert. The three battered space vessels and the silo mouth, with its slabs of glass, looked very vulnerable in the gray prestorm light.

"Who—?"

"I don't know!" Tiber shouted. "I think I know where Ripi is. Go warn the others. We don't have much time!"

"I knew I should have brought Tiber back with me." Ambryn paced in front of the shuttle. "I shouldn't have left him there, thinking about his fate."

"What did he tell you?" Soph peered into the eyepieces of her image display. The booster nozzle embedded in the wall of that passage . . . there. The vibrational image showed a tangle of tiny passages behind the metal.

"A whole bunch of stuff. Why the hell did you send Elward after him? Elward doesn't even like him!"

The exposure of the booby trap in the shuttle had terrified Ripi. It had showed him that his security was not as good as he had thought. So he had panicked and hid himself, going to ground like a gopher. Soph had devoted herself to searching out his place of concealment, and she thought she had finally found it. Vibrational analysis had found a lot of empty spaces behind seeming solid metal, but this was the only one that looked usable. And IR showed a small living shape huddled in there.

Soph stowed the display. He'd come out anyway, she hoped, when it came time to leave. But she liked keeping all the possibilities in mind. It might be necessary to yank him out.

"Elward wanted to go," she said. "He wanted to take a look around, see a few things. Don't worry."

Though now Soph was getting worried herself. It was taking much longer than it should have. The shuttle was ready to go. There was no reason to stay a moment longer.

"Tiber is looking for home." Ambryn managed to make herself sit down, though she kept crossing and uncrossing her legs. She was dressed as if for an adventure movie, with low boots, ribbed tights, and a high-shouldered jacket. She looked quite spectacular.

"Any indication of where that might be?" Soph said.

"No. But . . . Soph, I don't get the sense he wants to leave here."

"Why should he want to stay?"

"I don't know. The Gunners . . . the Gunners are a side issue. It was like a break of freedom when he thought about them. He does not see his true fate in them. He seems to think home may be here. What are you looking for, Soph?"

Soph couldn't have said why she found that question so annoying. Ripi's hiding place was in the passage that led to the shuttle in which Ambryn had skryed Tiber. Ambryn had said that Ripi's covert seemed an imitation of a Vronnan city. What did his tiny hiding place represent?

She decided that Ambryn deserved some kind of an answer.

"I'm no more sure of what I'm looking for than Tiber is of his home. Not long before Stephan died, he told me . . . you know, it was always hard to follow his thoughts. Even for him. He seemed to have a way of screening his thoughts from himself so that even he could not say how he reached the conclusions he did. He was like some kind of . . . prophet, I don't know. Hearing voices. He'd always know where lost things were. But even if they were important to him, he would never actually go to find them."

Soph described Stephan's death on Io. "Stephan had what, for lack of a better term, I would call a religion, there at the end of his life. He believed that something, some intelligence, inhabited the deep atmosphere of Jupiter. Possibly some alien species that had snuck in during the conflicts that tore the System apart after the Probe's arrival. He traveled the Jove system collecting stories from water dowsers, tech hunters, isolated ecstatics. He came to believe that, at the moment of maximum risk, the moment when your life hangs in the balance, uncertain of which way to tip, the Voice of Jove speaks to you. You hear something, you *understand* something. He was always after that. The ordinary conclusions of life had ceased to be enough for him.''

Ambryn seemed mesmerized. She leaned close to Soph. She radiated heat.

''Stephan knew there was something on Venus,'' Soph said. ''Something important.''

''Stephan learned this around Jupiter. And so you came here.'' Soph was amused to see what she thought was a hint of fear in those expressive eyes, as if Ambryn was suddenly wondering if this woman who had brought her here to this dangerous place was actually completely insane. She shouldn't have started on this subject, Soph thought. It was hard to make coherent, even to herself. And it lay, silent and still, deep under the last arguments she and Lightfoot had had.

''I . . . it affected my choice of projects,'' Soph said. ''Call it a whim.''

''Do you have whims, Soph?''

''Stephan did. I'll just have to use his.''

Footsteps pounded down the passage.

''This whole place is about to go up,'' Elward said.

''Those explosives came from the biopackage I was on,'' Soph said. ''I saw one. It had grown, and Kun pointed it out to me.''

''They're all over the mountainside,'' Elward said. ''I don't know how detonation occurs—''

''Lightning,'' Ambryn and Soph said simultaneously. They looked at each other, but it wasn't a bit funny. They were all in their couches, waiting for Tiber. Soph had yelled at Elward for not bringing him, but both of them had understood the pointlessness of that emotion.

''The Bgarth,'' Ambryn said in wonder. ''Those are Bgarth biologicals. I've had to deal with them before. I know how they . . .'' She seemed about to say something else, then thought better of it. ''Tiber paid the Bgarth off with those membranes. Not that they mind getting rid of Ripi. I'm sure this partially dead Bgarth body that he's using for his launch silo doesn't make them happy. Though it seems like they could just send someone up out of the ground to eat him. . . .''

''Giant explosive fungi,'' Elward said with what Soph thought was inappropriate enthusiasm. ''So when do they go up?''

''When the lightning hits.'' Ambryn pointed up at the clouds visible overhead. ''Stratoseeders created those clouds. The entire world is in league against Ripi.''

''Tiber!'' Soph shouted into her comm link. Still no answer. She looked at Elward. ''Why didn't he come with you?''

''I told you. He said he wanted to get Ripi.''

Soph looked across the silo at the embedded drive nozzle. Could she have been wrong about Ripi's location?

Both Ambryn and Elward watched Soph. They were so needy. If she said to go now, they would go, be out of the silo opening and up into the atmosphere. If she didn't, they would wait, wait, if need be, until the explosives detonated and brought the entire mountainside down on them, destroying Ripi's covert. She found herself shaking.

An explosion shook the shuttle, and she knew she had waited too long. ''Ambryn—''

''Wait!'' Elward said. ''That wasn't from outside.'' He pointed at a display screen. ''There. Look!''

Dust rose from the opposite side of the silo. The passage there had just collapsed. It was the one that led past where she had concluded that Ripi was probably hiding, Soph realized. And it led to where Tiber was. That passage was now closed.

''Tiber!'' Soph shouted into the communicator. And finally his voice answered.

''. . . cut off . . .'' Tiber's voice was faint, as if he was many miles away.

''There must be an alternate route,'' Soph said. ''You looked—''

''Ripi is dead.'' Tiber's voice grew stronger. ''The explosion caught him . . . tore him in half, buried him in rubble. I had just found him. And I'm cut off here.'' He paused, as if looking around. ''Both passages are closed. Soph. Go.''

"Tiber—"

"None of us has much time. If you wait . . . it won't help me. It would take weeks for you to get me out of here. And by that time I'll be dead anyway."

Ambryn leaned her head down over the controls, covering them with her hair. "Soph." Her voice was very quiet. "Soph, I think I can deactivate the explosives on the hillside. I learned it from the Guts—"

"It's a setup." Elward said. He looked at Soph.

"What do you mean?" Soph said.

"I . . ." He cleared his throat. "Soph. Tiber planted the explosives that blew that passage." He paused.

"Go on."

"I saw him finishing the job. He was right above the passage, planting them. Or that's what I think. I could be wrong."

"You're not wrong." Soph made a fist and rapped her knuckles on the bulkhead. She'd known it for a while now. No, not known it—*should* have known it. Lightfoot would have been contemptuous. "We have been set up. Used." She picked up the communicator. "Tiber!" No answer.

"But why?" Ambryn said. "Why would he want to stay here?"

"I don't think we'll ever know," Soph said. And the thought drove her crazy. There would never be any way to confirm her conclusions. She could be completely wrong, leaving behind someone completely innocent. . . . "Ambryn, I think we should just take off."

She expected instant acquiescence. Ambryn had spent the whole time here in absolute terror. But, instead, Ambryn turned away from the controls to look at her.

"Like I said, I can deactivate those explosives," she said. "They're Bgarth products. I've dealt with them. They're used in fracturing rocks. Without direct Bgarth management, they're pretty easy to circumvent."

"Why the hell didn't you tell us that before?" Elward asked.

"We were leaving. Taking off with Ripi and Tiber. That was it. Who cared if the place blew up once we were gone?"

"Not me. Good point, girl." Elward looked at Soph too.

"I think I know where Tiber is. That is, presuming he's not telling the truth about what happened."

"He's not," Soph said. "I bet you he doesn't even have Ripi. I think I know where Ripi is. But it doesn't matter."

"Maybe not to you," Elward says. "But it does to me. Ripi's our stake, Soph. He's worth money. If we just take off from here, who are we? Where do we go?"

"He's right," Ambryn said. "If we leave without Ripi, we're totally screwed. We have nothing. What do you have?"

Soph looked at them. "Ambryn. Take care of those explosives with your Bgarth kit. Elward. Go find that goddam Tiber and haul him back here—unconscious if necessary. And I'll get Ripi."

Elward grinned. "Tiber can cook. I knew there was a reason we need him."

Seven

1

The rubble shifted under Soph's feet. It looked like Ripi's escape path had been destroyed, as had no doubt been Tiber's intention. A loose rock fell from overhead and struck her on the shoulder. She fell and rolled down the rocks. She pushed herself up. She didn't have time to worry about it.

The drive nozzle was impervious, but she thought some of Ripi's tiny passages ran right under the rock here. An overnight bag climbed up next to her, drilled holes in the rock, and planted microexplosives. The detonation was a barely audible tick, and a section of the face fell away, revealing the tunnel. It looked like the tracks left by a wood-boring insect. It was as if Ripi had been an interloper in his own covert.

"Ripi! Come out. We need to escape."

And there he was, curled up in a depression in the floor. He looked up at her, as if she'd disturbed him at his nap.

"Do you have any enemies?" she asked.

"Thousands," he said without surprise. "Perhaps millions."

Now, *that* was a charming bit of arrogance. "Any who are likely to try to find you here on Venus?"

"My enemies are Vronnans." He had the patient air of

someone explaining a simple matter to a child. "Vronnans do not travel within this Solar System. I am the only one. If someone did, he would be unable to find me. The information would be unavailable to him."

"We found you," Soph said.

"But you are humans. Native to the System. You can contact information sources. But an unknown alien? No."

"Tiber is a human being," Soph said. "What if he guided someone else here?"

Ripi stared at her with his close-set dark eyes, and she knew he was finally reaching some of the conclusions that she had.

Then he dove under her feet. She grabbed at him, but he was past and gone, out the opening she had cut. By the time she was able to follow, the floor of the silo was deserted.

Rain pounded down on Elward as he crept across the wet rocks. They were loose and ready to slide down at any moment. Those explosives were really overkill for this thing. There. He was right above the Belt shuttle in which Tiber had been hiding. He was probably still in there. He was not expecting anyone to come after him.

Did the storm seem to be moving on? Elward couldn't tell. But maybe this one would move past, and Ambryn would have time to deactivate the explosives. He hoped so. Otherwise, she'd just ruin that dress. Despite himself, he smiled. She would have liked him having that thought. A bright flash of lightning blinded him. As he blinked, someone grabbed him and slammed his head against the rocks. The thunder in his head mixed with that outside, and the wet mud against his cheek felt like the sky, getting close.

He couldn't have been out more than a couple of seconds, but now he was inside and rain did not fall in his eyes as he looked up. A fuzzy sphere floated into his field of view. It had a face on it. Earth had a moon, he'd heard, a big one. Maybe this was what it looked like. The Man in the Moon. God, who'd want to see that thing floating in his sky? A wonder they hadn't blown the damn thing up.

"Sorry about that," Tiber said. "But I can't risk a lot of movement just at the moment."

"That's all right," Elward said. He could talk, but he couldn't move. He really couldn't move, though he could feel the floor under him and the cold dampness of his clothes. He put every ounce of willpower into moving his finger. Nothing. Tiber smiled at him, touched his head. Elward could feel it, feel the fingers stroking his hair. And the pressure of something, a band around his head.

A suspension strap. It cut his voluntary muscle impulses. E&J sometimes used it for pre-instructional detention. Made security a lot easier.

"It should be over soon," Tiber said. "Then I will release you."

"What will happen?" Elward said.

"I can go home."

"Where's home?"

"Home is Sukh."

"Sukh?"

"Sukh is Ripi-Arana-Hoc's daughter. The one he betrayed and abandoned and left without memories. She rescued me from those who attacked the *Prismatic Bezel*, destroyed everything, and took me. Things . . . happened to me. Sukh rescued me from them, gave me life. But just wait. In a few minutes, you'll get to meet her."

Through the gashes in the shuttle wall, Elward heard a long rumble of thunder. Thunder?

The shuttle shook as the mud and rock above Ripi's house roared down like an immense fist.

Ambryn clung to the jagged slab of glass. Rocks slammed against the other side, but the glass did not crack. She squeezed her eyes shut, certain that she'd guessed wrong, leapt for the wrong thing, and that what she had thought was the Bgarth mouth ring was sliding, with increasing speed, down the slope with the rest of the mountainside.

A fresh breeze blew through her hair. She unhunched her shoulders and straightened. The electrical storm had dispersed, and the air was crisp.

She'd done a good job. Only a few of the fungus explosives had detonated, dropping a load of rock and dirt on the dented spacecraft Ripi called home. Still, she'd waited a little too long. Wires had come up out of the soil and extended themselves until they were almost as tall as she was. They had wiggled like stop-motion photographs of sprouts seeking the sun. They had sensed the massive charge of the thundercloud hanging overhead and desperately wanted those electrons. She'd barely made it out before the lightning struck.

She looked out over the ring's edge. The landslide had sheered away the dirt and rock around it, and it now hung free. Immediately below her, a lump several times the size of a person, almost like a gigantic barnacle, swelled from the smooth side of the Bgarth body. She recognized it as a Bgarth override interface. She had never seen one.

She was just reaching down for it when the sky thundered. Had the storm returned? A small dark cloud against the now-clear blue—no! It was a descending spacecraft, which had hit the denser atmosphere at incautious speed. It roared down, sending fragments of ablative shielding flaming into the atmosphere, where they floated for a moment, like festival balloons, before winking out. As it finally slowed, it became not a spacecraft but a paradox, a heavy object suspended in air.

Ambryn watched in awe as the bulbous alien spacecraft settled ponderously into the waiting landing silo.

2

Soph pursued Ripi, praying that Ambryn was all right. She heard the explosions. Inside the silo, light brightened, then flared. She looked up. The Bgarth body itself seemed to be generating it from a thick ring partway up. Parts of the walls peeled away, knocking over poorly stowed gear, and quested upward like tentacles toward what was clearly an alien spacecraft. It lowered itself through the silo opening, blocking the sunlight from above. Now everything was the searing white light of the Bgarth ring.

The spacecraft cut its power a dozen or so meters above the floor. It smashed down through the Bgarth tentacles. Soph jumped into the air, then met the crushed and tilted floor as she came down. The tearing roar of the impact came an instant later. Soph slid down the torn metal toward the bulging shape of the alien spaceship.

Her elbow caught a sharp chunk of metal, and she grabbed on to it. The lights had gone out again, and the only light came from the opening high above. The alien ship had found a resting point not far below. Soph clambered back up the tilted floor.

She managed to grab on and swing herself up onto a level surface. The emergency life-support cart peeked out of its blister as if nervous about being seen. Through its double-bulge glass fuselage, Soph could see that it had inflated the pillows on each of the emergency cots. A tribute to Martian military medicine, Soph had time to think.

Then the spacecraft's hatch slammed open.

"Ripi . . . Ripi abandoned his daughter Sukh," Tiber said. "Left her without memories. You have to know Vronnans to know how significant that is. All because *he* wanted to live. Everything else led from that one act."

"So you came here to nail him," Elward said. "All that shit you did. Just to get here to help her out?"

"Yes. Just so she could get her revenge. And perhaps her memories."

He'd hauled Elward into the bleachers overlooking the silo. Tiber considerately propped Elward up so that he could see what was going on.

If he could have moved, he would have—to get away from what appeared in the hatch of the Vronnan spaceship.

Explosions, rending metal, disaster. Ambryn cowered back behind the protection of the glass slabs, afraid of seeing what was happening below. She was stuck up here, and there wasn't anything she could do.

Wait a minute. She still had part of her Bgarth kit with her. Fumbling, she pulled out a paracrine activator and reached down to the armored swell of the Bgarth override interface. These swellings had once been parasites on the ancestral Bgarth. With the grand indifference with which they incorporated parts of the universe into their bodies, the Bgarth had turned the parasites into emergency external control sites. A Bgarth that had lost function could be controlled remotely by one of its fellows until it could be . . . repaired, healed, whatever the hell you did with a Bgarth.

Maybe she could use it to do something.

She thought she could feel the huge barnacle quiver, though it was hard to tell with all the vibration from whatever was going on in the silo. Then, acquiescing all at once, its shell cleaved open with a dull crack. Before she could reconsider, Ambryn dropped down into the hot darkness inside the override interface.

3

An alien figure stood in the hatch. The body, supported by squat rear legs, was huge, swelling in an immense arch.

A Vronnan female. In the male, Soph knew, the middle two legs were shrunken. Ripi concealed his beneath his elaborate clothing. But the female's middle limbs were vastly larger and let her stand in centaur posture, her forelimbs—arms—raised in a dramatic gesture. She bellowed, her voice many-toned, like an organ. If that was intended for Ripi, it was wasted. He was hiding, and she'd have to dig him out of the ruins of his house.

It was good planning, Elward had to give Tiber that. Ripi ran into the observation bubble and stopped dead when he saw Tiber already there. Tiber took him with absolutely no trouble at all and hauled him right in. Maybe he wanted Ripi to get a look at his daughter, who was kicking up a gigantic fuss down below.

Elward waited, expecting the little alien to whip out some kind of weapon and cut Tiber up into tiny pieces, but instead he slumped in Tiber's grasp, like some little kid knowing he'd done wrong. It was that guilt thing that got you in the end.

"How did she make the arrangements with you?" Ripi said. "What Earth humans have contacts with Vronnans?"

"Never mind how." Tiber's voice was dangerous. And here Elward had thought Tiber kind of a blowhard, a bigfoot captain type who couldn't do anything without a big control couch and an obsequious crew.

"Your trap was right out in the open." Ripi sounded incredibly calm, but maybe these aliens showed hysteria in some other way—their smell or something. He'd have to ask Ambryn.

"That's your daughter," Tiber said. "Her name is Sukh. I don't think you ever learned it before you ran away."

"My daughter." Ripi stared down, fascinated. "She has come so far. So far."

"Fight him, you stupid son of a bitch!" Elward couldn't stand it anymore. Here he was, plopped on the floor, and he had to watch this idiot give his life away because he felt some weird kind of alien guilt. As if he was the first guy to ever abandon a child. They got over it, for God's sake. They learned to live their lives the same way anyone else did. It didn't make a goddam bit of difference.

Ripi jumped toward Elward, but Tiber plucked him right out of the air. As he did it, the long trailing edge of Ripi's fancy sleeve brushed across Elward's face. Before he knew what he was doing, Elward used the only part of his body that still worked and bit into it.

Tiber hadn't expected Elward's large weight to be added to Ripi's and fell off-balance, down to his knees. Elward felt a sharp pain in his jaw. The sleeve pulled him forward, and he rolled down onto Ripi. Together they sent Tiber sprawling.

Circus people did this jaw thing and spun around right under the tent. Their teeth didn't come out of their heads. Elward held on, getting dragged across the floor, feeling the pain as his loose body pounded on obstacles.

Elward spit out the sleeve when he fetched up at the bottom of the observation bubble.

"Come on, you moron!" he yelled. "Ripi! Before he grabs you again. Do it!"

Ripi dithered, unable for a moment to figure out what was wanted, then reached down and hit the release on the suspension strap.

Everything hurt, but Elward gathered himself together and

sprang up from the flexible glass. He slammed into Tiber just as he was coming down to finally take care of Ripi.

Elward head-butted him right in the pit of his stomach. Tiber went down hard. Dealing with wimpy aliens the size of an Airedale had clearly not prepared him for a real fight. Elward slammed heavy fists into Tiber's face—one, two. And three, just for good measure. When Elward saw the blood come out of his nose and spill all across that weird face of his, he knew that this was what he had been waiting for all along, since the first time he saw him, when Soph brought him out with her from under the ground.

Ripi was watching, but he didn't seem to be enjoying it.

"Got anything to defend against her? Why were you coming up here in the first place?"

The alien ship fired explosives up at the observation bubble and the glass cracked and sagged. Elward felt like someone sitting in a real wide-butt box at the arena, only the players were pissed and charging after him.

"Yes," Ripi said. A bulge in the wall popped open, and he did something inside of it.

"Let 'er rip!" Elward said.

The air was so full of flaming trash that for a moment Soph couldn't see what was happening. Then she realized—that firing was from the weapons pods Ripi had hung in the silo.

Soph flung herself into the Martian emergency med cart just as small-arms fire stitched across the impact-resistant tube of the medical bay.

"Analysis indicates that the patient is fully functional," a cool voice said. "Please discharge in favor of next patient."

Soph crouched behind a cot. Explosive fragments rattled on the tube. She could see the gleam of weapons lasers through the dust and smoke.

"Please do not malinger," the emergency vehicle said. "It will go on your next fitness report."

"I'm seeking shelter," Soph said, wondering how sophisticated its processor was.

"This is not a shelter. This is an emergency medical facility. You will be ejected," the vehicle said.

Its sheltering double cylinder opened up, the cots folded

into the walls, the rear tilted, and Soph found herself on the ground. She lay still. Mentally, she checked for broken bones. If the emergency vehicle had injured her, then it would now have a reason to let her in for treatment. Maybe that had been its entire motivation. Even simple operational devices, left alone to mull over their processing for long enough, developed interesting and perverse logic loops.

Soph rolled on her back. The firing had slackened. The Vronnan female—whoever she was—had just buttoned down and waited out the attack, sending out her own counter-battery fire. She'd destroyed all of Ripi's feeble weapons pods. Now she could move out without resistance.

4

Blinded by the darkness, Ambryn felt across the stiff folds of tissue inside the barnacle, sensing the different textures—sticky, slippery, rough—that marked interface points. After a few minutes, she got herself oriented and found the mouth-part control. It had several configurations—suitable, she suspected, for differing sizes of filterable food in the Bgarth's ancestral seas before they dug into the bedrock in pursuit of an absolutely unexploited ecological niche.

And the appropriate neurotransmitter was propane, a simple molecule. And the little lighter she used to melt on her decorative fingernail covers . . . or, hell, was it butane? Dammit!

Her fingers felt at the appropriate vial. A makeup kit always came in handy. She'd show Soph.

That is, if she was right about the propane.

She unscrewed the catalytic igniter, dropped it irretrievably into the folds beneath her feet, then tilted the nozzle over the reactive areas she pinched up with her other hand.

She couldn't smell it and hoped it wouldn't poison her in this enclosed space. The surrounding folds did seem to shudder and pull away a little. Otherwise, nothing.

Maybe this damn stuff was butane. She couldn't figure out any way to check. Screw it. She tilted it and actually poured liquid out on the receptor site. It made her dizzy.

Then she felt it, a deep rumbling all around her. She had

activated the sphincter closure reflex. The hydraulic-actuator-powered muscle around the mouth ring now started, ponderously, to shut the mouth, trapping the attacking Vronnan spacecraft inside the Bgarth landing silo.

A creaking echoed through the silo. Elward looked up. The opening overhead shrank as the huge vanes moved in. What had activated them? Maybe this dead Bgarth had decided to eat them, after all.

That huge Sukh realized that in a minute she would be stuck like a bug in a jar. She moved fast. The attacking spacecraft wailed, sucking oxygen in through pop-out intakes to power its atmospheric engines. The shattered observation bubble tilted, its supports blown away by Sukh's return fire. No more time to rubberneck. Elward scrabbled up and managed to reach a secure grip at the Bgarth wall. The bubble fell no farther. But he was stuck. There was no way to get up and out.

Ripi rolled past him. Elward couldn't grab him. He was holding on too tight with both hands. Ripi tumbled off the edge. Half-horrified, half-wanting to see the splat, Elward watched him shrink toward the floor.

He never got there. Instead, the spacecraft hissed powerfully. Garbage flew across the silo floor. Gas jetting out of a nozzle wailed at painful volume, like an emergency horn.

Elward did not believe what he was seeing. Ripi floated in midair. His clothes flapped. Elward couldn't read Vronnan facial expressions, so he couldn't tell if Ripi was scared, accepting, pissed, what. The spacecraft stood up on its landing legs, a nozzle sticking out from under its skirts, and shot a powerful jet of air up at Ripi, supporting him. Then, by slowly decreasing the pressure, the ship lowered Ripi delicately to the floor. He lay there, staring up.

"Move your ass!" Elward shouted. "She's not going to wait!"

Tiber hadn't fallen down into the silo, and he wasn't up here. What the hell had happened to him? Then he looked down and saw him.

* * *

Soph ran out into the silo, right under the ship that could kill her in an instant, and grabbed Ripi, thinking, Thank God, at least Elward's still alive. She heard him yelling from above. Ripi was light under his bulky clothes, and she had no problem dragging him.

"Sukh!" a voice shouted from above.

It was Tiber. He hung from the ruins of the observation bubble, reaching out to the ship with the gesture of a dying man on a life raft.

"Sukh! Don't leave me!"

Soph thought it was the most anguished cry she'd ever heard.

"Get back!" Soph shouted. "Takeoff backwash!"

She couldn't wait around to see if he understood. She dragged Ripi across the floor and threw him into the rear of the Martian med cart. She could see no emergency bunker to hide in. This was the closest thing to shelter she could find.

She pulled the cot pads over onto her and Ripi.

"This is not a human being," the vehicle said. "Not a human being!"

The shock of the takeoff blast turned the vehicle over.

Elward huddled against the wall as flames and dust blew past him. Everything shook as the spacecraft took off. Despite the risk, he turned his head and peeked out under his arm.

The Vronnan spacecraft smashed up through the half-closed vanes of the Bgarth mouth. Fragments showered down. Then it was gone.

The bright flames had blinded him, and he blinked at a big blue dot that obscured most of his vision. His head rang. He had no idea of what had happened to anyone else. Maybe he was the only one left alive.

Then, above the ringing in his ears, he heard Ambryn's voice.

"Hey! Anybody alive down there?"

5

"He knelt right here." Ambryn gestured dramatically over the rubble that covered the bent and torn silo floor. "Crying.

Wailing! He'd lost everything he'd dreamed of. His . . . mother. His only love!''

''In hot coals?'' Soph found this all too melodramatic. The flames of the unassisted oxygen-boosted takeoff had scorched the inside of the Bgarth silo. The metal floor was still hot.

''Like a martyr in the radioactive ruins of a city! Even his clothes were smoking. I'll never forget the sight. Here, this is where his knees were.''

Soph stared at the two marks indicated, close together but otherwise indistinguishable from the other gouges in the rubble, and shook her head in wide-eyed incomprehension. Her head hurt. She'd lain unconscious for at least fifteen minutes while the med cart tried to regain enough function to treat her.

''Tiber wanted to go with that ship.'' Elward reluctantly came to Ambryn's support. ''Ripi's daughter Sukh was aboard. She raised him, I guess. Something like that. He'd set this whole operation up so that he could see her again and go with her. That was the plan—for him.'' His back was scorched, but he seemed all right.

''So where is Tiber now?'' Soph asked. Damn it, she'd missed the most important events.

''Ran off!'' The whole thing excited Ambryn more than Soph thought decent. ''Before I could find a way down from the Bgarth mouth ring. And Elward was just getting down from that ledge. I don't know where he went.''

Soph looked over to where Ripi lay, almost catatonic, under a blanket. And beyond him, the blackened remains of the atmospheric shuttle. It would take weeks to get it operational again.

''Soph,'' Elward said. ''You knew. About Tiber. As soon as I told you—''

''I already knew. I just couldn't admit it. And that's dangerous. I thought my training had gotten me over that.''

''Our needs and desires are always involved,'' Ambryn said. ''They have to be.''

''They shouldn't be. Not to that extent.''

''How?'' Elward persisted. ''I thought you'd bought him all the way.''

''I did,'' Soph said. ''Maybe I still do. But it seems clear that he set this whole thing up as a way of getting back in touch with . . . Sukh, you called her? Ripi's daughter. He'd gone down to the Well to negotiate for these explosives to be sown over the covert as part of an ecomodule drop. That was why he talked to the Bgarth in the first place. But then Ambryn's attempt to contact him caused him to get sealed in.

''He never had any intention of returning to the *Argent*, but he ordered the second shuttle to be dropped here to conceal that fact from his crew. He—or an accomplice—placed the booby trap aboard.''

''But Elward was the one who found the booby trap,'' Ambryn said.

''Because Elward is smart and knows his job,'' Soph said. ''But if he hadn't . . . I think Tiber was just about to point it out himself. Remember? He needed to appear willing to leave. But he wanted us stuck here.''

''Then why not just deactivate the shuttle?'' Ambryn said.

''Because he wanted us to be able to get out,'' Soph said. ''He had his meeting with Sukh all planned. Once it was coming up, he tried to push us into taking off without him.''

''You think he wanted to keep us safe?'' Ambryn said.

''Yes,'' Soph said. ''I do.''

For a wonder, Elward did not snort.

Instead, he said, ''The house defenses are down, and even lazy E&J interrogators can get up here without tiring their tootsies. We need to get moving.''

''Soph,'' Ambryn said. ''What do we do?''

''I can get us out of here. Or, rather, you can, Ambryn, if you will pilot. I put *Len-3* on retainer. It must be roosting somewhere up in the Maxwells. A signal, and it'll be here in fifteen minutes. It even has rocket-assisted exo-atmospheric capability. We can probably make it across the pans down to Aphrodite and the eco-teams. It's risky, but it's our only choice.''

''If you had another choice,'' Ambryn said, ''would you take it?''

''What are you proposing?'' Soph said.

''Find Tiber,'' Ambryn said. ''Talk to him.''

"Yes," Soph said, feeling oddly tentative about the idea. What would she say?

"Hey, he wanted to screw us all," Elward said.

"He and the *Argent* are still our only hope," Ambryn said.

"How is it a hope?" Elward seemed irritated that people refused to give up. "You heard what Soph said. We got no way out."

Ambryn shrugged. "Perhaps the *Argent* can drop a shuttle into a low orbit, rendezvous with *Len-3* when it goes exo-atmospheric. I don't know, Elward. If you don't like it, you can just stay here and wait."

"Great," Elward said. "Just great. That's all my life is—a big smorgasbord of wonderful choices."

"Quit bitching," Ambryn said, "and fill your plate."

6

The shattered landing-ring vanes stood above Soph like semaphore signals. Their fragments littered the wet ground. The marks of Tiber's frantic run were easy enough to find. And the ground was unstable beneath her feet. She felt the rocks and mud shifting with every step.

"Tiber!"

The day was bright and looked full of hope.

"We have to talk. Please!"

She'd already summoned *Len-3*. She imagined how it must have perched on the edge of some high rock face, regarded with jaw-circling indifference by mountain goats. Upon receiving her signal, it had raised up on its legs, tilted forward, and slid silently off into the air, diving like a hunting owl, to swoop across the rock and mount into the sky.

"We might have a way out of here," she said. "If you cooperate with us."

"I lied to you."

His voice came from a hole at her feet. Startled, she shifted her weight and felt the rocks start to slide. He reached out and steadied her.

"We don't have much time." She squatted down next to where he sat against the side of the hole. His long hair swirled down to his shoulders. Burns covered his skin and his clothing, and the stink of fire struck her nostrils.

"Time? I think we have all of it that we need."

"Tiber! Listen to me." He looked at her, and she saw life come back into his eyes. "You lied to us, you lied to your crew, you used us all. You were never intending to go back up to the *Argent*, were you? You wanted to leave with Sukh. You wanted to give her father back to her."

He nodded.

"We know all that. It doesn't matter, not right now. E&J is on its way here. You can either shoot yourself now or tell the story to them. Ripi will be imprisoned somewhere else, and they'll lock him in a cage. No one will achieve anything."

"No need to threaten."

"I'm not threatening you. I'm informing you. I'm sorry we live in a universe where those two things are so often indistinguishable."

That almost seemed to amuse him. "So am I."

"The shuttle's down," she said. "So are Ripi's defenses. We have to get out of here, and we have to get out soon. I kept *Len-3* on retainer. It'll be here inside of ten minutes."

He looked at her, tugging burned hair away from his strange face. He really did look like a lion now. Lions: impressive, selfish, and devious, just like eagles and all other symbols of masculine pride.

"*Len-3* has limited suborbital capability," Soph said, trying not to reveal her own fear. "We can pop up above the atmosphere. Does the *Argent* have any way to rendezvous with a vehicle that's just barely exo-atmospheric?"

"In her hold, the *Argent* has a tethered dock." Tiber reluctantly returned to life. "If she comes close in to the dust clouds, she can drop it down to an orbit several hundred kilometers below. If we dock with it, she can pull us back up."

"That might risk a serious military response from the Skullhouse."

He shrugged, dismissing that as a minor inconvenience. There were drawbacks to making high-risk plans with someone who might be deeply suicidal, Soph reflected. But she didn't have a hell of a lot of choice.

"I want some way of guarding our safety." Soph was brisk. "As do Elward and Ambryn. Once we are aboard the *Argent*, our freedom of action will be extremely limited."

"Mine also," he said wearily. "I can't guarantee your safety. But I will support you as much as I can."

"I wish to go aboard without search of our effects," she said. "Once Ambryn, Elward, Ripi, and I have established our quarters in a mutually agreed upon area, we will, of course, wish to prevent the intrusion of unauthorized personnel. Ripi will remain in my custody. Where will the *Argent* head after Venus?"

He got to his feet and stood facing her.

"You will leave the ship at the first safe opportunity," he said. "Whether or not it is convenient. Just safe for you."

"Agreed," she said. "With Ripi."

"If he wishes."

"Of course."

"The *Argent* will head for Mercury," he said. "I have a question to ask there."

7

Ambryn spun *Len-3*'s engines up. The chatter of copter blades was just audible down the valley as E&J forces still wary of Ripi's defensive gear approached.

The cabin was crammed with gear. Elward had rigged a safety harness for Ripi.

The aircraft tilted, slid down the rubble slope, then, with a wailing burst of power, tore across the bright landscape and rose into the air.

A warning beep, then a rough jerk that snapped Soph's head into an instantly responding restraining harness. A single missile had been fired from an E&J copter. *Len-3* shrugged off this final assault and climbed. Ambryn hissed out a breath.

They tore across Ishtar, pressed into their couches by stiff acceleration. Soon, the wide expanse of the Sea of Atalanta opened up to the right. By this time they had climbed high enough that the pale curve of the atmosphere had become visible. The sun rose over them as they dove deeper into day.

"The dust will strip us," Soph said to Tiber. "If we get much higher."

"We're ready. Two degrees southing, Ambryn, and ten more kilometers in altitude." The closer he got to his ship, the more serene Tiber became.

They had left the bulk of the atmosphere behind. Soph had not told anyone, but she had doubted *Len-3*'s promotional claims. The plane had, after all, upgraded itself to exo-atmospheric capability without supervision. It wasn't as if the original aircraft, built more than a hundred years ago, had known any aerospace engineering. It had relied on contract workers, each kept in the dark as to what the others were up to.

"How are we doing?" she asked Ambryn.

Ambryn skinned lips back from white teeth. "I'm just hanging on for the ride."

"Good," Soph said.

She didn't hear any hiss of escaping air, and the rockets under the wings came smoothly into operation. The curving suborbital trajectory glowed on the display screen. Within the next ten minutes, *Len-3* would cut its rockets and arch back into the atmosphere, there to grab back on to the air with just the tips of its folded wings and come, after a long course, back to the surface. Though maybe space contained the inactive corpses of ultralights that had flown too high and gone into orbit. Dark wings might sail eternally above the atmosphere.

She stared forward. The planet glowed blue and dark below, its separate seas glimmering against the land that surrounded them. Was it . . . there. A small dot, growing rapidly. Now it was visibly a disk.

"Good, good," Tiber said under his breath. "Gently now, gently."

The disk became a concave dish. Hanging from its center, pulled along behind it, was an assemblage of spheres.

"That was once a high-vacuum research facility," Tiber said. "Superseded technology, for some reason we picked it up. The shield wasn't meant for this sort of friction, but just for pushing aside the usual dust and molecules found in interplanetary space. The vacuum behind it is several orders of magnitude harder. I'm willing to sacrifice the shield, since we're rarely able to lease it, but we must hurry. It can't stand this stress for long.''

An elephant's-trunk lock connector quested down from the research facility and felt out *Len-3*'s roof lock. Magnetic connectors clicked on. Ambryn turned the controls back over to *Len-3*'s autopilot.

Soph patted *Len-3*'s console. ''Maybe someday you can buy yourself a deepdrive,'' she said. ''Start saving now.''

She followed the others up the lock connector.

Len-3 disappeared into the atmosphere below. The interior of the research station had the swooping style of a century or so before, the same time period as *Len-3*'s original airframe. Soph wondered if they had recognized each other as coevals.

The research shield hung far below the *Argent* on a hundreds-of-kilometers-long tether. A flaring corona made up its perimeter, and flames blew past them on all sides. If the shield failed, their little cocoon would be torn to pieces in an instant. Soph felt the acceleration as they were reeled in from above.

The flames diminished, then disappeared as they left the dust cloud, and they were in darkness.

Its job successfully completed, the shield tried to fold itself, but, damaged, stuck halfway, like an umbrella abandoned in a garbage can.

Above them, the *Argent*. It had a wide stern, where the drive pods and life-support systems were, and curved up to an oddly pointy bow, as if it intended to enter an atmosphere someday. They rose up toward a hatch that had opened to reveal an open interior space, glowing from within.

Eight

A Previous Chapter from the Life of Ripi-Arana-Hoc

"Marriage," Ripi said, stunned.

"It's our most effective move." His mentor, Timp, was an ancient female who had long ago lost the use of her hind limbs. She crouched in a warm-water bath, nerve-maintaining eels slithering futilely against her flanks. "Our only move."

"I am ranking," Ripi said. "Valuable."

He tried to rise from the interview seat, but, of course, the restraints kept him motionless. The sensitive straps alerted Timp's two Guardians, whose long paired forelimbs slid out of their confinement: a warning. No Vronnan female would permit a possibly hostile male free movement in her private space.

"Most valuable as a sacrifice to peace with Bru clan," Timp said. "It is your very rank, unusual as it is, that makes you the ideal candidate. And your memories. Most valuable of all. Most valuable."

Timp munched thoughtfully on the delicate heart of a plant that had been growing in her chamber for decades, seemingly in anticipation of this desperate conversation. Its bitter scent filled the room, causing the sensitive filterplants on the wall to wrinkle up their comb leaves.

Timp had run the diplomatic side of Arana clan's relations for almost a century. Her mind held every detail of generations of agreements, alliances, linkages, a dense net that once had enabled Arana to pull itself forward among the exiled clans of Vron but now imprisoned it as it slowly shrank in influence, like a trapped and parasitized insect.

That status quo was what Ripi had spent his career struggling against. He had aroused much opposition. That opposition had clearly reached Timp's level.

"Bru's power is rising," Timp said. "Soon it will dominate this region of space. If we intend to continue our transit . . . we must have unlimited peace with them. And a penetration of their inner secrets. . . . You are to marry Lo-Bru-Tirni."

"She gave me honor," Ripi said dazedly. "Permitted my rank." He felt the almost paralyzing panic response that he recognized as sexual passion.

"She will give you more."

Lo-Bru-Tirni had commanded the spacecraft aboard which Ripi and an operational group had been carried to the asteroid belt of the Telstet system. There they had engaged a HarNagn colony that enforced a monopoly on mineral rights. Casualties were heavy, but together, the Arana and Bru forces had cleared the nest out and shared in the resulting wealth.

Ripi had imprinted on the powerful Lo, whose handling of her vessels had been ultimately professional. Those weeks that he and his force had spent aboard the Bru vessel glowed in his mind still. He would never have petitioned for that mating, of course. Doom lay that way.

His weakness had been obvious to all. Thus, he had achieved his most dearly desired destruction.

"The transfer of your memories into the Bru memory pool will cement our alliance," Timp said. "You will live on within that clan. Ripi-Arana-Hoc will never be erased." Traditional images of the ascent of his soul through the minds of his descendants flowed across the wall behind Timp.

Ripi knew that their effort was misguided. He would not have minded an early mating and dissolution, not for a good cause. Or at least so he told himself. But the Bru had clearly outmaneuvered Timp and her cronies.

His memory-holding children would be used for modeling. Their Arana memory traces would be intensively analyzed as they developed through their Bearers, and those memories would then be used against Arana clan. Traditional tactics would be analyzed, emotional weaknesses pinpointed. He knew, from long experience, that Bru aimed for absolute power in this region of space.

He would have to find a way to avoid his fate.

Ripi had found his Brother in Memory at a half-abandoned asteroid transfer station in the second asteroid belt of a K1 star devoid of habitable planets.

A Vronnan only truly existed with his clan, part of the interactive system with all the other species that had found homes within the Vronnan colonies over hundreds of thousands of years. But there were those Vronnans—exiled, fled, deranged—who lived apart, just as primitive Vronnans once had and as most Galactic species, less advanced than Vronnans, still did.

Ripi had been a junior member of a trade delegation dealing with a group of Ulanyi. The deal was for new membranes for the Arana deepdrive. It needed pieces of a modified Ulanyi placenta to survive, and what supported it now was dying. Every few centuries or so, something would go wrong that internal system maintenance couldn't handle, and new graft tissue would be necessary. That had happened to the Arana clanship.

Perhaps the Ulanyi had deliberately put the death time in to ensure their market. But then, all things died, even with sophisticated gene repair viruses busily keeping cancerous defects from spreading. The Ulanyi themselves discarded the placentas after they were born. It was only the Vronnans who had found such a use for them, which included a substrate for growing spacecraft.

When it reached the negotiation asteroid, the Arana clanship absorbed one end of it. All internal structures were rearranged to accommodate it, as if the ship were trying to invaginate and digest it. Such direct contact was always useful, for all sorts of defective and malfunctioning inhabitants of the clanship could then be filtered out without killing them directly. They just wandered along artificial habitability gradients into the new structure, to be left behind when the clanship finally detached itself.

As a result of generations of biological dumping, the asteroid's interior had achieved a factitious life of its own. Exiles rigged crude pumping mechanisms to transfer nutritive fluid. Creatures reverted to less-specialized primitive forms and hung in rock-cut chambers, their flesh carved off for food as they continued to live. A fusion reactor in the center generated more energy than anyone could possibly use, and the intelligent inhabitants, refugees of several species, had achieved a sort of primitive composite culture.

It was such a situation that must have been the original model for the clanship system in which all Vronnans now lived. Memories of that era were vague and disordered in all adult Vronnans, perhaps a consequence of the emotionally fraught conflicts of those millennia.

Or perhaps the sterile Helper semisibs, Ankur and his cousins, who supervised the transfer of memories into reproductively active Vronnans, had decided to edit those memories for reasons of their own. They themselves had no direct inherited memories, but their histories and traditions were vital things, jealously handed down through professional lines of descent.

Ripi had wandered away from the negotiations. The contact took months, according to slow but precise embryonic Ulanyi brain processes. Vronnans, particularly the younger males, never spent their entire time at the meeting.

But Ripi wandered much farther than any of his companions, who tended to huddle just outside the sealed polymer doors that marked the secret parts of Ulanyi territory. He brushed through tunnels filled with burgeoning Morth colonies. Those winged slugs seemed to find the asteroid congenial and, in fact, were approaching a population crisis, when they would be forced to swarm. Transport sellers already circled the asteroid, ready to make deals for the vast hollow spaces of their obsolete water transport tanks.

Ripi found his way to a huge interior space, a vacuole in

the asteroid. A primitive Vronnan nest hung in the vacuole's center. Ripi paused in shock. It had clearly been constructed from usually vestigial Vronnan glands, as had been done by primitive Vronnans before technological intervention in their reproductive schedules. Whereas modern Vronnan nests—clanships and clan cities—were kilometers across, this one was, at most, a hundred meters.

Plants grew densely throughout the surrounding chambers. They were relatively unmodified, only a few generations away from planetary surface, and still spread optimistic leaves, even though there was no solar energy to be caught in the warm, damp darkness, and the leaves were only foci for infection.

The plants were caught in dense webs of light-passage mycelia, which carried energy from the asteroid's fusion generator. The mycelia pumped energetic photons directly into the chloroplasts, having bucket-brigaded them down their endless molecular corridors, not spilling a single one into the outside environment.

It was a crude makeshift system, an indication of some serious fungal or viral plague that had destroyed specialized space-adapted plantings. Mycelia quested endlessly for chloroplasts to contact, while their energy-input endplates thrust into the face of the fusion flame, turning colliding hydrogen nuclei directly into photonic energy. It was a kludge, but it worked, keeping a complete shadow ecology in operation in the center of the asteroid. Ripi had seen more than one such asteroid filled with dry fungal mats that had once been intelligent beings. Whatever it took to survive.

The unforgivably primitive gland-grown nest should have sent Ripi screaming back to his delegation to squat humbly at the chief female's feet and listen to the chanted negotiations with the Ulanyi membrane sellers.

Instead, he found it perversely attractive. Even at that young age, when the idea of having progeny to suck the mind out of his skull seemed absurd, he had a queasy fascination with the forbidden. He pulled himself across on ropy mycelia trunk lines and shoved his way into a pulsing gate orifice. It was lined by a sphincter-keeper kept alive by clumsy semi-living feed tubes, dangerously exposed. Its tight slimy grip ran slowly up his body.

Within, a dank olfactory vestibule sorted his molecules across its sagging membranes. Supports had rotted and dropped their burden of sensory organ, which lay piled on itself and created spots of decay. Even the bony sphere of the olfactory cortex, all that was left of the original creature's nervous system, lay out on the glistening tasting papillae of the floor like a lost ball.

Two Guardians, of a much smaller subspecies than he was used to, popped out of their nests to threaten him. Their flesh-ripping jaws were hungry for soft meat, but he noticed that their lasers had seeped out their fluid and were useless. With the confidence of his hereditary rank, he challenged them and slapped their jaws with a biocommunicator stick, then waited for his pheromones to come through the vestibule's analytic surfaces to their primitive nervous systems. Guardians were descended from some distant branch of the Ulanyi. Some version of almost any creature evolved in this Galactic Arm could be found within Vronnan clan nests. No Vronnan thought that odd or even thought about it at all. It was just the way things were.

His identity diffused into the membranes around him, alerting the nest. Pheromones containing long-chain molecules coded with his genetic inheritance slid his genealogy into the binding sites and sent a signal into the chemical analysis centers within the bony sphere. The Guardians rested, spikes moving slightly, as if blown by a ventilator breeze, and waited, still not permitting him passage to the inner levels.

He squatted down to wait. The short forearm bones of his arms rested on the soft floor and gave him stability. Memory sorting took up the time. Any Vronnan had such a pile of unsystematic images and knowledge, stretching back millennia, that there was always room for more sophisticated cataloging. If they ignored him, in a few days or so he would leave.

It was in the hours he spent there in the vestibule, confronting the still-hungry Guardians, that the origins of his eventual diplomatic vocation could be found. Until his arrival at that asteroid, he had never been truly alone. From his birth, when he emerged from his Bearer already stuffed with the ancestral memories of his race, he had always been surrounded by the other beings, sentient and nonsentient, of the Arana clanship. All were bred to communicate and ask for instruction. His life had been filled by the constant sussuration of information transfer.

Here it was dead and silent. This caricature of a clanship was near death, seed spilled on rough sterile soil. He couldn't even tell if anything intelligent was left inside it.

Still, the smell had been there. Something, some distant relative of his family, had once dwelled here and left its traces. His curiosity was aroused. The Ulanyi had not spoken of this hybrid colony on the edge of their biological manufacturing center.

A voice spoke. It was rough, as if not having been used for many generations. A Vronnan voice, speaking the common root dialect, used for so long that children came forth with its rudiments spilling off their mouthparts.

"The sun crests the hill," it said. "The lacy trees hang silent as it floods the valleys with light. You are guilty. You have killed and are fleeing. But the beauty stops you. The rock path, smooth with the passage of a million feet, reflects the light and glows pink. Even the circulatory fluid, dried on your hands, so thick you can feel the layer of it cracking at the joint of your lower elbow, looks gorgeous in the light. Birds cry in the crests of the trees. Water tumbles between moss-covered rocks. Despite the pursuit, you pause, you look. You hear the beaters behind you, shouting your name. With sparkling blue wings, a blossom-sucking bird buzzes above your head, flicks past, and is gone.

"You run forward and escape your pursuers."

Ripi knelt in shock. "Brother," he said. "You remember."

"I remember. At the root, we are the same. I can smell it in your identity."

The memory was incomprehensibly old, dating back to some period before the existence of space travel, on the old planet Vron, before the wars destroyed it and the Vronnans fled in their earliest clanships.

A valve opened. The long-disused tissues creaked. A head poked forth: an old, half-blind Vronnan.

"I remember the Departure," the old Vronnan said.

Though he did not consciously recognize it, it was at this point, looking at the parasite-encrusted head of his Brother in Memory, that Ripi had the first inklings of a desperate plan for survival.

A thousand years before, Arana clan had been dug into the surface of a Probe-altered world. The crust was rich in minerals, water was plentiful, life abundant. It seemed that, at last, the Arana seed had found fertile soil. If the clan grew enough, it could split, hiving off subordinate clans, which would, in payment for their existences, give support to the parent clan. A rich net of associations would result, giving power in the local region of space.

It was not to be. Military conflict with an aggressive species dug into the crust of one of the planet's three moons led to greater and greater defensive expenditures. All expansion had to be stopped.

Specialized combat species had to be bred. Weapons bubbles sprouted and grew in the living sheath of the clan-city. Attempts to carry the war onto the moon proved futile. The mysterious beings who dwelled there did not negotiate and seemed impossible to kill. It was possible that they were not even truly alive, being the descendants of intelligent machines.

Finally, Arana clan-city was forced to encapsulate and depart. All resources had to be drawn to the creation of a clanship.

A deepdrive was grown in orbit. The original source of those tissues was forgotten. Some alien race had, at one time, given up the secret of interstellar travel to the Vronnans. It took most of Arana clan's life resources to grow the drive within its Ulanyi placenta, and they were vulnerable during the entire process.

Then units rose up from the surface and joined the deepdrive. Various species that had existed solely as eggs or diapaused embryos during Arana clan's tenure on the planetary surface were reactivated and allowed to be born. They helped construct the outer shell that protected the ship, grew into multitubed ventilation chambers, burst into glomeruli that filtered waste from water. All the specialized organs of space travel grew exactly as they should, though they had not been needed—or even thought of—for hundreds of years.

But the rancors and internal struggles attendant on the abandonment of Eden were never to be forgotten. The families were careful to breed in those memories, focusing and intensifying them so that their struggles, hurts, and enmities could finally, at some future time, find a fertile place to grow and reach fruition.

The Helper semisibs worked intensely on these tasks. Helpers, sterile themselves, had hope only in propagating those genes in the fertile caste that were most similar to those they themselves bore. And their skills gave them a precise knowledge of each fertilized ovum's genetic endowment. In order to maintain this power, they were always obedient.

Ten centuries later, Ripi's promising diplomatic career would come to a premature end as a distant consequence of these ancient hatreds.

Nine

1

Dr. Fulani peered at Ripi. "Ugly sumbitch, ain't he? That normal?" The *Argent*'s medico's mesh-reinforced legs were as long as Soph's entire body.

"I think so."

"One thing I don't have to worry about, then. Alien facial reconstructive surgery's a bit out of my line." The doctor cackled. "The crew's pissed at you all, understand. You're a foreign body. You'll have spiritual leukocytes all over you before you know it."

"That a threat?" Elward paused in his task of installing security lines through the stiff fabric of their shelter.

"Call it a diagnosis," Fulani said.

Soph gestured for Elward to be silent. "And you, Doctor? You have a position?"

"Me? Tell you the truth, I thought we were better off without Tiber. So I'm not thanking you for bringing him back to give us transcendent purpose." She put a finger alongside her nose. "Don't tell. My approval rating's in the toilet as it is." Her face was blotchy with generations of fungal skin rejuves. Soph wondered how old she actually was.

"Where *is* Tiber?" Ambryn asked.

She hung against a seeping mass covered with transparent tubes and filtration capsules. It was the outer wall of an Ulanyi placenta, used by the crew to distill psychoactive drugs. It smelled like a burning compost heap, but Ambryn had insisted on this positioning for their shelter so that she could study it.

"Getting ready for the big celebratory riot so that we can try to forget how much we all hate each other. Meanwhile, everyone's probably giving him lists of other crewbies' personal transgressions to mull over. We've been up here in orbit for months." Dr. Fulani looked thoughtful. "I should get mine in, now you mention it. That damn Archon, for example. That little pouter pigeon really gets on my nerves."

"Could you look at Ripi first?" Soph said.

"Ah, don't get your catheters knotted." Fulani peeled back Ripi's concealing robes. He was now conscious again and stared at her with close-set black eyes. He was, Ambryn thought, terrified. And why shouldn't he be? She had hauled him aboard the ship of someone who had proved to be an enemy. Ripi had lost whatever control of his destiny he might once have had.

"Talk to me," Fulani said. "You know what's normal, what's not. Pain? You feel pain? Sharp or dull? Abnormal constriction?"

"I had a mild fall," Ripi said. "The damage is relatively minor."

"Let's see if we can confirm that hypothesis, shall we? It's amazing how well damage can hide itself. Maybe your body is smarter than ours, but we should be sure." In her medical persona, Fulani was utterly serious, her eyes wide and probing.

Slowly, considering each answer before he spoke, Ripi responded.

"You know what amazes me most?" Elward lay on his back at the narrow bottom of their shelter. Covered hammocks hung overhead on taut lines. Elward had spent a while stringing them up.

The *Argent* was under acceleration. It was good to feel a little weight. He'd never experienced null-g before, but he'd already had enough. It made him feel like a ghost. But now they were heading to Mercury. He didn't know what to make of that at all. How had he ever let everything get out of hand this way?

"What amazes you, Elward?" Soph looked over the braces that spider-legged doc had put on Ripi and finally nodded approval. The little alien barely moved. Elward wondered if Ripi was sick.

"That I'm still alive."

Ambryn turned from her examination of the placenta and laughed. Now that he was getting used to her, he realized that she often sounded slightly hysterical. Of course, he'd never known her when she didn't have a good reason to be hysterical. "Me too. I thought that dust shield would burn up for sure."

"Me, I'm surprised I made it through that duel with the copter."

"All right, all right." Soph dropped lightly down next to him. "When the Vronnan spacecraft came down into the silo, I thought that was it."

"Huh," Elward said in a bemused tone. "That scared you?"

For an instant, Soph stared at him, then grinned and slapped him lightly on the arm. He was startled by how good that made him feel. For a minute, anyway.

"Soph," Ambryn said, deliberately casual. "What arrangements have you made on Mercury?"

"Ah?" Soph seemed annoyed by the question. "What do you mean?"

Ambryn pushed her head closer against the placenta and made a great show of intent scrutiny. "You need to contract for a vessel at Caloris to get off the *Argent*. I think I have a way you can do that. There's a group of construction monkeys under the Gun, doing work for that crazy human colony that's dug into the crust. They'll probably be willing to lease or sell a booster and an environmental capsule."

Soph was tired of thinking things up, Elward could see that. Still, she wasn't sure she wanted Ambryn's help. That woman was too clingy. Soph had probably been looking forward to getting away from it.

"You know these people?" Soph asked reluctantly.

"I did a skrying for a few of them, years ago, on my way to Venus." Ambryn was enthusiastic. "It would be interesting to see what happened to them, anyway."

"What about that embryo thing?" Elward said. "Isn't that what you were hot to get to this whole time?"

"It's . . ." Ambryn put her hand against the placental surface. "There was an embryo in here once. I think. But it's been what we call 'psychically dissolved.' It's a disorganized mass of needs and . . . services."

"Services?" Soph said.

"It ducts emotion, for one thing. The crew uses it for their pep rallies. Syncs up whatever it is they use for brains."

"So was coming here futile?" Elward said. "Meaningless?"

"No," Ambryn said quickly. "Oh, no. There's a lot to be learned from it. It needs . . . it has strange needs. Someone else's, maybe, I can't quite tell. It's . . ." Her voice grew quieter. "It's not what I wanted, but it's something. It's a rare opportunity to get in touch with even this much of a mind."

"So why the hell is the first thing you want to do is leave and supervise some stupid ship lease?" Refusal to admit your own motivations had always irritated Elward. He didn't understand how people could do that.

"I want to help," Ambryn said. "That's all. You and Soph are heading off for Luna with Ripi and—"

"Whoa." Elward sat up. "Who said I was going to Luna?"

"I—" Soph was uncomfortable. "I thought that you would—"

"Would what? Do whatever you told me?"

"You prefer to stay aboard the *Argent*?" Soph tried to hide her disappointment, but he could see it. So maybe she was just pretending to hide it.

"I don't know. But I don't need to go with you. I don't *need* to do anything. So don't assume it. Look, I didn't ask to get hauled along on this. I was all fine, just doing my job, happy in Golgot."

"Hey!" Ambryn waded in. "If you hadn't decided to get

brave and whack that E&J copter with your dick, you'd be safe and rich in Golgot, where you say you want to be."

"Screw you, muff mouth. I don't need your—"

"Stop it, both of you!" Soph looked at them with something like fear. "You have no idea how dangerous this is. We're just a tiny redoubt aboard this ship. We have to stick together."

She pulled herself up against Ripi, as if to protect him. Her prize. The thing she'd come after. And she'd gotten it. What more could she want?

"I don't know that it's so important," Elward said.

Thumping music pounded through the shelter. Voices howled outside. It sounded like the entire crew of the *Argent*, trying to sing. Soph, Elward, and Ambryn pulled together. They were poorly armed. It would be impossible to stand against the crew if they chose to attack.

"Soph! Elward! Ambryn!" It was Tiber's voice, sounding strong above the music. "Please come out and join the party. We want to thank you!"

If you took a packed mass of soap bubbles of varying sizes, punched out the faces, and turned the lines of intersection into a fibrous black composite, you would have had the framework that filled the interior of the *Argent*. Functional spaces and brightly colored privacy shelters clung to the framework like bodily organs. Their own makeshift shelter, Ambryn noted, was no different, though somewhat lumpier.

The entire crew, some twenty people, had climbed out and hung themselves from the framework from straps on their clothing. Tasklights crawled along the struts. Each crew member seemed to have a specific one dedicated to him. They glowed like angels, though Ambryn could smell the stink of unwashed bodies above the resin smoke of their pipes. God, they smoked placental secretions to get high. It was an unspeakably primitive thing to do with those biological membranes. Still, she felt the rush up into her skull. She could feel the emotional ducting of what was left of the embryo.

Tiber stood above them, casting huge shadows into the bow high overhead. He wore a suit of many layers of thick folded silk, tight at the wrists and ankles. Something about its tentative lines looked like he'd copied it from an unconfident memory. Still, the dark green fabric had an effect. It suited him and made the swollen bones of his face look more alien. Ambryn felt like questioning her assumption that he was, in fact, a human being.

"Mercury!" he cried. The crew cheered, as if it was their heart's desire. He'd already prepped them. The pounding music made Ambryn's head hurt. She noted that more than one crew member wore yellow earplugs.

The rusty-ball-bearing image of Mercury floated up through the ship's center.

"I saw the truth on Venus!" Tiber worked the crowd like a preacher. "We will see more truth on Mercury!" They danced to the music, chanted responses to his phrases. He told of his travails on Venus, suitably edited. They wailed as he was imprisoned below the surface. They cheered as he saw the sun, then groaned as Enforcement & Joy threatened. "I was saved!" Wild cheers. "I was saved by Elward Bakst. By Ambryn Chretien. And by Sophonisba Trost!"

Despite their covert hostility, they cheered the three interlopers who had saved their idol. Ambryn saw Elward skulking at the edges of the crowd, no longer willing to admit to association with her and Soph but uncertain of where else to go. Soph stood up and bowed graciously, so Ambryn followed suit. She didn't like Soph's attitude toward Tiber. Soph seemed to respect him too much, even like him. First it had been Elward. Soph had poor taste in young men, it seemed.

Then Tiber launched into an account of Ripi's escape, with even greater gaps and fictions covering his complicity in Sukh's assault. "Engineer," he said. "Show us."

A wide-shouldered woman with a heavy jaw, her big fingers covered with metal rings of a dozen colors, manipulated an image display. Mercury disappeared, and a view of Venus from low orbit replaced it. The dust clouds melded perfectly with the thick smoke from the pipes.

Ambryn recognized central Ishtar and the mass of the Maxwells. A spacecraft rose up, moving much too quickly through the thick lower atmosphere, leaving a hot stream behind it, like a meteor in reverse. Sukh's ship, escaping from Ripi's covert.

Atmospheric detonations shook the craft. E&J had gone completely crazy, using such massive weapons this close to population centers. One came close to hitting the Vronnan vessel.

The Engineer called up spectral information, which indicated the amount of surface damage Sukh's ship had suffered, and then fell into a trance over it.

"Please," Tiber said as energy leaked from the revival meeting. "Engineer. It is not necessary—" Reluctantly, the Engineer turned off the spectral displays. She turned and smiled shyly at Ambryn, who, startled, smiled back.

"Our attackers did not escape unscathed. They are so seriously damaged that they will not be able to follow us to Mercury. Mercury, where we will take our first steps toward destiny!"

The crew cheered again. Ambryn felt weakness in her joints. Those missiles . . . if Sukh hadn't taken the heat first, *Len-3* would never have made it. But it did look as though Sukh had taken a beating. She wouldn't be much of a threat for a while.

Tiber still loved Sukh. Ambryn could see that. But he made the copious tears part of the show. He flicked them off the ends of his fingers into the audience. The crew writhed passionately together, even Fulani, who grunted in protest.

"My knees, dammit," she said. "My knees."

The music grew even louder and the party began.

Three half-naked crew members covered with shiny insulation bounced up and down between two resilient membranes, hands on each other's bald heads. Bioluminescent blue tattoos on their shoulders gleamed through their grease covering as through a layer of ice.

"Undines," the Archon said. She had dreadlocked hair and wore an impact uniform covered with weapons points. "Undina's a prison asteroid run by the inmates. They lease each other out for income. Those three broke indenture. We're all exiles here. See him?"

Elward looked at a sad-looking dwarfish man with odd cheek extensions. "Yeah."

"The Sharif. He's a refugee Turtle-server from Ganymede. He lived his life in the bark of one of those yggrasils the Turtles grow from the core out to the ice rafts on the surface. The good luck sighting of an ice-swimming Turtle dignitary at his coming-of-age party is his only mental landmark. It's all he talks about. It gives his soul a kind of purity, I suppose, but it's really boring."

"And you?" Elward found her disquietingly exciting.

She smiled, revealing teeth filed to points. Her face was heavily tattooed with swirls and jagged lines. "Egeria. Another asteroid—if you don't know. We're bounty hunters. I was a good one, but I overran my expense account, became a target instead of a hunter."

"So you joined Tiber's merry band."

She winced. "Sometimes survival has a high price. Look, there's Fulani. She thinks she runs this place."

Fulani danced with a fat man with bandoliers of hypodermics criss-crossed on his chest. His title was Sirdar, and he was the one who distilled stuff from the placentas for these hopping ship conferences. Ambryn had already had a fight with him over what that had done to the placentas. Fulani's long arms and legs flopped in time to the music, but her eyes kept up a cold scan of everything going on around.

"You don't like her?" Elward said.

"None of us like each other. That's not the point."

"I have a question for you," Elward said. "Do you protect Tiber? I mean, personally?"

"Am I his bodyguard?" The Archon seemed to find the idea amusing. "His flesh is his own business."

"Good, good. You know, I . . . I hit him."

Her eyes flashed. "Hit Tiber?"

"Yes. I punched him in the face. More than once, actually. Back on Venus."

"What did you do?" She was excited. He could see that. He'd counted on it. "Tell me. Please be precise."

He leaned toward her. The music was making his head hurt. He told her what he had done, each punch like the movement of a symphony.

"Now that's a bond between us," she said. "Once I did pretty much the same thing to him. Worse, actually. Much worse."

"And then he made you his security chief?"

"Who better? That's a bond too. I told you, liking's not the point." She put her hands on his chest. Her huge breasts were lower here in the gravity, but he didn't mind that, not at all. "There are bonds of all kinds, Elward. Maybe you should think about making a few with us."

Why did that seem to make more sense than keeping with Soph? "Sounds great," he said.

She tugged him by the hand. Together, their egos vanishing like dust thrown into a whirlwind, they dropped together into the howling crew of the *Argent*.

"The last time I tried this, I took out the ventilation in the aft port quarter." Fulani slipped a scalpel under a power cable looped onto a support strut. Shredded repair tape dangled from previous patches to the cable. "I don't got a lot of engineering, tell the truth. I go on medical instinct." The ultrasonic blade sliced through the sheathing. The lights stayed on, but the oppressive thumping music went dead. "Ah. I'm smarter than I thought. I always surprise myself." She popped out her earplugs. "That music's a high price to pay for crew solidarity, you ask me. Someone always seals the connections under high-impact plastic so that the damn thing can't be turned off."

Soph saw a loose hand sticking out from under a pile of unlaundered ship's coveralls. She tugged, and the Turtle-worshipping Sharif popped out. Close up, Soph could see the scales he'd inserted in his skin. The loose bundles must have fallen over on him during the mad bouncing dance the crew had indulged themselves in for at least two hours.

Fulani peeled back his eyelid and examined his pupil with a pinlight. "Ah, of course, the usual. He keeps running this memory regression thing whenever he parties. Like nothing good will ever happen to him again. I know just how he feels." She pushed on his chest to expel air, then popped a cartridge under his nose.

He gasped and awoke. His eyes focused on Soph. "I saw

the Preceptor as he swam the cold ice sea, the day of my coming of age. He was covered with lights! It was an honor, understand. The luck of my life was established then."

"Yeah, yeah, yeah," Fulani said. "Time for bed, Sharif. Party's over."

The Sharif grabbed Soph's hand. "Trust everyone, believe no one. All the *Argent* see the truth but lie. I will return to Ganymede. The Turtles will take me back."

"I'm sure they will," Soph said.

Ganymedean humans had moved into the huge treelike yggrasils the Turtles had grown in Ganymede's seas. As far as anyone knew, the Turtles regarded the interloping humans as pests but had not, so far, tried to exterminate them.

Whimpering over lost glories, the Sharif crawled to the purple lozenge of his personal quarters. The rest of the crew lay like soldiers killed in battle. Fulani walked among them, aspirating vomit, stabilizing heart rates, detoxing blood, making sure no one died from an excess of celebration. As each crew member had fallen unconscious, his tasklight had gone out. The interior of the *Argent* was now almost completely dark.

"Now where's that dear captain of ours?" Fulani said. "You don't suppose he made it back to his coffin under his own power, do you?"

"I think I saw him heading that way," Soph said. She hoped Fulani would forgive her the lie.

One set of lights remained, illuminating Ambryn and the Engineer as they sat down by the drive pods that the Engineer maintained. The Engineer was slowly and shyly telling Ambryn her theory about the placentas, about how they were meant to house a deepdrive. Soph sensed that the wide-faced, slow-moving woman would have liked to have become a deepdrive herself. Ambryn was noncommittal about the possibility. Soph admired her graciousness. The Engineer had fallen hard, and Ambryn dealt delicately with her.

Tiber lay snoring underneath the shelter Elward had put up, against the placenta itself. The rest of the crew members had specialized in their drugs, while he had taken them all. What had happened to him must have been hard, Soph thought, for him to seek such oblivion.

No one had ever known what happened to the *Prismatic Bezel.* The Martians had launched the sublight colonization vessel toward a Probe-modified world thirty years before. A light-year or so out, it had vanished. Its fate was one of the great mysteries. If what Tiber had told Elward was true, before her lay the solution.

Tiber opened his eyes. "Sukh raised me," he said. He reached up an arm and Soph pulled him up until he was sitting. "Not well. She didn't understand human beings. But as well as she could. She rescued me from what happened to the *Prismatic Bezel.* My family was dead, all that I had known was gone, I was crying, and a huge Vronnan female loomed out of the smoke and screams and took me away."

"Where?" Soph said. "Where did she take you?"

Tiber shook his head in bewilderment. "I don't know. I never saw the outside of it. Only the inside."

"But surely you—"

"It was not a real world, that place where she took me. Sukh knew something of human beings. So she raised me, as well as she could, with simulation devices programmed with human responses. I was old enough to know that these were not real, that the figures that held my hand, that threw me into the air, that warmed and comforted me when I hurt myself were nothing but generated images. But I knew that behind them was a reality, something that was caring for me."

Tears flowed from his eyes, and Soph held him. It wasn't until she did it that she realized she had wanted to do it all along. He was a powerful man—and afraid. She thought she could protect him.

"It wasn't until Venus that I realized the true reason Sukh kept me alive. She had raised someone who could slip through the humans of the Solar System and find her father, Ripi-Arana-Hoc, for her. If I had not been useful for that I would not have lived."

2

Ambryn watched the dark side of Mercury swell ahead, visible only as an absence of stars on the greater blackness of the universe. The vacuum shuttle she piloted was, if anything, in worse shape than the rest of the *Argent*'s equipment. It would never have made it down to the surface of a planet with an atmosphere. With the Engineer's help, she had done her best to make it spaceworthy. As it was, she hoped she would be coming back from the surface in something more functional.

"You all right there, Captain?" Fulani examined Tiber's physiological readout.

"I'm fine." Ambryn was pleased to hear impatience, even irritation, in Tiber's voice. These unmelodramatic emotions made him easier to take.

"Just doing my job." Fulani had added herself to the shuttle roster before the descent to Mercury. She hung closely around Tiber ever since rescuing him from Soph, in the aftermath of the big party a few weeks before. She'd immediately sedated him and kept Soph from learning anything more. Ambryn could tell how frustrated Soph was but was unable to tell how much was intellectual and how much was sexual. Usually she knew right off, but Soph was hard to read.

Fulani wore the red quilted robe she used to warm up before operating. She reached into it, revealing the sculpture of her mesh-reinforced legs. Their shape was exquisite, and patches of smooth, vat-grown skin glowed under the mesh. Ambryn saw the cool run of a vein on the doctor's inner thigh and felt an inconvenient surge of lust.

The Engineer had not satisfied that. At the end, just before going to sleep against one of her drive pods, the Engineer had hugged her, pulling Ambryn close to her hard chest, and left the imprint of her many rings in the back of her head. Ambryn supposed that it was the most physical contact the woman had gotten in years.

Fulani's exaggerated formal hips were revealed to be equipment racks carrying med support gear and personal items. "Tea?" Steam rose from the thermos.

Ambryn accepted a titanium cup that soon became too hot to hold. Fulani, she saw now, wore black ridged insulators over her delicate surgeon's finger pads.

She and Fulani sat close on narrow seats recycled from an excavation dozer, now-useless blade and tread armrest controls dangling loose wires. Ambryn stuffed her hot cup into a hole where an indicator had been ripped from the padding and shook her fingers. Fulani gave no sign of noticing.

The great circle of Caloris expanded below them. The basin's thirteen-hundred-kilometer diameter subtended one quarter of the entire planet. The asteroid impact had shifted Mercury's entire crust, causing vulcanism that left the basin smooth, a perfect plain for the construction of the Gun.

A curving line of shallow impact craters across the basin marked where the encapsulated Gunner infants had originally hit and dug themselves into the dust. The pattern of day/night, heat/cold, one-hundred-seventy-six Earth days in duration, had stimulated maturation. A century later, mature Gunners, enclosed in vacuum-proof integuments, had crawled out onto the surface of their new world and immediately gotten to work on their grand project.

No mature adults had accompanied the unconscious infants. So they either had their information genetically encoded or had, as part of the complex maturation shells, a teaching system that raised each of them to functional adulthood.

It had been theorized that they were actually no more intelligent than Terran termites and that the Gun was an instinctive reproductive device of some sort, one that had not yet reached maturity and fired the isotope barges as some grandiose alien equivalent of nocturnal emission.

Tiber wanted to ask the Gunners a question. As Ambryn had explained to him, the Gunners had desperate needs. They had lost the vessel in which their pupae had arrived in the Solar System. Its whereabouts were, apparently, of great significance, and they were so desperate that they regularly paid well for obviously false coordinates.

They had needs, and so did Tiber. Ambryn was willing to help him, in the interests of finding out more.

Under her direction, the shuttle slowed, dragged its tail, tilted back, and settled onto its support legs. From here, the straight-trussed trough of the Gun was so huge it was incomprehensible, blocking out half the sky, as if the façade of the universe had been peeled away to reveal its crude substructure. It would fall. Now that she was in its shadow, Ambryn was sure that it would fall.

Ambryn's spacesuit had been made for someone taller than she was, and it kept trying to stretch her out to fit, with an insistent tension at the wrists and ankles. And whoever had used it last, probably decades before, hadn't cleaned it out. It stank.

They made their way into the structures beneath the Gun. Ambryn could see some of the access shafts that led to the human city more than a kilometer below the surface, where it huddled against the onslaught of solar particles. That city was of no interest to Tiber, Ambryn, and Fulani, save as it affected their plans to contact the Gunners. To prevent interference, Tiber had been forced to pay the colony leaders a substantial fee. This fee, which the Gunners had nothing to do with, was the key to the colony's continued survival. The Gunners had become their sole natural resource. While no longer interested in answering any questions about the Gunners themselves, the humans managed to make a good living from those in the Solar System who were still curious.

"Let's curl up back here," Fulani said. "If we're careful, we can probably survive for . . . oh, hours at least." She glared at Tiber through the flowing globe of her helmet.

"No need to be alarmist." Tiber strode over to the diamond-crystal window and peered out at the structures that made up the base of the Gun. His spacesuit had been recut from some other model, and the welds were plainly visible.

"Alarmist! Particle flux is so intense I'm surprised the momentum transfer doesn't slide us across the floor. I'll need mast-cell repair when we get back up to the *Argent*. Replacement, maybe."

"I thought this place was safe," Ambryn said.

"As safe as it gets, I suppose." Fulani gloomily contemplated the radiation counter on her wrist.

They had found shelter in the Gun's information processing center. Cosmic ray damage could throw off important calculations, even with robust error-correcting algorithms, so the Gunners had been forced to shield their computers heavily. A dense sheet of crushed nuclei even screened neutron flux. Despite years of research, no one had been able to figure out that technology either.

Ambryn stood next to Tiber and looked out at the Gunners. Three of them hunched along in the viciously radioactive work area. Their bodies were covered with complex laceworks of tissue that distended and shrank, causing constant ripples of motion.

The truck-sized Gunners, with their eight pairs of stubby legs, looked like something evolved to live under incredibly heavy gravity. They swam through the low gravity of Mercury as if underwater, the manipulator palps at the base of each leg waving gaily as they floated down to take another complicated step.

Two transparent blisters, one to either side of the otherwise minuscule head, seemed to contain sensory apparatus, perhaps even the radiation sensing organs that some had hypothesized. Maybe the complex organs just visible inside the blisters were really symbionts that had adapted to life as part of a Gunner's body. The Gunners did seem to have smaller organs, like vestigial eyes and nostrils, on the tiny head between the blisters. And whatever was inside kept moving constantly as the Gunner went placidly about its business.

''Show them what we have, Ambryn,'' Tiber said. ''And we will talk.''

The three Gunners had stopped just short of the shielding, as if the invisible particles whizzing through their bodies were in some way essential to them.

Tiber walked out to the edge of protection and stood in front of the gigantic multilegged creatures like a mahout seeking just the right mount.

Ambryn fumbled with her display gear and, as they had previously arranged, the image of a spacecraft came slowly into existence, a lumpy container being tugged along by a ramscoop that sucked up interstellar hydrogen and compressed it to a fusion flame. The stars behind it were distorted but not dramatically so. It couldn't have been moving at more than half light speed. She'd bought it as part of a collection of random images from around the near Galaxy and used the image in a few skryings, but it had taken Tiber to tell her what, exactly, it was an image of.

"You know," Ambryn said, "I've heard it hypothesized that the Gunner barge-drive is the ancestor to all deep-drives."

"You can hear almost anything, you listen long enough," Fulani said.

"The Gunners have been around a long time. Millions of years maybe. Some have seen anomalous Gunner flares in the Large Magellanic Cloud, hundreds of thousands of light-years away."

"What the hell is he playing at?" Fulani asked. "That's nothing faster than light. That brassiere thing there's a damn sublight ramscoop. And, yeah, you can find ramscoops hundreds of thousands of years old floating around, you look in the right place. The races that built them are extinct, though. Not Gunners. Just sad-sack colonists that never made it anywhere."

The thing the ramscoop pulled, heavy and lumpy, at least a kilometer long, contained the swelling Gunner pupae. And those eight pairs of projections from its back that might have been comm antennae or weapons. But Ambryn knew what she was seeing. It was a gigantic Gunner body, the pupae living inside it. The heavy projections, cracked by the cold of interstellar space and eroded by centuries of dust and micrometeoroid impact, were what had once been the legs.

As she watched, delivery capsules emerged from the body, apparently pushed by muscles within. They jerked and emerged only slowly, as if reluctant to brave the light of the distant sun, which, Ambryn thought by the apparent spectrum, was probably Sol.

This last segment was not part of the original image sequence. Tiber had added it from some private image store of his own. Ambryn wondered how much of it was true—and how much purely his imagination. She hoped the image addition wouldn't start bleeding through and editing the previous strip, making it completely invalid. Truth was hard enough to find.

"They arrive as pupae," Ambryn said. "There's essentially a different subspecies of Gunner on each world, depending on the photoperiod. I don't know if a day as short as Earth's would be possible for them. But the isotope barges *do* move faster than light. Maybe someone else, with different ambitions, evolved deepdrives from that segment. I don't know how much evolution was necessary. The flare barge version they have here might be the deepdrive equivalent of . . . an *Australopithecus*, or something.''

Tiber pointed up, sketched lines against the image backdrop of stars. The Gunners around him paid no visible attention. Ambryn felt a vibration through the soles of her feet. Something was happening with the Gun.

The Gunners rotated on their countless legs, delicately avoiding Tiber, and walked off. Their fringes erected and fell and then glared in the Mercurian sun as the dust flowed around their feet like thick oil.

''They will speak to me further,'' Tiber said, ''when they have the information I need. No need for you two to wait here. Ambryn, I think, has a ship to purchase. You can go with her, Doctor, and I will meet you both back at the *Argent* when you rendezvous.''

''No, sir,'' Fulani said. ''You know my job. You can do whatever you want, but I'm coming with you.''

Tiber's face darkened. Ambryn thought he looked quite frightening. ''Doctor. There is no need—''

''There is every need.'' Fulani was unimpressed by her commander's anger. ''We lost you once. We don't want to lose you again. The entire crew is agreed, and I'm their representative. It's simple prudence.''

They loved him so much that they weren't ever going to let him go, Ambryn saw. No matter what Tiber himself wanted, he was going to have to take the *Argent* crew along with him.

''Don't you care what I'm after?'' Tiber asked as he turned away, accepting Fulani's supervision without acknowledging it.

''Tell me. I'm sure it's fascinating.'' For someone compelled by charisma, Fulani was remarkably resentful, Ambryn thought.

''They lost their seed vessel. Their mother. They were conceived inside it and were finally expelled from it as it neared the Sun. After that, it was supposed to have gone curving into the Sun's atmosphere, thus sending up a signal prominence with specific spectral characteristics. That way all other Gunners in the Galaxy would know that a new solar system had been settled by their species."

"So what?"

"So they need someone to find it. It is both blasphemy and tragedy that it did not reach its determined end. Their mother's soul will not achieve her final rest until the prominence emerges from the Sun. That prominence is a signal to God."

"And you have information as to the whereabouts of Mom's body," Fulani said.

"I think that, together, the Gunners and I can work it out."

Following Tiber was mad. Ambryn could see that and could see that Fulani knew it. But what other choice did the *Argent* crew have? They had gotten themselves good and stuck.

"And what do you intend on asking them?" Fulani said.

Tiber looked startled at the question, though it was a reasonable one. He really had never learned to conceal his emotions, Ambryn thought.

"The . . . many things are lost. We . . . I seek a place of safety for the *Argent*. The Gunners know all the hiding places. We can be concealed."

Sukh, Ambryn thought. He was going to look for Sukh and wondered if the Gunners knew where she was. He was a man obsessed.

"Great," Fulani said, staring at her captain. "Just great."

3

After identifying himself to the scanner that protected the shelter, Elward pushed his way into Soph's private space. A swirl of movement in the floating trash marked an air current from holes Soph had punched into a ventilation duct. Crew emotions of suspicion and anger, which could not be expressed openly against Tiber himself, had coalesced around Soph, whom they saw as a dangerous interloper, a separate power center. In Tiber's absence, hostility had grown to the point that the Tribune and the Ensign had cut her power, but

Soph had run a tap line to a conduit in the hull itself, one they couldn't switch off without affecting ship function.

"Elward," Soph said. "How goes the *Argent*?"

The cheeriness of the question made him uncomfortable. In Tiber's absence, the *Argent* seemed like the place he had always been looking for. No one seemed to be in charge, and he could make things happen. He had plans for this place. But Tiber would be back. What then? The Archon might be happy that Elward had punched him in the face, but he wasn't sure Tiber was.

"Good, I see." Soph said with a smile.

"God, Soph, I'm sorry."

"For what?"

"We came up here together, after all. You still have things to do, places to go."

"So I'll do them and go to them. You've lost your home. Someday you have to find another."

"I don't know that Golgot was ever home. It was just the place that I lived."

Her acceptance of his separation from her was more painful than anger would have been. Was that deliberate? Every time he felt something like love for her, he felt suspicious. She seemed too smart to ever have anyone love her by accident.

Soph floated cross-legged amid a mass of coiled corrugated air tubes, a urine distiller, and even three ancient blue-green solar panels he had helped her drag in before the siege closed down.

She smiled at him and reached out a short-fingered hand. She looked worn, older than usual, with lines around her brilliant dark eyes. He took her hand.

"Oh, Elward, what a mess." With a mother's intent tenderness, she pulled at the fragments and dust that covered his clothes and hair. The air-filtration system in this area had long been knocked out, and all the detritus natural to a null-g environment had been collecting ever since.

"I've thought about punching a hole out through the hull here," Soph said. "I'll suck the dust out, then reseal it. Let the crew send me another of their damn petitions. I can't stand the mess."

"Don't be crazy, Soph. You'd—" Then he saw the vacuum-seal fabric that covered her hammock, the air-recirculation lines running to pumps equipped with CO_2 traps, the squat three-nozzled shape of a reaction drive, the black lozenges of magnetic cosmic ray blockers adding their fibers to the tangle. "God, you could live in vacuum."

She nodded. "If I have to."

"But—" Solar panels, urine distillers, food stores. "You're not going to blow the entire side of the ship out and escape!"

"Not in my immediate plans. But one should be ready. The crew seems rather sullen, don't you think?"

"What'll you do then? Float around Mercury until you mummify?"

"Don't be upset with me, Elward. I'm just trying to take possible circumstances into account. Is Tiber still down visiting the Gunner oracle?"

"Is that what he's doing? I don't really get it. You know, Soph, he was gone a long time back on Venus."

"He was."

"Well, the crew got used to it. I can feel it, just being here. They kept the ship working, made contingency plans. Particularly Dr. Fulani." He looked around, but if someone had inserted an eavesdropping device, there was no way he'd be able to see it. "And you and I know that he didn't even *want* to come back up. I think they sense that. Once he gets whatever information he needs from those things down on Mercury, what will he want to do next?" He shook his head. "They love him, they need him, but maybe they just need to have him around. Not to make decisions for them anymore but just to bring luck."

"What will they do then? What are their plans? You know, Elward, those pep rallies have been keeping me awake. Can't you guys make decisions without all that chanting?"

"I don't know, it feels kind of good, moving together," Elward said. He took a breath. "You know, Soph, you can join up, gain some control over the situation. I don't know what will happen when Tiber comes back, what he'll say, what we'll do. It may help your mission if you join on. The crew will be glad to have you, I can say."

"Sure." Soph brushed away floating debris. "They've been very welcoming."

"They don't know what they're doing. They're running scared. To be frank, Soph, *I* could use you. You have no idea how crazy some of these people are."

"No thanks. I'm finding too much out. Look at this. He produced it with his chest glands."

A structure with the papery texture of a wasp nest hung behind the hammocks. Stringy lengths of foam connected to Elward's taut lines.

"He's emotionally and physiologically off-balance," Soph said. "He's been spilling information. I know his story now, how he lived, how he came to Venus. All the complex structure of the Vronnan clanship."

"Incredible." Ripi moved inside the nest like a shifting grub. Elward patted the hard surface and, when Soph's head was turned, slid a tool within. He wondered if Ripi would figure out how to use it. "Soph. I don't know if you can leave with him."

Her eyes were sharp. He didn't like her looking at him that way. "What do you mean?"

"I mean just that. You've got Ambryn down on Mercury trying to rustle you up some transportation. That's fine, well within your rights. But Ripi . . . we're likely to need him. The *Argent*, I mean. Ripi is the only valuable resource we have, now. Now that he's free of Venus, everyone will be interested in him. And the *Argent* is a mess. We may even have to deal with Sukh—if no one else bites."

"My agreement with Tiber includes my control over Ripi."

"Tiber's decisions are not entirely . . . final. Not as far as the crew of the *Argent* is concerned. He is sometimes unreliable. His generosity outstrips his resources. So they tell me."

"Elward." She put her hands on his shoulders. It was only at times like this that he realized how tiny she really was. He felt that he could grab her and hold her like a child. "Try to take Ripi and you have a fight on your hands. Do you understand that?''

He heard the rustle of her luggage overhead. It wasn't even worth checking out what weapons was now focused on him. ''Look, it wasn't just you that took him. It was me and Ambryn too. You don't own him. He's not your slave.''

''He's not staying aboard the *Argent*, Elward.''

Ripi stirred in his nest. Soph grabbed a squeeze bottle filled with dark, rust-red liquid and popped it into a heater meant for thawing oxygen cylinders. She'd stepped the current down with Elward's help, in happier times, just a few weeks before.

''A formula Dr. Fulani and I came up with,'' she said. ''It seems to be keeping him alive.''

He wanted to tell her he was sorry. He didn't mean to find joy in the hot crew assemblies, the idea of unity and belonging. But he did. Soph's need to see what lay beneath the surface of things seemed cold by comparison.

''It's not personal,'' he said.

''You take care of yourself, Elward. But Ripi leaves with me.''

As he left, Soph floated over to the nest with the bottle in her hand. Ripi had communicated his desire to stay aboard the *Argent*. He had his own plans. Elward didn't know what they were. He hoped Ripi had the sense to conceal the tool that would let him penetrate the shelter's security layers from inside.

4

''Did you ever find it?'' The four-handed construction monkey, Martyshka, hung over Ambryn's head in a harness. She had a cute little monkey face with big eyes and big teeth.

''Find what?'' Ambryn asked.

''The truth.''

Ambryn remembered her own boasting aboard the *Imhotep*, the Venus-bound construction monkey ship, years ago. Had she really been heading to Venus to learn the truth? ''No.''

''Of course not.'' Martyshka slapped the harness with a

decorated pig trotter of a foot and raised herself higher, as if for dominance. "You don't find the truth. You build it."

The waffle-vaulted tunnel, one of the maze the construction monkeys had dug out underneath the Gun, was about five meters high in the center and stuffed with gear and supplies. A ventilator made a dangerous-sounding flapping noise.

"I need a long-range shuttle," Ambryn said. "Three-to-four-person. I sent you the specs."

"We don't have one," Martyshka said.

The air failed. Ambryn fumbled for her air mask. The crew of the *Imhotep* was famous for ad hoc design . . . she gasped a breath. Defeat had stolen the air. "But you told me—"

"Don't fret, Ambryn. We can build one. We need one anyway, to get ourselves off this gravity ball. Do you want to pilot us up? You're better at tolerating high g's than we are."

"Sure," Ambryn said. "I think we can make a deal."

Martyshka's modified feet dangled just above Ambryn's head. In infancy—or even before birth—they had been sliced up between the phalanges and actuators stuck in between the now-long toes to provide motion muscles. In repose, the obscenely long toes curved weakly together and looked gross and useless. Realizing Ambryn's attention, Martyshka spread her toes wide, like the ribs of an umbrella. Her modified hip joint let her bring her leg up high enough that the foot could hold something while the hand worked on it.

As she remembered, she and Martyshka had flirted a little on that long-ago trip, but nothing had come of it. Still, you could do a lot with that foot.

"Build one? Out of what?" Ambryn asked.

"Look around you. We have everything you need. Most of it's in use now, often for a non-design purpose, but we're about to finish our job and leave. Perhaps you would like that thruster there." She pointed with her foot. "It can manage nearly two g's. We will need it to get off the surface, but after that, we can sell it to you. It will be a long time before we need that gravity-escape capability again—if I have anything to say about it. And if we need it, we can redevelop it."

The thruster was old, and the *Imhotep* construction monkeys had heavily rebuilt it. Meant for purely vacuum use, its feed tubes and control lines were completely exposed. Ambryn peered more closely and saw argument made metal.

Each module, circuit, and valve had, shining next to it, one or more pearly dots. Touch one, and it expanded into a holographic notice from whoever had last performed maintenance on the part, which was standard procedure for complex systems.

But these notices denounced and argued with each other. Some had even, through metalevel conflict, tried to edit the contents of other maintenance messages, leading to lines of garbled text.

Generations of modifications sprawled archaeologically, full of second thoughts, revisions, even parallel structures duplicating function. Normally, such design debates would be carried on in an interaction space somewhere. But here they were actual bent tubes and snapped-in circuits.

"Oh, don't worry, it still works," Martyshka said. "Better than ever, in fact."

"This is your entertainment, I take it."

"This job for the colony is a simple one. It's interesting that they want expansion when their world is so contracted, but maybe they've learned something from the Gunners at long last."

Ambryn doubted it. The *Imhotep* had drastically underbid the job to give this human colony, which survived only by shakedowns of curious visitors to the Gun, something it had no need of. The construction monkeys were after something else, something they were excavating from these endless tunnels and chambers.

"And what about the life-support capsule?" Ambryn said.

"We can chop off part of ours." Martyshka's harness slid away down the tunnel. Ambryn followed, kicking her way through construction litter. As they passed various pieces of gear, Martyshka muttered, "We'll need to run the nitroxy lines around the water reservoir . . . foam out the seams . . . change the pores on that osmotic filter and turn it into a waste freeze-drier. . . ."

Ambryn was a little abashed to see the woman again. She had been young and thrilled with ambition, the last time she had talked to Martyshka. Now she was little better than a refugee, with nothing to show for her sojourn on Venus but an added burden of years.

A bulbous body-transport module sat on its own booster at the bottom of an excavated shaft that presumably reached to the surface. Its oxygen and water lines were also perilously exposed. Martyshka's cable swung her up into the open hatch, where her harness clicked onto another cable. Ambryn had to find the maintenance footholds where they were obscured by after-market piping and make her way up without damaging anything that might be responsible for keeping her alive later.

Martyshka looked down at her. "You know, I always wondered what had happened to you."

Ambryn had not thought of Martyshka more than once or twice in the intervening time. Now that seemed like an immense oversight. And an unnecessary distraction.

"I'm afraid we won't have much time to catch up on things," she said and felt the pain as the other woman turned her head away.

5

Soph had heard the rally greeting Tiber and Fulani's return from Mercury. Ambryn had transferred to the construction monkey shuttle and would come up to dock with the *Argent* in a day or so. And that would be it. Soph would take Ripi and head for Luna, where she could name her price. Ambryn would stay to study her placentas, and Elward would stay as a full member of the *Argent* crew. Their personal tensions would fit right into the general hostilities of the *Argent*. She would miss them both.

"Soph." Weapons activated, tracked. That wasn't Ripi's voice. It was Tiber's.

The Vronnan nest shook and fell apart in the null-g. Tiber climbed out of it. His large hands floated up, white in the dark. "I'm sorry, Soph."

"Where the hell is he?"

Ripi was gone. Someone had cut through the security barriers and pulled him out without setting off an alarm. She'd been skunked. She couldn't believe it. Wait. The wall had been penetrated from *inside*. Ripi must have spent long hours working his way through, bit by bit.

"Ripi wants to stay aboard the *Argent*," Tiber said. "There's something important for him here. Not for me. Not any more."

Elward. That bastard. Here she'd just been having tender thoughts about him, and he'd come in here, ostensibly to talk with her, but really to slip Ripi the gear he needed to escape from her. Perhaps others had had the opportunity, but she knew Elward. That last sneaking look as he had left . . .

She hadn't been kidnapping Ripi. Had she? She had just been relying on his having nowhere else in the universe to go.

Ripi was gone. She'd never be able to haul him out of the *Argent*. He'd used her to get off Venus, just as Lightfoot had warned. Then he had dropped her. Soph looked into the dark hole, with the ominous thumping music beyond. She'd lost. Bit by bit, since leaving Luna, she'd lost everything. No, it had started long before that. It had started when Stephan died.

"Ambryn said you would let me go with you," Tiber said.

"What?"

"We talked about it while waiting for the Gunners' answer. I need to escape. I need to leave the *Argent*."

"Where do you want to go?"

"Home," he said. "Home."

"Do you know where that is?"

She did her best to be businesslike, but she was frightened of herself. He was so appealing like this, with all of his compelling drive gone. The frightening thing was that if he was always like this, it would not have been appealing. You need a façade in order to have cracks in it.

"It's what I'm trying to find out," he said. "I want to escape. I want to be free. There was a time I was free. I remember it. I made lunch. There, in that launch silo. All of us together."

"Yes." How long did it take to develop nostalgia for something? "It was very good."

"I was free once. Just like that. Just like that moment. Nothing driving me. No need. Just life. Isn't that the way it's supposed to be?"

It wasn't true of anyone Soph knew. "Yes. That's the way it's supposed to be."

"Please." He was crying now. "It may be my only chance."

She took hold of him, just the way she had the last time, before Fulani had come and taken him away to protect him from himself.

"It's all right, Tiber," she said. "It's all right." He'd hurt himself, he'd come home crying. The universe could seem a terrible mass of painful accidents. But if you had someone to hold you, it could all make sense, after all.

He moved against her, and she felt a surge of heat. Behind the tears, she felt his strength, the power of that huge head. His arms tightened around her until she could barely breathe.

Dammit, she'd thought about it enough, hadn't she? She realized that she had. Lightfoot would have mocked her for not knowing she was thinking about something. And why was she thinking of him now?

Making love in free fall was, in many ways, as erotic as docking two spacecraft. The technical aspects tended to overwhelm the messy arbitrariness of real physical sex. There was no weight, no sense of pressure.

She pulled Tiber into one of the covered hammocks Elward had strung across the space. His breath chuffed. The hammock pushed them together. She tried to calm him by stroking the back of his head, where she felt scars under his thick hair, but he shook as if in a fever.

Animals bred in captivity often lost the ability to mate in the wild. Soph felt that right away as he grappled with her, now too hard, now letting go when he should be holding on.

"Shh," she said. "Calm down."

"Calm? Is it about calm?"

"Shhh."

He did not make her feel like a girl again. Something

about his aggressive clumsiness should have, the revelation of fear and longing, but instead it made her feel infinitely old.

"It's all right," she said. "It's all right."

"Isn't that what women say when it isn't right?" he said.

Trust that to be the one real thing he knew about women.

"Please. It's not important."

"That's the other thing they say."

"Tiber." She put her arms around his wide chest and squeezed hard. "I am a human being. And I will hold you."

"I want to," he said. "I need to. I have always been alone."

Soph wanted to tell him that the bare act of insertion was not what mattered. But that would be a mistake—and a lie besides. It had been a while for her too, and she had felt a clearing surge of lust. But now that surge settled down to a nagging sense of pressure.

"Ambryn said this would happen," he muttered.

Soph froze. "You talked about this?"

"We talked about a lot of things. I can't talk to my crew. They don't want my reality. They have their sex. They combine in all ways. But, though I participate, I'm always separate."

"I'm sure you had an extremely enlightening conversation. Did Ambryn tell you that what I really needed was a good fuck?"

His sigh was full of pain, but now she didn't care. He wasn't the only one who could feel pain, damn it. She turned her head and looked out through the steamed transparent fabric at the darkness of the shelter. She had no idea of how she had come to be here.

Tiber pulled her toward him and she felt the strength of his arms. For the first time, she felt fear. She was alone in a trap with him, this creature with its shaggy mane and its powerful breath. And, in males, what followed frustration and disappointment was most often anger.

But his touch, for the first time, was delicate.

"Soph," he said. "There was no harm in it. I don't feel what I should, so I think instead."

"You didn't think enough."

Before he could hold her back, she unzipped the hammock and floated out of it. The air felt frigid on her bare skin and she felt goose pimples all over her. She wished it was colder so that it could quick-freeze her right down to the marrow. He floated past her, a shadow springing across her sight, to the acrid swell of the placenta that made up the far wall.

"Soph." He moved the flat pads of his fingertips across the swollen surface of the placenta. "There's still a chance for us."

"What chance?" she said.

"Here." He took her into his arms and pulled her against the sagging side of the placenta.

"Did Ambryn tell you about this too?"

"You'll see what I need. I don't. I can't. Look. See what it is."

Whatever was left of the Ulanyi embryo could duct emotions. The crew used it as just another way of getting high. But there was more to it than that. Soph knew that as soon as she opened herself up to it.

She felt her own heat and then Tiber's directly, like a sudden flare behind her eyes. His smooth skin was hot, and his breath across her shoulder burned. His long hair tickled her face.

She started to see it: what he needed. She saw through his eyes, felt with his body. Something loomed far above. Something that held him tight, kept him from moving, kept him pressed hard against joy.

She took the hint and pinioned his arms. They floated, so confinement was difficult. She searched for a moment and found a packing strap. He whimpered as it went on.

"My side," he said.

"Here?" Soph touched his ribs.

"Lower, lower. There! Now hard. Draw blood, dammit. Hard! Yes. There she is. There!"

Her fingernails tore his skin, releasing the tight knot of pleasure stuck in his side. It filled his guts.

"Who is it?" Soph whispered.

"I never knew the one who used me. Sukh killed her. Sukh killed them all."

Soph saw what Tiber made love to. Joints glistening with polish, hind limbs braced to exert maximum muscular pressure, head raised up proudly, Soph loomed over Tiber in the guise of a full-sized Vronnan female.

She did what he wanted. Her massive forelimbs pressed against his chest and the ovipositor pushed its way through the skin of his side.

Tiber's body melted under her magnificence.

6

The news had come while Elward and the Archon were making love—and operational plans. Tiber had attempted suicide by sticking a sharpened hydraulic line into his side. Elward hoped that the collateral rioting by the crew hadn't seriously damaged the ship. Excess enthusiasm was dangerous in enclosed spaces—an axiom of orbital crowd control. But without excess enthusiasm, the *Argent* was nothing but an unsalvageworthy hulk.

He'd assisted the Archon in making the arrests. Soph they'd found, sobbing, with Tiber. Ambryn they'd hit right when she came off the spacecraft into the docking bay. There weren't any *charges*, as far as Elward knew. There was only spiritual guilt. These women had done something to Tiber. They were responsible. The crew needed scapegoats, and the choice was obvious.

Tiber's body floated in the ship's center, the crew packed in around it. They hummed gently to themselves, a sound Elward found immensely irritating. Tiber was naked. An endoscope line snaked out of the wound in his side. The display was all blobby and vague, and Elward couldn't make out what he was seeing.

"He cleaned the toxic hydraulic fluid out first." Dr. Fulani floated by Tiber's head and brandished a tube with a crudely sharpened end. "The damage is purely physical."

"He'll live?" The Archon looked beseeching.

"Yes. He will live." The crew's humming grew louder.

"Let's take a look," the Archon said.

Dr. Fulani directed the endoscope, and the image on the screen shifted. "The hydraulic line penetrated the muscle layers of the external and internal obliques,'' she said. ''But beyond that, there is surprisingly little tissue damage.'' The image floated up what looked like a long passage. ''There's a layer of smooth muscle here, much like that surrounding the intestines. But it is not part of the intestine. It is not part of the normal human anatomy at all.''

Elward would have expected consternation among the crew at this news, but they barely responded. Maybe they'd always known there was something particularly odd about their captain.

Elward supposed that, in some sense, this little medical investigation he was watching was actually the trial, though no one mentioned either Soph or Ambryn. The crew had to suspect that Tiber had tried to desert them on Venus. Maybe they even suspected that he had been trying to arrange to run away with Soph—Elward certainly did. But Tiber couldn't be guilty of anything. Therefore, Soph and Ambryn had to be.

''The tube followed the path of the smooth muscle,'' Dr. Fulani said. ''It scraped its surface but never penetrated it. What looks like a serious wound is really just superficial damage.'' The endoscope ran into a dead end. ''Here is the closed end of the passage, just anterior to the muscles of the descending colon and rectum. As you can see, there has been past trauma and surgical repair. Blood vessels have been tied off. And here are the remains of some sort of differentiated support tissue.''

For all Elward knew, she was making the whole thing up. All he could see were differently shaped blobs.

''From what's left, it looks folded over on itself many times to make an immense osmotic surface, like that found in the placenta and kidney. Most of it was torn away in some earlier medical intervention.'' She turned off the endoscopic image.

Tiber groaned, and his crew moved in closer to provide comfort. The humming now buzzed in Elward's teeth. He caught Fulani's eye. Was that a message there in that grim face? Or was it a trap that would put him right in the same cage as Soph and Ambryn?

He'd soon find out.

7

Soph was done with crying. She slumped against Ambryn in the surprisingly sturdy cage the Undines had built out of the useless remnants of the dust shield that had brought them up from Venus. She had told Ambryn the story, and Ambryn had listened.

"Oh, Ambryn," she said. "I was weak, so weak."

"Thank God," Ambryn murmured. "It's time for some weakness. So was it Sukh that Tiber saw?" There was a little more left of that embryo's brain than she had thought—if it could do what Soph described.

"No. There was a sense of Sukh to it, but the Vronnan female that assaulted him was someone else. It seems that some group of Vronnans took Tiber from the *Prismatic Bezel*. Then, some indeterminate time later, Sukh rescued him and raised him in a simulated environment. Later she dropped him into human space somehow and used him to winkle Ripi out of hiding. She needed a human to penetrate Ripi's defenses."

Talking about conclusions calmed Soph down. Ambryn wasn't sure that was what Soph needed. "That female Vronnan, whoever she was. She raped him. Or was it a fantasy?"

"A fantasy?"

"Let's call it an imaginative emotional incarnation that explains the difference between what he is and what he thinks he should be."

"I think it was real," Soph said. "He must have been young, and the act realigned his whole mind. Oh, Ambryn, it was shameful, so shameful to him." Soph began to cry again. "Revealing it to me . . . he orgasmed when she stood above him. His soul dissolved in joy. So when we were . . . finished, he wouldn't look at me."

"And then he fled in shame, because you had seen it? And tried to kill himself."

"Yes."

"I don't think that was why," Ambryn said.

"Why then?"

"His shame was not that you had seen but that he'd enjoyed it so much. Maybe he'd never before even consciously perceived what it was that he loved. He'd never confronted it with his body. Until that moment."

"He's not dead," Soph said. "I know that, at least. He stuck that line in, right where the ovipositor, or whatever it was, had gone. It should have done serious damage. Instead, he went into some odd sort of shock." She looked at Ambryn. "He came to me. Ripi had escaped, he wants to stay with the *Argent*, for whatever reason he has . . . and Tiber came to me."

Time to fess up. Ambryn hadn't thought she'd ever be confronting Soph like this. She'd figured she'd come aboard, Soph would leave with Ripi, and they'd never see each other again. It was like a last gift, something she thought Soph had needed.

"Yes, I told him," Ambryn said. "He asked." She remembered Tiber as he huddled against her in the darkness of the shuttle, just before they parted. His control had been cracking, even then. "He doesn't know what human beings are for. He's like, I don't know, an animal bred in captivity, never exposed to members of its own kind. Sex is not natural to him, any more than it is for anyone. Oh, I suppose the urge is, somewhere deep down. But the actual relation to another human being is something we all need to learn. He needed help."

"And you thought I needed it too." Soph cried silently now, tears pushing their way out from behind closed lids. She huddled against the side of the cage. "And I did."

Ambryn had thought Soph's emotions too weak. That was how she had defended herself against the other woman's overwhelming competence. But that wasn't the case at all. Ambryn looked at the small, shuddering figure before her and, for the first time, felt herself melt.

"These two slats back here are weak," Soph whispered. "If we work them, we might be able to get out."

"Shhh!" Ambryn said. "Someone's coming."

"You guys are really gumming things up." Fulani pulled herself down next to the cage and spread her endless legs out to either side.

“You here to rattle our cage, Doctor?” Ambryn said.

Fulani smiled. “Be nice now, Ambryn. There’s two ways this matter can be handled. One, we can kill you.”

The Engineer grunted. She’d come in with Fulani but hadn’t said a word. She huddled against the cage, and Ambryn had suffered herself to have her fingers held.

“But you know who’d have to handle that particular little job?” Fulani said. “Me. I’d have to inject you, certify death, et cetera. A pain in the butt, in other words.”

“Sorry to be so much trouble,” Soph said.

“You have no idea how much trouble you are. Tiber was bad enough to begin with, but now his brain’s floating completely untethered. As if that wasn’t enough, we’ve got this alien crawling around with his own load of ambitions. All sorts of desires stuck together in a big wad, and not a one of them mine, got it? Your fault, every bit of it.”

While holding Ambryn’s fingers with one hand, the Engineer worked at the cage slats with the other. Without saying anything or looking at Dr. Fulani, Soph helped her.

“The other way this thing can be handled,” Ambryn prompted.

“Oh, yes. Yes. That interests you, I expect.” Fulani looked across the docking bay to the airlock. The spacecraft Ambryn had picked up from the construction monkey was docked on the other side of it. “The other way is you escape. Dramatic, daring. Taking with you just the shirts on your backs and maybe a couple of your more important self-directing makeup cases.”

Soph sucked a breath. She didn’t want to go, not now, Ambryn knew. She’d lost Ripi, Tiber too. And, just when all the mysteries seemed about to be revealed, she was being forced to leave. And Ambryn herself was losing the opportunity to study whatever Ulanyi mind lurked in that placenta. A mind the Engineer had told her wanted to become a deepdrive.

But there really wasn’t any choice.

“When?” Soph said.

Fulani looked at the Engineer, who nodded. “Right now.”

One last lingering squeeze, and the Engineer followed Fulani out of the docking bay.

Soph rolled against the loosened slats. They pulled away from their frame with a dry creaking, and she was out. Ambryn saw three of Soph's bags in the air, just floating there, as if someone had dropped them. Who had handled that? Fulani and the Engineer had been busy here.

Ambryn was bigger and had more trouble getting out. The slats scraped across her skin and tore a hem on her sleeve. Dammit, as if things weren't bad enough.

She dove into the airlock. As the door closed behind her, she turned. Someone watched from the inner airlock, hanging tightly on to the frame, as if unused to free fall. A big man. It looked a lot like Elward.

8

Elward dug frantically through the mass of gear floating in Soph's shelter, setting off collision chain reactions that eventually involved every object in the space.

Fulani had double-crossed him. He had worked with her and that silent Engineer to get Soph and Ambryn off the *Argent*. But when the Archon started to figure out who was responsible, all the evidence pointed to Elward. It was really pretty neat, and he supposed he didn't blame Fulani for it. After all, she lived here. This was her place. It would never be Elward's.

The Archon would nail him, no matter what their personal connection. And the crew was out for blood. Soph and Ambryn had escaped. Elward would have to be the sacrifice for everything. No one could save him.

Maybe Soph and Ambryn still orbited not too far away, shaking down their new interplanetary vessel. He tried to think about that as a real possibility. It made sense, after all. Really, it did.

Soph had rigged explosive all through the hull. Elward moved a couple of wads, just to put his mark on it, then pulled equipment out of the free-floating piles of junk and snapped it together. Soph had made everything ready. It was quite remarkable: liquid oxygen tanks from one of the emergency vessels in the loading bay, centrifugal ventilation motors, a mesh of particle shield powered by a nuclear decay pod. Carbon dioxide filters, even a packet of fecal decay bacteria.

An alarm buzzed. It wouldn't take anyone long to get through the security seal. He climbed into the hammock. It smelled like sex. Elward wrinkled his nose and pressed the activator.

The thunder of escaping air was much louder than the grunt of the explosive. Floating garbage fought to get out through the torn-back petals of the flower Elward had ripped in the ship's side. The hammock wobbled on its stays and inflated. Elward's ears popped from the pressure drop.

The hammock material was more flexible than he had anticipated. It ballooned out, tugged at the stay lines, and made disturbing stretching noises. He stared at the sides, as if they would be too embarrassed to blow out while being watched, and released the lines.

The bulging hammock popped forward, surged along with the last chunks of debris . . . and bounced back from the peeled-back opening in the hull. The inflated hammock was too big to fit through.

"Shit!" After a moment's thought, he shut off the air flow from the tanks, slapped on a breathing mask, and valved air back out of the hammock. The fabric collapsed around him.

He gathered the loose material under his arms, as if he was holding up a blanket while getting out of bed to check on the window, then, with encumbered arms, reached out to pull himself and the hammock through the opening.

The hull edges were sharp, he could feel them hungrily checking out his protection. He pushed carefully, relying on the fabric's slickness. He was narrower now, not the turgid balloon of before, and there was room to get through, just as he had originally planned.

Light flared at the side of his head. He squinted, and found himself looking into the oculars of the repair spider already working manipulators at the edge of the torn hull. No one aboard the *Argent* had yet sent it a command to oppose Elward's motion, and all it did was wait for the hammock fabric to slide out of its work area before going back to reweaving the hull fibers.

Then he hung from the *Argent*'s side, a line connecting

him to the drive unit still inside. And the fabric on his face was slowly suffocating him. He flailed down through the clinging folds and opened up the valves on the air tanks.

Nothing happened. Instead of freeing him, the fabric clung more tenaciously. For a long moment of blind panic he flailed away at it. He was trapped, he couldn't breathe, he was dead . . . he stopped himself and thought deliberately, though the pounding of his heart in his ears made it hard to form a coherent thought.

He hooked his feet under the harness holding the tanks, pulled himself down through the fabric bulges, and felt blindly below at the valves. A fold of fabric had gotten stuck under the harness and was holding the air tanks closed. He tugged, and it popped free.

The blessed feel of cold breathable air blew up around him. The fabric ballooned. He watched tensely for tears, patch kit in hand. God, he was dumb. He hadn't arranged the escaping garbage to make sure no sharp chunks careened off him on the way out, and he had underestimated the inflated size of the hammock so that he had hit the sharp edges of the explosive-ripped hole. If Soph found him tumbling through space, dead from a tear in his containment, she'd probably see at a glance how dumb he'd been.

He was fine, he was fine, there was no leak. So he turned and yanked the drive unit out through the tear. The squat shape sailed out of the hull tear—and the repair spider reached out a manipulator arm and snagged it. Someone in the *Argent* had finally gotten smart.

He hung taut from the *Argent.* The spider didn't have the capacity, but someone in an airsuit would come out soon and reel him in, hand over hand. He was sure the Archon would be glad to have a final chat with him.

He pulled out the drive control and palmed it to full thrust.

A white glare illuminated the broad side of the *Argent.* But the line didn't move. That damn spider was hanging on. He cut the drive, then slammed it on full again. He was sure the nozzles weren't made for this treatment, but he didn't have much choice.

Off, on, flipping changes in the nozzle directions. Those

transients had to hit the thing harder . . . got it! The drive unit sailed past, a chunk of the repair spider still clinging to it.

The drive caught up the slack and piled Elward into the rear of the bulging hammock with a yank. Along with it came the sound of tearing, a popping in his ears, and Elward lost air. Fabric did not collapse around him this time, because the drive was at full thrust and pulled everything taut.

The top seams had ripped with the sudden stressing of the line attachment points. Elward climbed up with seam sealer and groped. A burn and vacuum-suck on his fingertips revealed the stressed seam.

He squeezed the tube. The organized gel obeyed its calculated tropisms, spreading out against the vacuum and cold, directed by the brush of escaping air molecules across its back. That rush of air stopped, but there was another one, which Elward could hear as a sharp whistling. Just a few pinpoints on the seam opposite had sprung open. A few dabs with the sealer, and they closed up too.

The tanks did what must by now have been a weary repetitive job and refilled the hammock with air. Elward slumped down. It was as if he was being carried at the bottom of a duffle bag. He could lie on his back and look up at the three bright pinpoints of the rockets as they tugged him along. Nice. The safety line held, he'd set up the connections right. And he was alive. What more could he ask for?

Soph and Ambryn's ship, for one thing. He looked out through the transparent sheet at the stars and the fingernail paring of Mercury, with the impossibly bright disk of the Sun beyond it. The *Argent* had vanished behind him into the infinite blackness. As he looked out at the wash of stars, he knew what he had known all along. Soph and Ambryn were gone.

Elward was covered with bruises, and bending his left elbow made him feel as if a bone was tearing through muscle. He felt it with his right hand. No shattered fragments of bone or anything. He bent it again, wincing.

Equipment was piled up around him, bouncing on the flexible fabric as Elward moved. He'd done his best on short notice to anchor it to the hammock, but most of those stabilization points had torn loose during one or another of his acrobatic stunts. He took a few minutes to stack cases on top of each other and did his best to snap-strap them together. Soph's luggage organized itself.

Everything shifted to one side, and one of his stacks collapsed. Things seemed a little lighter. Decreased acceleration. Elward squinted up at the rocket engine pod.

Only two pinpoints now. Thrust was down to two-thirds. Its internal programs had tilted the engine slightly on its axis to compensate, but Elward wasn't sure how good a job it was doing.

He'd like to blame the *Argent* crew for bad maintenance, but the drive pods were grower-sealed, never maintained, never opened. And they were supposed to last for centuries before use, even if you slammed them into an iron-nickel asteroid at a good fraction of light speed.

A few minutes later, a second engine died. Only a single pinpoint of flame now pulled him away from the *Argent*. But wait—a flicker of light, like a corona of the reaction flame, barely visible. Elward dug through a bag, pulled out a flashlight, and directed it up at the engine pod, some thirty meters away.

The two nonfunctioning nozzles gaped blankly at him, giving no indication as to their cause of failure. But over by the still-functioning one . . . Elward peered past the actinic brightness of the rocket, screening it with one hand while he probed with the flashlight.

And, for an instant, he saw it, hanging precariously off the reaction drive pod with two limbs while a third performed its deadly task: the repair spider from the *Argent* hull. Its bottom had been torn off, and control ribbons and connector rods dangled out. Still, it had retained enough function to respond to a command from the receding *Argent* to destroy the pod. Elward felt a moment of misplaced admiration for the thing, as if it was some kind of dedicated commando, sacrificing its life for the good of its fellows.

He blinked his eyes against the drive's flare and turned away. There was no way for him to climb up there and do battle with it. But the drive control was still smooth in his palm.

After a silent prayer to an unknown deity—he really should pick one, it would make moments like this a lot easier to take—he cut the remaining drive. Once again he drifted weightlessly. Maybe the thing would think its job was done and quit. But no, there was another flicker. It would keep cutting until it ceased to function.

This little circle here was probably the attitude override. He'd never used such a control, but it had to be one of the common symbologies used in interplanetary transportation. Centuries of use had smoothed the systems until they seemed like something natural, co-evolved with humans. Using them required no thought, just reaction.

So the devices were designed to make you think—if that was absolutely necessary. The palm control poked sharp points into his skin as he tried to turn it, a warning of the inadequacy of human comprehension when it came to navigating in space. You don't just point things by feel, the control told him. You depend on gadgets like me that are much smarter than you could ever be. Understand?

Elward understood, but he pushed down and sacrificed some blood in the cause of human supremacy. The wheel clicked over to its maximum negative extension, pointing up past perpendicular. The drive pod had no true reverse. This was as close as it got, with the nozzle pointed back at an angle. Elward could feel some play in it: thirty degrees or so of back and forth. And the proprioceptive feedback of the control let him know that, as it moved, the nozzle was bumping into something. Like Elward's left elbow, it had lost its full range of motion.

Another flicker of light from the drive pod. The repair spider had probably been stimulated into more frantic action by the bumping of the nozzle.

Elward braced himself and flicked the drive on again. The drive pod swung to the side like a slingshot, and all tension vanished from the line connecting it to the inflated hammock. The drive pod swung past, pulled the line taut again, and the stars started orbiting, faster and faster.

Elward wiggled the attitude corrector, back and forth. If he had it right, at its maximum, the place where its movement was blocked, the drive nozzle was jabbing a fiercely hot flame against the underside of that goddam repair spider.

Something bumped against the outside of the hammock. Elward jerked his head around. For a moment, it looked like some alien bug, desperately trying to get in at him so that it could rip him apart.

It was the repair spider, its side melted and torn, its one remaining limb waving. Its oculars glittered for an instant, then it slid off into space and disappeared.

Elward returned control to the drive pod's own processor. After a few moments, the sickening swerve of the surrounding stars came to a halt. The drive pod, with its single functional nozzle, tugged gently at the connecting line, increased its flow, and resumed pulling Elward on the chosen trajectory.

He slumped down against the toppled equipment and looked out through the fabric at the universe. So many stars . . . You couldn't see the night sky from the surface of Venus, not really. The dust cloud screened out most of the dimmer stars, so it was always like being in the city, no matter where you were. But now, there was no air, no glow, and every place you looked they kept coming, just when you thought you had seen them all there were more and more, shoved in spaces where you would have sworn there wasn't enough darkness for another one. The Sun itself, though so bright it tightened the side of his face, was just another star. If he put his hand over it, the stars near it were just as bright as any of the others. Everyone was equal out here.

Here it was, what he'd been looking for: his kingdom. His own little piece of the universe. He could feel around, find out what he ruled. Soph's solar panels had deployed. He had food, air, distilled water. Edible fungi could grow on his sterilized shit. This fabric was a suit, a stylish garment. He would walk with it among the stars, swishing his sleeves. He'd kick the planets, rub the asteroids in his hair, swallow the comets. And it was all his. He didn't have to worry about belonging to anyone. No one's feelings mattered, not even his own. It was all physics. He could feel atoms banging against each other all around him. He'd never realized how mushy everything had been down in Golgot. Here everything was clear.

Wearing a crown of stars, Elward Bakst strode forward into the universe.

Ten

1

The road down from the rim of the crater Copernicus was not much more than a rough grade at this altitude, but Soph drove recklessly, bouncing her car high.

Kun lived in an abandoned construction shelter. He'd hidden there after returning from the disastrous expedition to Venus, and it had taken her a while to find him. She had wanted to tell him what had happened on Venus. He didn't want to hear it.

Instead, he tried to involve her in yet another tech-hunting mission, this one to the Asteroid Belt. He had recruited a band of impossibly young enthusiasts. They had sat cross-legged on the frost-covered floor of the construction shelter and presented their case with every evidence of calm sanity. It seemed that there was a Morth nest in the asteroid 324 Bamberga that was to be the target of a raid by Morth from 451 Patientia as the two asteroids came into conjunction. The Patientia Morth wanted to hire human mercenaries to assist in the assault. It seemed a good chance to examine the innards of a recently destroyed Morth nest, once the fight was over. The fact that neither Kun nor his young colleagues had any military experience seemed a minor objection.

The road grew smoother lower down the rim. In response

to a signal that told her the road ahead was blocked, she swerved left of her intended route, past piles of excavation spoil. The only sign of life was the blinking of a lonely amber indicator light.

The idea of a new tech-hunting mission left her with nothing but bone-deep weariness, but she couldn't think of anything else to do with her time. Besides, quite to her surprise, she found herself close to broke. She'd made money selling some of Ripi's data and had her share of the cash from the sale of the construction monkey ship in which she had come from Mercury. The amount could have lasted her a while, but she'd felt impelled to spend it extravagantly. She'd redecorated her apartments in the wall of Archimedes. Soph rather thought Ambryn would have liked the effect of the dark red wood with inset crystals, the swooping couches with human hands as feet, the yellow porcelain pots in the pebble-filled streams. But the pressures of the long journey from Mercury had been too much. Ambryn had gone down to Earth, the planet she had fled so many years before, and Soph never expected to see her again. And, damn it, wasn't this a stupid moment for that thought to give her a pang?

A bridge crossed a dust-flow ravine. But a mishandled construction crane had sprung a truss out of position. The car advised her not to attempt crossing and plotted another route.

What the hell was being built way out here? Cranes hung overhead like quizzical diplodoci waiting for an interloping mammal to be on its way. Her car was locked into deep wheel trenches left by construction vehicles. Their constant passage had welded the dust together. This road seemed to lead nowhere.

She squinted at a tiny shape ahead. As she approached, it grew clearer. A big, full-bellied man stood patiently by the roadside. His wrinkled inner airsuit was bare of equipment and outer layer, as if he'd wandered away from his fitting room before donning the rest of his gear.

Fighting down the urge to just accelerate and get the hell out of there, Soph stopped the car. There was nothing visible around—not a shelter, not a vehicle. She stared at the man. He raised a hand in a casual gesture of greeting, as if he'd been expecting her and was pleasantly surprised to find her early.

"Son of a bitch," Soph said, and opened the airlock to let Lightfoot in.

The restaurant's glass floor glowed blue, but from the angle of the ebony-walled cloakroom, Soph could not see down through it. The attendant gave the shoulder of her gown one last brush.

Lightfoot was dressed with his usual elegance, making his ponderous body into a confident statement of authority. Despite that, he seemed puzzled, a little confused, as if he had no idea of what he was doing here in the cloakroom of the Doc Kraken Restaurant, where reservations usually had to be made six months in advance.

The attendant nodded graciously, exactly as if he had not just searched both of them thoroughly for surveillance gear. The white of his sensor-gloved hands now bore the gore of confiscated equipment. Soph swept out to their table, ignoring, for the moment, what lay beneath her feet, visible through the glass. The white cliffs of Copernicus rim loomed above, visible through the high windows.

The hem of her long skirt brushed the rough glass of the floor with a flare of sparks. Her face was powdered bone white, matching the cliffs, and her lips were dark brown-red. Her hair remained in the black bowl cut that had, over time, become a trademark. Lightfoot followed sedately, a step behind. They looked like quite a couple, she knew.

"See those segments?" Lightfoot pointed down through the floor. "They're stingers. I think they work through focused electromagnetic pulse. EMPs are usually only made by nuclear detonations. They knock out unshielded microelectronics. If you put Doc Kraken in the right place, once he gets himself put together, I bet he could hunt spacecraft."

The toroidal segments floated separately, spinning like tires. Sometimes one would freeze, just for a second, so that its cilia, each the size of a human arm, glittered like tree branches caught in an ice storm. Beyond was the cryptic high-pressure-fluid-ice environment in which Doc Kraken had evolved. A rippling plain of a solid ice phase bore spiky plants on it.

"Well, Lightfoot," she said. "I survived. You didn't think I would, did you?"

He looked at her for a long moment. "That's right. I didn't think you would. That's a lovely dress, by the way."

The stiff fabric rustled as she pulled her shoulders back. "I did all right—if that's what you're getting at. How's the house?"

"Sold it." He grimaced. "I kept thinking there was someone else there. I'd go searching and get lost. It made me appreciate that little place we had in Chaplygin, remember? When Stephan was a boy."

She did remember. Chaplygin was Farside, where there was nothing but stars in the sky and the circum-Lunar asteroids of the Diadem. It had been a little dark place, like a shoe box someone had forgotten in a closet, and Soph hadn't much cared for it. The synthetic wood cabinetwork had quickly lost its polish. But they'd been young. Younger, anyway, in Lightfoot's case. As soon as he could, Stephan had climbed up the cabinets in the kitchen and dove off until he cut his forehead. Blood had spattered all over the counters, and Soph had at first thought some hot sauce had spilled. The crescent scar had been visible under Stephan's close-cropped hair the last time Soph and Lightfoot had seen him, just before he left for Jupiter.

"We've lived a lot of places, Lightfoot. It's a wonder you remember any of them."

"Please, Soph. You're not actually going to go out into the Belt after Morth nest-maintenance tech, are you?"

"And what the hell business is it of yours?"

"None," he said. "None at all." He poured her a glass of wine from an impatient bottle that squirted it out rather than relying on Luna's languid gravity. "I'm not good at this. I'm sorry."

"Don't shadow me, Lightfoot. I know you have contacts everywhere. You can find out what I'm doing—if that's what you want. But don't lurk around in the shadows. If you need to keep in practice, do it with something important."

"This is important. You have to understand."

"Dammit, Lightfoot. I'm tired of being your project. I don't care if you have too much money already. You should find something else to do with your time." And she *was* tired. She'd been tired ever since arriving on Luna. She kept waiting for it to go away, but maybe this was how old age happened. One day you were no longer yourself, and had to learn to live with a dull ache that never went away. Maybe you got used to it. Maybe you died eventually.

"I understand." That was always his response when he was going to disregard what she had said. "All I want to know is: do you account the Venus mission a success?"

"Are you debriefing me?"

"Don't you think you need it?"

He had the defining ability of a spouse or a parent: he could tell her something true, reasonable, even necessary, in such a way that she wanted to reject it in a rage.

"What I need is some peace and quiet," she said. "A rest."

"You should rest only when you're done with something."

"Only, with you, nothing's ever done."

Under their feet, the defensive segments began to link up with the other free-swimming portions of Kraken's anatomy. Kraken was a communal structure, like a portuguese man-of-war, and he had come apart for maintenance. Slithering shapes like moray eels with rows of sharp-clawed legs along their bellies hunted through the body segments seeking interlopers, those creatures more definable as parasites than as members of the Kraken community.

To eat dinner while watching Doc Kraken was the most expensive show on Luna. This restaurant was how Kraken financed his millennial trip through this arm of the Galaxy. Reportedly, he'd already traveled thousands of light-years, working as a tourist sight the whole way.

"Soph—"

"God, Lightfoot, stop talking to me."

He hid his eyes with his hand. It was long and bony, with swollen joints. It looked carved from wood as a model to demonstrate the movements of the human hand, something kept in the cabinets of a Renaissance artist/scientist along with the quartz crystals and the stuffed raven.

Soph reached out and pulled his hand away from his face. He blinked rapidly, as if the light was too bright. Facing everything clearly every day caused him pain. It was a discipline he had forced on himself. He had forced it on Stephan too, a burden no child should have, forgetting the long years he himself had had to get used to it. But he'd never forced Soph. He'd just left his mind lying out like a gift, hoping she would accept it. After Stephan's death, which she had blamed Lightfoot for, she had no longer wanted the crystalline lens of his mind anywhere near where she needed to see.

Lightfoot had let his hair go gray, but it wasn't the aristocratic pewtered look now in fashion. This was the no longer obedient hair of a sad and aging man. Stephan was dead, and Soph still refused to look at what Lightfoot was trying to show her. Maybe it was time she stopped refusing.

"Lightfoot. I abandoned everything. I failed so completely I can't even begin to comprehend it."

"Tell me," he said. "Tell me everything."

"It's amazing how often success depends on the screwups of the competition. . . ." she began.

Kraken had taken shape. The stinger segments now bristled from an armored carapace whose hexagonal segments were the shells of linked crablike creatures.

"Ripi has secrets," Lightfoot said. "He didn't tell you everything. But his secrets are not the important ones."

"Tiber," Soph said. "I know almost nothing about him."

She hadn't told Lightfoot she'd made love with Tiber. She wasn't going to.

"What *do* we know, then?" he said.

"He's Martian, and was a young boy on the *Prismatic Bezel* when it left the Solar System on its interstellar colonization mission. The ship was hit by some sort of Vronnan force used to interstellar assaults, and he was taken for . . . reproduction? Some other process? I don't know. The experience scarred him.

"Sometime later, he came into the hands of Sukh, Ripi-Arana-Hoc's Memoriless daughter. Ripi had fled the Bru clanship without transferring any of his memories to her. All she possessed were the most ancient of them, the ones he shared with his poor Brother in Memory. Sukh took Tiber from his kidnappers by force, and I doubt any of them survived. She raised him with the aid of environment-simulation machines to some approximation of normal human adulthood. Then she used him to ferret Ripi out of human space.''

``Do we know anything about how he arrived in the System?'' Lightfoot asked. ``How he appeared among men?''

``No, not really.'' Soph chewed her thumb. ``The first I know of him, he is already on the work crew at the orbital dock of MeshMatrix Krystal, working on what would become the *Argent*. He did mention a man he knew on MMK, someone named Hlobane, who helped him. Taught him to cook. Aside from that, it's a blank.''

``Hlobane?'' The name meant something, but Lightfoot was noncommittal. ``But Tiber had knowledge useful to the construction of the *Argent*, probably learned during his sojournings among the Vronnans.''

``Right. He then used that knowledge to hijack the *Argent*. Sometime later, he used it to lure Ripi into hiring the *Argent* in his escape from Venus. There was something about the *Argent*, with its dying Ulanyi placentas, that Ripi needed. . . .''

``Was that the reason Ripi stayed aboard?'' Lightfoot asked.

``I think it was.'' Soph had thought about it. ``He was terrified of Tiber, who was Sukh's tool. But his need was strong enough to make him stay behind.''

``And then there's your friend Elward.''

``If he's still aboard the *Argent*, I doubt he's getting along with anyone.'' Despite her suppressed worries about Elward's fate, Soph smiled at the thought of him trying to get along with that mad crew on a day-to-day basis.

``At any rate, the *Argent* is gone, heading God knows where,'' Lightfoot said. ``And Sukh's ship is untraceable as well. You have no idea what panic swept the inner System after that little hit on Venus. It's been a long time, over a century, at least, since any alien vessel attempted any such military adventure. Even damaged, it managed to evade investigation."

"So we have nothing." Soph felt resentful. "You've gotten me all excited, stirred up things I'd managed to forget, and . . . there's just a big hole."

"Not nothing. Not quite." Lightfoot was patient. "We have Tiber, and his past. That can be uncovered, I think. How he came into human space, and under what circumstances. One reason we can't figure out where anything is going is because we really do not understand where it has already been."

It was amazing, how quickly she felt a team with him again. She didn't even mind his use of the word "we." He'd always been the best project manager she'd ever met. It was just that having a brilliant project manager as a husband had never quite worked out as well as it should have.

"So where do *I* go from here?" she said.

He nodded up at the high windows overhead. A glittering point had risen above the crater rim, and Soph wondered if Lightfoot had timed the conversation for this dramatic point.

"MeshMatrix Krystal," he said. "Where the *Argent* was built and where Tiber lived out his time among human beings. I've been in contact with various people on MMK. . . . Forgive my temerity. Your Hlobane happens to be one of them. I think he might be willing to help you out."

"I'll forgive you if it pans out," Soph said. "Otherwise, it was unwarranted interference."

"I don't know," the shuttle pilot said. "The thing looks like it's about to come apart. The impact of the Rock probably left fractures that never healed."

MeshMatrix Krystal loomed ahead, covered with ice spikes so that it looked like a slowly rotating sea urchin. The Rock, the iron-nickel asteroid that had been crunched into the center of the snow-and-iceball that was now called the Halo, stuck out into space at one pole like a pimento in an albino olive.

"It's been there a long time, Sarah." It was just like Lightfoot to hire Soph an attractive young woman as an escort pilot. He didn't want her sympathies engaged with any more attractive young men.

"Has to happen sometime, right?" Luna shrank beneath them. "They must get a lot of leaks. Melting's natural, they cram too many functions together in a place where there shouldn't be anything at all."

"Maybe," Soph said as the spiky ecocyst approached. "But I think it's an ad."

The spikes gleamed with subtle algal colors ranging from dark red to bluish green.

"An ad?" Sarah said. "For ice? We have to buy it regardless."

"Not necessarily from them. Besides, pure H_2O's not all they sell. It's clear they know what they're doing, isn't it? It's not easy to keep algal blooms alive in water ice exposed to open vacuum."

"An interesting problem, now you mention it." Sarah got lost in thought. Her pouf of white hair reflected the indicator lights in the otherwise dark cabin.

Soph had expected that they would have flipped over by now, decelerating for docking. The spiky ecocyst swelled entirely too quickly in the transparent nose of the shuttle. The rocky end had the usual docking facilities, but they weren't heading there. Hlobane was an ice dweller and lived on the exterior of the Halo, somewhere amid the ice spikes. Everyone in MeshMatrix Krystal had originally lived in the Rock, but rougher types had spread through ice tunnels in the Halo, developing their own culture as they went.

"They're still leaks," Sarah said. "You get stress releases, the water comes out. Can't avoid it. So they take advantage of the inevitable, make it look deliberate and a sign of their cleverness. Nice technique."

A red dot blinked, down between two spikes with flat hexagonal crystals at their tips. Its light refracted up through the ice. The ecocyst swelled as they circled it, closer and closer. Soph felt the increase in weight as they whipped tighter.

"You know, their approach instructions didn't make much sense," Sarah said. "In fact, they sound kind of suicidal."

What was it with the pilots Soph ended up flying with? "You didn't think to mention this before?"

"This is a learning experience for me. I figured you knew everything that was going on. I cleared the flight path with you."

"With Lightfoot."

"Yeah, well, same thing, right? Don't you guys work together?"

Damn him. Just when he'd finally managed to make her feel something for him, he did something like this. Their trajectory grew impossibly tight, a spiral held to the ecocyst's surface by a steady blast of side-directed rocket. Each orbit took no more than two or three seconds. The same ice spikes came past, each time higher, their widening bases closing in. The red dot strobed in until, with a last descent, the shuttle slapped into it, and its bright red smears dripped back along the hull.

A solid sheet of ice loomed ahead. If it was the last thing she was going to see, then she should *see* it. Soph stared forward. They smashed through the sheet, sending flinders flying. Beyond it was another, and another, hitting so fast they merged into a steady rumble.

The ship finally gave up all momentum and came to a halt in a pile of bluish snow. Soph looked up and behind. They lay in a curving ice tunnel. Shattered fragments of the successive ice sheets stood, in steady succession, back out of sight.

Sprays of mist into the cold atmosphere, and ice crystals grew visibly. The ice sheets that had slowed the shuttle's frantic career reformed in seconds and once again blocked the tunnel, testimony to the skill of MMK's water-sciences subdivision.

"No magnetic braking?" Soph asked.

"There's barely any metal aboard this tub. It's mostly crystal-grown." Sarah's eyes danced with delight.

"Plus, this was more fun."

"You know it."

Just like youth, to stick risks where they didn't need to be. Soph looked out at the walls of ice. "I didn't bring a parka."

"Not as cold as it looks."

"How do you know? You've never been out there."

"I read the promotional materials. After all, this is—"

"A learning experience, I know. Thanks for the ride." Soph unsnapped herself. "How do you get your shuttle out?"

"They'll start melting me out soon. You better get going."

"Thanks, Sarah. I hope you're learning enough."

"Good luck to you, Ms. Trost."

Water streamed past as jets of steam melted their way into the surrounding ice. Soph jumped out the hatch and clambered across an ice bridge that arched high above swirls of boiling water. She turned to see its glittering shards topple away behind her. With a loud cracking and hissing, the shuttle sank, blue slabs tilting up around it, and vanished.

Soph grabbed at a railing and looked down. The colloidal ice refroze instantly over the shuttle. The layer thickened and left it entombed like a frozen mammoth. Had the MMK staff decided to imprison the insolent Sarah and keep her for further study?

No. Below the ship moved ice manipulators. She could see the frantic boiling of adolescent water confused about its phase, being solid, gas, and liquid simultaneously. Within a few seconds, the shuttle had melted all the way through the thick ice layer. Inertia grabbed it, and it was gone, catapulted off at the tangent. For an instant, she had a distorted view of the stars directly under her feet, then the ice grew thick again.

Stairs cascaded down, slick and dripping icicles. She turned and started the long climb.

2

"Do you want to see what's left of the old place?" Uncle Otho asked. "It's actually got a bit of melancholy drama. A place for a poet to sit." The aircraft's wings shuddered, and they left the ground.

"What's left?" Ambryn felt startled for a moment, then remembered. The house she had grown up in had been abandoned, then semiofficially looted and burned under the doctrine of embryo turnover. The Egg had hatched, and Pyx, its embryo, now an adult Ulanyi, was imprisoned somewhere for crimes she had not yet managed to understand.

"Surprise," Otho said. "You've not become sentimental, have you?"

"There have been a lot of changes, but nothing that dramatic."

"Relief." They climbed steeply. "You always hated that place."

"I did. But when you run away from something, you want it to remain behind."

Uncle Otho examined her closely, then smiled. He had always been the one she would complain to, because he would listen without telling her she was being unreasonable, an irresistible temptation to everyone else. Where Ambryn was big, ruddy, smooth-skinned, he was small and dark, with carved-looking wrinkles and graceful fingers. He did not look any older than she remembered, but then he had always seemed ancient.

"Do you still want to see it?" he asked.

"I'm sure you have other, more interesting things to show me." She strove for detachment.

"I think I do."

The shuttle from Earth orbit had landed on the banks of the Bow River, amid the overgrown ruins of what had once been a city called Calgary. The front range of the Rockies bulked just below the horizon to the west, while to the east, north, and south stretched the vast plains at the center of the North American continent, the center of Ulanyi/human cooperation on Earth. Otho had come in one of the family's aircraft to get her.

He had brought her a delicate spray of miniature roses of dizzying scent. The single bumblebee that had come along seemed to have become drunk on the smell. It lay in a stupor on the worn leather control panel, wings moving slowly in the apian equivalent of a snore.

Ambryn looked down at the spots of darker green as the clouds' shadows grazed placidly across the endless grasslands and, despite herself, saw the blur of tears. They weren't entirely for this vision of her childhood home. She remembered Soph's cold departure after they had sold the construction monkey booster for much less than its true worth, simply to be quit of it.

Only one thing had kept her from swimming after Soph and embarrassing herself completely, and that was the knowledge that Soph would someday have to face the mysteries she was avoiding. And when she did, Ambryn would hold part of the solution, because the secret of the *Argent*'s departure from MeshMatrix Krystal lay back in the center of her own family. Pyx had been a major conspirator, part of the reason Ambryn had gotten interested in the *Argent* and gotten involved with Soph in the first place. Both she and Soph would have to accept the tangling up of their fates.

"Who shall I say is calling?" Otho said. "How have you been redefined since we saw you last?"

"Regrettably, I have to say that I'm much the same. I've lived on Venus most of the time. In Golgot, the big city on Aphrodite."

"I'm familiar. You look well. It must have suited you. But you did not rise to high office? A tooth on the Mandible? No?"

She shifted, feeling she was disappointing him. "I was a fortune-teller. An alien haruspex. Particularly popular on Venus."

"Foreigners must eat that skrying right up. A good living?"

"If you work at it."

Otho laughed. "And you didn't work at it. Not half hard enough. Ah, you always were a lazy little thing, dear Ambryn. Cursed by too much brains so that you never had to work very hard."

"Are you trying to toughen me up for the family meeting?"

"You don't want toughness, Ambryn. If anything, you've always had far too much. You find some truth?"

"A bit."

"More than most, then."

"I'm looking for more."

"Ah, an explanation. Why you are home. And why you're unlikely to stay, even to please an old man who will not make it around the Sun more than one or two more times."

Ambryn kissed his furrowed cheek. "You've learned the secret of manipulation, Uncle Otho. That people love it. It makes them feel worth the effort."

"If they loved it, I'd be more successful at it."

"So," Ambryn said. "What should I watch out for?"

"Everything. You're an outsider now, regardless of who you once were. It will be like learning to walk again. With land mines under the carpet."

"Oh, that makes me so happy to be back."

"Regrets. We're nomads now, we Chretiens. We walk the loamy soil, herd the buffalo, hunt the wapiti." He rubbed his shoulder in memory of some outdoor mishap. "It wouldn't be so bad if we had an adult Ulanyi to follow, to give us meaning. We're wandering in the wilderness, Ambryn. Soon separate bands will creep off into the whispering darkness, and the Chretiens will disappear."

He banked the aircraft. Below, standing on a slight rise of ground surrounded on three sides by a meander of a swift-flowing river, stood a conventicle castle, with all of the typical extravagance of architecture of a family secure in its possession of an Ulanyi Egg. Pavilions overhung the water. Different colors of crops interrupted the green of the grass. An attendant village huddled on the other side of the river. For an instant, she thought she was home, and gasped. But this was nothing like the place where she had grown up.

Ambryn had had her own room atop a tower, a dramatic place her mother had thought secure. But Ambryn, already an avid climber, had regularly swung herself out through an alarm-disabled escape hatch and crawled down the rough stone of the tower to meet . . . whoever it was at the time. This castle had no such tower. Hers had had a high octagonal roof that had developed astounding gleaming icicles during the long winter.

"Hergild," Otho said. "A growing power, if you want to know. To climb back up, Chretien may have to displace them."

"Are you showing me this to bug me? I wouldn't undo my decisions, even if I had the power."

Otho sucked thoughtfully on a slender eyestick, blew the delicate aerosol out his nostrils, where it formed a delicate rime and gleamed for a moment before evaporating. Sharply trimmed eyebrows raised, he offered her the case. She waved it away.

"Too mild a bad habit to be interesting," she said.

"Don't be harsh, Ambryn. There's information down there for you."

"There's no Ambryn tower."

"Perhaps you revealed the flaws in the concept."

"Ah, their poor daughters. To be punished for my experience."

"I'm sure they have their ways of getting around family restrictions."

They circled again. He had cut the engine back to almost nothing, extending the wings, and Ambryn could hear the whistle of the air across the airfoils. She felt like a ghost.

Afternoon settled toward the horizon, and Hergild Castle cast shadows to the east, across the peaked roofs of the village. The rotunda rose in the house's center. Within it sat the Hergild Egg, in solemn splendor amid its support equipment. Everyone in Hergild, including the embryo itself, dreaded the inevitable day of its birth.

"How much was Pyx involved in the *Argent* project?" Ambryn asked.

"A deep question and one no Chretien has been able to answer. Not much, if at all, is my suspicion."

"But surely, with the involvement of the Gregsons . . ." The Gregsons had been friends of Ambryn's grandparents, and their part in the original *Argent* conspiracy, the attempt to raise Ulanyi embryos under complete human control, was well known.

"The Gregsons are dead now and never revealed their contacts with any Ulanyi. You remember them, I'm sure. Not pleasant at a dinner party, but tough. Wild human supremacists . . . and, you know, I think they would rather just have banished all Ulanyi from the surface of Earth. They had no real interest in spiritual domination. As far as I know, they never had much contact with Pyx. Your mother, you remember, was quite protective of him."

Ambryn couldn't imagine growing up without seeing the world reinterpreted through an embryo's perception. Still, the result was a suspicion that the Ulanyi were nothing more than a consensus hallucination. None of the aliens who had entered the System were real, and deepdrives were not means of interstellar travel but just a way of giving human nightmares and needs physical realization. There lay the origins of skrying.

"But what was Pyx charged with?" she asked.

"Oh, the usual Ulanyi sins: perverse thinking, refusal to be born, fear of reproducing, that sort of thing." Otho pulled at his lower lip. "At any rate, Pyx is currently under sentence of death in an ice cell in the Halo of MeshMatrix Krystal. Since the *Argent* was hijacked from a construction bay in the Rock, at the opposite pole of MMK, that indicates that someone sees a connection."

"Poor Pyx," Ambryn send, remembering the mind with which she had grown up. How was he doing with a body? "I'm sure he's cold. He's alone. He's frightened. And the Chretiens have abandoned him. But, Otho, you don't think his crime had anything to do with the *Argent*."

"Me?" Otho seemed startled. "You know me, Ambryn. A mess of opinions, none of interest to anyone."

"I'm interested, Otho." She put her hand on his shoulder. "Always."

He rubbed her hand. "So nice and always so much trouble. Much as I love you, Ambryn, I'm glad I'm your uncle and not your parent."

"Don't try to change the subject. Or pick a fight. You'll still have to tell me."

"Pyx's guilt, it seems, is vastly deeper than involvement in a mere conspiracy plot with human beings, though, somehow, his obsessions were of interest to the *Argent* conspirators. That was what eventually led the Ulanyi Pure Mind sect to him after they succeeded in getting the ship hijacked and out of their jurisdiction. But Pyx had not had any real connection with the conspiracy. What he feared was birth. His own birth. He was looking for some way to avoid it, some way to reach transcendence without ever feeling the air on him, seeing the light, ever having any direct sense impression. And in there, somewhere, lies the crime for which he is to be devoured."

Otho, as Ambryn had suspected, had thought a lot about Pyx's fate. She wanted his opinion before she got to the Chretien encampment and heard the mass of theories, conspiratorial and wild, that were surely common family currency.

"The Chretiens gave Pyx up, didn't they? Someone informed, in the wake of the *Argent* fiasco, to avoid getting sucked up along with the Gregsons and the rest."

"The family has dealt with that." Otho was clearly uncomfortable with the entire subject. "It has to be regarded as a closed issue. They told me that I should be discreet—for now."

"Sure, Otho. The witch hunts are in the past. I don't want to mix in."

They? Who ran family affairs now? Ambryn's mother had already been dead when Ambryn left. Ambryn had been the product of a stored ovum, an indulgence of her mother's declining years. Ambryn had a sudden painful stab of guilt at the thought of how difficult those years had really been.

"How long for them?" Ambryn pointed down at Hergild.

"Oh, decades yet. Don't they look serene?"

"I've always loved serenity."

Uncle Otho laughed, relieved at leaving a sensitive topic. "Disappointment for you, then. The family's riven with infighting over what to do next. A new Egg must be acquired or the family will cease to be organized by conventicle and fall apart into its constituents. We may become ordinary village dwellers."

A new Egg. Ambryn sensed something unspoken behind what Otho had told her. That wasn't like him. Pyx and the new Egg. . . . "When Pyx was arrested—"

"You will be interested to know that old friend Martine is now a power in the Chretien family. Your mother's influence. There's even talk of making her the next Maintainer, as successor to your mother, should an Egg be acquired."

Ambryn felt a flush across her cheeks. "Martine? In the Chretien family?"

"Well, yes. We rather got to like her, you know, during your . . . association."

"Association? We were screwing, Otho."

Otho chuckled, not at all offended. "I've become fond of her myself, I must admit. She's an ill-tempered little seer. I can see why you were so taken with her."

"Great."

"You want your old house to hang around, and your old lovers to disappear, right?"

"That would be nice."

"Life is more instructive than comforting, Ambryn."

"Platitudes, Uncle Otho. I'm surprised at you."

"Don't be. As I grow older, I take the job of uncle more seriously."

"The first thing in life you ever took seriously, then."

"We all have to start somewhere."

Martine had been Ambryn's first real lover. Real, because unlike Ambryn's other girls, she had been unwilling, finding girl love to be a childish affectation. Martine had had a real boyfriend, a broad-shouldered man a few years older who wore well-cut suits and had a beautiful singing voice. Martine had clearly done as well as she could, and Ambryn could see that Martine was distressed at not being satisfied. Well, you had to give them a try, after all.

Ambryn seduced Martine one afternoon after a school field trip, a particularly neurosecretory interview with a dying Egg, an Ulanyi embryo who, for complex biological reasons, was never to come to term and would end its existence without leaving its placenta. Even though healthy embryos played at considering their adult stage as tantamount to living death, this involuntary in-placenta death was a tragedy, and someone had decided that human children should be exposed to it. The humans of Earth concealed their tightening grasp of power over the Ulanyi by dramatically regarding an Ulanyi death as much more important than that of any human. Mourning ceremonies were a decoration on the soft glove of power.

And both Ambryn and Martine had, with youth's natural attraction to the tragic and morbid, felt the internal gloom of the dying Ulanyi. Afterward, Ambryn suggested that they lay down and comfort each other. She had a wonderful daybed in her room, it was perfect for socializing. It was the culmination of Ambryn's long campaign. Deep emotion was always useful in seduction. It didn't matter which emotion it was.

In addition to a tight, wiry body, Martine was sharply intelligent, with a mind as heedlessly energetic as her body. Between bouts of actual sex, Ambryn preferred to lounge, let the sweat dry, maybe drink something, while Martine insisted on restarting some intricate argument whose premises Ambryn had already forgotten. When Ambryn figured out that the harder and more effectively she argued with her, the more furiously Martine made love, Ambryn hyperoxygenated the drowsy flames of her intellect and astonished her teachers. All ashes now.

Ambryn was afraid. She'd left Martine behind when she fled the restrictions of her embryo-worshipping family. So the family, ever-flexible, had taken Martine as sacrifice in Ambryn's place.

And Uncle Otho was the most flexible of all Chretiens. Bachelor uncles are the shepherds of genes and customs, preserving those most in tune with themselves and expelling those they do not approve of.

"Look." Ambryn pointed out of the window. "Who is that?"

Otho didn't even look. Maybe it was part of his guided tour, her preparation for finally seeing what had become of her family.

"Nordhoffs," he said. "Their Egg, named Chrism, hatched a year ago. She has not mated yet, not even once. She's one of those adults who actually enjoys her own body, looks like. A throwback."

She could see the strutting shape of the adult Chrism, ahead of the long train of bactrian camels that carried the goods of the Nordhoff family on their resentful backs. Chrism was large, but her shell was still soft. It was only after reproduction that her armor would thicken, spikes would grow on her limbs, and her jaws would gain muscle: Ulanyi females defended their embryos.

Ambryn had heard that these changes could be carried even farther with proper hormonal control, creating a death-dealing creature called an Executioner, useful in certain circumstances. Human intervention in Ulanyi reproduction made sure that specialized form never appeared on Earth, but they did exist in the Asteroid Belt. From what Soph had told her, though, the Executioner form was standard for post-reproductive Ulanyi females in Vronnan civilization. The Vronnans called them Guardians. It seemed that everyone who gained control of Ulanyi reproduction had a different goal in mind.

A small herd of buffalo cropped the grass two kilometers or so to the north, and Chrism seemed interested in them. She was about the same size and perhaps found their company more congenial than the nattering humans who never let her be.

It was late enough that the Nordhoff family head, whoever that was, had ordered a stop. Soph could see tents blossoming on the grass, water parties heading out to a stream nearby, animal handlers negotiating with their camels. A group of armed young people followed Chrism at a respectful distance. If she bolted, as adult Ulanyi sometimes did, they would follow—all night if necessary. They had to be present if a mating occurred to prevent damage to either Ulanyi and to lay claim to any resulting embryo. That had never been part of Ambryn's life. Pyx had been born before her own birth. She wondered if things would have been different if her adolescence had been spent sleeping on the grass and diving amid the flailing, deadly limbs of mating Ulanyi to prevent their killing each other before fertilization occurred.

Probably not. She would just have been the same in a different way.

The tents of the Chretien encampment lay atop a riverside bluff amid some stubby oak trees. Ambryn thought she detected something demoralized in the arrangement of glowing geometric shapes. It entirely lacked the purposeful confidence of the Nordhoff band, with their organizing obsession with their adult-phase Ulanyi. ''Dammit,'' Otho muttered. ''You'd think they could maintain those landing lights a little better.''

An area of flat land had been set aside as a landing strip, but only a scattering of glowing dots marked it off against the darkening earth. Ambryn could just see the shadows of the storage huts that held the rest of the Chretiens' limited mechanical transport equipment: perhaps another aircraft or two, and a few riverboats for supplies. Ambryn thought about offering to help Uncle Otho with the night landing but, looking at his grim face, realized that such an offer would not be welcomed. Even the easygoing Otho was feeling the strain of the family's situation.

In any event, they landed without difficulty. It had been Otho, after all, who had originally taught Ambryn to fly the difficult thermals of the Front Range. Ambryn helped push the light aircraft over to its hangar.

The Chretiens had clearly been in residence for some time. The trail up the bluff from the riverbank was worn wide and was starting to erode. Some halfhearted attempts had been made to bolster the trail and create some less-destructive switchbacks, but most of those bringing water and fish up from the river ignored them. Ambryn foresaw trouble. The agreements guiding settlement and nomadism in the Ulanyi plains were ancient and could be enforced harshly. The Chretiens risked family annihilation if they stayed in one place for too much longer without an Ulanyi Egg to give them sanction.

Lights glowed on high poles ahead. A huge fire burned in the pit in the middle of the encampment, the carcasses of two deer and one wild pig turning in it, sending up their rich odor. Cheers greeted Ambryn as she walked into the circle of light, and she felt dizzy to see so many familiar faces at once. She stepped forward and was embraced by her family.

Ambryn walked cautiously between the trees, once stumbling into some prickly bushes that she misinterpreted as oak branch shadows. She blamed that on the wine, even though she really hadn't drunk that much. She'd been too busy catching up with everyone.

The encampment was quiet now. Ambryn luxuriated in the feeling of the cool air across her face, the smell of the damp earth, the hooting of an owl somewhere on the other side of the river. The feeling would soon fade, she knew, and she would once again long for the roaring confusion of a place like Golgot, but for now, it cradled her soul.

There was her assigned tent, glowing a faint purple. Opening the flap sent up a swirl of rose petals. Masses of the flowers filled the tent. She could see the fluted legs of what had to be a lightweight reproduction of her favorite daybed among the blossoms. She got an erotic charge just out of seeing those cloven-hoofed feet.

"I knew Otho would do the elegant thing," a voice said. "The precise gesture. That didn't seem right. Not for you."

Ambryn picked up a handful of fallen petals and let them sift between her fingers, feeling their dusty silk.

"No, Martine," she said. "Excess has always been the way to my heart."

There, on the daybed, a high-arched foot in a silver sandal, Atalanta at rest. Heart pounding, Ambryn pushed her way through the nodding blooms and stood over her old lover.

Martine had aged, and her skin had drawn tauter over bone and muscle. It made her eyes look larger. And her texture was, like the petals, elegantly dusty. She moved her feet, and Ambryn sat down. A hummingbird flicked by overhead, intrigued by the scent of Ambryn's hair, then buzzed away.

Light came from two lanterns. It gave the scene a romantic glow. Martine always had been a master stage manager.

"I'm not here to threaten your position," Ambryn said.

"I didn't think you were."

And Ambryn did see from the tilt of Martine's head that she had lost none of that old confidence. Ambryn had seduced her, but now it seemed that seduction wasn't power, not the way she had thought.

"So why did you think I was here?" Ambryn asked.

"Where else would you go? This is home, after all, isn't it?"

"There are things I need to know," Ambryn said.

"And you think the Chretiens might be able to help?" Martine said. "What is it?"

"The Chretiens. . . . Don't get too cocky, Martine. It is still my family, after all."

"I'm sorry." Martine looked contrite, exactly as if the slip had been accidental. "Tell me what you need."

"Pyx. I don't know how, but I need to talk to him. To get into that ice cell of his somehow. I was aboard the *Argent*, you know. For quite some time. I had some communication with whatever was still alive within the placenta. I may know something of use to someone else, something I could trade."

"Maybe it's of use to all of us," Martine said. Ambryn didn't think that what she *needed* was any surprise to Martine. It never had been.

"How is it of use to all of us?" Ambryn leaned back against Martine, not looking at her. Martine's skin was hot, just as she remembered. Martine always felt like her bones were on fire.

"It's interesting that you should want to get in to see Pyx. As you may know, the Chretiens cooperated with the Ulanyi Pure Mind investigation into the *Argent* conspiracy. Only as far as they needed to, but it seemed to satisfy the Pure Mind investigators. But the main thing is, as a consequence of cooperation, the Chretiens have won the right to Pyx's child—if there is one as a consequence of his execution. It's just that someone has to go and . . . get it."

Ambryn felt a chill, as if that damn ice asteroid was resting right on the back of her neck. "And you think that I can recover the new embryo?"

Martine shrugged, as if the matter were not really of any importance. "You always were Pyx's favorite, Ambryn. It would require his cooperation too. We can get you up there. That is, if you still think your questions are important."

Knowing it was stupid, knowing that there was nothing but trouble in it, Ambryn kissed Martine gently on her hard, dry lips. She could see the artery pulsing in Martine's throat. She seemed so fragile sometimes, this endlessly manipulative woman. If Ambryn hadn't requested to talk to Pyx, what way would Martine have found to maneuver her into stepping into Pyx's execution cell? The Chretien family needed her to do it. And Martine's main interest was now the Chretien family. Not Ambryn.

"My questions are still important," Ambryn said.

"Good." Martine's quick fingers undid Ambryn's long hair so that it fell over both of them.

Eleven

1

"The first thing is inventing the demand,'' Martyshka told Elward. ''Without, of course, seeming to do so.''

''Got it,'' Elward said. The pale globe of Luna was visible through a porthole. He'd gotten so used to the interior of the *Imhotep* that he had at first thought that its light was some sort of condensation on the glass. ''I can do the mysterious stranger role, sure. Let's see: I got secret knowledge, but I'm a bit of a natural, innocent, you know, so I give stuff away without really realizing it, and smarter people take advantage of me.''

Martyshka inclined her head, impressed. ''Ambryn said you were a smart one.''

For some reason, that pleased him. ''She had time to talk?''

''Really, Elward. That was pretty much all we did.''

''Huh. Doesn't sound like Ambryn.''

''I don't think you know Ambryn Chretien at all.'' Martyshka smiled so it did not seem like a rebuke, which wrinkled up her monkey face.

''Maybe not. Do you miss her?'' Elward been on this tub long enough to be able to ask personal questions like that. He kind of liked it.

"Yes. Do you find that odd?"

Elward thought about it. "You know . . . no, I don't." Ambryn and Soph must have fought after they left the *Argent*. He couldn't see how they wouldn't have. "Do you want to find her again?"

"Yes. You do too."

"No, I . . . well, what if I do?"

"We can reach some kind of arrangement."

The construction monkeys had achieved their mission on Mercury and were en route to the circum-Lunar asteroids, but they had decided to poke around the old *Argent* for a while to see what information they could pick up. Ambryn seemed to have gotten Martyshka interested in that tedious subject. What they had picked up was Elward. Despite the fact that it meant he was alive, he still felt regret at the end of his personal kingdom. No other place would ever be so full of meaning for him.

An environmental globe floated up between them. It glowed in the darkness and cast soft shadows across the equipment-laden walls.

Over a thousand of these globes had been buried in a mass of waste out beyond the base of the Gun, remains of the first period of human investigation of the Gunners and their structure. The current much shrunken population of the human colony had long ago forgotten the entertainments of earlier generations.

The *Imhotep* had bid unrealistically low for the rebuilding contract, because historical research had revealed the presence of this obsolete technology. And obsolete technology, reincarnated as fashion, was, as Elward had learned, the main income source for the crew of the *Imhotep*. In fact, it had made them rich and enabled them to indulge in their own expensive hobbies. Living in free fall was never cheap in the first place. To rebuild one's living space on a regular basis took massive resources.

Restoring the globes to some semblance of function had been the crew's hobby on the voyage from Mercury to Luna. The high-intensity sun in the center of each globe had usually ceased to function or had shifted frequency. The living creatures inside had died, gone into dormant states, or shifted populations into scavenging regimes. The construction monkeys had found the globes just at the declining knee in the curve. A few more decades and most of the life in them would have been beyond recovery.

As it was, about half of the globes had had irrecoverable ecological collapses. Restoring the central suns had been the first order of business. After that, the dead globes had been sterilized and reseeded with spores and eggs from a variety of sources, many of them Venusian and thus of dubious ancestry. Just as a result of statistics, some of the globes had to contain largely Probe-origin ecologies: mysterious duplicates of Earth biologies by alien agencies.

Elward caught the floating globe and looked into it. A swimming bug spread out its wing covers so that a batlike shadow was cast out onto the globe's surface. Snails kept greedy algae from covering the sun and absconding with all of its photons for their own chloroplasts.

"This is a bit of a speculative enterprise," Martyshka said. "A little different than our usual line. Our last shipment for the MeshMatrix Krystal passé-tech market was a line of combat figurines, made of stacks of metal disks held together by superconducting magnets. The defective movements of the magnetic fields were a difficult-to-repair problem and engaged our customers' attention for a long time."

He'd help Martyshka out with Ambryn. Hell, he wouldn't mind seeing that long-fingernailed little clothes horse again himself. But what he was really after was Tiber—and through him, Soph. He didn't understand the guy—and he knew Soph never would—unless he got down into Tiber's grimy past and looked himself. Tiber had spent an important part of his life in MeshMatrix Krystal. Elward had lost all the anchors in his life, so Tiber's past was as good a place to start looking for some as any. Eventually, he'd find Soph again. She'd end up there too, he was sure of it, looking for the same thing. He hoped by the time he saw her again, he'd have something to offer.

The light from the globe glowed green and yellow on Martyshka's face. Seaweed waved, tiny fish with vivid red stripes darted between reaching fingers of coral.

"We have too many globes with us," Martyshka said. "If

we shipped them in from the *Imhotep*, we would drown our own market. We must first stimulate those desperate to gain status by their originality. Our little combat scenarios are no doubt out of fashion by now, played with by the little brothers of those who originally introduced them into MMK society. So they are looking for something else. Something new. But if they know how many globes we hold in reserve, they'll stay away. Part of the pleasure is the rarity. So the new product has to come in an unexpected guise."

"And I can provide it to them." Elward still wasn't sure if he bought the idea.

"That's right. The mysterious traveler. It would help if someone assaulted you and stole the one that you carry. . . ."

"Sure. I'll try to work that out. Maybe if they killed me, it would be even more convincing."

"Reality is not convincing," Martyshka said. "Artifice is convincing."

Elward's destination aboard MMK was a small eatery. Flaring grow lights permitted a dense growth of glossy leaves. Above, bare trunks continued upward until another cluster of lights marked some other enterprise. The actual rock ceiling was high above. In between was darkness and mesh-sided storage platforms. Elward slid into a vacant seat in the restaurant and slung his bag of globes onto the table in front of him.

Laughing groups sat among the seeping leaves and hanging orchids, sipping drinks out of high cups made of bamboo segments. He heard discussions, arguments, a woman's tears, clanking plates, the rumble of piping . . . there. The sliding sound of metal on metal and small, precise impacts. Martyshka had turned on a combat figure for him aboard the *Imhotep* so that he could identify it, and his ears had been sifting for the sound.

Elward's waiter invited him into the back to examine the restaurant's still. A fermented extract from a specialized bamboo was vacuum-distilled, then aged in swollen bamboo casks.

"It's good," another patron, a balding man with long,

nervous fingers, said. "I haven't gone blind, at least." He squinted and stumbled into a chair.

"Nice, Praeger," the waiter said, snapping a cloth. "We're trying to build a market."

"No, really," Praeger said. "Vacuum distilling's safer than heat. No toxic fractions cracking off the still. And it's not as if there's any shortage of vacuum."

"Looks like there are a lot of fans," Elward said, examining the list of testimonials.

"Deservedly. Really."

Elward got a bamboo glass full of the house rum, mixed with fruit juice. He and Praeger chatted, and it turned out that Praeger was a member of the passé-tech posse that hung out here and invited him back into their private area to continue drinking. He was intrigued by Elward's mysterious burden, which Elward had been careful to say nothing about.

Toxic spills of lubricant and fuel had poisoned the plant growth, and the club room was surrounded by dried branches, some of them with ends idly whittled into dangerous spikes. Machinery that would have been better off in some sealed area lay piled in the corners. A young man and woman, both with long hair clipped back with packing straps, desultorily played a game on the table.

Their fighting figures stalked across their field of combat, a scarred metal plate, their feet clicking down with each step. Despite himself, Elward found himself interested in the movement of the figures, which were made of stacked metal disks held together by magnetic fields.

They had been popular more than seventy years before on a series of asteroid ecocysts in the Belt, as well as Deimos and Phobos. They had worn versions of historical armor, and, at the height of their craze, deadly serious combat contests had determined distributions of water and oxygen. Then their popularity had fallen off, many of their superconducting coils reused for other purposes and the rest tossed out into those bee-swarm orbital dumps that made approaches to old ecocysts so dangerous.

This particular passé-tech trend had started on MMK itself when a ship construction contractor had brought back a load of the old devices to be recycled. The passé-tech posse had gone through the pile of discards and rebuilt three complete sets of the combat figures, one of which was later found to be mismatched, to the owner's dismay—and loss of status.

But now the wheel of lifetrend had turned, and the devices were losing popularity again. No crowd gathered around the two combatants, shouting encouragement and making keen judgments about technology and technique. The devices that stood in combative attitudes along the walls had pollen sifted across their shoulders.

Martyshka had picked her marketing moment superbly.

Elward lay a dust-fused lump on the table. After repairing them, the construction monkeys had restored the globes to their appearance when excavated.

"Hey," he said. "You guys have tools, right?"

Praeger frowned. "What the hell is that thing? A geode?"

"Not from Earth, I don't think. Mercury, the guy said. No geodes there."

"What, then?" Praeger waved a hand at the other two globes in Elward's mesh sack. "You carry them to keep from floating away? You're Venusian, right?"

"Yeah." Elward had been careful to emphasize his flat, yokelish accent. "No geodes on Venus either, unless the Probe dropped them. Maybe they're Gunner eggs or something."

"So where did you get these things?" Praeger was impatient.

"As I understand it, there was an excavation at the base of the big Gun. . . ." He told an edited version of how the globes had actually turned up, mentioning neither the *Imhotep* nor how many globes there were. "I ran into a Martian. He'd picked them up at some kind of junk sale, brought them along. But he was out of money and needed to get back home."

"So you bought them without checking to see what they were?"

"Sure. That's how I got them so cheap. He didn't know what he had, so why should I let him in on it? Did you say you had tools?"

"So what *did* he have?"

"Let's see."

Elward sat and dissected off the coating of fused Mercurian dust. Praeger, with nervous hands, produced a vacuum device that scoured the dust off the table as soon as it appeared. A few of the rest of the posse gathered around to see what emerged as the dust fell away.

The second globe Elward excavated was, deliberately, one that did not work. The first one lay on the table next to him, glowing mysteriously, fish and crustaceans swirling, and seemed to spell out messages to someone intelligent enough to perceive them. This second one was still dark, the glass sphere encrusted inside with encapsulated organisms, the fluid dull with spores and decay products. Despite the cleanness of the environmental sphere's design, with its delicate decorations of spun bronze, the globe looked like a hunk of waste, something excreted by a space-going alien.

He looked at it in irritation. "I got taken. It's just a piece of junk."

Praeger looked up from his intent investigation of the functional globe. His gaze was distant. He was getting drawn in.

"Let me see it."

"Sure," Elward said. He examined the globe more closely. "Maybe it just needs a good shake."

He held it up, as if ready to rap it on the table edge, but let Praeger snatch it from his hands.

"I'm not really here for this stuff," Elward said. "I'm looking for an old friend. He's probably gone now, but I want to pick up his trail."

"Who?" Praeger had clipped on a monocular viewer with a sharp beam of white light. The gold head brace rested in his thinning hair like a crown.

"Guy name of Tiber. He was kind of notorious around here for a while, I understand."

"Hmm." Praeger was unimpressed. "I've heard the name. Old stuff."

"Pretty old." Elward had hoped for this. It wasn't as if everyone in the Solar System was obsessed with the poor guy. "But still important to me."

"What can you tell me about him?" Praeger said.

"He worked food service, diners, that kind of thing. Liked to cook small-time. He was kind of odd-looking, though." He described Tiber.

A light glowed inside the globe and grew brighter. Others of the passé-tech posse gathered around, their old fighting machines momentarily forgotten. After getting a gesture of permission from Elward, they started excavating the third globe. That one, Martyshka had made sure, was even harder and more interesting to fix.

"I think I may have something for you," Praeger unclipped his viewer and turned off its light. "At least I know who to contact to find out."

His eyes glowed as he looked at the globe. It looked like Martyshka had her first customer ready to buy.

2

High above Soph's head, ice hung in curtains. A species of cold-loving bat had dug colonies into the ice and hunted up through cracks into lower-gravity areas. Around her spread wide leaves, shining dark green beneath a waxy cuticle that protected them against the bone-chilling air.

Beyond stood thick stands of pump bamboo, each stalk as big around as Soph's waist. Their vestigial leaves did little to provide the plants with energy from the light that flared down between dangling ice sheets. Nutritive fluid flowed from generators below.

Pump bamboo had been developed on Venus but had proved useful anywhere adaptable water-supply systems were necessary. It sprouted in response to demand and died away when demand disappeared. This species could grow through the ice layers that divided up MMK's cold pole, and each one carrying a different osmolality of solute-containing water, tugging along osmotic and evaporative pressure gradients. They kept the cold pole's entire water-zone system in balance. Far from being the solid chunk of ice it appeared from space, the Halo was a constantly changing organism.

But this bamboo stand had developed other functions. Soph saw makeshift structures built on platforms dug into the smooth green trunks. Plastic sheet shelters spilled water condensation and left icicles dangling from the platform edges.

Faces peered out of the shelters, entertainment screens glowing blue behind them. Someone slid down a stripped trunk and ran off into the ground mist. A dependent ecology of mosses and gigantic fungi grew on the substrate of bat guano and human by-products.

"There's a system here, and you got to understand it."

The three people who emerged from the bamboo colony wore regalia of gold foil from some ancient planetary probe. The big woman clearly dominated the two skinny men. The fiberglass in the men's quilted cloaks dug through the poorly stitched seams and left welts on their skin. They wore bat-fur hoods with the wings crossed over their foreheads.

The woman disdained such external insulation. Her loose bra barely restrained her vast breasts, and her pink flesh sagged over her blue-fur bikini bottoms. A skin-covered blood warmer hung below the bra like a failed third breast, its glowing power indicator a radioactive nipple. With that and the closed-cell foam modifications to her fat layers, she could sleep naked on ice. In fact, she did look red-eyed and grumpy, as if just woken up. Icicles clung to the ends of her stringy red hair.

"It's a good system, and it works." The woman spoke carefully, as if continuing an argument.

"I'm sure it does," Soph said. "But I'm here to see Hlobane."

"Hlobane?" The woman drew herself up, as if Soph had uttered an obscenity. The two men chortled.

"That's right."

"No one comes to see him. He's in internal exile."

"I still want to see him," Soph said.

The big woman glowered at her suspiciously. "Is something up? Are they finally over this hijacking thing upstairs?"

"I can tell you this," Soph said. "In a bit, everything's going to get wound up, one way or another."

"That's just a way of saying nothing at all."

Soph spread her hands in apology. "Maybe Hlobane can tell you something—after I've talked to him."

"I have half a mind to label you labor pool, lady. Assign you a tent out at the edge of town, let you wait for a bamboo-cleaning assignment."

There was no way Soph could get out of here. She wondered how many other people with legitimate business appointments ended up as indentured servants aboard MeshMatrix Krystal. It seemed an inefficient way of filling labor applications, but it had the merit of being completely arbitrary. They must occasionally have ended up with a valuable employee indeed.

She examined the men facing her. She could take them—easily. They relied on the threat of the club but clearly had no idea of how to really use them. Their pale guts were wide open.

The big woman grinned, seeing her thoughts. "No need to get fancy. Let's haul you down to poor Hlobane. He lives right on the outer rim of the Halo, you know. No one ever talks to him any more. He'll be happy of the company."

"The anchors," Soph said, staring out at vacuum, the gleaming bulk of MeshMatrix Krystal above. Hlobane's little house hung straight off the icy ecocyst surface on long cables. "Just in ice? They can't be as precarious as they look."

"I'm making a political point here." The big man in the center of the room continued to strap on his pangolin-plated armor. "I have to. They're exactly as precarious as they look."

"So this isn't exile, Hlobane? It's personal choice?"

"Let's just say that making it look like choice keeps me happy. Is that all right with you?"

Hlobane's receding hair revealed a gleaming ebony forehead. His blocky jaw rested on his chest like one boulder set on top of another. He'd cooked lunch for Soph, and it had been excellent. He'd made it all himself from expensive raw ingredients. She hadn't had such a pleasant lunch since Tiber had cooked for them back at Ripi's. Soph was startled to find herself looking back at that place nostalgically.

"Tiber would be sorry to see the consequences of his actions," Soph said. "I'm sure he never meant for you to be hurt."

That made Hlobane smile. "Is that your way of saying that you're sorry you insulted me? The last time I saw him, Tiber barely recognized me. He was possessed, driven. So are you. I can see it. That's a loss of free will, no matter what it gets you. You should look into it."

Hlobane's cabin hung down amid the gigantic ice stalactites, its tethering cables sunk into the ice. The stalactites, products of generations of venting and freezing, internal melting, and creeping extrusions of experimental high-pressure ice composites, were unpredictable structures. In fact . . . Soph stood on tiptoes and looked down over a polished metal sill. A cable anchor, pulled free, dangled straight down below them, its mesh catching the light, growing, then falling again into darkness as the ecocyst rotated.

"The last time you saw him . . ." Soph said. "What was the first time?"

"Let me ask you a question." Hlobane snapped on padded wrist guards. "What was the last time *you* saw Tiber?"

"Aboard the *Argent*," she said.

Hlobane was emphatically silent.

There was no way to get information without giving it. "He'd attempted suicide," Soph said. "Or something that looked a lot like it. His motives were ambiguous, but he was going to survive. He didn't do himself any serious damage. Physical damage, at any rate."

"Oh, Tiber." Tiber had said that Hlobane had protected him. The concern in Hlobane's eyes was obvious. "That urge to self-destruction wasn't there when I first met him. But after . . . when he started his work on the *Argent*, I could see it. It had come to the surface." He picked up a gigantic compound bow.

"What the hell is that?" Soph said.

"My hobby. I find it relaxing, and it impresses the Halo dwellers. They're the future of MMK, you know. Tough. Like Livilla, the three-breasted woman who brought you down here. She was a criminal when I hired her. Fleeing something . . . it doesn't matter what. But she's moving up. She's someone to watch. So I advise her. It's my only hope. I've been out of the loop since the *Argent* disappeared from its construction bay. Tiber was mine. I'd produced him. I was responsible.'' Hlobane nocked a long metal arrow that looked like a primitive rocket, with fins that were mesh in transparent matrix.

''How did you . . . produce him?'' Soph asked.

''I found Tiber hanging in Prisoner Maintenance, in the core of the Rock. It was a service MMK ran for the Terrans during the Earth–Mars War. We provided maintenance for storing Martian POWs until they could be repatriated. . . . Are you wondering what I'm doing?''

Soph now saw that he had thick padding painted with a ringed target on the back of his ornate helmet. ''Yes, in fact.''

''Don't worry about my losing the thread of my account. I've thought about it often enough. Come here for a moment. Look through this eyepiece.''

It was just a refractive circle in the flexible clear wall. Above, Hlobane's circular hanging cabin had a pitched roof with eaves, just like any mountain dwelling on Earth. Precipitation came from the ice ecocyst above, and the roof, with its grooves, spilled it off so that it did not accumulate.

She pushed her eye against the ocular. For a long moment, nothing was clear. It looked like an endoscopic view of the lumen of some impossibly elongated human organ, extending away infinitely between dangling secretory projections. The image curved strangely, obviously heavily processed, and she couldn't figure out what it represented.

''But Tiber, for some reason, had never been repatriated,'' Hlobane said. ''No one had any claims on him. There were a few of those in there, even a couple of years after the war was over. I checked through the bodies that were left over, in preparation for clearing it out, just sending them back, even if it meant they would just be unemployables back on Mars. Here. I'll increase the magnification.''

The eyepiece's focal plane hurtled forward. She traveled between what she now realized were ice stalactites. The image, somehow, curved around the surface of MMK. And there, ahead, a quirky high-peaked cabin with transparent walls and, within, the backs of two people, who stood peering into an optical device.

"All the way around the universe," she said. "Just like they told us at school. Infinite but bounded. But how—?"

"Processed image, integrated up from cameras. I just wanted to show you the route."

"The route?"

"Of my arrows. MMK has a hefty magnetic field, of course, to hold off the charged particles spiralling through Earth's magnetic field. This arrow has its own field. If I fire it properly, it curves around the ecocyst and"—he slapped the back of his helmet—"hits me right here."

"That's very strange, Hlobane."

He seemed hurt. "Use your imagination. Useful practice for military encounters around black holes, for one thing. But it's a game. Just a game."

He pulled back on the huge bow and fired. The arrow streaked right through the flexible wall and disappeared.

"But in Tiber's head, I detected what looked like top-secret military tech codes. Now, the war was long over, but military work often leads to civilian development later. I figured that some information about Martian military technology could give us hints about postwar Martian investment possibilities."

Hlobane stood stock-still. His head jerked forward, then snapped back. A long arrow now extended from the back of his head. Not a bull's-eye but quite impressive. Soph wondered if he knew how dumb he now looked. He nocked another arrow, fired, then grimaced.

"Better get down," he said. "Now. Angle's a little off."

Soph dropped to the floor.

Peering over his shoulder, Hlobane continued. "But I was completely wrong. The codes—if that's what they were—had nothing behind them. Tiber had no knowledge whatsoever of Martian military affairs and couldn't even remember the name of the warship on which he had supposedly been serving. In fact, aside from his official category of POW, there was no evidence he had ever served in the Martian military."

The misaimed arrow ripped through the cabin with a pop and whizzed just above Soph's head. Hlobane watched its course back out the other wall and winced.

"Right into a stalactite. Melted in. I'll have to climb out there to get it. You a climber?"

"Not on your life."

Hlobane sighed. "Surface control gets pissed if I leave those things hanging around. Interferes with the sensing system. Like a speck in MMK's eye."

"I'm not climbing out there to get it for you, Hlobane." Soph stood back up.

He fired the next arrow without even seeming to aim. Soph flinched, then stood absolutely still, looking at him.

"So you had to release him into the free-labor pool once he proved useless?" Soph said.

A tiny thwock, and the arrow joined the other sticking out of the back of Hlobane's head.

"Not at base level. He had a marketable skill: he could cook."

Soph looked back at the elaborate kitchen in which Hlobane had made her lunch. "You taught him."

Hlobane folded up the giant bow. "Yes, I did. But he was a quick study. It was all a revelation to him. He'd never eaten anything not extruded. And he turned out to be quite good at it. Good enough to get a job in a diner near the construction bays. I used to visit him there. He was happy. It was the first place he'd ever fit into where his obsessions, whatever they were, didn't matter."

"He had a relapse," Soph said. "Short-order cooks don't hijack interplanetary spacecraft."

"They don't keep high office in MMK either." Hlobane was acridly amused at himself.

"So what happened to him?"

"I don't know." Hlobane sat down, turned away from her. "One day he was happy at his work, his new life. The next, he needed to do something. He was no longer his own man. Suddenly he moved into the *Argent* project, with knowledge that had nothing to do with Martian military secrets. And it was for someone else. He never said, but I could tell, just by looking into his eyes. He did it all for someone else."

Sukh. Soph knew that perfectly well. For some reason, after being independent, having escaped her domination, Tiber had returned to it.

"What *happened*?" she said.

"He was involved in the conspiracy to create an independent platform for raising Ulanyi embryos. What could he have known about that? But it was a high-level MeshMatrix Krystal plan, in cooperation with certain forces on Earth: the Gregsons, others. . . . He was advised by a psychotic Ulanyi embryo—Pyx. I don't think they've killed him yet, but it's just a matter of time. But Tiber double-crossed them too in the end and took off with the ship. He'd been paid off by the Ulanyi Pure Mind group. There's a struggling Ulanyi colony in the Belt, and they send agitators in. Executioners too, which even human-friendly Ulanyi use for enforcement. They breed them tough out there, without humans to calm them down.

"The hijacking was the last straw for my career. Someone had to be blamed, and I was it. I had brought Tiber into MMK, so I was responsible."

"So you won't tell me what happened to Tiber at that diner?" Soph said.

"I can't. I don't know."

She sensed that something vicious had happened to Tiber there at his comfortable cook's job, and the result had been the reactivation of his Sukh-driven passion, one that, momentarily at least, he had forgotten. But Hlobane had no interest in finding out how far from protecting his friend he had really been. He had his own pain.

"Don't be angry with me." Hlobane sat hunched over. "There's nothing to be discovered there. But Tiber's obsessions lay farther back in his past. He never talked about it. But I think I know someone who can tell you a little more about it."

"Who?"

"Commander Riemann-Vesper. She commanded the *Vesper*, the Terran spacecraft that recovered Tiber from the wreckage of the Martian warship on which he had served."

Soph thought about a long journey down to Earth in pursuit of some bare testimony about the mechanics of rescuing someone from a wrecked spacecraft and repressed a sigh. "Where is she?"

"We all have our obsessions. Commander Riemann-

Vesper has retired to the empty tunnels of Prisoner Maintenance, deep in the Rock. Right where Tiber was kept." Still hunched over, he scribbled on a datacard. "I don't have much influence right now, but no one cares about that place. This should get you in. Livilla will show you the way."

MeshMatrix Krystal had not been built. Like the rest of the circum-Lunars of the Diadem, it had been hauled into orbit with large boosters, set to spinning, and then carved out inside in a manner not substantially different than primitive mining. The Probe arrived on Venus early in MeshMatrix Krystal's existence, and in the chaos following that revelation, the careful future mapped out for it had been forgotten. When the asteroid had been reoccupied, by humans no longer convinced that a virgin universe lay at their fingertips, development had been chaotic, and the tunneling that underlay the Rock's surface now resembled the mad scribbling of wood worms.

Prisoner Maintenance occupied the Rock's axis. Now that the prisoners were gone, it was used to store null-g equipment. Even with that, it was mostly empty.

Livilla led Soph to the abandoned facility. She had said almost nothing for the entire convoluted path upward from the ice-filled reception area. As a rendezvous location, she just gave Soph a string of corridor designations, as if their meeting place was to be nothing more than a coordinate point, and then left her to her business. Livilla had been desperately eager to get to another engagement. Now Soph pulled her way through Prisoner Maintenance, looking at a location indicator Hlobane had given her.

Lights came on around her, showing the endless four-unit bays to either side and above and below. During its peak, just as the end of the Earth–Mars War was being negotiated, the place had held thousands of Martian prisoners in groups of four, suspended in these bays, their intestines deactivated, their brains on hold, their skins kept moist in the warm humidity. Most ransomed prisoners suffered from serious fungal infections.

Sometimes, Soph knew, prolonged imprisonment had bizarre hormonal effects, leading to schizoid psychoses, acromegaly, deforming benign tumors, and an irresistible sense of having spoken with God. The dark chambers of Prisoner Maintenance were the Martian equivalent of the deserts of Judea and Arabia, as far as creating new religious movements went.

Tiber had hung in here way past spec time, and it was not impossible that bored Prisoner Maintenance employees had played hormonal games with their only remaining toy. The origins of most of his mystery could lie, prosaically, here in this brain-dead prison case.

Her wrist indicator flashed. Soph slowed.

For a moment, Soph thought that the lighted bay was filled with nothing but hair. Burnt-butter hair, extravagantly curled, its sulfur bonds rearranged into complex structures, felted here, standing out in stiff sprays there.

"Commander Riemann-Vesper?" Soph said uncertainly.

Two remotely powered waldoes emerged from the hair like fish from a mass of seaweed, moving it aside with a hissing of air jets. A face slowly appeared in the depths. It was tiny and pure white, a porcelain doll's face. Blue eyes were revealed as eyelashes as improbably long as the hair drifted open.

"I hold that rank and had the honor to command the *Vesper*." The voice came from a speaker mounted on the wall. It clattered with harsh overtones, like commands echoing down the corridors of a ship under fire.

"I'm glad you consented to speak with me," Soph said.

"It's a subject on which I have been waiting to speak."

The doll face's heavy-lashed lids were now fully open. The eyes behind them were real, human, and Soph could just see crinkles of skin around them.

More waldoes came into view as the hair drew away to the sides, forming a dramatic curtain hang, with the doll figure as the star of the stage. Beneath the face was a shrunken but still recognizably human body. False stuffed arms in elaborate padded sleeves embroidered with gold thread crossed in front of the breasts. Where the legs should have been was nothing but a satin curve beaded with pearls, like a giant pincushion. Riemann-Vesper looked like a portrait of Queen Elizabeth I as reimagined for a doll's theater.

Clamps held luggage to the walls. Several of the bags bent in right angles, as if they contained some odd musical instrument. Two pairs, one larger than the other. For some reason, Soph's eyes kept straying to them.

"Demyelination," Commander Riemann-Vesper said. "The curse of direct-control linkups. Don't know where it first came from, but it spread operator to operator. This one was subviral, so subviral it was barely a protein. A nice example of minimal-length information coding. I think they study it in signal school now. It ate the myelin right off our nerves and increased the axonal noise level until any real signals got swamped. Our limbs stopped working as the muscles ceased to understand what they were being told. You imagine them yelling, 'What? What? I can't hear you over that *goddam racket*!' "

A hail of tiny hissing waldoes transferred momentum by bouncing off Riemann-Vesper's shoulders and pushed her toward Soph. Something was wrong with the commander's movement programs. It should have taken her will to move and translated it into smooth remote waldo movements that had the correct effect. Soph thought she should go in for maintenance.

"How did you find Tiber?" Soph asked after a period of silence. Perhaps Riemann-Vesper had forgotten why she was here and thought she had come to ask about neurodegenerative diseases among Earth–Mars War veterans.

"I was getting to that," Commander Riemann-Vesper said with some asperity. "I just want you to understand. Don't just focus on the target. See what's around it, what it's attached to."

"Sorry."

Waldoes turned Riemann-Vesper until her padded pincushion bottom rose up out of her swirling hair.

"You know," she said. "When your limbs stop working, you really don't need to have them connected to you, though you might still want them around."

Soph cursed herself. She'd broken protocol, and now the woman was going to punish her by giving her more irrelevant information. Well, that was what she deserved.

"I had them removed. Legs, arms too. And I had good

legs, don't think I didn't.'' Riemann-Vesper lowered her voice. ''I keep them toned. The skin on them is really very nice. Soft. Particularly the inner thighs. I can see why people used to pay attention to them.''

''You still keep them?'' Soph couldn't have said why that startled her.

''Why, sure I do. Not too much trouble to maintain, after all, just some stimulation to keep the muscles in shape, some glucose perfusion. . . . I never thought I'd get to like my own limbs so much. I never saw them the right way. They were mine, connected to me. Now, sometimes, I just wrap my legs around me, knees just under my breasts. Then the arms touch me, hold me. I still have a lot of feeling in parts of my skin. It's like nothing I ever imagined.''

Her real eyes closed, but the doll's eyes remained open, so Soph found herself looking at the old woman's wrinkled lids and the REM flicker of bulging corneas beneath them.

The eyes snapped open. ''It happened in the second year of the war, during the Hidalgo operation. It's absurd. We range all through space, but we cling to those little pebbles, as if they were the only thing that was real. But the fight for 944 Hidalgo was something. Oh, you know it? It wasn't really one of the big—''

''My son,'' Soph said when her throat had opened again. ''Stephan. He was in a Terran attack cluster near that asteroid.'' Doing nothing, according to him. They'd hunkered down, screened by some rock and ice, and waited things out. He'd spent his time floating on a tether, listening for Jove.

''The wing near Jupiter's Leading Trojans, sure. The orbit of 944 Hidalgo has a honking big eccentricity and tilts way out of the ecliptic besides, but at that point it was passing near the orbit of Jupiter. It was a quite a battle, Miss. . . . I've forgotten your name. Mrs. Stephan's mother, I guess they used to call you.''

It was a stab right to her heart. ''That's what they used to call me. What happened at Hidalgo?''

''The *Vesper* was screening flank, above the ecliptic. It was one of those stupid things. There had been some kind of chance encounter—meaningless, really—but vessels kept getting sucked in. Nothing decisive occurred, of course.

Nothing decisive happened during that entire war. It was just a gigantic potlatch, an attempt to show the aliens in the System how many spaceships humans could destroy for no reason whatsoever. Anyway, it was almost all over when we found a partially destroyed Martian support vessel, named the *Greatorex*.

"The *Greatorex* had been lost on recon in those Trojans of yours, weeks before. Supposedly, some surviving crew member reactivated the drives but died before they got to base. But its velocity relative to Hidalgo was zero. That didn't fit the scenario."

Soph remained silent.

"I decided to board and investigate. Areas of the *Greatorex* that had not been completely destroyed were sargassos of shattered equipment, severed limbs, shredded clothing. You swam through them, pushing aside frozen body parts. But it was the first place any of us had been outside of the *Vesper* for a good year. We wanted to get out and explore. We wanted to make a discovery. . . . We did. One of my crew felt a vibration through his gauntlet. It seemed that someone was still alive in a sealed space and was pounding to be let out. It was a thrilling moment. We quickly built a rescue airlock, cut through the bulkhead, and pulled him into a sealed transport to take aboard the *Vesper*. Your friend Tiber."

"He was a crewman?" Soph asked. "Aboard the *Greatorex*?"

"We found him aboard." The waldoes rotated Commander Riemann-Vesper back and forth in a total body head shake. "He was an odd-looking man, you know. We were all startled by it. Swollen facial bones, fingers of a frog. How *did* he enter the Martian military with such an obvious glandular disorder?" So much for Soph's theory that his glandular abnormalities had originated in MMK Prisoner Maintenance. "In retrospect—and believe me, I have a lot of retrospect—perhaps there was evidence that the airtight space in which we found him had been hastily repaired and refilled with air, that it was not just coincidence. But we weren't looking for anything like that. It may be just my imagination. We did not have time for further investigation. We detected a warship in the vicinity.''

Back to the war stories. ''I hope you gave the Martians hell,'' Soph said.

Riemann-Vesper's hair rustled as the waldoes dug through it. And a recurrent knock somewhere in one of the cases sounded like something trying to get out.

''It wasn't a Martian warship,'' Riemann-Vesper said. ''And it certainly wasn't one of ours.''

''What?''

''I was suspicious, even at the time. The vessel's traces did not match Martian design specs. Later, when the glorious peace was concluded, I made an information request under treaty provisions. At the time we rescued Tiber, after the conclusion of the Hidalgo broil, there was no Martian vessel for many AUs in any direction.''

''The Martian government could have been keeping secrets,'' Soph said. ''They do that, you know. They wouldn't give them all up just because they'd lost a war.''

''No, of course not. But I confirmed it with our intelligence. It took me some time, understand. You don't give up all your secrets because you've won a war either. All Martian vessels were accounted for, and none were near our volume.

''He infected us,'' Riemann-Vesper said with sudden viciousness. ''Tiber was a biological booby trap, set for us. He was immune to the nerve disease, but he carried it with him. It was when we took him aboard that he achieved his purpose.''

''I have never heard of any such Martian project.''

''Now, Mrs. Stephan's mother, haven't we just concluded, with truly classical logic, that our Tiber was not Martian? Who would want to infect us? Find that mysterious vessel, and you have your answer.'' Limbs rustled in their cases, arms and legs waiting for Soph to leave so that they could caress their mistress. ''When you find out, kindly don't let me know. The answer would be of no use to me.''

Twelve

1

"Did you hear?" Praeger said. "Bina found a globe buried in a pile of abandoned shock struts up near the Halo ice face." He shook his head. "Who knows how long it had been lying around in there?"

Elward did. About two days. He'd been working his ass off, seeding globes in various out-of-the-way corners of the Rock. He'd even glued one into an elaborate stone sculpture in a MeshMatrix Krystal municipal park, where it looked like just another of the hero's cannonballs. He hoped that it would seem like it had been there for decades, ignored by everyone. Elward couldn't remember the last time he had had so much fun.

"You want to be out there, looking?" Elward asked. "Afraid of getting scooped?"

"Nah." That clearly *was* what worried Praeger, but he wasn't about to admit it. He poured more sweetener into his coffee. "I've done a little research. The globes were popular in the Caloris colony on Mercury, maybe a century ago. I think they went a little nuts when they couldn't figure out fact one about the Gunners and started creating their own worlds. It became an obsession." He tasted his coffee, pursed his lips, added a few crystals of bitterer. ''We'll have to find a way to get them direct.''

''Praeger,'' Elward said. He was starting to like the wizened little passé-tech freak, but he was impatient. ''Are we here for a reason?''

''The food's not good?''

Elward's plate now held only streaks of ostrich egg yolk and pressed meat loaf. ''The food's fine. That's not why I'm here.''

Behind the counter, catalytic heaters glowed at various temperatures. Cooks with insulation slopped casually onto their naked chests and arms moved through the rippling heat, turning meat slabs with impervious fingers.

The diner clung to a wall of rock in a vacuole in a low-g region of MMK. The opposite wall of the vast space, big enough to hold spacecraft, was ice, glowing blue from within. Here was the boundary between Rock and Halo. And above, toward the null-g axis, Elward could see spaceship parts migrating slowly toward the ship construction bays at the pole.

''Your friend Tiber,'' Praeger said. ''I've been doing a little research. He's long gone, not likely to come back.''

''Let me decide that,'' Elward said.

''Okay. At any rate, he was an odd one.''

Elward shrugged. ''The System's an odd place.''

''How long do you think I can keep giving you information without you telling me anything?''

''He was raised by one of those teaching systems with total sensory control. There may have been defects in the software. Reality doesn't mean the same thing to him as it does to most people.''

''Those things can build weird personalities,'' Praeger said, showing an odd enthusiasm. ''They alter the apparent laws of the universe at will. Think of the personalities they generate as artifacts. It might be worth looking into, as a hobby.''

''Difficult collectible,'' Elward said.

''Hey, there's always someone who points out why something is impossible.''

Elward looked at the glowing kitchen area. ''You say he worked here?''

''Yeah. For quite a while, it seems.''

''What happened to him?'' Elward asked.

Praeger looked uncomfortable. ''I'm not sure I've gotten it all clear.''

''Give me the raw stuff, Praeger. I can take it.''

Elward had allowed Praeger to buy his three globes, for much less than they would eventually be worth. Now Praeger felt guilty, and was willing to help Elward out in his quixotic search for his old friend. Tiber had apparently worked in this shipyard diner after arriving at MMK and before becoming a key figure on the *Argent* project.

''Is your friend all right?'' Praeger asked. ''Now, I mean?''

Elward thought of his last sight of Tiber, white-faced, unconscious, a self-inflicted wound in his side. ''Sure, far as I know.''

''Then I would suggest you leave him be.'' Praeger was earnest. ''Wherever he is. Let him keep his secrets.''

''Spill it, Praeger,'' Elward said. ''I think you owe me.''

Praeger sat hunched tightly for a long moment, then uncoiled. ''He was some kind of unrepatriated Martian POW,'' Praeger said. ''No one had ever reclaimed him. Is that why you're here?''

''I'm acting on behalf of his . . . family, yes.''

''Someone pulled him out of detention, eventually. But they didn't have any use for him or something, because they just dumped him out into the MMK free-labor pool. He ended up working here. He liked it, to all accounts.''

At the opposite end of the eating area, a massive, mostly naked woman was being sprayed by a waiter holding a giant silver nozzle above his head. The woman wore blue-fur bikini bottoms, her flesh slopping over. Did she really have three breasts? Elward couldn't make himself interested in the answer.

The spray froze when it hit the air and coated her body with frost. Her stringy red hair seemed to have snow on it. She kept her eyes closed, occasionally raising an arm to get the blessed cold into a hidden area.

Across the table from her, a young woman ate soup while reading a leather-covered book, and a little girl, her dark hair rebellious under a velvet cap that had worked partway loose from its anchorings, stuck out her tongue to catch the snowflakes that wandered away without landing on the big woman's bódy. Her bowl of soup steamed ignored in front of her.

Praeger noted Elward's interest. "Those Halo dwellers have gone too far in adapting to their environment. It was kind of a joke at first, but now it's become a little too real. I don't like it."

The woman was silver now, a saggy mountain covered in moonlit snow. The little girl, prodded by her mother, tried to eat her soup, but the spoon missed her mouth with the wonder of it. The mother wiped her daughter's mouth exasperatedly.

"Her." Praeger nodded at the big woman. "Livilla. Talk to her. I checked around, and she's the one. She knows what happened to your friend here. And she's willing to talk."

The woman's eyes glittered at Elward across the diner.

"She doesn't look too willing," Elward said.

"It's a need, then. She has something to say, and you're the one to hear it. Take advantage of it."

"Thanks, Praeger." Elward got up.

Praeger grabbed his hand. "I thought about not telling you, once I found out. But that didn't seem fair."

"It wouldn't have been. Good luck finding more of the globes."

The little girl and her mother bustled as they got up to leave. The girl gave the approaching Elward an unreadably significant look, then ducked down under the table. Livilla shifted to look at him and dropped a cascade of frost crystals.

The mother stood at the door, looking for her daughter, not worried yet. Elward had made it most of the way across the eating area when the girl popped up and threw a snowball. Its accuracy was impeccable, and it smacked him right on the side of the head. He slipped and fell on the slick floor.

The girl, appalled at the dramatic consequences, darted past him to her mother.

"You didn't . . . *touch* her, did you?" the mother asked.

"Yik." The girl glanced at Livilla. "No. I got it from the floor. Not from *her*."

The woman stepped over to Elward and hauled him to his feet, as if he was another of her children, causing trouble.

"Nice shot," he said.

Behind Mother, the girl smiled.

"You're all right?"

"He's all right," Livilla growled. "I can take care of him."

Her hand clamped onto Elward's wrist like a manacle. Elward had time for one last glance back at Praeger, who had returned his attention to getting the flavor balance of his coffee perfectly correct, and then he was hauled out of the diner into a corridor cold with ice. Mist swirled around their feet.

"You're Praeger's buddy?" Livilla said. "And you're curious. Everyone's curious these days. Fine. Let me show you Tiber's secret. You can tell me what you think of it. Don't spare my feelings, now."

2

"I thought everyone had forgotten me in here," said the guard, whose nameplate called him NICK PELHAM, as Ambryn floated uncomfortably in the security cube, being checked for potential escape gear. "It's been a long time since anyone's come to visit our state prisoner."

"Who was the last one?" Ambryn asked.

His face closed up. "That's a security matter."

"Fine. I hope you won't tell anyone else about me, then."

"Oh, certainly not." Pelham, startlingly, blushed. "You know, these search regs are ancient. Back from when we had tons of prisoners. Martian POWs, all that. Now there's nothing but Pyx, and he isn't long for this world. I should just let you in."

He didn't, of course. Instead, he watched carefully as the detection cube tested her, trying to get surveillance gear to betray itself. Images of the insides of Ambryn's body flashed on displays she couldn't see from where she floated, and she knew, from what Martine had told her, that he derived a sexual satisfaction from what he perceived. His breathing was audibly rougher.

He was a petty sexual criminal of some sort and had grown old in security service, never being granted the physical contact once so important to him. So he had transferred his need to his security data.

Martine had given Ambryn the emotional rundown, with what Ambryn had thought was a bit too much satisfaction. Still, Ambryn had secreted a few easily detectable security penetration aids on her person. She had to get Pyx's child back out again, and this was part of the deal—or so Martine had told her.

Things went as Martine had predicted. The alarms went off. Ambryn was forced to allow the insertion of deactivators, which scrambled the transducers hidden in her flesh, and the guard got his extremely attenuated satisfaction. Should Ambryn have felt soiled? After all, as far as Pelham's underlying emotions were concerned, he had just stripped and raped her.

Pelham turned to her, his pale eyes, she saw with surprise, gleaming with tears.

"Damn you," he said.

"Excuse me?"

"You think just because I . . ." He turned away, ostensibly to reexamine a screen. "I begged them to take it away altogether. The need. The memory of the things I've done. No, they said. You're a criminal. You need to be punished, not relieved. Besides, it makes you good at your job. It makes you pay attention. I thought I'd forgotten all about it."

"I'm sorry."

"Go," he said. "Go see that doomed creature and be damned."

"I don't have a lot of time," Livilla said. "I have to meet a party."

"Sure." Elward puffed vapor in the cold air. "So you knew Tiber. How?"

"At the diner. It used to be my favorite place to . . . pick up people."

They floated in a storage space near the Rock's axis. Mesh

held several large pieces of equipment against one wall. A layer of oily soot showed that it had been a long time since they'd been moved. Some part of the spacecraft business ground heavily behind rock. He could feel it grunting in the pit of his stomach.

"He worked there. A cook," Livilla said. "You know, I haven't been back here since." She looked around. "Brings back memories. We used to hang around that diner: me, Pelham, and Jig. It was a lighter time then. MMK was hopping, no one cared about things much. We'd spend late hours there. Mist came off the ice face, and sometimes you could see things in it, if you stared at it long enough.

"It was Jig that first got the idea. Jig . . . You know, those damn Egerians are crazy, the whole rock full of them. They're always bounty-hunting loose criminals. And you know, almost everything is a crime somewhere. They get a lot of work. But Jig had screwed up somehow and was on the run from her own people. Fat lot of good those fancy sharpened teeth did with the food she could afford here."

The chill that ran through Elward's body was almost erotic in its intensity. "Whatever happened to Jig?"

"Boy, we're full of questions, aren't we? After what we did to him, she joined up, got on the *Argent* team. Can you believe that? Pelham and I took it in the neck in the responsibility investigations after the *Argent* disappeared, as if we'd had something to do with it, and she took off with the ship."

So Jig had achieved the rank of Archon aboard the *Argent* and taken that as her identity, so thoroughly that Elward had never even learned her name. Even now he would continue to think of her as the Archon. He missed those sharp teeth.

"Tiber was a man with secrets," Livilla said. "Secrets he didn't know himself. You could see that. Oh, he was happy enough. Kind of dumb-looking, really. And there was something else about him. . . . We were tough then, working face-to-face enforcement, local persuasion, that kind of stuff. You get grated yourself, even when you're doing well. We weren't doing well. As I remember it, each of us had gotten some pounding that week. I had a new tooth trying to work its way into my jaw—I'd gotten the original kicked out by some Terran businessman's bodyguard."

"I've dealt with worse," he said.

She eyed him. "Maybe you have. Anyway, we were spoiling. And, like I said, there was something about him. You seek out the weakness, you do, when you're in a certain frame. He needed something, and we thought we could provide it. Crime's victim is not always unwilling. Sometimes he wants it. Needs it. So that it isn't really even crime at all."

"Bullshit," Elward said. "You're just an accessory after the fact. Part of the original crime."

"We brought him here. Why did we do it? It wasn't our way, not usually. Maybe the crime cried to be finished up—if that's the way you want to look at it. So we were its victims too—"

"Cut the crap. Just tell me what the fuck you did. You brought him here."

"We . . . hurt him. We tied him up, and we hurt him. But it was Pelham who went the rest of the way, I swear. Pelham always did. He raped Tiber, right up against this mesh."

Elward didn't know why, but somehow he had expected something more . . . transcendent. An imaginative crime. A drama. Instead . . . well, he'd been there himself. Crimes cried out to be completed, repeated endlessly, recycled and stale.

"And something happened to Tiber," he said.

Livilla grabbed his arms and pushed his face into the greasy mesh. "It all . . . woke something up inside him. Something he'd kept down. He kept saying 'I remember too much. It got stuck and I remember too much!' Pelham had a guilt fit, like he always did, and Jig and I hauled Tiber to a med center.

"After that, he wasn't the same. Something took him over. He left the diner. He had knowledge, specialized knowledge about those damn placentas they raise on Earth. Now tell me, how would he know anything at all about that? He was a goddam Martian POW, right? All they have on Mars is those greasy Gkh, and Martians don't seem to know anything about their own aliens. So where'd he learn all that stuff?"

"I don't know."

"Think a little, friend. I'm sure you know more than you think."

He did. He knew he never wanted to go through this again. He relaxed against the mesh, as if acquiescing. Livilla loosened her grip in response. Elward kicked her savagely in the stomach. She sailed free, fetching up against the opposite side of the space. He braced himself against another attack. None came.

Livilla was crying. "Shit," she said. "I wasn't jumping you. I don't do that for fun anymore. Just by way of work, and no one's paying me right now." She looked at him as if it was all his fault. "You know, Pelham's got a job now. Guard at an ice-storage facility for bad Ulanyi. Who knows what the hell Ulanyi have to do in order to be considered bad? There's only one in there now. One from Earth, named Pyx. He had something to do with Tiber too. Isn't that a hoot? All any of us does, now, gets us hooked right back up with Tiber. Our victim. Ruler of our fates. Pelham's still hot there, at his desk. But he can never do anything."

"I'm not interested in your stupid personal problems," Elward said, still breathing hard. He felt triumph. Not over her. Over himself. It had been that old Enforcement & Joy lockgrip, the one you put right on yourself, and he'd broken out of it. Maybe not everything had to happen over and over.

"Hlobane has promised me a place if he succeeds in gaining power in MMK," she said. "Is that what's left for me? A uniform, an office, a set of stuff to do?"

"If it's a good job," Elward said, "take it."

Her fat face was slack. "Good advice. So what do you want to know about?"

"Tell me about Pyx." Elward remembered Ambryn mentioning the name. It had something to do with her family. Some kind of cult thing.

Livilla floated helplessly in the air. "Pyx is about to die. That's set. He's almost dead as it is. But a bunch of Ulanyi worshippers is up from Earth to pick up the embryo he's implanted in the Executioner while the Executioner's been killing him. It's not only humans who mix this stuff up."

"Save the sexual philosophy." Elward had to admit he was enjoying pushing Livilla around. He knew it wouldn't last. Basically, she was mean. Some old guilt had weakened her, that was all. He had to use it for all it was worth before she hardened up again. "The Chretien family?"

"You think you know a lot, don't you? A representative from the family. Who's going to be screwed. Once the Executioner has a child, she won't abide by any deals. Those Earth people are so stupid. She'll take care of Pyx and then Miss Ambryn Chretien as a little extra snack." She gave Elward a sharp glance. "Ah, I thought you weren't just doing Ulanyi research for pure love of knowledge. You know her?"

"Never mind if I know her."

"Doesn't matter if you do. She's dead meat. Pelham might have helped her, but she was mean to him. Pelham's sensitive. Of course, there are other ways in and out of that cell. There always are. Ice sublimes, melts, reforms. The joy of the Halo. Someone could get in—if he wanted. But Pelham doesn't give a shit anymore. That girl, Ambryn, isn't getting out alive."

Elward took hold of Livilla. "Yes, she is."

3

"Pyx!" The ice walls amplified the fear in Ambryn's voice.

"Over here, mama. Over here."

The floor's protective padding had been stripped off by the obsessive passage of Pyx's sharp-clawed feet. Mist swirled around Ambryn's knees as she stepped over tangled hoses that raised their ridged backs out of the ice, heading for the chittering voice.

"Oh, too bad. Just who I want to see. Dear Ambryn. Dearest. Before I fuck and I die."

Pyx huddled in a pit he had torn in the floor and turned slowly around and around even as he talked. Stalks of pipe bamboo had been shredded under his claws and in response had grown large tumorous growths in a futile attempt to defend their structures.

"You could refuse," Ambryn said.

"Refuse to fuck? As if I would. Besides, it's too late.

Much too late. My lady has achieved her protective form. Now she will protect the community against her mate."

"She's supposed to defend your offspring," Ambryn said. She had heard of the Executioner form, but she had never seen one. Post-reproductive female Executioners were used by the Ulanyi for political enforcement.

"She will do that too. Did you realize that, dear Ambryn? She will. She will defend my child, which you would take away. Once she has done her job and killed me."

Ambryn felt fear and shame, both. Shame, because she really was here to take away Pyx's offspring. She was no different from the rest of the Chretiens. To them, an Egg was a tool for their own domination, and Pyx's condemnation and death an unfortunate setback that could be turned to advantage.

Fear, because she had not anticipated the fact that the Executioner would be the mother of Pyx's child, that it was this very reproduction that *made* her an Executioner. Would she really give the Egg up as agreed? Why should she?

"Help me, Pyx," she said. "Help me make the right decision."

"You're so stupid! You humans. How the hell do we let you into us the way we do? Ulanyi. Our minds are just fiction. Invented. You've got to show me I exist. Please, Ambryn. Don't leave me now. Leave me and I'll kill you. Wa!"

Ambryn remembered the wise and intelligent voice that had spoken to her from inside the Chretien family Egg. She did recognize some of the tones in this chittering creature. Ulanyi ended their lives with frantic sex-obsessed adolescence. She supposed that that made more sense than the human arrangement.

"If I'm here to provide spiritual solace, you have to help me," she said briskly. "Come out of that hole."

Until that moment, he had just been a knot of body segments and limbs. She almost gasped as he revealed himself. His body armor, remnants of his original Egg casing, shrunk and stuck by adhesion points onto his otherwise vulnerable body, was scarred and shattered by impacts.

"I'm ashamed of my sins too," he said.

Ambryn couldn't stand it anymore. "What the hell did you do, Pyx?"

"You mean, what did I find out?" He chortled, more quietly than before. "What is useful to you?"

"I mean talk to me. That's what you need, isn't it? Help in defining the universe?"

"We Ulanyi will always need help with that, won't we? It's the way we're built. Someone did it to us, millions of years ago. Probe Builders? Vronnans? Ulanyi have an important place in Vronnan nests and have since anyone can remember. Just as humans have. For there are many humans aboard the clanships. . . . Are we both created species? You and me? The placenta is an artificial creation that brings a version of reality in to us. Your neocortex is no different."

"Pyx—"

"Wawawa! Not enough sex. Where is she? Where is the mother of my child, so soon to be created, so soon to be enslaved?" With spastic repetitiveness, he slammed a forelimb against a wall. Above the sound of the impact, Ambryn could hear the creaking of breaking tissue.

"Stop it!" Ambryn shouted.

"Why?" But he did and settled himself down onto the ice. "Saves the Executioner, my spouse, my mate, from having to bind me. You humans know yourselves least of all, don't you think? Other examples of your species wander around the stars, and you think yourselves the only ones, here in this little sanctuary, the Solar System. And all you think about, in here, is how to get out. How to get a deepdrive. Maybe that's why they thought what I did was such a crime."

Damn it. With everything he said, he raised a hundred questions. She'd never figure anything out. "You tried to steal a deepdrive?"

"Wawawa! You don't steal a deepdrive, Ambryn. You grow it. You grow it on the pattern of your own mind. The mind of your own species. Just as we Ulanyi have been grown. Each star-traveling species has its own model. Who knows where those little space-bending minds first came from?"

"The Gunners," Ambryn said.

For the first time, she sensed that Pyx was taken aback. "The Gunners . . . yes, dear Ambryn, that may well be it. Those suicidal rudimentary little minds they grow that leap so eagerly into the Sun. But the Gunners may simply have stolen those minds from someone else. There was, perhaps, a time when some intelligent mind did something for the very first time, but no one remembers that. What we remember is the first time a mind stole something another mind had already created. And thus interstellar civilization was invented."

It was his last energies, Ambryn could see. He was dying, even without the final quietus of the Executioner, and his mind had flared up just before the final darkness. Would that he were making sense. If only he would say something *useful*.

"I thought it would be a way of never being born." His voice had grown quieter. He shuddered a little in his dug-out crater but did not move. "I talked . . . that was my crime, you know . . . I talked with the Vronnan deepdrive. They should never have brought the damn thing into the System. Of course, given the troubles . . ."

Ambryn did not dare breathe.

"Vronnans have almost-conscious deepdrives, you know. No one else does, but then that's how they do things. Everything around them has to have a mind, a will, a feeling. All alive. The Vronnans are never alone. Vronnan deepdrives live inside a distant descendant of an Ulanyi placenta. That keeps their minds alive. . . . So was it insane of me, dear Ambryn?"

"What?"

"To want to join it? The deepdrive is not well, you know. Not well at all. The depredations of past years. The disasters that brought that clanship here. The Vronnan wars, caused by that damn Ripi on Venus. Everything. The drive sickens. I wanted to save it and thus save myself."

Ambryn suddenly saw the entire plot in a new light. "So the *Argent* was intended to save the Vronnan deepdrive. But where—"

"Originally, yes. Such was my plan. The placentas can nurture a deepdrive. But it was my private need. As the operation proceeded, its goals, ineluctably, changed. Before I knew it, the *Argent* had become a platform for Ulanyi embryos alone. You see, dear Ambryn, no one believed my visions. They had no faith in a deepdrive in the Solar System. There was no indication of such a thing. But the time was ripe for a move against the Ulanyi who, they felt, had gained greater and greater control over the lives of human beings. A way of reasserting a balance. The Ulanyi Pure Mind saw it differently, of course. And it was a crime, my need. At least here in the System, where we have made our home. We are to resist the siren seductions of deepdrive minds."

"You set up the hijacking," Ambryn said. "Not the Ulanyi Pure Mind. There was no outside plot. It was all you. You convinced Tiber to do it. You wanted him to take you along. But he didn't."

"I am not the only one with needs. The *Argent* was meant for that deepdrive, but the uses—" Pyx looked out past her. "I'm afraid, Ambryn, that we are both due to be cheated. Perhaps there are some truths that are never to be conveyed."

Ambryn turned to look. The passage she had come in through had vanished, already covered over with a thick layer of ice.

"What—"

"She's here. At last she's here! Save yourself, Ambryn. You'll have time. Run!"

A puff of steam and the Ulanyi Executioner stepped through the ice wall, which immediately refroze behind her. She was an exceptionally large Ulanyi, and her disproportionately elongated forelimbs had mining lasers implanted in them.

"Livilla!" Soph shouted again. Her voice cracked back at her from the rock-melt walls. Were these indeed the right coordinates? She'd asked a sad, balding man in the corridor, and he had, after long hesitation, pointed her here. Maybe he'd had his own motivations for misleading her. She should have gone on to the lights of what looked like an eating place just beyond. Someone there might have been more sensible. "Livilla!"

"I'm here, goddammit." Livilla had been floating, all

curled up, amid some mesh-held equipment. If she hadn't seen fit to respond, Soph probably would never have found her. ''And I'm done. I've got a life to deal with, and you're sitting right on top of it. I'm taking you out to the Rock hub.''

''Can I get to the shipyards?'' Soph said. There would be little enough to gather there. All direct information was still secured.

''That's your own business. I don't know what's what out there in the Rock.''

Livilla, Soph could see, was not to be argued with. Not now, not here. And without her, Soph would just wander the MMK at random. She didn't have the time.

''Hlobane,'' Soph said. ''Take me—''

''He ain't seeing you no more. Rock pole.''

She'd have to regroup there. What had happened to Livilla? Who had she spoken with? Soph felt like something had been stolen from her, some vital piece of information.

''Besides,'' Livilla said. ''There's someone up there in rockland who probably needs to talk to you. Hlobane said that, anyway. A good final destination for you.''

''Who?''

Livilla smirked. ''You know, you all think you're so smart. You come in here, swagger around, break things open to see what's inside. It ever occur to you that it's not your business? That we know what we need to know? That guy, big shot from Luna, I guess. Like you. Came up, bulled his way around—nowhere. Like you. Now he's just relaxing in a little resort room, drinking mint tea and playing chess.''

Lightfoot. It had to be. Soph's anger at Livilla spilled over onto him. What the hell was he doing here?

''Don't waste my time, then,'' Soph said. ''Get moving.''

A sea lay at the Halo's center. Most ecocysts did have a hollow center, but they usually provided an expanse of open land, with at most a lake or two. The water sellers of MMK disdained such weakness, such need to put feet on solid ground.

The sea swirled with storm. Elward clung to the handles by the hatch, feeling his feet floating, and looked down the axis of the vast water-swirling tube. Waves, once formed, tended to grow, their feathery tops weightless.

Livilla's instructions had been grudging. But he didn't think she had been lying. There, moored in the stormy water, floated a raft, ten meters or so away. On it was a pavilion with curving eaves. Windows glowed yellow. It looked very cheery. The Chretiens were there, waiting for the outcome of their plan. Despite Livilla's conclusions, Elward wasn't sure what that plan was. All he knew was that Ambryn was in deep shit.

The sky was stormy water as well, whitecaps filling in for clouds. An iceberg loomed above him. Penguins and cormorants swarmed over it. The penguins had taken to the low gravity with joy. They almost seemed to fly as they dove in high arcs into the water, and they flipped out of it as they swam, like enthusiastic dolphins. Livilla had told him that they occasionally attempted assaults on the tethered rafts, swarming up the sides like pirate crews, breaking into the food stores. Despite extensive breeding, their flesh remained unpleasant-tasting. The only thing that would eat them was the internal sea's one orca, whose muscles had been attenuated so that it would not become airborne in pursuit of prey. Instead, it slid along the sea bottom and gently nipped swimming penguins from the surface like single grapes.

There was nowhere to stand, no way to get over to that raft. Damn that Livilla. Elward could see little boats with outriggers bobbing by the raft's side. The Chretiens had all gone over there and clearly did not expect any more guests.

He was in the water before he knew it. For a second, he managed to convince himself that he was almost warm, that it was like getting caught in a rainstorm.

It was longnight, condensed and made liquid. It struck right down into his bones. And, he now remembered, he didn't really swim very well. No need for it in the streets of Golgot. For a second, he thought about giving it up, but the place he'd been hanging from, by the hatch, was much farther away than he'd thought.

Well, dying here would be really stupid. Keeping his head as far up out of the waves as he could, he pulled his way toward the raft in a clumsy breaststroke.

There. That wasn't so bad. Once you got used to it, the water seemed almost warm. Well, not warm . . . but his teeth had stopped chattering. That was something. But the raft didn't seem to be getting any closer.

Ice water stung his nostrils, and he almost choked. Damn it. His legs had gotten really heavy. He guessed they were his legs. They were attached to him. But he couldn't really feel them. He pulled as hard as he could with his arms, wondering if something had grabbed him from below. Maybe a walrus had gotten his tusks tangled in Elward's pants. That would be pretty funny—once he got out of the water.

But the raft still was no closer. A wave washed right over his head. He almost didn't bother to come back up. The raft. He reached for it, even though it was still miles away, but he couldn't feel anything. Now his arms were gone too. Wasn't that a hell of a thing?

4

The Executioner wrapped herself almost completely around Pyx, and their abdomens pressed closely together. There was something stately about it, like a formal salute between two fully rigged sailing ships of enemy powers. Limbs slid along limbs, and the air filled with a deep humming that almost tickled.

Though no human had ever witnessed an Ulanyi mating, Ambryn did not stay to watch. There was no way the Executioner had ever intended to give her child up to humans. Only desperate need had deluded the Chretiens into thinking she would. Pyx still loved Ambryn. But in a few minutes, Pyx would be dead.

She slid across the misty ice, seeking a path of escape. But there was none. The solid ice walls curved back on themselves. For the first time, she felt how cold it was in here. Thick mist bubbled from the pit Pyx had dug while tormenting himself. Bamboo pipes cracked and broke. Soon she would be just a frozen mummy. She wasn't even dressed for this. She didn't want to die.

* * *

Elward choked on the hot liquid being poured down his throat and sat up. It took a lot of work, his muscles didn't work at all . . . no, there was something around him, holding him. It was a big bag, heavy. But it was full of heat. He could feel it. Slowly baking in.

His fingers and toes hurt.

The man pouring the liquid fire put the flask back into a pocket in a shoulder bag. He was an old bird, with big white eyebrows. He squatted back on his haunches. His outfit gleamed black.

"Ambryn. . . ." Elward managed to choke. "Trouble. You a Chretien?"

"Shock." The man's eyes widened. "You *know* her?"

"We've been . . ." He finally got control of his breathing. "We've been through a lot together. Venus . . . after . . . Who are you, may I ask?"

The man inclined his head slightly. He was a classy piece of work, Elward had to give him that. "Otho. Ambryn's uncle."

"Ah. The one she likes." He remembered just the vaguest mention.

Elward hadn't ever done it very much, but now he knew the satisfaction of making someone happy. Otho's eyes glittered.

"I'm afraid I don't have much time for pleasantries," Otho said. "I was looking over the edge of the raft—lucky for you—when your head popped up out of the water. But Ambryn—"

"So you know she's about to get whacked." Elward could see that what Otho wore was an insulating diving suit. It did not fit him very well. It was made for someone much larger. Behind him lay a pile of underwater breathing gear.

"I—what do you know about it?"

Elward pulled himself out of his heated bag. He was still frozen right up to his skin, but he couldn't spend much time worrying about it.

They were in some kind of aquatic kitchen area. The air had a crisp ozone-and-iodine smell, and it scrubbed, wet and salty, across Elward's exposed skin, making him shiver. Water bubbled in dark tanks filled with scuttling crustaceans and spilled out of filters onto the pressed-fiber floorboards. He could hear someone wailing and pounding on the walls. It was an adult, not a child.

"I know someone on the Ulanyi side of this operation is pulling a double-cross, and Ambryn's going to get killed as a result. And you know it too. What the hell is that racket?"

The screams subsided to whimpers.

"That's Martine. Ambryn ever mention her?"

"No."

"She planned this handoff. But she didn't know that the mother of Pyx's child was to be his Executioner. Ambryn can't get an embryo away from her. The Ulanyi are risking a bigger breach than anyone could have thought." The wailing rose in volume again. "When Martine found out, she wanted to rescue Ambryn immediately. Of course, we could not permit it. The Chretiens need Martine too badly."

"Oh, like this Martine didn't realize her value from the beginning." It looked like theater was a Chretien family trait. "So you volunteered? You probably don't even have a route down. You'd be crawling blind." It would be scary enough as it was, Elward thought, given the possibility that Livilla simply wanted to kill him.

"Martine . . ." Otho shivered himself. "A nice play . . . Either she gets the Egg or she gets her old lover Ambryn out of the way. And you're right, she must have known we'd never let her risk herself."

They both listened to the steady weeping from the next room. At least the woman was willing to put the work in, Elward thought.

"I don't have a lot of time," Elward said. "You can think about it while I'm down there. Get out of the suit, give me the breathing gear. Now. I have the route down the cell. One of Hlobane's people gave it to me. Seems she felt guilty—or responsive to pressure."

Elward pulled open lockers. There was a hell of a lot less diving gear than Livilla had sworn was here. And Otho had the only suit that would fit him. Had Livilla just been trying to get rid of him? Imagine that. He did find a suit that would fit Ambryn. He didn't have time to make sure it worked.

"Gratitude," Otho said as he pulled the suit off his bony chest. "You must really care about her."

"Nah. I don't even like her. She talks too much, right? But . . . you don't let someone go down for talking too much. It just ain't right."

Otho smiled, finally relaxing the suspicion that had kept his shoulders tense, even as he obeyed Elward's instructions. "You must really care about her."

"If that makes you more comfortable," Elward said. "Yeah."

Every thirty meters or so, a filtration endplate marked the joining of two bamboo segments. Elward had to cut his way through each one. As he got farther out to the perimeter of MeshMatrix Krystal, the gravity grew greater and his head-down position more unpleasant. The fluid was stagnant. This particular pump bamboo had been dead for some time. Flukes rippled around his head, looking for entry to his flesh. Ulanyi parasites of some sort, their penetrating mouthparts left scratches across his air hoses.

The access to the bamboo had been right under the Chretiens' raft. As Elward had squeezed into it, he had thought that maybe he should have let the skinny Otho take the job, after all. For him, it was a tight squeeze. And maybe Otho could have found it on his own. A huge crevasse had been melted down, exposing the access. If Otho had had the nerve, he could have stuck his head in and started swimming down, down, down. From what Elward had seen of him, he might just have done it.

The tube grew narrower. Had he picked the right opening? Had there been another one, one he had missed? This one went nowhere, he would suffocate here head-down, he was dead. It took all of his willpower to keep himself from thrashing around. Pushing with toes and fingers, he crept forward. The tube closed around his shoulders. He expelled a breath and kept going.

A last squeeze and his shoulders were free. Something had damaged the pump bamboo here. The stuff had grown wildly, leaving a swollen reservoir. The flukes were even worse here. He listened for a moment but couldn't hear anything, so he cut his way out.

The near-freezing fluid poured out into the even colder air, forming frost and mist. Elward rolled out into some kind of ice crater. For a moment, he couldn't see anything, just ice walls, mist, and the shattered remains of the pump bamboo.

"Who—Elward?"

It was Ambryn, disconcertingly well-dressed, kneeling and digging in the ice, as if for a lost earring. Beyond her, two gigantic aliens were wrapped around each other. Laser lights made the ice glow.

"Let's go." He tossed her the rolled-up suit. "Pronto."

"I never thought I'd be happy to see you."

"I love you too. Hurry your ass. What is this thing?" While she put the suit on, he touched the thick pipe Ambryn had been digging for.

"Hot pipe. Superheated steam for carving ice."

"Smart girl. The only weapon in here, ah?"

"Closest thing I could find. But feel it. It's rigid, not like the ice hoses. You can't point the damn thing."

"So how were you going to cut—"

She tossed him a reel of wire. "Monofilament line. I had it in the seam of my jacket. Security didn't catch it."

"Hah." Elward looked up at the big aliens. They were done. The bigger one, the Executioner, now had a translucent sac hanging from the underside of its—her—abdomen. He prodded the thick joint in the steam line, grateful that he wouldn't have to try to use it. "You ready?"

"Ready." Ambryn wore her gleaming black suit.

It would take the Executioner a few seconds to perform her duty on Pyx. That would give them enough time to—

The Executioner sprang right over Pyx and landed between them and the pump bamboo exit. It raised its laser arms.

"Ambryn!" Pyx said. "I am spent. I am dead."

"Pyx!" Ambryn said. "She's going to kill me."

Pyx smashed into the Executioner. Huge limbs flailed. "Flee!"

Laser light flared. But the battling Ulanyi were still between them and the escape route.

Elward rolled the monofilament onto its thumbguards. Always have a backup. Never assume that you're safe. Too bad this was such a lame backup. He shaved the joint. Composite flaked off. Another pass—steam jetted out of the junction with a thin scream.

Mist filled the air, so dense you could feel it. Ambryn blundered against him. "The ice line. That's a weapon too. Down here."

She tugged him along a ridged ice line. He began to see her plan. He found a place where the flexible pipe had kinked up. He wrapped the monofilament around it.

"Get them both," she said. "We can sort them out later."

They felt a blast of heat, followed by the bitter smell of charred flesh. The Executioner had sent a bolt of high-energy coherent light through Pyx's brain, killing him instantly. Pyx toppled.

"See you later," she said and disappeared into the mist.

Screwed again, dammit. She was going to let him take the fall. . . . Elward pulled the thumb guard behind him as he crawled, trying to leave the line loose. He didn't want to slice through the ice pipe too soon, which would give the game away. He didn't want to lose any fingers either. There was too much to think about.

The greenish beam of the laser flickered through the thick mist, but most of its energy was absorbed by the water molecules. But maybe the Executioner was just target-locating.

The escaping steam still screamed. Elward heard a lumbering, then a bellow as the Executioner, incautious, encountered the hot stream. Was she trying to pile ice on it, block it, freeze it up? Good luck, Elward thought, and crouched down to wait for the Executioner's invisible approach.

But then, in a matter of seconds, the jet of steam stopped. Probably some monitor down the line had noticed the pressure drop. Goddam safety engineers. As if they didn't have more important things to worry about.

The Executioner came out of the thinning mist at him. It held its laser fire and reached out at Elward's head with its foreclaws.

"Hey, you!" Ambryn shouted from somewhere to the left, beyond the cold pipe he had rigged. "You've got the wrong target.'' She threw a chunk of ice and hit the Executioner in the head.

The Executioner jumped instantly toward Ambryn's voice. Elward barely saw it move.

He fell backward and yanked on the thumb guard. It was like he was not holding on to anything at all. Maybe the Executioner's claw had severed the filament—then it cut through the cold line. Ice bubbled screamingly up, shooting fragments of the froth that had already formed.

The bubbling ice trapped the Executioner's lower limbs, climbed up her sides, and imprisoned her. But her laser-equipped upper limbs were still free. And the mist had almost dissipated.

Without even thinking about it, Elward dove and skidded himself right between the Executioner's pinioned legs. From what he could tell, the lasers couldn't fire right underneath. Maybe he was wrong. He'd find out.

He bumped into Ambryn, and they both fell back in shock.

Then Ambryn laughed. ''Only safe place.''

''I thought you had—''

''Elward, I wouldn't leave you like that. Here.'' Ambryn grabbed at the edge of a thick, soft swelling: the new embryo, in its placental precursor.

''Got a knife?'' Ambryn asked.

''Sure. Those I got.'' Elward handed Ambryn a rolled-up blade and Ambryn snapped it open.

''Now, bucko, it's your turn,'' Ambryn said. ''Can you distract her for a few seconds?''

Elward looked up at the creature above them. She was still, every muscle tense, waiting for an opportunity. ''Sure.''

''Let's see if I can remember my Ulanyi anatomy. . . .'' Ambryn reached up and cut, her eyes closed.

Elward rolled out under the Executioner's rear and jumped up on her back. A spike-tipped limb whipped by, but it didn't seem to be able to reach him. The entire creature writhed. The ice cracked with its struggles. Elward jabbed his knife at an exposed joint, but an inner layer shrugged off his point.

Then the Executioner bucked and keened. Her upper limbs stuck straight up. Ambryn had done something underneath.

"Do not kill it," the Executioner said. "Please." The human words did not come easily to it.

"I don't intend to," Ambryn said. "And I don't intend to kill you either."

Elward jerked in surprise. "Let's get with it, Ambryn. Are you talking deal with this thing? Let's just take care of it and dive." Though it looked like it would be a hell of a lot of work to kill it.

"I think we can get some information and get out of here safely."

"And in return?"

"She keeps her child," Ambryn said.

"What? I thought you came down here to get the damn thing for your family."

"I'm no longer sure why I came down here, Elward. But it was mostly to talk with Pyx. She knows more of what he had to say than I do. He was your mate, correct? And you were his interrogator."

"Speak slowly," the Executioner said. "I have little knowledge of your language."

"Born and bred separate, right? Off on one of the Ulanyi-controlled Belt asteroids."

"You are the first human beings I have seen. I desire that you are the last also."

"Maybe we can work that out," Ambryn said. "I want to know what Pyx told you."

"He told me many things."

"About his crime. About the deepdrive. And where it is."

"I cannot tell."

"Then the Chretiens get their new Egg," Ambryn said. "And you die knowing your child will be raised by humans."

The Executioner's limbs jerked. Elward was impressed by the savagery in Ambryn's tone. She wasn't screwing around. She'd kill the Executioner, if she had to. Hell, she'd kill the kid too, and let everyone get screwed. He liked that.

"Will you free my child? Will it be mine?"

"If you talk. And if you give us a way out of here. Yes."

The Executioner thought about it for a long time. Elward

wondered if he could feel the buzz of its neurons under its shell.

"Pyx did not talk about many other things," the Executioner said. "He wanted to go to where the deepdrive was. That was his crime. That was why I killed the father of this child."

"Do we have a deal?" Ambryn said.

"I do not understand."

"Will you give me the information about the deepdrive and free us from this ice cave, in exchange for your life and your child's?"

"Yes," the Executioner said. "I need mist."

"All right." Before Elward could say anything, Ambryn strolled right out onto the ice and sought out the monofilament thumb guards in the frothy ice. It took a few minutes to chop one free.

"Ambryn," Elward said. "Are you sure this is a good idea?"

"You have a better one?"

She was on the verge of losing it, Elward thought. He could hear it. Better not to argue. "Nah. Go ahead. I'll deal with whatever comes up." He waited tensely for the Executioner to fry her with one blast of her laser. But the Ulanyi just stood and waited.

It took Ambryn quite a while to find another steam line. Then she did the same to it as Elward had done to the other. The chamber filled with thick mist.

Laser light glowed, then flickered. Slowly, as the Executioner manipulated what were usually her weapons, a hologram appeared. Chunks of something—rock? ice?—floated against a more distant backdrop of stars.

They looked like asteroids.

"When Pyx spoke to the deepdrive," the Executioner said, "this was what was around it."

"Are you getting this, Elward?" Ambryn said.

"I'll do my best," he said, knowing that the images would fade before he could draw them, or describe them, or whatever the hell she expected him to do with them.

"Never mind," Ambryn said. "I think . . . I think I can remember it."

"Great." Elward realized that he was almost frozen. He could no longer feel his grip on the Executioner's back.

"Look, Ambryn," he said. "Your family's plans are too complicated for me to keep track of. But, you know, Otho was going to dive right down to look for you, even though he didn't know exactly how he was going to get in. He realized I had a better chance and gave me the gear."

"Otho . . . he's not so smart, you know. Martine played him too."

"He said that he didn't think Martine knew that the Executioner would try to kill you too."

Ambryn looked at him. "Don't be too sure about what Martine doesn't know. She sent me down here because she knew I had the best chance. She knew Pyx would defend me."

"Now free me completely," the Executioner said. "And we can go."

"Ambryn?" Elward said. He felt completely dependent on her.

"Let's get to work. We have some ice to chip."

Thirteen

1

Livilla dumped Soph in a black-walled hallway in the high-g area of the Rock. She walked off, steaming visibly in the moist air, without another word.

Soph slid through the doorway, checking for booby traps. Yellow light spilled from inside. Lightfoot's room came into view, inch by inch: clothes on the floor, a bed so disordered it looked like someone had been having nightmares on it, a small desk covered with stacks of display screens.

He sat at the desk, not working but pensively playing with a light pen, sketching random lines on a floating screen, then smearing them with his finger until they looked like oil slicks.

"You bastard," she said.

He twitched in shock. "That must be my dear wife."

"Ex-wife. Please."

"Certainly. Come in. We have things to talk about."

"You sent me on a mission." She spoke with the precise diction of rage. "We discussed it, we planned it. I had things to do, things to find out. It's been hard. Goddam hard, Lightfoot." She waited for him to interrupt. He didn't say anything. "And what do you do? You decide to take a luxury jaunt out here, just to check things out, a happy bigfoot. So what the hell am I doing out here?''

''I don't think you've ever understood,'' he said after a long pause.

''Understood what?''

''What it is that I do. And what it means for what you are able to do.''

''We're not married anymore, Lightfoot. I don't want to have any reasonable-seeming discussion about how everything's really my fault. I'm not interested in *theory*.''

''Dammit!'' he shouted. ''You just won't listen, will you? You ask a bunch of questions, but you're not at all interested in the answers. Okay. Scream at me all you want, if it makes you feel better.''

He had to be faking it. Lightfoot never got angry. The more vicious the fight became, the calmer he was, until she became furious enough to kill him. He was yelling at her now to calm her down.

That made her smile. They were both so stupid.

''Okay,'' she said. ''Explain it to me.''

''Soph, have I ever told you that you have the best expression of martyred patience that I have ever encountered?''

''I'm sure you have, some time or other.''

Lightfoot was no slouch at martyred patience himself, she noted. ''I started my professional life as a field tech hunter. You know that. You've even called up some of my old reports. You wanted to know who I was, back in the early days when we first had met. What did you think?''

''Think?''

''Yes. About my reports. Remember the impression you had right at the time. Don't pull any punches. We're having an argument, remember.''

''I haven't forgotten.''

Soph did remember the guilty thrill she'd gotten from reading the unexpurgated reports of Lightfoot's youthful expeditions—another example of Lightfoot's quirky dispassion. Anyone else would have hidden them, or at least edited out some of the more embarrassing sections.

Lightfoot had appeared to her full-grown, plump and dignified, a man seemingly in disdainful control of any situation.

The reports told a different story. The high-noise environment of fieldwork had confused the anxious young Lightfoot and he had found himself incapable of plucking useful information out of the distracting flickers of irrelevant facts. He had irritated local contacts, missed vital opportunities, and concluded one mission by being dumped out of the airlock of a Callistan space station, to be rescued, at ruinous expense, by a passing supply boat.

"So?" Lightfoot said.

"I *was* startled. Clearly, by the time I had met you, you had . . . learned a lot."

"Ha. You are very kind, dear wife."

"Ex-wife."

"Whatever. The only thing I had learned is what I had no gift for. But it was my romantic ideal. Fieldwork. I wanted to be out there, disguised as an air filter distributor or an indentured worker, seeing the underside of human/alien life. But I was no good at it. No damn good at all. So I moved back to the office and ran operations from there."

Soph refused to be mollified.

"You aren't in your office now, Lightfoot. You're here, trying to make my work irrelevant."

"No. I'm trying to give you the resources to make your work have meaning. This *is* my office."

Soph sighed and dug through the left drawer of the desk. Lightfoot had his habits . . . there, behind the air ionizer, a bottle. She raised eyebrows at him, and he nodded. She pulled it out and unscrewed the top, which was made of two nested glasses. Lightfoot used alcohol to lower his barriers to other human beings and never drank alone. She poured bourbon into the cups and handed him one.

"What resources?" Soph asked.

He was silent a moment. "I've hired an interplanetary vessel. Its name is the *Imhotep*. You know of them, I think. You came from Mercury to Luna aboard their converted surface-to-orbit mass driver."

To ease her shock, Soph poured the bourbon down her throat. She didn't feel anything, but when she looked, her cup was empty.

"Where are you planning on going?" she said.

"That's what you're supposed to tell me. Outer System, I suspect. The ship is ready to depart, though they're still in the process of modifying the main hull's structure to hold a particle-beam weapon I was able to purchase from an arms distributor on Laurion who owed me a favor or three. He threw in a couple of cases of small arms he'd been intending to ship down to Southeast Asia for the guerrilla war against the HarNagn."

Laurion, one of the other circum-Lunar asteroids of the Diadem, was well known as a source of weapons, one reason their exports were so closely watched. But Lightfoot always did have people who owed him favors.

"Don't look so startled, Soph. It's an investment. A good one, if I know you."

He'd just thrown himself headlong off a cliff in the presumption that she would catch him. But she didn't have enough to offer him. Vague suspicions, hints . . . Had he set this up so that she could let him down?

His eyes were bright as they looked at her. It had been a long time since she'd seen that expression on his face—not since before Stephan's death.

"But a ship is not enough to do the job," Lightfoot said. "Even with weapons aboard. We need intelligence, will, activity . . . *staff*, preferably someone familiar with the situation. I had several long discussions with Martyshka, the *Imhotep*'s manager. She indicates that she has information that might be of interest to you."

2

"I feel like these people are idiots," Ambryn said as they floated through the crowded market area that blocked entry to the spacecraft docks at the hub. "Doomed idiots. I mean, don't they know what sort of things are going on back in the Halo?"

She and Elward swooped along with all the other travelers in a vortex stream that spiraled along the outer wall of the swollen hollow cylinder of the hub. The market area was half a kilometer long and at least a hundred meters across at its widest. Tethered suns floated at the axis, sending off streamers of coronas. A second transport spiral sent a stream of people the opposite way. Ambryn watched them sailing against the tangle of glowing advertisements that made up the entire wall of the hub cylinder: Institute scholars with decorations of jet, a small boy holding firmly onto a blinking guide tab and not looking around at the confusion, three Lunarian women with glowing hair and a dozen mesh shopping bags each arguing over a map display over where to go next. Who needed aliens?

"It's no different than anywhere else." As if to annoy her, Elward stopped at a vendor's float and examined a wide hat with plastic icicles all around the brim. It said: I FROZE MY BUTT OFF IN THE HALO! in silver letters. "Always something hidden, something that seems kind of fun—until it reaches up and grabs you by the throat. Gives a little thrill to places like this here. Just like in Golgot." He had recovered the fragments of Soph's luggage he had brought out of the *Argent* from the locker in which they had been stored, and they clung around his waist.

"Come *on*!" She jerked him away, wondering at her own temerity. He used to scare the hell out of her.

Instead of resisting, he chuckled and came along. Maybe fighting a huge fierce creature together was the best way to build trust, she thought. The airstream caught them and they continued their flight toward the docking areas.

"You know, the *Imhotep* seems like home now," Elward said. "As I understand that particular word, that is." He looked at her, and she felt an intimacy that surprised her. Particularly here, in the midst of these bustling crowds, all flying in streams. Both unused to this method of transportation, they held hands, like brother and sister. "Tell me, Ambryn. Did you like getting home again?"

"In a way, I did. It ended badly. But if Martine hadn't taken my place . . . if I could have been of use, then it would really have been home."

"You were of use. Your use to them is over."

"That's why it's not home anymore."

"I never had a home, you know," Elward said. "Not a real one, with people I was related to and stuff. But then it's one of those words that everyone uses, but each person means different. A wallpaper word, covers up all the cracks, lets us pretend we understand each other."

"There's never been a place you felt comfortable, even for a moment? Home is only in memory, you know. You only understand it afterward."

Elward was the one who had contacted the *Imhotep*. Ambryn had been startled—and more than a little disturbed—to find out his close association with the construction monkeys and with Martyshka in particular. Martyshka was a past encounter. Ambryn preferred that her past encounters stay . . . past.

But there had been little option. MMK had grown inhospitable to both of them, and the *Imhotep* had offered refuge. Temporary refuge, it seemed, for the entire ship was abustle with some new long-range operation. Someone had hired it, and whoever that was was unlikely to need either of them. Neither Elward nor Ambryn had any idea of what they were going to do next.

"But you know where home really was?" Elward said.

"No."

"Think about it. I didn't know it then, but it was in those damn stinky tunnels under Ripi's. Remember?"

"I remember."

"We saved everyone we needed to save and ourselves too. All together."

And immediately afterward, aboard the *Argent*, had fallen apart, Ambryn thought. "Yes."

"That was it, you want to know. The closest I've gotten."

"Pretty close for me too," Ambryn whispered.

"For her?"

"Soph? Maybe. She talked about that apartment in Archimedes . . . but she never found home again after her son Stephan died. He must have been quite a man."

"To grow up with her as his mother? Must have been. And poor Tiber." This was the first time Ambryn had heard Elward speak of Tiber with anything but wary contempt. "He's looking for home too, isn't he?"

"I don't know what he's looking for," Ambryn said.

"Well, I guess that makes it unanimous," Elward said. "No one knows where the hell home is."

They approached the curved end of the cylinder. A constant shout and sound of bells and honking horns came from people hanging around the various access gates, trying to get the attention of those they were trying to meet. Vendors blundered through with streamer-waving floaters.

Did Ambryn hear her own name being shouted? The waving masses of hands looked like seaweed. She couldn't make out any individuals. The vortex stream swept them by.

"Hey, *hey*!" Soph's bags fought like dogs that had just seen a cat strolling insolently by. Wheels popped out, jewelry drawers presented themselves, air jets fired randomly. Elward yanked at them. "What the hell?"

He looked up and, with sharper eyes than Ambryn's, found who was shouting at them.

"Soph!" His rough bellow rang Ambryn's ears.

Now she could see Soph too, waving madly as they flew past. Nice outfit, Ambryn had time to think, navy with white trim. While she looked like hell, wet and stained with Ulanyi embryo secretions.

Elward grabbed a climbing line out of a conveniently open bag and tossed the end weight. Soph, laughing, leaned out, knocking a package from the hands of the beefy matron next to her, and grabbed hold of it.

"Hold on, sweetheart," Elward said.

"We can hit the distribution platform and be with her in five minutes," Ambryn protested.

"So don't hold on."

At the last minute, though, she did. The tightening line yanked them through the stiff cold breeze of the outer vortex, probably setting off alarms in pedestrian traffic control.

Soph hauled them in, hand over hand, while apologizing frantically to the angry woman next to her. They swept perilously close to the axial suns, but Ambryn's hair was too wet to react much to the coronal static charges. Despite her resolve, she found herself waving and yelling too. As they approached, Elward swung his legs out and neatly captured the foil-wrapped gift box as it drifted past. He handed it to its owner. Then he reached up and took Soph's hand.

3

"You know, Elward, I just missed you," Soph said. "When I found Livilla, you must have just left." She remembered the heavy woman leaning thoughtfully over the scene of her ancient crimes. Soph had had no idea. . . .

"That's okay," Elward said. "I don't think I was ready to meet yet."

"And Tiber . . ." She didn't want to know what had been done to him. But she had to know.

Elward closed his eyes. "They kidnapped him, assaulted him, raped him. Right there in the center of the whole asteroid. Livilla showed me. The man who actually did it was named Pelham. Pelham got arrested, reprogrammed. And Jig joined the *Argent* crew and became the Archon. Balls, on Tiber's part, to keep her. Though I guess that one of the reasons she helped kidnap him in the first place was because she had . . . a *thing* for him. People don't always show that in the best way, I guess. You should have seen the way she cried over him at your trial aboard the *Argent*."

"Pelham," Ambryn said. "He was the gate guard for Pyx's cell. They all got tied in a knot and never got themselves untied."

"Like us," Elward said. "Ah, Soph?"

Soph couldn't have said why that statement pleased her so much.

The *Imhotep* was outbound, at as great an acceleration as the construction monkeys were willing to tolerate for the amount they were being paid. Its goal was the Leading Trojan asteroids of Jupiter, the area where Tiber had first appeared. Every planet had gravitationally stable lagrangian points sixty degrees ahead and sixty degrees behind its location in its orbit, but only Jupiter was large enough to collect a substantial amount of mass there. A relatively dense grouping of several dozen asteroids, the largest being Hector, with a diameter of one hundred and eighty kilometers, preceded Jupiter with the bustling solemnity of ladies-in-waiting.

They sat lightly in a conference space lined with tumbles of thick fabric, as if they were stored Christmas tree ornaments. Soph still felt the aftereffects of their emotional reunion. Her tears had crusted around her eyes.

Lightfoot sat a little apart from them, quiet and watchful. Both Ambryn and Elward dealt with him warily, as if he was an only partially tamed wild animal.

"Tiber had thrown off his past, come to MeshMatrix Krystal, and found a life," Soph said. "The attack was just chance. Without it, he could still be cooking—and happy."

"Livilla said they sensed his weakness and gave him what he really wanted." The compassion in Elward's voice was new. Soph too was startled to hear it. He had never had anything but contempt for the idiosyncratic weaknesses of others.

"It wasn't his fault," Soph said.

"I didn't say it was."

"And it all came back. He'd slipped the leash. He'd gotten away from her. But after the attack, it all returned. His knowledge, all the things Sukh had planned. He realized that there was no escape. He understood that the only thing he could do was repeat what had already happened to him."

"Soph," Ambryn said. "Please. It wasn't your fault either."

"I suppose not."

Lightfoot carefully said nothing but looked intently at whoever was speaking, lending automatic significance to the words.

"So what do we got?" Elward said. "Soph trekked to the tombs of Prisoner Maintenance, I fell in the ocean, Ambryn almost got eaten by a big alien bug. And now we have Tiber's little biography, all the way from being born in a sealed cabin aboard a Martian warship, to suspended prisoner, to failed information source, to chef, to rape victim, to project leader, to hijacker. To us. Is that it? Our big payoff? Do we know everything now?"

"We know that the *Argent* had deeper purposes," Ambryn said. She explained what Pyx had told her before he died: the dying deepdrive calling out across the spaces of the Solar System and the building of the *Argent* to go heal it. There was grief in her voice as she spoke: for Pyx, for herself as a member of the Chretien family.

''The deepdrive that the *Argent* was intended to heal,'' Soph said. ''Where do you think it came from?''

Ambryn raised eyebrows. ''I think . . . well, where else? It has to be a Vronnan clanship. As far as we know, the Vronnans have no other deepdrives. Just those half-conscious minds in their giant clanships.''

''There was the one Ripi used to get here in the first place,'' Elward said.

''A one-shot.'' Lightfoot made his first contribution. ''I think we have the first glimmerings of a taxonomy of deepdrives. I've been thinking about what Ms. Chretien has presented to us, combined with my long unsuccessful years of seeking out a functioning deepdrive. The minds that Pyx described to you are the true deepdrives, the ones each species coexists with and that can go from one star system to another.

''But, clearly, these true deepdrives have ways of producing single-use units. Budding, sprouting, building—I won't even attempt to characterize it. But Ripi caused one to come into being in the skin of the Bru clanship. Once it was used to cross interstellar space, its function was over.''

Despite herself, Soph found herself again impressed by the way Lightfoot had integrated all of the information. There was as much noise in a mass of reports as there was in the field from which those reports were made and yet he was able to function in the first environment and not in the second. Nevertheless, it was galling too. She had gathered most of that data herself. Had she been too close to see the truth? But, of course, deepdrives were Lightfoot's big obsession. He wanted to give the fire of the stars into the hands of human beings.

''This is just a guess, of course,'' Lightfoot said. ''An initial hypothesis. So—a Vronnan clanship. Where, Soph?''

''If I'm right,'' she said grudgingly, ''the Leading Trojans of Jupiter.'' She gave, in more detail, Riemann-Vesper's account of finding Tiber. ''And our son, Stephan.'' Without looking at him, she felt Lightfoot's startled reaction. ''He . . . well, he's behind all of what I have done, somehow. I make no apology for that. But he too felt a mind in the Trojans. During the war. I don't know how.''

''Home,'' Elward said. ''They're all going home.'' Everyone in the room looked at him. ''This clanship thing. It has a deepdrive, right? A way of getting through interstellar space. It, like, snuck into the Solar System somehow.''

''Alien spacecraft seem to transit the Solar System regularly,'' Lightfoot said. ''We have little way of detecting a ship under deepdrive.''

''Okay, fine. But that lumpy thing that hit us at Ripi's—''

''Sukh's spacecraft,'' Ambryn said.

''Right. That didn't have a deepdrive, did it? Or did it pop in here with one of those one-shots you're guessing at?''

''I don't think so,'' Soph said after thinking about it. ''That thing looked like a straight interplanetary vessel. Remember, Ripi's was an illicit growth, specifically intended for an escape across interstellar space.''

''A tumor,'' Elward said.

''Just so. A tumor in the outer membranes of the Bru clanship. So if what we think about Sukh's assault ship is true—''

''It was brought here by a clanship that *did* have a deepdrive,'' Ambryn said.

''Home.'' Lightfoot brought the discussion back to his desired topic. ''We're putting Sukh at the Vronnan clanship. Her ship is damaged. She most likely needs repair, and there's no safe haven for her in the Solar System. The others?''

''Tiber was raised somewhere,'' Elward said. ''By Sukh. She used all sorts of imagery, a whole simulation system. Where? Aboard her spacecraft?''

''Aboard the stranded clanship,'' Ambryn said. She watched Elward intently, as if he was her child, performing in a school play.

He shrugged. ''Seems reasonable. Home. Tiber wants to get there.''

''Ripi.'' Lightfoot watched Elward closely too, but that was just his way, not because he was seeing something new in someone he had thought he knew everything about.

"He wanted to stay aboard the *Argent*." Elward looked away from Soph. "I helped him do it."

"He wants to get back to Vronnan space," Soph said. She and Elward would have to deal with their problems later. "There's been war there, and Ripi-Arana-Hoc is suddenly a valuable resource. That's what started this whole thing off."

"And how better," Lightfoot said, "than through using a repaired—healed—Vronnan deepdrive?"

"He was after the *Argent* the entire time," Soph said. "That was what he wanted. For precisely that reason. He hadn't anticipated Sukh, and Tiber's involvement made things difficult for him, but he still needed those placentas. To save the deepdrive. To get—"

"Home," Elward said.

They thought about this, all in silence.

"And I know where it is," Ambryn said at last.

"Sure," Elward said. "Those Leading Trojans Soph is so excited by."

"I mean more specifically. We could search there for months and still not find it. But the Executioner told me." She looked apprehensive, remembering, as if the Executioner was just waiting to burst through the wall. "Pyx no longer remembered, but they'd carried out an extensive interrogation. They knew the location of the mind that Pyx had contacted . . . the deepdrive. And the deepdrive senses the gravity of things around it. In exchange for her life—and her child—the Executioner told me where it was."

"How?" Lightfoot asked. "How could she tell you a gravitational map?"

"She didn't do it in words," Ambryn said and began to sketch the image that the Executioner had shown her.

4

"Soph." Lightfoot sat up on the floor and rubbed his eyes when she dropped through the hatch, as if she'd shown up unexpectedly. "I have a question."

"What?" He'd called her away from a planning session with Ambryn and Elward, and Soph suspected that he was jealous of her closeness with them. "Couldn't it wait?"

"No, it couldn't."

He brushed fingers over a stack of old data screens, which fluttered off an inflated seat. The construction monkeys had built him a weird little aerie out on the end of a sling cable. Soph didn't think he'd want to know about the modification work they did to the attachment collar while it was still spinning.

"All right." She sat. "Is it an operational question?"

"Not at all."

"Then why—"

He was silhouetted by the light of his display screen. It showed the Leading Trojans, enhanced so that you could actually see the asteroids against the dense background of stars. "Stephan was out here during the war. Coincidence, you think?" He looked frightened.

"Not coincidence. More like causality." She would much rather have dealt with the risks of their violent deaths in the approaching operation. "I talked with him a lot, those last weeks before he left for Io. I can't pretend that I knew they were the last. I had no sense of that, no deep mother's intuition. If I'd had it, I wouldn't have let him drive me so crazy. But something he said—some connection—tipped the scales in my later decision to go to Venus with Kammer and Kun."

"But how?" Lightfoot was stunned. "I might accept his faith: that near the moment of death you hear the Voice of Jove. If the Voice of Jove turns out to be itself the dying deepdrive of the Vronnan clanship . . . he never again came close, did he? He heard it, but he didn't know where or how. Close to death, floating out on his tether behind his ship during the actions around Hidalgo . . . so he went back. Again and again, not really knowing what it was he was looking for. Soph, think of the work, the dedicated, desperate . . . and I thought he was just scatterbrained, an adolescent way beyond his time, enjoying himself by sliding on Ioan lava flows. . . ."

"Lightfoot—"

"But, Soph." He took her hand in a painful grip. "How Venus?"

"What?"

"I could buy all that, see some kind of . . . *mechanistic* explanation for the last part of Stephan's life, a dying deep-drive instead of God, a mere mistaken interpretation, but . . . how could he have known that Ripi was on Venus? That . . . deepdrive didn't know that. From what I can figure out, it wouldn't know anything much, except . . . well, I don't know what it would know. But no one aboard the Arana clanship knew where Ripi was. That was why Sukh sent Tiber out into the worlds of men to find him. How did Stephan . . . ?"

The human mind is inherently fallible. It sees patterns where there is only random clustering, overestimates and underestimates odds depending on emotional need, ignores obvious facts that contradict already established conclusions. Hopes and fears become detailed memories. And absolutely correct conclusions are drawn from completely inadequate evidence.

Years of tech hunting, under Lightfoot's tutelage, had taught Soph to recognize and acknowledge these errors, if not entirely to eliminate them. So should she acknowledge her errors to him now?

"I don't think he did know," Soph said after thinking about it for a long time.

"What?" Lightfoot asked wearily.

"I don't know, Lightfoot! I don't know." She was weary herself. "I don't know."

"Tell me *exactly* what it is that you don't know."

"Don't, Lightfoot."

He opened his mouth to say something else, to press down harder, but then just kept it open and breathed slowly and evenly through it. She fancied she could hear him loosening his tight throat and imagined rusted-stuck clamps being hammered open with sledgehammers. They were both working hard. Was it worth the labor?

"I carried Stephan along with me to Venus," she said. "Why not? It was a mission born of faith. We'd talked about various plans when he was home the last time. We ranged all over the Solar System. We did talk about Venus . . . I think. Oh, Lightfoot, it was such a rough time, then and after. . . ."

"You carried him with you." Lightfoot said. "He never

told you that any secret lay on Venus, but you needed to go, so you read that into his words. It's coincidence after all. I can see why people wish coincidence had meaning."

"I really don't know anymore," she said. "Maybe Ambryn does actually see something true in her alien entrails."

The supports of the cabin vibrated beneath her. Somewhere in the *Imhotep*'s structure, construction monkeys toiled at their endless task of rebuilding their spacecraft. She closed her eyes and pressed her forehead against the curve of the wall.

Given Soph's information from Commander Riemann-Vesper, Ambryn's from the Executioner, and some scraps and hints of observations Lightfoot had managed to correlate from the battle of 944 Hidalgo, Martyshka had a specific location to aim for. Was this location, amid a group of flying mountains in a lagrangian point in Jupiter's orbit, any more of a real goal than her Stephan-inspired dreams of Venus?

"We're sitting in this little cabin slung off a construction monkey vessel, en route to the Trojans," Lightfoot said. "What pulls us there is a long chain of connections. But those connections existed before you even left for Venus. Clanship to Tiber, Tiber to *Argent*, *Argent* to clanship deepdrive, Sukh to Tiber, Sukh to Ripi, Ripi to clanship. Clanship deepdrive to Stephan. It was all there."

"Are you saying that I somehow perceived all those connections before figuring anything out?" Soph said. "That all I've been doing for the past year is *remembering*? Or that Stephan did?"

"Maybe it was your memory of him that knew it. He lives on in you. . . ."

"We should live on in him instead," Soph said. "Only we don't."

"Yes, yes." Lightfoot rubbed his wrinkled forehead. He was a big, dignified man, but he had curled up on the floor, creasing his inappropriately fine suit.

Soph slid up next to him. Their marriage was the opposite of entropy. Their differences got magnified, rather than worn down into evenness. Marriages like theirs either generated a lot of power or ended spectacularly. No matter how hard she tried to make it clear, this one never seemed to have ended. And she did want to feel that power once again.

Now that Lightfoot, driven by old grief, was sliding into a mysticism not too different from Soph's belief in Stephan's supernaturally prescient advice, she was driven away from it to find a haven in rationality.

"I guessed, Lightfoot," she said. "I used a distorted memory of Stephan's words to cover that guess, make it seem reasonable. I guessed that Ripi was important, never having any idea of where that importance lay. The guess paid off. But that doesn't make the guess retroactively sensible. I was looking for something else."

"Columbus was looking for China when he sailed from Spain," Lightfoot said. "Sensible people knew that the world was indeed round but also knew that it was too big for him to reach China by going west. Hell, Eratosthenes had figured out that the world's diameter was almost thirteen thousand kilometers back in the third century B.C.E. Columbus's ships would disappear into what, in terms of the available technology, was essentially an infinite expanse of ocean. Only he ran into the Americas on the way. Which, incidentally, he never realized. He kept believing that he was somewhere in the outer territories of Cathay until his death. And so the world was changed."

"So did he, unconsciously, perceive the truth?" Soph asked. As soon as her head touched his shoulder, she felt sleepy. It had been years since she'd slept like this.

"Maybe. Sometimes it did seem that he realized he had stumbled on something vastly greater than a new route for shipping cloves. That the mystical kingdom of Cathay was not actually China at all."

"So which are we flying toward?" Soph asked. "China or Cathay?"

"Let's see if there's a Vronnan clanship in the Leading Trojans at all. We've all been talking about it as if its existence is proven, but it is nothing but supposition. Let's find it and then we can figure out if there's any truth in it all or if we've just tripped over it all by accident."

"That's a good idea, Lightfoot," she said and fell asleep on his shoulder.

Fourteen

1

"There's a lot of post-explosive debris.'' Martyshka floated in a spherical control space, all four of her limbs dancing across command points. ''It spreads from at least two foci.''

The *Imhotep* approached a small chondritic asteroid, outlier of the Trojan group. It looked like any other asteroid, a chunk left over from planetary construction, like scrap lumber. But between them and the asteroid lay something else.

''There's one focus for you,'' Ambryn said. Information swam around her. She had her own control area, but its functionality was so limited that she felt like a child with a toy. She tapped in and the image swelled.

''Oh, God,'' Soph said. ''Is anyone—''

''Life still aboard.'' Martyshka was brisk. It had only been through intricately negotiated agreement that anyone other than she and Ambryn were inside the *Imhotep*'s bridge. Soph, Elward, and Lightfoot were confined to a cagelike arrangement with the controls to Lightfoot's particle-beam gun, like captured prisoners. All wore airsuits.

The image of the *Argent* floated above them. An explosion had creased the wide stern. Ambryn felt a moment of sharp sympathy for the Engineer, whose precious, balky engines had to have been damaged.

The rents in the hull had been sealed, and lines of bracing were just visible, holding the weakened structure together. Infrared readings showed most of it holding heat.

Once the *Argent* had been identified, Martyshka scanned beyond it. ''The other focus is some thousand kilometers beyond. Almost on top of it but still distinct.''

The only thing left of the other ship was a segment of hull and the melted remains of what might have been drive pods.

Ambryn sensed the flicker of computer identification as the *Imhotep* tracked every fragment spreading out from the ship-to-ship encounter and classified it. Two wide starburst patterns slowly came into existence, overlapping each other, with a big hole in the pattern where the asteroid had caught the shrapnel. Guesses about composition and identity puffed around Martyshka's head.

''The *Argent* did not destroy that other ship,'' Soph said. ''She had no weapons aboard. Not like that.''

''Perhaps they found a hulk and blew it up,'' Martyshka said. ''Went aboard and planted explosives. They were damaged by an unexpected fragment.''

''You don't believe that,'' Soph said.

''Soph.'' Ambryn knew that Martyshka would be frantic at this interruption to her thoughts. ''Let her—''

Ambryn's helmet sucked onto its seal and air puffed up around her neck.

The alien spacecraft rose slowly and dramatically above the distant asteroid.

''Ah, there's the beast,'' Lightfoot said, with every sign of satisfaction. He pulled himself down to the controls of his bootleg particle-beam weapon, which had been worked into the intricate pattern of gear on the bridge's walls.

''That's not Sukh's ship,'' Ambryn said.

''Then whose?'' Martyshka sounded annoyed. Ambryn had briefed her on all the players.

''It's Vronnan.'' Soph looked intently. ''It looks a lot like the one-shot interstellar vessel in which Ripi arrived in the Solar System. Gear's been added to the exterior. But I bet that thing budded off a living clanship.''

"And came here from Outside?" Information poured from the readouts, so much that Ambryn couldn't keep up with it.

"Armed, armed," Martyshka said. "Has to be. The *Argent* didn't blow up that other vessel. This one did. Perhaps it attacked the *Argent* as well."

Ambryn spared a glance at her. Martyshka floated confidently in her control space, a hundred lines of data playing over her skin. Her efficient energy made her seem old, as if she had fought such battles many times before. Ambryn knew the image would stick with her for as long as she lived. However long that was going to be.

". . . dangerous . . ." A voice crackled over Ambryn's comm line. ". . . think so . . ."

"*Argent*? *Argent*?" Ambryn shouted, even though it wasn't necessary. "Who's over there?"

A pause. "Well, if it isn't our fancy-pants Miss Ambryn Chretien." It was Dr. Fulani. "Forget something? I'll check Lost and Found . . ."

"Dr. Fulani." Soph broke in. "Can you give us any information about the Vronnan vessel?"

"My Lord. Are you all up there?"

"Yes," Soph said. "Elward too—if you want to know."

"So he *did* get scooped up by that whirligig. This is the same ship, isn't it? Elward, you're luckier than God."

The Vronnan vessel drifted closer.

"Fulani—" Soph said.

"Don't worry about her. She saved our asses, I think. She blew up the ship that was threatening us. Then she disappeared behind Hector. This is the first we've seen of her since."

"Who is that?" Soph was clearly ready to burst. "Who is aboard the Vronnan vessel? What happened to Sukh?"

Ambryn examined the destroyed hulk more carefully. Could that be the remains of Sukh's vessel? There really wasn't enough left to tell, but maybe Martyshka would be able to integrate it back up from the spreading fragments. If Sukh was dead, it would take care of a few problems.

"Well, Soph, you probably know a lot more about it than I do. You listened to Ripi's stories, after all. But near as I can tell, the name is Lo-Bru-Tirni. Says she's Ripi's wife.

And the mother of whoever was commanding the ship that attacked us. Sukh, you say her name was? Hell of a thing, eh?''

''Okay,'' Fulani said. ''Time for some straight talk. Tiber never intended to come back from Venus, did he? Ah, I can tell just by looking at you, Ambryn. You can tell me now. He's gone.''

''No. He thought he could leave with Sukh.''

They floated in Fulani's medical office. A thrown-up screen showed construction monkeys crawling over the damaged portion of the *Argent*'s stern. Ambryn could see the large form of the Engineer as she attempted to direct their work.

''We all would've been better off, I think.'' Fulani sighed. ''As it was, he hauled us all the way out here. The orbit of Jupiter! Not even *at* Jupiter but at a bunch of crumbs that got caught in the fold of its pocket. Then he dumps us again! Took off in our last vacuum shuttle with Ripi. We go through shuttles like butt wipes.''

''Where did they go?''

''Home, he said.'' Fulani grimaced. ''That thing doesn't have much of a range. He must have been raised in vacuum.''

''And Sukh—''

''Damn, what a mess. You know, I didn't have to take this gig. I could have beat those malpractice allegations at Malahyde . . . it was a hormonal problem, nothing I could have anticipated, my free-fall medicine was a little rusty. . . .'' Ambryn could see how old Fulani really was, under the mosaic of rejuves. The *Argent* had to have been the only place she could have gone.

Fulani remembered herself. ''That warship was waiting for us. Sukh's warship, the one that hit Venus, right? Tiber must have known. He was hauling us out here to meet her or something.''

''She needed Ripi. He's her father. He has her memories.''

''Dear, you say that as if it all makes perfect sense. I'm not sure it even makes any sense for *them*, for these Vronnans. I think what we've got here is crazy aliens. Even other *aliens* can't figure them out. How does your skrying handle something like that?''

''I care about their guts, not their brains,'' Ambryn said. ''I'm interested in human fate.''

''Well, those aliens seemed to have played Tiber's fate pretty good. Maybe that's just an edge condition your system isn't designed to handle. I'd advise you to look into it. But Sukh was here with that little warship of hers. I swear, Tiber left us open, let her hit our engines so we couldn't get away, so it was all up to her. I've looked at the image stores. Her ship looks like hell, it's been through a lot. I don't think she could have done anything unless we let her.''

''And then Tiber took the shuttle and left?''

Fulani shook her head. ''Not right then and there. Because that *other* ship appeared. It was like a bedroom farce played in outer space. Sukh hadn't expected that, I could tell. Tiber neither. There was some kind of confrontation, all sorts of alien screaming on various frequencies. I got records if you want to listen. They sort of stared at each other, then Sukh fired some kind of sneaky missile, the track's just a big wiggle. The other ship fired back . . . and Sukh's ship blew up.''

''Just like that?''

''Seems absurd, right? Bad design or something. But like I said, the thing had been through the wringer. Once Sukh's ship was gone, the other one, Lo's, kind of retreated, as if it couldn't believe what had happened either. Of course, she'd just vaporized her daughter. Maybe these aliens take that kind of thing seriously. And Tiber fell apart. This was the end. We'd brought him back from the dead, patched him up, put him back up on his pedestal, worshipped him, licked his toes, the works, and now he had nothing again. And we'd gotten lax, I have to admit. For a while, we'd guarded him, kept watch, but the system had fallen apart. That Archon, she struts a good game, but it's that tedious day-to-day shit that's the real test of a security chief, and she's got a little too much theater on her. Tiber grabbed Ripi, took off in the vacuum shuttle.''

''So now he's out there, somewhere.''

''Dead.'' Fulani stated it as a fact. ''As soon as the Engineer gets those engines repaired . . . What the hell *are* they doing out there?" Some kind of squabble seemed to have developed between the Engineer and her construction monkey subcontractors.

"Probably debating some fundamental modification to the engine functions," Ambryn said. She didn't know why she found that so funny, but she found herself laughing.

"All I want to do is get the hell out of here." Fulani was fierce. "Do you understand that?"

"I do."

2

The air was full of the sounds and smells of an implied life that had never lived within these barren walls. Creatures chittered and moaned. Communicative smells, acrid and sweet, spiraled through the air, forming delicate architectures of scent that the human nose, blunt-sensing and one-dimensional, was incapable of perceiving.

Something seemed to grunt by, with a heavy tread that vibrated in the walls, despite the nonexistent gravity—the sensory images had not been reprogrammed for free fall. Soph wondered if Lo-Bru-Tirni felt disoriented or if it made perfect sense to her.

Despite herself, Soph backed against the wall and scanned the dark space of Lo-Bru-Tirni's audience room. Nothing. But she could feel the heat that came from the creature, and a directed puff of air made it seem that it had brushed past her arm. The bulbs in the wall took on a hint of the grainy texture of probing laser light. Without anything specific, she could see the creature's essence: a Guardian, one of Lo-Bru-Tirni's imaginary bodyguards, here to look after her in her interview with the free-running human beings. And Guardians, it seemed, were distant descendants of Ulanyi, having made a comfortable home within the Vronnan clan nests.

Lo-Bru-Tirni floated in what would be her support couch under acceleration. It was clearly meant to interface with something living. Hollow spaces underneath should have been a habitat for some sort of maintenance creature. Lo's integument was cracked and peeling, and one of her hind limbs had developed a nerve defect and shuddered. Soph remembered Ripi's description of Timp, his aging female mentor. Perhaps loss of rear limb nerves was a common effect of aging in Vronnan females. Or perhaps it was just a side effect of negotiation in the Vronnan diplomatic class. All that endless sitting.

And there, partially concealed by the massiveness of her middle limbs, the ovipositors. Soph's eyes kept straying to them.

"Where are they?" Soph asked. "Where are Tiber and Ripi-Arana-Hoc?"

A purse perched on Soph's shoulder. Not much of her luggage had made it through the vicissitudes of her life since escaping from the *Argent*, but she had been careful to keep the one that had stored the results of her communications with Ripi-Arana-Hoc. Her bag spit Vronnan at Lo-Bru-Tirni.

"They have returned to the beginning. They are now aboard the Arana clanship."

"Arana? Is that what's here in the Trojans? Ripi's original clanship? But how . . . ?"

Even through the medium of her translating purse, Soph could feel the solemn dignity of Lo-Bru-Tirni's manner.

"The story is complex but not without interest."

It took a good number of months before the Bru clan leaders concluded that Lo-Bru-Tirni had had nothing to do with her mate's escape and let her out of severe detention. By that time, the total situation was so serious that the destruction of her life seemed a minor inconvenience. She retired to unmarried female quarters. Stigmatized by her association with Ripi and her one surviving Handicapped daughter, she remained alone.

The war that had broken out between Arana and Bru in the wake of Ripi's betrayal of both of them eventually involved a good part of Vronnan civilization, as alliances pulled other clans into the conflict. Despite its precarious political position, Arana proved to be militarily successful in engagements amid distant asteroid belts and near the sullen surfaces of dying red dwarves, as well as in the social assassination encounters more typical of Vronnan conflict resolution. Clearly, Arana contingency plans based on political failure had long been in the works. Lo wondered how many of those contingency plans were the product of her beloved if insane spouse Ripi-Arana-Hoc. He had always been ready for political breakdown. In her darker moments, she had thought that he longed for it. Lo-Bru-Tirni, as one of Bru clan's most respected military commanders, was frustrated by her distance from events. Even though she was free, suspicion kept her from any direct military action.

It was in this situation of sudden Bru reverses that Ankur, Ripi's sterile Helper semisib, who had masterminded the fake memory transfer that had permitted Ripi's escape, made a proposal that freed him from right under the descending jaws of the Guardian assigned to execute him.

Fertile Vronnans suspected the sterile Helper caste, even as they depended on them for their very existence, Vronnan reproduction being the tangled, technologized business that it was. Most of the raising of post-eruption infants was taken care of by the sterile semisibs.

Sterile semisibs had originally arisen from unfertilized ova. Over many millennia, it turned out that clans that did not eat their sterile semisibs but instead trained them in nest maintenance and defense had more fertile children that lived into adulthood. In that sense, Helpers were the original symbionts in Vronnan nests, templates for all the rest. As memory transfer technology leaked into Vronnan culture, and was unified with the sophisticated placental membranes derived from Ulanyi precursors, and the nervous tissues of what looked very much like human beings, Helpers took over the technology of reproduction. Most adult fertile Vronnans knew nothing whatsoever about it.

Helpers brought in the organisms that made up the functions of the Vronnan nest. Thousands of years of intense genetic modification created a variety of specialized creatures, and eventually everything from food production to waste removal was performed by dependent organisms. Machinery might have done the same, but Helper power depended on control of reproduction, and clans that attempted to replace Helper functions with machinery tended to die out.

Ankur knew the life of the Arana clan, and, particularly, the biology of its human beings. No one in Vronnan culture knew the origins of these creatures, which had joined the nests early in their prehistory. Some of the fertiles suspected that the Helpers knew more about early Vronnan history than they were telling. Since Helpers supervised the memory transfer that was the central life sacrament of Vronnan civilization, they could influence which memories transferred and which finally vanished from the meme pool. And a culture that depended on nonphysical means of transferring race memory found that it had no way to independently check its own self-perception.

Ankur proposed an interesting form of biological warfare to the old female clan heads of Bru. The humans aboard the Arana clanship were a reproductively isolated population, with a narrowed range of genetic variation. He had in his possession a crystallized prion that would cause severe but nonfatal myelin damage to the possessors of a certain group of genes. The damage would be just enough that the human central nervous system could no longer be used for the transmission of Arana memories. The clan would be forced to sue for peace before a generation of Handicapped children were born and its entire culture was wiped out.

In return, Ankur wanted to leave Bru with the infant Sukh. Since Sukh possessed none of her father's memories, she was useless to Bru purposes. The deal was made, and none of Lo-Bru-Tirni's objections were considered. This was a state matter, not a personal one. As, in fact, her marriage had been—to everyone but herself.

Lo found herself hoping that Ripi had survived somewhere out in the insane universe, despite the sin this implied to her as the mother of Handicapped children. The two of them had served together with honor in the Telstet system and she too thought that, in another world, their mating might have happened voluntarily. That it had been forced on him for state reasons was a nightmare to her.

Ankur disappeared with her daughter Sukh, who grew up hostile to both sides in the expanding conflict. Lo heard stories about Sukh but was not sure whether to credit them. The hybrid asteroid colony to which Ankur took her was violent, and she grew up fighting, as a Handicapped Vronnan usually did. She defended her increasingly weak foster parent until the day when he died in an assault. Her revenge against his killers left the interior of the colony a devastated wasteland.

After Sukh escaped the moribund colony, her mind packed with whatever information Ankur had seen fit to put in there, she raised an army of other lost Vronnans: those without memories, those with the wrong memories, those from clans that had reached the end of their spans and fallen apart. Sukh's group of renegades formed an independent force of some importance during the wars that sparked off the Arana–Bru conflict and flared throughout Vronnan space. They hitched rides on clanships, peeling off when the destination system was reached.

But it was clear that what Sukh most desperately sought the entire time was the location of her dear Running Father, Ripi. Ripi had vanished into the mysterious Sol System, where loose human beings, who had lived for hundreds of thousands of years without another intelligent species until the arrival of the Probe, were now slowly working their way into the symbiotic niches for which they were best suited.

In between paid military operations, Sukh sought information coming out of Sol System. Information did trickle out via Ulanyi couriers, Tibrini supply vessels, trade ships. But there was no way to find where Ripi had gone to ground, the prerequisite for a quick, sharp operation, violating human space.

Meanwhile, the Bru biological warfare plan went forward. The human population of the Arana clanship was infected with the tailored prion, which was brought in on supposedly neutral trade goods. It spread through the human population. But Ankur had either miscalculated or lied deliberately about the effects. The damage turned out to be severe, and many of the humans died. But the memory effect Ankur had predicted held true. The humans aboard the Arana clanship were no longer capable of mediating Vronnan memory transfer.

At this point, the Arana should have sued for peace. Their act would have been greeted with relief throughout Vronnan space and a transfer of human populations arranged. The Arana clan memory would have been preserved.

Instead, driven to the last extremity by the conflict, the Arana committed a perversion, one that would leave them forever outcast among the Vronnans. They launched a sublight assault on a lumbering Earth-human colonization vessel that was, at that point, just leaving the most distant confines of Sol System and kidnapped its off-brand humans for the purposes of reproduction and memory transfer.

It was the *Prismatic Bezel.*

Humans were not livestock to the Vronnans, or slaves. While they might at one time have been simply hosts to Vronnan infants, they were now an intelligent co-species, one that had lived with the Vronnans for so long that it was impossible to imagine the world without them. To kidnap and rape nonconsenting human beings was a savage and unforgivable crime. It was desperate enough that it gave a serious boost to the peace process in Vronnan space. One thing was agreed to: the Arana clan had to be punished.

Despite their detestation of the crime, other Vronnan forces were reluctant to travel vast distances to confront the desperate Arana clanship where it lay, in the Oort cometary cloud around the Solar System, where it had concealed itself. Everyone agreed that it was a crime, but who was to make sacrifices in order to punish it?

Fortunately for the Vronnans, the tool for punishment lay readily at hand: Sukh's military force. In return for a free operational hand, Sukh agreed to take care of the problem aboard her father's old clanship. Her force was carried to the Arana clanship's position.

No one in Vronnan space had ever inquired too deeply into what happened aboard the Arana clanship, and its captive, the *Prismatic Bezel.* All that was known was that Sukh's spaceships did their job. Moving with suicidal daring, they boldly approached the Arana clanship and dove in to the assault, suffering heavy casualties in the process. They slaughtered the offending Arana clan, which did not defend itself forcefully, conscious of its guilt. Sukh seized control of the Arana clanship.

Sukh then, without outside authorization, moved the Arana clanship. Though the deepdrive was already injured, the clanship was operational enough to slip inside the Solar System, to hide itself in the Leading Trojans of Jupiter. Forces elsewhere in Vronnan space became worried that she was attempting to start her own independent clan, using the old Arana clanship resources as a power base. Perhaps she even planned some domination over the humans of the Solar System, which would have caused war, not just within Vronnan space but with other species who had a stake in human beings. A larger military incursion by Vronnan forces into the Solar System was threatened.

But Sukh had other plans. She released her forces, and they trickled back and vanished into the complexities of Vronnan civilization. The Arana clanship remained concealed in the rocks of the Trojans, damaged but alive. The human beings of the Solar System remained completely unaware of the vast conflict they had so narrowly avoided.

A few years later, Sukh, alone in her vessel, left the remains of the Arana clanship and moved toward Venus.

"Fulani wouldn't let me go back aboard the *Argent*," Elward said.

"Why would you want to?" Ambryn fiddled with the shuttle's controls. "The place was a pigsty."

"Because I wanted to. I wanted to see—"

"The Archon? Or should I call her Jig?"

Elward did not take offense. "I don't think she'd like that. Oh, no. I think I might have enjoyed calling her that."

"Fulani's just covering her own ass," Ambryn said. "She managed to blame everything on you, once you were gone—"

"Dead," Elward said. "She thought."

"Hey, did anyone ask you to use Soph's big escape bubble? That was strictly a desperation move. You *should* be dead. Pure luck that the *Imhotep* was nosing around and picked you up." Soph got the sense that Ambryn was more than a little jealous of Elward's revealed long relationship with Martyshka and the construction monkeys. "It was a sensible play on Fulani's part, given the situation. Otherwise, she and the Engineer would have ended up in the cage they let me and Soph out of."

"Sounds like you and she had quite a talk."

"We did."

Soph watched the image of the chondritic asteroid recede

behind them, radar-detected variation in density as darker blobs inside. Ambryn piloted the spacecraft toward the Arana clanship, deeper in the concentration of the Trojans. The *Argent* and Lo-Bru-Tirni's ship shrank and vanished. Hector loomed ahead.

''So what the hell is our Lo doing way out here?'' Ambryn said. ''Looking for hubby?''

''I can't really explain her motivations,'' Soph said. ''But apparently there was concern about what had happened here at the Arana clanship. Once again, no Vronnans were particularly interested in checking it out, so Lo-Bru-Tirni volunteered.''

''They didn't think it odd? She's from the Bru, Arana's enemy clan. Her husband fled, her daughter became their rogue enforcer . . .''

''Remember that a budship is a one-way ticket. Unless the deepdrive aboard the Arana clanship somehow gets revived, Lo-Bru-Tirni is stuck here in the Solar System along with the rest of us. How many volunteers do you suppose there were for that particular suicide mission?''

When Soph had last seen them, Lo-Bru-Tirni, Martyshka, Fulani, and Lightfoot had all been floating in Lo's audience chamber, negotiating salvage rights. They had looked like a bunch of old sharpers sitting down to a game of poker, Soph thought. They might have been doing it for years.

Martyshka had leased them this shuttle to continue their exploration while the real decisions got made. Lightfoot would be handling the mission from aboard the *Imhotep*. No matter where he was or what was going on, Lightfoot always had to have a back office.

''Any guesses as to what actually happened to Sukh?''

''She tried to kill Mom,'' Elward said. ''She got what was coming to her.''

''Maybe that's true,'' Soph said.

''You think it was too easy, don't you, Soph?'' Ambryn said.

''It's not the ease that disturbs me. It's the festival explosion. Destroyed Sukh's vessel completely and spread it out beyond recovery. I just don't like disappeared bodies.''

''Not a lot left after a vacuum military encounter,'' Ambryn said. "The *Greatorex*'s partial survival was unusual. That's why Sukh used it. Usually there's nothing bigger than a scorched pinky fingernail left to investigate."

Soph was still uncomfortable with the way Sukh's vessel had behaved like a piñata but couldn't articulate it. Instead, she tried to relax and watched the screens. The three of them sat in companionable silence for some time.

"There's another asteroid behind Hector," Ambryn said. "Except the charts don't show one. Maybe the radar's malfunctioning."

"Well," Elward said. "Look the hell at that thing."

3

The Arana clanship was, at its largest extent, at least three kilometers across. That would have made it a small asteroid, particularly in the shadow of the one-hundred-eighty-kilometer diameter of Hector. But, unlike the circum-Lunars, the largest artificial satellites in the System, it did not seem to be based on any naturally occurring structure. It looked like it had been built.

Or grown.

Whatever the clanship had once been, it had suffered grievously. Vast explosions had torn through the humped outer surface, revealing intricate onion layers of structure. It still spun slowly, maintaining gravity at its outer edge, so any loose debris had been slung off into space. Whatever had happened, by this time the pieces had been so far dispersed that there would be no way to reconstruct the disaster. Sukh had done a serious job on Daddy's ancestral clanship, the one from which her memories had never come.

As Soph examined it, the initial monolithic impression disappeared. It was not a single structure, built somewhere for a purpose. It more resembled a vast coral reef, full of structures that had found it convenient to grow together. Still, taken as a whole, the Arana clanship was the largest self-contained structure Soph had ever seen.

She supposed that made sense, given what she knew of the Vronnans and their means of transferring memory. The problem with any of the theoretical massive structures that might lie somewhere out in space, the giant star-enclosing spheres, the millennial starships, the ringworlds, the planet-girdling constructions, all rumored and spoken of by aliens passing through the Solar System, was not the physical engineering but the social. How did you maintain an organization made up of individuals for long enough to build the damn thing? The grandchildren would revolt against the now-meaningless megalomaniac ozymandiasing of their forebears and depart the never-to-be-completed structure to live out their lives somewhere that made sense.

The Vronnans had tried to overcome this problem with generational memory transfer on a dangerous scale so that the obsessions of the sires were transferred, unchanged, into their descendants. In fact, those who fled, refusing to pass down their demands, were, like Ripi, considered criminals, passed beyond the bounds of civilization.

"There!" Ambryn said. "That looks like—"

"I think it is," Soph said. Below them, a detonation had crisped deck structures up like burnt sheets of paper. Revealed at the bottom of the crater was the smooth back of a separate spacecraft. Explosions had torn through it, but Soph thought she recognized the design of the *Prismatic Bezel.*

Now that they were closer, she could see that life had continued past the time of destruction. For example, new connections had grown up around the *Bezel*'s hull. It looked now as if it had been stolen by ants, carried down into their nest, and used as the center of their activities, replacing the vanished queen.

"Now, you say Lo-Bru-Tirni's been in contact with these . . . well, whoever lives in there," Ambryn said.

"So she told me. I have no idea how many intelligent species there are aboard a Vronnan clanship—"

"It's amazing how much we don't know, isn't it?" Ambryn said.

"The more for Soph to find out," Elward said.

"Your loyalty is touching," Ambryn said.

"Lo-Bru-Tirni has communicated with the humans aboard," Soph said. "At least they seem to be humans. It remains to be seen what kind."

Ambryn maneuvered the ship inward. The Arana clanship

swelled until it was everything. The torn levels of the destroyed sections rose up around them and became cliffs that bulked against the stars.

The ring of assault craft still clung to the *Prismatic Bezel*'s waist, just as Tiber had described them. Their backs shone purple-black. Were they heavily modified creatures, descended from some ancestral limpet, or had the Vronnans built them, the way normal species built things? The seams between them were almost invisible. They must have been special-constructed for the *Bezel* assault, since they matched up with the hull perfectly.

"Looks like someone has been trying to fix the thing," Elward said.

Soph looked more closely at the torn-back hull at the stern. The dim forms of the massive Martian drive pods were just visible. Explosions had torn away the shielding.

But someone had been working. Not with emergently complex creatures but with homely tools, which now hung in neatly clamped racks along the spine of an engine whose shell had been neatly welded shut. It looked like parts had been taken from other engines to repair it.

"Escape," Ambryn said. "Maybe they had no other way and decided to try the *Bezel*. I wonder if they ever got anywhere. Probably not, if they're still here."

"I don't think so," Soph said. "The ship is braced in. See the reinforcement? And that was done after Sukh's assault. It's harder to remove now than it was before."

Ambryn looked at the honeycomb matrix that had grown to encase the *Bezel*'s blunt nose.

"Okay," she said. "So the engine thing is just somebody's hobby. Must get kind of boring, hanging around out here."

"They must have lost their rotational engines," Soph said. "So they've modified the *Bezel* for that use. They direct its drives at the tangent. They're trying to spin the clanship up to full gravity. Far from wanting to desert this thing, they want to maintain it."

"Who?" Ambryn asked.

"Maybe them," Elward said.

They looked up. Three human figures, faces invisible behind reflective visors, hung from the honeycomb above. One of them held an unnecessarily large plasma weapon in both arms.

4

The cylindrical airlock was large enough for a dozen people—or perhaps for one vastly larger creature. The walls were gouged with what looked like claw marks, and a taut storage cocoon hanging on to the wall with suckers gave hints of what looked like an airsuit for an elephant. Or perhaps it wasn't a suit but the embryo of something that would grow up to be the size of an elephant. Other cocoons held more normally sized vacuum gear. The cocoon skins swelled out and then relaxed, as if getting used to having air pressure against them again.

"This airlock is derived from something that was once alive," Ambryn said, kneeling and touching the bonelike ribbing where the cylinder flattened into a floor. "A huge tube worm or something. At first glance it looks almost like Bgarth body modification, but it's actually something completely different. Some other planet of origin entirely."

"Does it eat things?" Elward asked. "Are we lunch?"

"We'd be more of a light snack," Ambryn said. "But it's really just an airlock. And an ancient one. I think it's got some age-related hormonal problems."

And Soph saw the stress creases in the cylinder walls, where they seemed to have grown thicker than the design indicated. Chisel marks along the edge of the circular inner door showed where someone had made sure the seal was still airtight against the burgeoning of the airlock body.

Elward eyed the three Arana humans. "And what's their status? Captors, hosts, escorts, what?"

"You need to know how truculent to look?" Ambryn said.

"I don't know that word," Elward said sourly.

"Don't get mad," Ambryn said. "Call them guides if that makes you happy."

"Knowing what's going on makes me happy."

"How often are you happy?"

"Odd thing, Ambryn," Elward said. "Less and less as time goes on."

Their guides were two women—one blonde, one dark-haired—and one man, all of them young, with the characteristics of an interior race: pale skin, wide eyes, fine features. Soph looked for hints that they were a separate species from Earth humans but saw nothing definitive. Even with *Homo sapiens*, an isolated population like this would have experienced substantial genetic drift, leading to defining traits. But these people had to be related to people from Earth. Tiber, in fact, looked much more alien.

The massive plasma gun had crudely welded handles for human use. It seemed to have originally been designed for something like an Ulanyi Executioner. In the better light of the airlock's glowstrip, Soph could see that drops of molten metal had spattered around a pinhole in the charge chamber. The thing was useless.

The fairer of the two women clicked it into a holder, which seemed to consist of two pairs of canines. The teeth slid around the tube and pulled it into the wall. She then stripped off her airsuit and stuffed it into a small cocoon, which sucked it up.

The woman had biosupport packs on her neck and spine for calcium and electrolyte balance. Something, probably excessive travel into the null-g center of the vessel, had left her with osteoporosis. Even with the metabolic correctors, the fine bones of her forearms and lower legs had been reinforced with adhesive mesh, and at least three of the fingers on her left hand had broken and healed badly, leaving it only partially functional. She pulled on a loose gown, tightened a few straps, and was suddenly dressed.

The man had what looked like ringworm, which left livid marks on his almost transparent, blue-veined skin. Despite their success at surviving here, the environment was not entirely friendly.

The man gestured at Soph and said something in their buzzing language. In response, she pushed herself back up against the wall. The huge elephant-airsuit cocoon moved away with a sound of releasing suckers.

"Careful, Soph," Elward said. "That gun was a dud. Maybe they had to get us in here to take care of us."

"We have to trust them," Soph said. "Otherwise, we get nowhere."

The other woman, who had short dark hair and no visible medical problems, smiled at Elward. She looked as nervous as he did. Who knew when these people had ever seen a human not a member of their tribe? Even if some of the *Bezel* crew had survived their savage arrival at the Arana clanship, that had been decades before.

"Look out, Soph!" Elward said.

Something grabbed Soph around the neck. An instant of uncomfortable tightness and then it relaxed into a warm pressure. She reached up and felt something like a squid tentacle clinging to her.

"What do you suppose these are, Soph?" Ambryn did her best to seem calm. Soph could see a similar tentacle encircling her neck. Maybe Elward had been right.

Soph felt a sharp pain in the side of her neck. The thing was sucking her blood, it would drain her in a few minutes . . . the pressure released.

"Goddammit! Goddammit!" Elward had evaded his own tentacle and had grabbed the man, a thin youth with an oddly prominent chest, as if wings had once attached themselves to his sternum. The man did not struggle but spoke in a calming buzz to Elward as one would to a dangerous maniac.

"It's a blood test, Elward," Soph said, rubbing the side of her neck. The tentacle had vanished into a horn-covered bump on the wall. How many other things were concealed in these thick walls? A tech-hunting team could have spent weeks looking over this little place alone.

"I'm fine! I don't need a blood test."

"Elward." Soph was surprised to hear Ambryn speak with calm authority. "Let that poor guy go and stop screwing around. They need to know if we carry any infectious diseases. They've had one bad experience already. In an enclosed culture like this, a new infection can spread like wildfire."

Elward did as he was asked. He stood against the wall, eyes closed, like a man awaiting execution, the tentacle pressed against his neck as the thin man rubbed his own neck and exchanged a ''Do we really have to deal with these idiots?'' look with his two companions.

The blonde woman with the biosupport packs nodded back: ''Yes, we do.''

The man turned and rubbed an area near the circular inner door. A few seconds later, it gasped open, letting in warm, humid air.

''Whatever it was, it looks like we passed,'' Ambryn said.

''I wonder what the test showed?'' Soph said. ''I'd like to see a genome comparison.''

''To see how closely related we are?'' Ambryn eyed their guides. ''Who knows? We never gave Tiber a blood test, did we?''

''I'd like to give *them* a blood test,'' Elward muttered.

After the brightness of the airlock, it was hard to see in the dappled shadows inside the clanship. The air was filled with the calls of animals, low thumps, high shrieks. Thick smells fought each other. The air was hot, and Soph found herself sweating almost instantly. Lights floated high overhead, but only vagrant beams penetrated down to the soft floor on which they stood. The bulbous forms that loomed around them seemed, at first, like huge oily mushrooms, but slowly came into view as some kind of shelled creatures who puffed air from wheezy lungs.

''Living air filters?'' Ambryn said.

''Someone should change the damn things,'' Elward said. ''Isn't anyone taking care of this place?''

''They've been through a lot,'' Soph said.

''So have we,'' Elward said.

A dense growth of lichen had clogged many of the shelled creatures' air holes, and at least one of them had died and been stripped by scavengers, leaving only a ghostly exoskeleton, like a gigantic barnacle, holes eaten through it. Something with wide, glowing eyes had made its home in the abandoned shell and peered out at them, just the tips of its claws visible around the edges of a hole.

Ambryn gasped and held Soph's arm in a painful grip. Soph looked up. Perched above them on one of the lower levels of the wide meshwork that filled the space, the model for the much smaller one that had made up the structure of the *Argent*, was a Guardian—what Ambryn knew as an Ulanyi Executioner. Its laser-equipped forearms pointed down at them. Soph wondered whether that particular surgical modification of the post-reproductive female form had been invented by the Ulanyi themselves or by the Vronnans. Since it was useful, the practice had spread.

Their three guides trotted on along a trail that sloped upward, ignoring the gloomily lowering Guardian. Ambryn, relaxing her muscles with a visible effort, followed.

A group of humans waited for them beyond. Water dripped all around. Thick leaves held pools filled with hundreds of small creatures.

At the center of the group of a dozen or so was the woman who was clearly their leader. She rode on the back of what looked like an early model dinosaur, with a huge bony head and spraddled legs. Her thick body was swathed in layers of loose silk, tight around her wrists and ankles, as well as across her belly. Her dark hair thrust atop her swollen head like a volcanic eruption. She said something to them in a baritone voice.

Soph bowed in return, followed by Ambryn and Elward.

"Thank you for your guidance," Soph said.

Their guides had a lot more than that to say. They explained a lot of things to their Queen.

"They're probably complaining about your bad attitude," Ambryn whispered to Elward.

"They ain't seen nothing yet."

Soph tried not to stare, because the woman bore, on her face and body, some of the answers to Soph's questions. She had the same spatulate frog fingers and distended facial bones that Tiber had. On him they had looked like an idiosyncratic deformation. Now that Soph could see another example before her, this one a success, even a triumph, it began to look like a perfectly natural state of the human condition. She could see too where Tiber had copied his formal uniform.

The big creature shifted beneath its royal rider, flicking its tongue at insects that had ventured too close.

"Soph," Ambryn said. "Do you see?"

"Shh!"

And Soph did see. The Queen's legs dangled down within the thick folds of silk, the muscles shrunken and useless. Her nervous system must have suffered serious damage from the demyelination disease.

"Tiber brought it to us," Ambryn said quietly. "To the humans of the Solar System. The infection started among those who had found him aboard the Martian ship. Then it spread from MeshMatrix Krystal in the years that he was there."

Soph realized that it was true. But it seemed that only a very few Earth humans suffered from the demyelination. Commander Riemann-Vesper had, unfortunately, proved to be susceptible.

Now that she was looking for it, she saw more evidence of the disease's depredations: a withered arm here, a constantly twitching muscle there.

The Queen looked down at them and nodded once, with a sort of satisfaction, as if showing the damage the disease had done had been her actual purpose in meeting them. Then her mount turned and lumbered up the path. Everyone else followed.

As they climbed along what looked like the back of a massive tree trunk, high into the hollow meshwork that extended in all directions, Soph saw how both the *Argent* and Lo-Bru-Tirni's ship had attempted to mimic this space. Now that her eyes were attuned to the confusing shadows that fell from the high lights, she saw that they were surrounded by living things. Things like pillbugs the size of rats clambered along upside down, seeking out what had been forgotten. A bouncing creature like a wallaby with an iridescent scaled surface crossed back and forth above the humans, as if wondering when to drop something on their heads.

At one point, they had to step aside as a team of large-headed emus dressed in concealing, equipment-festooned robes, forelimbs nowhere visible, came through carrying what looked like a gigantic, translucent cicada grub, developing wings just visible under its paper-thin shell. The grub's mouthparts worked frantically, reaching out for the humans, who pressed as far away as they could without falling off their precarious path. The Arana humans did not acknowledge the unblinking emus, who seemed intent on their task. They were not a species Soph had ever heard of.

Unlike the others, Ambryn leaned toward the grub, looking interestedly at its crystalline jaws. It snapped out at her with surprising speed. Ambryn fell back, saved from tumbling over the side only by a quick grab by Elward. An emu squealed, in rage or warning, and they redoubled their pace.

"Ambryn—" Soph began warningly.

"Did you see? I think that's what they use to keep the airlocks from growing out of control. The teeth on that thing seem to match the chiseling around the airlock door. So it's some kind of aftermarket modification."

"There's too much, Ambryn," Soph said. "We could spend weeks at any spot in this place and learn only a small part of what's there."

"No sense in getting eaten before your time," Elward said. "Or do you feel you're growing out of control?"

"Shut up, Elward."

The path finally climbed up through the ceiling into a different sort of space, more of a regular passage, though the thick covering on the walls proved to be a sort of fungus. Their escorts tore pieces off to chew on as they walked.

The human-occupied areas formed a dense network of passages throughout the clanship, Soph noted. As they kept on, through lower and lower gravity, they could see into connections with other regions of the clanship: a Vronnan meeting hall supported by what looked like the rib bones of some immense creature; a Guardian reproductive site, its soft walls and floor covered with supportive caves; an abyssal tank once filled with specialized molluscs, now an empty space littered with shattered shells, the water spilling out through explosively vaporized intake valves. In many places, the thick growth on the walls had died, revealing the understructure.

Soph could see what a small part of the entire colony the supposedly dominant Vronnans really were. The vast volume of this interstellar ecocyst had, at one time, supported at least a million sentient creatures: human beings, Guardians, scavengers, pilots. Of that number, she guessed that no more than tens of thousands—if that many—had been Vronnans.

They paused, a long while later, in front of what looked very much like a storefront. Brighter light came from within, and regular shapes indicated the presence of manufactured, rather than grown, objects.

"Welcome to the Arana clanship," a quiet voice said from within. "We've waited a long time for someone to find us."

The voice spoke with a distinct Martian accent.

"She is the Memory Giver. Memory Giver Tuqi. Not quite their Queen . . . but certainly their chief. She granted me this space, this memorial. Normally, bodies are recycled. Though after the battles, many rotted. There were so many. So many . . ."

The man's name was Kirby Wu. His skin was dark and coppery, and had not faded in decades inside the Arana clanship. His white hair fell to his bony shoulders. He had grown up in the caldera of the volcano Pavonis, on Mars, in an environment built by the alien Gkh. Until its destruction, he had been a member of the crew of the *Prismatic Bezel.*

The space they were in was the burial place of the rest of the crew of that vessel. The bodies were encased in simple sprayed matrix, like mummies, but their possessions were displayed on racks: clothing, jewelry, books, toys, cooking utensils, crystals.

Wu had apparently lived out most of his life aboard the Arana clanship here, among the dead bodies of his former crew mates.

"There are kingdoms to be won here," Elward said. "If the place is as disorganized as you say." He scratched patterns in the thick humus of the floor, as if drawing maps of conquest.

"I suppose that's true. Only a matter of time before someone tries. There are areas of the clanship that none of us have been into since Sukh's departure after her occupation."

"How many of you survived Sukh's attack on the clanship?" Ambryn said. "I mean, I'm surprised—"

"To find anyone alive?" Wu was an austere stick figure, particularly in contrast to the huge Memory Giver, who had embraced him before turning him over to what must have seemed to her members of his own tribe. "I'm surprised myself. Dozens of us survived that first assault, Miss Chretien. They stormed aboard, Vronnans, those Guardians . . . we would have called them Ulanyi Executioners, I think, back in the System. But I forget, we are in the System, aren't we? It's deep underground here, you have to understand. I haven't seen the stars in a decade. But the Arana brought us aboard for a specific purpose. They wanted memory transfer. The Arana humans could no longer perform their function."

"Because of the nerve plague," Soph said.

"Yes. We had never known where it came from. Now you have explained it. Ankur's disease, I guess we'll call it. Demyelination. The memories became stuck." He nodded down the passage outside the memorial. The Arana humans had retreated down, just out of sight, but their murmuring was audible. "Memory Giver Tuqi fears she is the last of her kind. She transferred the memories of thirteen Vronnan clutches. About forty individuals in total, some of them quite important to the Arana. They grow in a sort of anatomical pouch and are expelled while still quite small. But by then the essential memories have been transferred, with the human brain as a transducer."

Wu managed a kind of reflected pride in the achievement. Apparently, he had made himself a sort of adviser, though he had never entirely fit in with the tribes of Arana humans.

"The memory transfer operation could not have evolved naturally. Vronnans have vague myths about how the process came about because they have no memories from that time. The sterile Helpers, who do not inherit memories, keep their own traditions.

"The human being lies in a state of suspended animation within the fluid-filled abdomen of what was once a predator that stored prey there as living food for its children. The predator's reproduction is now strictly controlled, and its ability to keep living things alive in a suspended state highly refined, with a food and oxygen supply pumped into the arteries. The neural cables, which may ultimately be derived from human nerve tissue, run into that abdomen and join the human brain at the base of the skull."

Soph remembered the scars she had felt on the back of Tiber's head. He had borne the traces of what had happened to him all over his body, and she had never been able to understand.

"We knew nothing of this when they came to take us for reproduction and memory transfer," Wu said. "No explanation, just force. We had been put here, it turns out, because it was next to the memory chamber, where all the biological equipment necessary to the memory transfer lived. They wanted the children most of all.

"We fought them. We all fought them. The Vronnans could have separated us, kept us completely defenseless, but they were not used to managing human beings. In Vronnan civilization, humans manage themselves. Many of us died. Most of the children . . . died." Wu paused for a moment to breathe.

"We of the *Bezel* had seen signs of the other humans, these humans of Arana, and thought of them as enemies. But they came to help us. They were sick, their world had been destroyed, but they came to help us. There was no saving the children that had been taken and no war to be made against their co-dwellers the Arana Vronnans, but they left us food, made it into the sealed kennel areas where we were being kept. We had just started to establish communication with them when the rogue Vronnan force attacked."

"Sukh," Ambryn said. "And her renegade troops."

"It was savage. We did not see most of it, but apparently it was a massacre. Sukh and her troops appeared as some sort of supply ship, mimicking Arana ID signals—that may have been Ankur's contribution to Sukh's education. The battle went on for a week or more, ranging throughout the clanship. That was when most of it was destroyed.

"Eventually, the Arana clan was dead. All of them. And then Sukh and her troops came for us."

"Why?" Ambryn asked. "They were there to save you. They were there because the Arana had kidnapped you."

Wu shook his head. "Sukh was punishing perversion, not rescuing us. In fact, we represented part of the perversion. We were not Arana humans, we were not humans associated with any Vronnans. We were filth." He gestured around at the scene of Arana human civilization. "They managed to save us, Memory Giver Tuqi and her people. Some few of us, of which I am now the only one left alive."

"And Tiber?" Soph asked.

"I knew his parents. They died early, before they could know what had happened to their son. Sukh took Tiber after it was all over. She took him to the region of the clanship she and her force made her own. That area is still almost inaccessible. Huge areas of vacuum and high radiation keep it incredibly distant, as if it was another continent. And she stayed there for a long time before she finally left."

The life energy seemed to go out of Wu as he spoke. Soph wondered if he had survived this long simply to do what he had just done: tell the story to someone who could understand it.

"Tiber has returned to the Arana clanship," Soph said.

"I know," Wu said. "He came back to the place where he was raised, out in the territories that Sukh ruled."

Soph was surprised. "You know? But how—?"

"Because he has managed to find a way out of there," Wu said.

"Yes," Tiber said quietly from behind the memorial cases. "I am here."

5

In later years, Tiber would grow to realize how deep Sukh's planning went. For a long time, he had thought that she had taken him from the slaughter aboard the Arana clanship as some sort of symbol of kindness, something plucked from the blood to show the continuity of life.

But Sukh had only one obsession, and the continuity of life was not it.

Tiber knew that his family had been killed along with the rest during Sukh's reduction of the Arana clanship. Aside from the flickering memories he had pulled out during his long-ago conversation with Elward, everything was blank. Too many savage disasters had slid across his mind like sharp-stoned rock slides, annihilating some memories and burying others so deeply that they could not be recovered without endangering the stability of the personality that had finally arisen from the ruins.

The Arana had kidnapped the humans from the *Prismatic Bezel* for reproduction, for the necessary transfer of memories. And reproduction was what the young Tiber had started to be used for.

Carrying a Vronnan clutch was apparently a piercingly pleasurable experience for a human being. Among Vronnan humans, it led to high status. You floated in an Ulanyi placenta, and alien thoughts drifted through on their way to the infants growing in your side.

"I don't remember what happened," Tiber said. "Perhaps something did. As far as I can understand, Sukh attacked just as they were beginning. The physiology of Earth humans apparently differs in some significant way from that of Vronnan humans."

He was regal again, as if his desperate suicide attempt had never happened. As if they had never made love. Soph looked at him, searching for a crack in the façade, but there was none.

Soph knew that the deep image of being penetrated—violated—by a Vronnan female underlay his entire personality. If he didn't want to remember that consciously, it was entirely his business, regardless of what she wanted to find out from him.

"Sukh raised me," Tiber said. "She took learning equipment from the *Bezel*. I learned all about Mars as it had been when they left. I thought I did a pretty good job of pretending to be a human being."

"You didn't have to pretend," Soph said. "You're a natural genius."

"Yeah," Elward said. "She did a pretty good job, considering."

"She inserted you aboard the Martian warship," Ambryn said.

"Yes. I was supposed to be recovered by the Martians and hauled back to Mars, where I had connections, resources I could tap into secretly with my gene patterns. Instead, I was taken by the Terrans and ended up on MeshMatrix Krystal. For a long time, I forgot all about who I was and what I was supposed to do. I thought I was just a regular person, with my own life to lead. Then it all changed. . . .''

It was incredible, Soph thought. Unfamiliar with human beings, brought up by sophisticated machines aboard a ruined spacecraft by a monomaniacal alien, then dropped in completely the wrong place . . . he had still succeeded in his mission, through brilliant expedients. Sukh, hiding out in the periphery of the Solar System, needed a native guide to make his way through the mysterious worlds of humans and find the one being she needed: Ripi-Arana-Hoc, her father, the person who had stolen her memory and left her a Handicapped outlaw in her own civilization.

And Tiber had done as he was bid. He had searched out Ripi and offered him something that got through the layers of paranoiac security the fugitive Vronnan had thrown up around his fortress in the Maxwells: a return to the Arana clanship and potential return to power in Vronnan space. But Ripi, with Soph, Elward, and Ambryn's help, managed to escape his kidnapping, leaving Tiber bereft and Sukh enraged.

''You love her,'' Soph said softly.

''I did. You have to remember, she did save me from''—he smiled tightly—''a fate worse than death. Or so it seemed. I was not prepared. I did not understand, couldn't . . . understand. The humans here, they've lived their lives aboard the clanship. Their lives are permeated by understanding of this. If I had been educated, would I have responded differently?''

''It was rape,'' Ambryn said. ''The fact that we can make love doesn't mean we can't be raped.''

''But that's not why I'm here,'' Tiber said.

''Home,'' Soph said. ''You've come home.''

''Yes,'' he said. ''At long last.''

''You didn't know where the clanship was, did you?'' Ambryn said. ''When you finally remembered yourself, aboard MeshMatrix Krystal, you had no idea of where you had come from.''

''No. I was reborn. I didn't care. Not then.''

''But the Gunners knew,'' Ambryn said. ''They track every pebble floating around the Solar System, hoping to find some evidence of their mother's fate. We offered them some fake information about her, and they couldn't resist the urge to check it out. They never can. So they traded you the clanship's location for it."

"They had noted the Arana clanship's entry, and the battles following. Not that they had any understanding of it—or even interest. But they did have the vessel's orbit." Tiber looked sad. "I hope that someday they do find their mother."

"Is that the only reason you're here?" Soph said. "To take a look at home?"

"Yes." Tiber seemed affronted by the question, as if it was not entirely polite.

"Did you find the place where you were raised? You and Ripi?"

"Yes."

Ripi was among the humans. In the long pauses of their conversation, Soph could hear him, speaking in the buzzing of the local human language. Soliciting votes? Enjoining silence? She didn't like having him loose and unsupervised like this. He'd already caused enough trouble.

Tiber stood deep in thought, remembering what he had found of his home. Soph could see that it had not satisfied him. And how could it? To see the old machines that had generated the simulations by which you had been raised . . . it was scarcely listening to the creaking rafters of your old family home.

"How did you survive?" Soph said.

"What do you mean?"

"That area was the center of Sukh's rule when she had power aboard this clanship." Soph herself wasn't sure what conclusion she was headed toward. "But military forces must have penetrated there after her departure. Did you see anyone?"

"No." Tiber was suddenly quiet. "No. The place she raised me was isolated. I saw no signs. No one disturbed us. No one even seemed to notice that we were there."

"And you didn't find that odd?"

Soph fumbled for her comm gear. Several times already she had felt the tingle of Lightfoot's trying to get in touch with her, but she had put him off with a signal that said, essentially, "All fine. Will speak later."

It was now later.

"Soph." Lightfoot's voice crackled in her ear. "What's wrong?"

"Sukh's alive."

"That's a good working hypothesis," he said. "To be on the safe side."

"No. I have better evidence. Tiber went into the heart of the area of the ship she had ruled. No one disturbed him. And no one tried to prevent his passage over here, to where the Arana humans still live." She briefly described the Memorial and where they were. "There are all sorts of independent forces on the loose over there. At the very least, he would have been stopped and escorted here as we were."

"She kept everyone away from him." Lightfoot understood instantly. "Him and Tiber. She wanted them to make their way there, to you. Evacuate, Soph. Now."

People were shouting down the hall. Screams of fear, of rage. The floor vibrated with heavy limbs smashing down.

"I'm afraid we're a little too late for that, Lightfoot."

"We're coming in, then."

"*No.* If there's trouble, someone must remain safe. Just hang tight until it's over."

"Soph." Despite the strain, he sounded almost amused. "Try not to treat my recording of this conversation as a basis for the quotation carved in the base of your memorial, and tell me what you need."

"I just did."

"Where are the other humans, the ones of Arana?"

"They are poorly armed. Apparently, Sukh destroyed all personal weapons during her tenure here, and they have been able to build only makeshift ones. There's not much metal aboard this place."

"No personal weapons? I *am* coming in, Soph."

Despite her fear, Soph smiled. "You going to come in and distribute weapons to the natives?" She remembered the cases of small arms Lightfoot had collected.

"Oh, no. That would just make them suspicious, and I don't have time to deal with that. I'm going to sell them."

"Get a good price."

"I intend to. Do you know where Ripi is?"

A memorial case shattered. Wu shouted in anger. Soph looked up. A Guardian, laser arms at the ready, trotted in with the tiny Ripi held in its subsidiary limbs like a baby. Behind, escorted by two more Guardians, strutted the proud female form of Sukh.

"Yes, Lightfoot," she said. "I do."

Soph gave up struggling with her bonds and looked around the memory chamber. It was made almost entirely of living creatures, all of which provided part of its functions. The floor rippled slowly. Something moved slowly inside a translucent vacuole in the wall. A dense network of circulatory vessels pulsed behind thin membranes. She almost gasped. Something very much like a human eye regarded her from the ceiling. Octopi had eyes that looked just like human ones, she reminded herself. It was a reasonable design, certain to be discovered again and again. That one had not come from a human being.

She was almost sure of it.

Ripi floated on the tongues of the supportmouth, just as his Brother in Memory had. A mindnurse, which looked like an air-breathing jellyfish with an added hydrostatic skeleton, hung above him.

The straps that held her seemed pliable, but her grip slid off of them. They were at least half-alive. Cold air played on her naked skin. Behind her, she sensed the opening into which she would sink and where memory transfer would occur.

They had killed Wu. Unable to stand the ruin of his carefully constructed Memorial, he had attempted resistance, and one of Sukh's Guardians had smashed him against a wall. Elward too had been beaten, though he was still alive. Soph couldn't see him, but she could hear him cursing under his breath.

"I feel like a sacrificial virgin," Soph said.

Ambryn looked up from her huddled position at Soph's feet. "Is that necessary for memory transfer? Perhaps you should inform someone that you don't fit the requirements."

"I don't think it's that . . . but Memory Giver Tuqi was young when she bore her first Vronnan memory. And Tiber couldn't have been more than six or seven . . . I don't think my nervous system will be able to do whatever is necessary."

"Sukh is going to kill you." Elward spoke clearly and slowly.

"Sukh is going to do whatever the hell she wants," Soph said.

Guardians, forbidden entry, stalked around the entrances to the memory chamber. Sukh had brought humans with her, those renegades who had joined her during her incursion of the Arana clanship. Enemies of Memory Giver Tuqi's clan. Three of them now lay ostentatiously asleep in corners of the room, gaining calm for their tasks. They would assist, as other humans always did, in the transfer of memories from Father to child. They were the Bearers. All Vronnans remembered them. They wore ceremonial clothing, bright fabrics with swirls of silver and gold.

By jabbing what looked like giant bee stingers into the wall, they had already stimulated the modified predator that would store Soph in its abdomen during the memory transfer procedure. Its open mouth, rimmed by vestigial teeth, gaped in the wall, and a thick tongue lolled down to the floor. Deeper in its maw, Soph could see the sharp points that would inject her with muscle paralyzers, anesthetics, and metabolism suppressors as the creature slowly swallowed her.

Elward finally managed to sit up and into Soph's field of view. Drying blood covered his face. In his arms, absurdly, he held a decorative paper umbrella. He had stolen it from the memory racks of the *Bezel* crew. Soph wondered if it reminded him of something from his own childhood, if he had started to wonder whether he had mysteriously grown up here and forgotten all about it. He picked shreds off of it with his fingernails and let them flutter to the floor.

"You are right," Ripi said from the supportmouth. "It won't work. Your nervous system is not suitable. But no infants are available."

"Don't the Arana have any?" Ambryn said with cool brutality. "Isn't that their fate, after all?"

"Not for Sukh. Not for me. We are accursed. The memories I bear are no longer precious but are memories of hell. She could get an infant but only at the risk of serious casualties as she moves deeper into the clanship. She is not ready for such an effort. And it would most likely fail.''

Soph felt the vibration of steps, and Sukh stepped into the memory chamber. She was a much more impressive creature than Lo-Bru-Tirni, her mother, though some of that was due to the armor she wore. Her centaur shape loomed over everything.

Sukh had destroyed the Arana clan because of their perverse use of Earth-normal human beings for memory transfer. And here, driven by the same necessity, she was committing the same sin. But Soph, looking at the Vronnan's wide staring eyes, suspected that Sukh wasn't thinking about anything anymore. For all that the memory transfer procedure had an entirely artificial, contrived origin, it had become as deep as any other reproductive urge. Sukh, a salmon swimming upstream in time, had to get those memories into her head—or die trying.

''She will get some memories,'' Ripi said. ''A few.''

''But it will kill me.'' Soph was surprised at her own dispassion. There would be no transformation for her, no matter how unlooked for. She would never become a Memory Giver. She would never become anything other than what she was. Her change had come a long time ago, when she gave birth to Stephan.

''Yes,'' Ripi said. ''You will die.'' He managed to turn his head to the side, away from both Soph and the looming Sukh, the first sign of weakness he had shown. ''You will die and then I will die. Since my death is inevitable in any case, it would save you if I died first.''

''Sure,'' Soph said. ''Sure it would.''

She should have known that his comments had a meaning and would find their mark. He was a ruler, a prince of the kingdom, and he understood the weaknesses of his people. The paralysis was wearing off, because he slowly moved his arms until his hands rested on his abdomen, fingers around a spot between his vestigial limbs. It looked like a position for meditation.

From his slumped, defeated position, Elward moved with

blinding swiftness. He rolled over, sprang, and stabbed Ripi with the decorative umbrella, putting all the weight of his wide shoulders into it. The umbrella had a stiff handle and a sharp tip. It went into the soft plectrum between Ripi's vestigial second limbs.

Before Elward could pull the umbrella out to stab again, Sukh swung her massive forelimb. Elward ducked, but she was incredibly fast. The forelimb's armored length caught him on the side of the head with an oddly tiny thunk, and he went down. From the looseness of his body, Soph was sure that Elward Bakst was dead.

Sobbing, Ambryn gathered herself together at Soph's feet.

"No, Ambryn," Soph said.

"But—"

"It won't do any good."

"None of it will," Ambryn said. She pressed her wet face against Soph's legs, and Soph was able to feel a moment of irritation that she, bound up for sacrifice, was expected to be a source of comfort to someone else.

She looked at Ripi. Was he satisfied with what he had achieved? He had done his best to indicate the location for a killing blow. His pinkish blood bubbled around the umbrella and as he shuddered, the broken ribs and tearing tissue paper sifted down into the supportmouth, which flicked each tiny piece out as it fell.

Ripi rolled in an attempt to drive the umbrella farther in, but Sukh grabbed him and yanked it out again. With an almost comforting gesture, she pressed against the wound until the bleeding slowed.

"How long will this take?" Soph said.

"Days," Ripi answered. "I die slowly. Perhaps before she succeeds in transferring all the memories. I can only hope."

Soph knew that he hadn't tried to kill himself in order to save her. He had done it to deny his own hated Handicapped daughter that which she most wanted.

Sukh exposed her ovipositors and pressed their sharp tips against Soph's bare chest. Sukh was going to be her own mother, it looked like, Soph thought dizzily. Was the intromission of eggs a necessary precursor to memory transfer?

She held on to the intellectual question to keep from screaming.

Sukh pulled her ovipositors back and half-turned to look at something in the memory chamber doorway. Soph, gasping for breath, was almost angry at the respite. Couldn't this creature keep her mind on what she was doing? Finally, reluctantly, she turned her head to see what Sukh was staring at.

Tiber stood in the doorway. He wore the robes he had worn while presiding over the *Argent*. Then they had looked idiosyncratic, some odd invention of his own. Soph now saw them anew, as the prerogative of a human Memory Giver.

He said something plaintive to Sukh, and Soph realized that he had, until this moment, concealed his knowledge of the Vronnan language. He had, in fact, concealed almost everything.

"What?" Soph said. "Ripi! What is he saying?"

"What you might expect." Ripi was disgusted. "He should be the one to bear the memories. She raised him to provide her with those memories, and she should take it to its logical conclusion. Please take him."

"She's not going for it," Soph said.

"It would be too much, even for her." Ripi was calm, observing the scene from the supportmouth, making it look like a soft couch. "She is not that insane, to use him."

Sukh turned completely away from Soph and loomed over Tiber. Her voice boomed out, the threat obvious, but Tiber did not step back. He just stood, his arms in his robe, suppliant but demanding.

She would kill him, Soph thought. No matter their past, how she had rescued him, raised him, used him . . . she was too far gone now. She would not be balked of her prey.

Still Sukh stood poised over Tiber. One sweep of her arms, the same way she had killed Elward . . . but she did not move. For a long time, neither did he.

Then he reached into his Memory Giver's robes and pulled out a blunt-barrelled pistol, clumsily catching it on the thick fabric. Sukh, overconfident about her renewed rule over the entire Arana clanship, had not checked carefully enough for it.

Still she did not move. He spoke again. She did not reply. He pointed the gun at her.

The motionless tableau was more than Soph could bear. Someone had to do *something*. She took breath into her lungs to scream at them.

Explosions rocked the room, and for an instant she thought they came from within herself. Soph did scream, but no one could hear her. It sounded like Lightfoot's marketing efforts had finally paid off. Now that she had a moment to think, she could identify the fire of various personal arms, now in the hands of the Arana clanship's humans. She heard the thump of an explosive bullet entering thick flesh. A Guardian pounded limbs against the walls in agony, then fell heavily to the floor.

Sukh stood over Tiber, the human being she had raised, and still did not move. Finally he pulled the trigger.

The explosion that killed Sukh was not even audible above the sounds of the greater battle. She stood still for a moment longer, then toppled forward, right onto Tiber and out of Soph's line of sight.

Within a few moments, the firing had stopped, and all was silence.

"This isn't hurting you, is it?" Ambryn dragged Soph across the floor by her shoulders, showing unexpected strength. She had killed the creature that held Soph by hacking savagely at it with a knife she had taken from Kirby Wu's body. Its many straplike appendages now littered the floor, curling in on themselves as if searching for something to hold on to.

"I can barely feel anything," Soph said. "Don't worry. Is he . . ."

"I don't know, I don't know! Tiber thinks he's—Tiber thinks Elward is alive."

Tiber murmured something, but Soph couldn't make it out.

"Roll me over and prop me up," she said, "so that I can see."

"You need medical care too, Soph." But Ambryn did as she was bid and leaned Soph up against the base of the supportmouth so that Soph could see the injured Tiber, his left arm broken and hanging limp, kneeling over the recumbent form of Elward. Tiber had cleared Elward's throat of vomit and mucus and administered artificial respiration. But blood covered the right side of Elward's head, and Soph suspected a serious skull fracture. His right pupil, when Tiber pulled the eyelid back, was contracted to a tight pinpoint, while the other was normal.

"Me," Ripi said. "Pull me out of here."

"Why the hell should I do that?" Ambryn crawled over and touched Elward's hand. Gently, so as not to get into Tiber's way.

"Help him out," Soph said. "Don't be petty."

"I'm not *petty*."

Soph was still unable to move. She could see that Tiber could not help Elward.

"Cut open the wall," Ripi said as Ambryn pulled him from the tender caresses of the supportmouth's tongues and lowered him to the floor. "There, at that swelling. Use those knives the Bearers brought. Let the mind transfer tissues take hold of him. They contain functions that assist the human brain."

"Why—" Ambryn was ready to argue.

"It could do no harm."

"He's right," Tiber said. "It could keep his mind alive."

"Hurry, then!" Ambryn said. She darted across the room. The Bearers brought by Sukh had fled, leaving their gear. She dug among it and came up brandishing what looked like a machete. She flinched and almost dropped it. "It's alive. I can feel it grabbing at me."

"Cut carefully," Ripi said. "Do not damage the function."

"I'm not much of a midwife." Then she cut a single slash across the bulge in the wall, as if she'd been doing it her whole life. Thick fluid spilled out, with a harsh metallic scent, like scorched blood.

Ambryn and Tiber together lifted the limp body of Elward and thrust him into the open abdomen. The creature's mouth, balked of even the taste of its prey, opened and closed, punching holes in its own tongue.

"My mate," Ripi said. "Lo-Bru-Tirni. She is here?"

"You know she is," Soph said. "You had to have deliberately avoided her, in coming here to the Arana clanship. Do you fear her?''

''My duty, by Vronnan standards, is still to die,'' he said. ''No matter that my memories will now go nowhere. But I think I can be useful enough to avoid that. I must speak with her.''

''What about?'' Ambryn did not turn away from Elward. Soph was sure she was unhappy that Ripi was not dead along with his daughter.

''Vronnan authority has fallen apart across a wide area of space,'' Ripi said in a detached tone. ''We have the still-living deepdrive aboard the Arana clanship. If the placentas aboard the *Argent* can serve their intended purpose, perhaps it can be brought to health. Perhaps you humans from the Solar System would like a chance of influence in Vronnan space.''

''Talk galactic conquest with Lightfoot,'' Soph said. ''He has the big ambitions.''

''I am looking forward to it.''

''Soph!'' Ambryn reached down and hauled Soph up so that she could see into the abdomen.

Elward's eyes were open. The pinpoint pupil had dilated until the iris was almost entirely black. A thick band of some kind of tissue, gleaming like a beetle's back, had crept out under his skull so that he looked like he was in the forest, resting his head back on a gnarled tree root, looking up at the sky. But the sky was a dripping mass of tissue only a few centimeters away from his face.

Then he smiled, as if he really was looking at the clouds. It transformed his face, and Soph realized how little she had ever really seen him smile. He hadn't had much to make him happy, not the whole time she had known him. She thought that was her fault.

''Elward,'' she whispered. ''What do you see?''

''I knew it was just an interruption,'' he said. Though he smiled, his breath was shallow, and the words came out slurred. Soph had to struggle to understand him.

''What was?''

''I walked into the stars. The universe was all mine. I was

just starting out when . . . when I got interrupted.'' He crinkled his forehead. ''There was something I had to do. . . .''

''You did it, Elward,'' Soph said, hardly able to breathe herself. ''You did everything you had to.''

''The deepdrive calls out to you,'' Ripi said from the floor. ''To human beings. It means to go. It wants to leave this solar system behind.''

''Shut up,'' Ambryn said.

''And your minds are the way it will do it!''

''Elward,'' Soph said, ignoring the frantic proclamations of the Vronnan, though they spoke of what human beings had been dreaming of.

With a jerk, he raised his right arm and pushed his hand against the dripping abdominal tissue. ''I can touch the stars,'' he said. ''You know, they aren't hot at all. I always thought—''

His arm fell back, and his head tilted to the side.

''Elward!'' Ambryn cried.

Soph reached in and took his hand. She thought it tightened a little on hers before he died. What she could see of Elward's face was peaceful.

She hoped it was true. She hoped that somewhere, Elward, at peace at last, strode out toward the stars.